THE
ELECTION

WILLIAM L. LITTLE

Order this book online at www.trafford.com
or email orders@trafford.com

Most Trafford titles are also available at major online book retailers.

© Copyright 2015 William L. Little.
All rights reserved. No part of this publication may be reproduced, stored in a retrieval system, or transmitted, in any form or by any means, electronic, mechanical, photocopying, recording, or otherwise, without the written prior permission of the author.

Printed in the United States of America.

ISBN: 978-1-4907-5156-6 (sc)
ISBN: 978-1-4907-5157-3 (hc)

Library of Congress Control Number: 2014922039

Because of the dynamic nature of the Internet, any web addresses or links contained in this book may have changed since publication and may no longer be valid. The views expressed in this work are solely those of the author and do not necessarily reflect the views of the publisher, and the publisher hereby disclaims any responsibility for them.

Any people depicted in stock imagery provided by Thinkstock are models, and such images are being used for illustrative purposes only.
Certain stock imagery © Thinkstock.

Trafford rev. 01/12/2015

Trafford
PUBLISHING   www.trafford.com
North America & international
toll-free: 1 888 232 4444 (USA & Canada)
fax: 812 355 4082

Prologue
Late Summer 1924

A thick cloud of late August dust engulfed the Overland touring car as it traveled down the narrow, worn country road. It passed, on either side, an unending scene: cornfields, some half harvested, others, waiting with crops higher than the car itself. The new, shiny, black, chauffeur driven vehicle, with its once brightly polished brass head lamps and trim, was now a dull, nondescript, mud spattered gray; the dramatic change brought about by the prairie's unpredictable weather. There had been a brief morning shower while driving towards Flintville; and now there was this hot, dry afternoon of August dust on the trip into Crescent. The usually rolled-up isinglass curtains were now down and snapped into place to protect the single passenger in the back seat.

It had been a long time, two and a half years, since he had been home to Crescent. He was tired, needed a few days rest; time to clear his head, "mend a few fences", get things "back on track" before the hectic schedule of the next two months. The sharp edge of his high starched collar chafed his neck. His throat was dry. He closed his eyes and tried to lean back against the hard leather seat; but the ride was too rough, and his driver, Baron, was both unfamiliar with the road and too intent on pushing for the car's top speed of twenty-five miles an hour to make the trip comfortable enough for sleep.

He opened his eyes wide, pulled himself up erect, picked up his hat, carefully checking it for dust. Satisfied he put it down and turned to brushing off the sleeve of his gray serge topcoat, which he had neatly folded on the seat beside him. Again he shifted himself around trying to get more relaxed. Next year, thanks to him, the promised new rail spur from Colton would be completed right into Crescent. That would make such journeys more pleasant and perhaps even exciting.

Finally, through the haze of the side curtains, he recognized the outline of Murdock's dairy barn with its huge advertisement for Cuban cigars painted on its side. There was also the eye-watering odor of the strong urine and manure mixture that permeated the fields and barns at Murdock's. Some things never changed. They were now only a couple of miles from Crescent. Subconsciously he pulled his comb from his inside coat pocket and ran it through his silver hair. He mindfully straightened his tie. There would probably be a group there to meet him, plus the Walker County Journal reporter, of course. Just before they reached town, he had Baron stop and roll the side curtains up and wipe off the windshield, so he could see better. As they continued, he put on his hat and adjusted it carefully; then let his tongue moisten his lips.

When they turned the corner off Main Street, on to Elm Avenue and had reached the blacksmith's shop he noticed there was a new building being constructed in the piece of property jus north of it and a new large sign, which read "Ward J. Kessel & Son" over the shop itself. He felt a strange feeling of anger and confusion coming over him. He clenched his fists and gritted his teeth; but by the time he was at the granary and he could clearly see in the distance all the people gathered in front of the fire hall, some of them pointing and waving in his direction, he had relaxed.

The minute the car stopped, not waiting for Baron, he swung the car door open to greet the small crowd there to welcome him. He waved and smiled broadly, but with all of his well-known dignity intact.

There was Luke Mason and several members of the local Elks Club band, with a touch of uncertainty, starting to play the Star Spangled Banner.

Someone began to clap and few cheers could be heard. He looked around at the familiar faces in front of him; obviously pleased by the presence of most of them. As he stepped down from the running board of the car, he reached forward to take the outstretched hand of Bruce McHenry, Crescent's fire chief, and said, "It's wonderful to be home. I just want you to know how...."

Without warning, almost unheard over the music, there was a loud "snap" like the crack of a whip, and another, and another. His hand still extended to McHenry, his eyes widened, the color drained from his face, and his voice stopped in mid-sentence. He dropped to one knee and then the other before crumbling, face down, in the street without completing his thought.

Oblivious to the event, the band continued. Other than that, there was a dull silence until finally, a woman screamed, and the crowd pushed forward, toward him. Unaware of what had happened, Bruce and two or three other men tried to help him to his feet. The music trailed off in disarray.

Matt Harwood, who had been standing a few feet behind and to the left of McHenry, stood motionless, his feet wide apart, numbness coming up from his groin, to his chest, to his head, as he looked over at the limp figure the men were trying to hold upright. The hat had fallen off and lay upside down on the ground. A small, bright red spot quickly spread outward, staining the front of the starched, white shirt; and blood oozed out and over the lower teeth, collecting in the corner of the stilled, open, smiling mouth.

Matt turned away, but he could not move, he felt as if he were going to vomit. He was dizzy, there was a pounding in his head, and his arms became tense, but his legs weakened as if they were about to buckle. He could hear Bruce's deep voice booming out "Matt, Matt, get the God damn doctor, Matt!" But there was a rushing sound and the pushing of bodies around and past him. Then all was blank. Faintly, in the distance, Matt could hear: "Matthew, Mathew! The damned doctor, Matt! Someone! Hell!

Chapter 1
Summer, 1918

The sun spilled its long, lacy shadows through the rows of poplars lining the streets of Crescent and a crazy rickrack of dawn grays and yellows stretched across fields, between fence pickets, over lawns, porch railings and swings, bringing with its colors a slow, half-awareness of being watched. Eyelids lifted their weighted corners. Nostrils sucked in the coming warmth. Combs were hastily drawn through hair too long and tangled; and a sleepy-eyed, shirtless man, his pants depending on a single suspender strap, waddled down a path and closed an unpainted shanty door behind him.

A hundred kitchen grates were violently shaken for the daily fire; while cows, here and there, were comforted by calloused hands. Occasional electric lights snapped on into glaring contrast; but mostly wavy candle flames and lamps sputtering on coal oil wicks signaled the awakening.

Women's voices, ranging from soft to screeching, pulled reluctant men and sons from the snores and grunts of careless sleep to greet the caress and harness of another day. And in the distance, there was the faint "put-put-put" of an automobile coming out of the flat prairie farm country along the narrow dirt road from Flintville: Dr. Phillips ending an all-night siege with flu at the Cramer's and a new son for the Seeker's to replace one just killed on a hill somewhere in France.

Matthew Harwood was happy that morning. He ran his fingers through his thick yellow mop of hair. Who in that whole "damn one horse town" could feel better, he thought to himself as he walked down the quiet street toward the feed store on Elm Avenue.

A tint of self-satisfaction highlighted the glint of his hazel eyes. New job, new pair of socks straight from Murphy's Emporium, and a new girl lined up for the dance over at the Grange Hall; all that and a morning with nothing to think about but how many bags of grain he could sack before noon. Maybe he would have a bit of Indian wrestling with "Ward" Kessel after lunch, before he loaded the grain on the wagon and headed for Flintville.

It wasn't every "fresh-from-high-school" kid that had a job "right off" with someone as fussy as Mr. Dodson. "Nope", Matthew said aloud as he kicked a stone from the wooden sidewalk and watched it bounce down the newly paved street of Elm Avenue, "not very damn many like me. Guess I'll get married to this here Ellie...she looks pretty...healthy as a hog...and well, I'll bet she can kiss like nobody else in Flintville."

"Morning, Matthew." It was Mrs. Cross beating her rugs over the railing of her front porch. Everybody said she started beating them early so she could keep track of every-thing everybody did and said everywhere in the whole of Walker County.

"Your father back in town; yet?"

"Nope."

"That's a shame, Matthew. Him leaving your mother all alone while he tramps all over this country making eyes at dance hall girls."

"She isn't 'all alone', Mrs. Cross," Matt said with a slight twist of a smile on the left side of his mouth. "That is, not quite alone. Not with ten of us there to keep her company, now and then."

"Yeah," he thought again, as he picked up a stone and threw it as far down the street as he could. "I'm going to try that girl's kisses tomorrow night."

"Hey, Matt, what in hell you doing up before your ma milks the cows?"

The voice was as coarse as sandpaper scraping across the surface of the calm morning. Bruce McHenry pushed wide the doors of Crescent's just-completed fire station. He dunked his head in the rain barrel by the red maple tree before Matt could even say "Hello" and then made so much noise blowing the water out of his nose that he sounded like a mating stallion. He wiped his face with the tail of his undershirt and belched once or twice for accent. "Well, guess I'm about as bright as that damn sun after all that, wouldn't you say, Matt?"

Bruce McHenry was Matt's favorite uncle on his mother's side.

"Uncle Bruce, you are the noisiest damn man in town. Why, you'll...."

"If you're about to say my taking my morning toilet is going to wake my dignified and 'Most Reverend' neighbor, save your breath, because I've heard the complaint before." Bruce blew his nose. "And I hope to hell it does," he added. "By-the-by, boy, don't let your ma hear you using no words like 'damn'. Why, I tell you, Matt, it'd kill her to know you were going to hell."

Matt stood looking at his uncle. Being in his presence always gave Matt a pleasant feeling of calm amusement. "But he sure did talk a lot."

"Coming over tomorrow night to help christen the new gas-putting fire engine with the rest of the volunteers?"

"Nope."

"What?"

"Said, 'nope'."

"How can you say 'nope' when you're the second vice-captain of the volunteers and you have a five-minute speech to make?"

"I'm going to the dance over at Flintville."

"What a hell of an explanation. What do you think those other four volunteers will think about you deserting? They'll class you just as they would a slacker from the Army."

"Don't care."

"Matthew, I think you're a liar clean and fair, 'cause the whole town will be here for the ice cream and free beer. There won't be any girls left over, even from your own flock of sisters, to be traipsing to Flintville for no farm dance."

"I've got that all figured out, Uncle Bruce. She isn't from Crescent."

"What you mean she ain't from Crescent?"

"Just that; she lives in Flintville."

Bruce McHenry's face showed concern for the first time. "Now, Matt, since your dad's not around, we'd better have a talk. You know, it isn't that speech. To be just plain honest about it, that gives me another half hour to express myself. And it isn't the part of you being the second vice captain of them volunteers and not showing up. If the place goes up in flames again like it did last time, I'll be there to direct the volunteers for you. But, Matt, this here going to a dance with a one, single SHE. Boy, don't you know that's dangerous?"

"Awe, for hell's sakes," Matt tried to break in.

"There you go cussing again. Now you listen. This whole idea kind of riles up the bachelor in me. How do you suppose I kept my priceless freedom these forty-nine years?"

"Don't know."

"Sure as hell not by going off with some certain individual 'She' to dances where that 'She' might get some extra fancy ideas about me being the papa of her ten offspring."

"Uncle Bruce, it's me that's got the ideas."

"You stick to crowds; it's safer that way. Go to your dance, you deserter, but stick to the crowds." Bruce turned and started back into the fire station.

Matt started to walk on down the street, chuckling to himself. Suddenly there was a verbal roar from Bruce that again broke the silent morning: "Matt! Matt, what in Christ's name do you mean its YOU that got the ideas? You got her with child?"

Certainly now Crescent had awakened from its slumber. Mrs. Cross's rug beating stopped, careful not to drown out any stray words. The Reverend's asthmatic cough suddenly set up a rhythmic refrain from his open bedroom window. And up and down the street unseen eyes peered out in silent observance while a rooster chimed a contribution of its own from the distance.

"What's her name?" Matt started back to the fire station. "I said what's her name?"

"Ellie," he answered.

"Ellie, who?"

"Just Ellie."

"Ain't she got a proper family name?"

"I don't know." Matt felt like a small boy again, as if he had been caught playing hooky from school.

"What kind of a girl can she be if she ain't got no proper name? What's her dad got to say about this? Does her dad know about you two? How you going to be able to support a wife and a bunch of offspring when you'll probably get caught in the draft before the year's up? God only knows if you'll get back alive!"

"Uncle Bruce, I only met her yesterday at Coolie's Drug Store. Just had a soda, that's all, a soda."

There was a long pause while his uncle thought in silence. When he spoke again, his words were soft and calm. "Why didn't you say so? You gave me a scare. Now do as I say: make it a crowd, even if you have to take the whole volunteer squad. And for the sake of my peace of mind, find out her proper family name."

Mrs. Cross's rug started to slap the railing once more. Reverend Pritchard's cough stopped and the unseen eyes turned back in disappointment at the morning which had promised so much and given so little: nothing but a Friday's usual chores.

Matt took a deep breath and composed himself. How could you get mad at someone like Uncle Bruce? He searched the street for another stone to throw and thought momentarily about Crescent's powerful new fire engine: "only gas-driven engine in sixty miles."

"Nope," Matt said aloud, "The volunteers will have to wait. I'm going to find out if she's got a proper name so I'll know what to call her pa."

Cyrus P. Dodson was the "best dressed" man in Crescent according to the annual listing found next to the Emporium's spring advertisement in the Walker County Journal.

Cyrus P. Dodson was the most punctual man in Crescent according to the large pendulum clock, which took sole honors as decoration over his roll-top desk; and by the tick of his prized railroad watch, which he bought at auction for one dollar and fifty cents when Alfred Wilkins retired from the Union Pacific and came home to die.

Cyrus P. Dodson was the grouchiest man, not only in Crescent, but: in all of Walker County; according to his wife, Myrtle Wilkins Dodson, and four of her five grown daughters, sired by Alfred Wilkins, one-time fireman for the Union Pacific and the Chicago Northwestern.

"It is six-oh-three, Matthew," Mr. Dodson said without turning from the invoice he was writing. "You know, Matthew, time is the prime resource in business. Success is but the proper management of that resource."

"Morning, Mr. Dodson."

Matt scarcely heard his employer's remark; and Mr. Dodson, unaware of Matt's leaving through the warehouse door, continued on with the dissertation from Benjamin Franklin's Poor Richard's Almanac.

Matt liked the smell of grain. He spread a burlap bag wide open, catching the edge over the two large nails he had rigged on one of the posts, then opened the door to the bin where the corn was stored.

The sun had been shining down on the east side of the granary since dawn, giving a promise of what the noon day would be by the heat already stored up in the bins. Putting his shirt over the rail of the stall, Matthew made a mental reminder for himself: to keep that shirt clean today. All of them at home had decided to try and conserve on Mother's ironing. Even with seven girls in the house, she still would let no one else touch that part of her daily work. Matt took the heavy scoop shovel and pushed it deep in the cushion of the grain.

The Election

"Enough corn there to feed a rain cloud full of pigeons," Cyrus said from the doorway, "but it's just a trickle, just a trickle in that old river down there compared to the feed we will store when we build those new elevators."

Cyrus was ready to do the ink work on his ledger; he had taken his coat off and was now putting on his black muslin sleeve protectors.

"People here in Crescent don't believe that, Matthew; and those in Flintville even less imaginative. When the time comes, they will probably have a railroad spur over from Colton; bypassing Flintville altogether."

Cyrus P. Dodson had not spoken so many words all at one time since Matt had started working for him. But in spite of his surprise at the sudden verbal outburst, Matt kept shoveling the grain into the sacks.

"I'll tell you, Matthew, you keep working the way you have this past week (with the exception of being late this morning); and with no son for me to pass this business onto, you'll have a bright future in the grain and feed business. All we need is devotion to a purpose. And work! I must get the ledger posted; can't spend all day talking to you."

Even a trickle in "that old Smith River down there" would be a welcome relief not only to Crescent but to all of Walker County, Matt thought as he stopped for a short breather. Things were still green but there had been no rain for three weeks and people were bringing the subject of rain more and more to the foreground. Mr. Dodson was no doubt the best businessman in Crescent; even a member of the bank's board of directors. Without knowing why, Matt began to shovel faster and faster, losing all sight of time until Cyrus called to him, reminding him that it was twelve o'clock.

He washed himself in the watering trough behind the granary and sprawled out on the cool grass under the clump of cottonwood trees waiting for his basket of lunch being delivered to him by Margo, next to the youngest of the seven Miss Harwoods who claimed him as their brother.

Margo was a dawdler, a talker and a dreamer living in a void of adventures nobody else could ever share, unless they were eight years old.

"You're snoring, Matt," she whispered softly in his ear, then dropped the heavy lunch basket to the ground and sat down in the middle of his bare midriff.

"Where you been?" he said waking up from his near drugged sleep.

"Oh, Matt, you snore something awful; just like hogs."

"Don't you know it's past noon? Where you been? Want me to starve on a hard job like this?"

He grabbed her around the waist and pulled her to the ground, tickling her as he kissed her on both cheeks.

"Now tell me where in this little one horse town you've been hiding."

"Over to see the new engine. And, Matt, there's more gold on it than you ever seen in your whole life," Margo said straightening herself up from the tussle.

"I expect if the truth be known, it's more like plain brass."

"Uh, uh, gold! Uncle Bruce showed me," Margo's expression was a mixture of anger and disappointment.

"Just plain brass. Same as you'll find in the foot rail at the saloon," Matt teased further.

"If your brother knew how much the city council paid for that engine, Miss Margo, he'd know well and good that all that glitters on the machine must be gold," Cyrus Dodson said in a very serious manner as he stood over them. "Matt, I'm going home for my dinner; it's now twelve-eighteen I'll be back before one to unlock the door."

"Sure, Mr. Dodson," Matt replied out of his newly acquired habit of servitude.

"Miss Margo, do me a favor and ask your Uncle Bruce to let you see his gold spittoon someday. Tell him that I told you to ask him," Cyrus said with a smile.

The two watched in silence for a moment while the dignified man walked away, his head high, his black derby squared, his silver-handled cane tapping the ground with each step.

"I told you; I told you it was gold," Margo said with conviction. "Just like Papa says, you never listen to nobody, Matthew, except yourself."

"Swear you are, I swear."

"You swear I are what?"

"You are becoming an old woman before Mom is, Margo."

"Well, you heard him say it's gold."

Matt laughed, "All right, it's gold! Now, what kind of sandwiches you bring?"

"Some beef and some plum butter, I guess," she said. "I don't for real know; but I put the horseradish in anyway and there's three tomatoes," she added sitting down next to the basket.

"Oh, someone ask you to stay for lunch?"

"Where's Ward," she asked ignoring his question.

"He's a little late, but he'll be here soon. And as I said, Margo, someone ask you for lunch?"

"Ward asked me yesterday; besides, you didn't even say 'thanks' like you should." Her last remark put a stop to conversation and the two of them ate in silence.

"Milk in the fruit jar. Rhubarb in the other," she finally commented after Matt had eaten three beef sandwiches without a breather.

Ward Kessle stood six foot four inches and was easily three feet wide at the shoulders. He was the kind of man Cyrus Dodson took pride in ignoring; the kind of man little girls enjoyed talking with, asking questions of, and idolizing with wide-eyed wonder; the kind of man big girls didn't want to dance with because he ignored regular Saturday baths.

"Only if I might happen to feel in the mood," he would laugh. "Not one soul in this world big enough to make me fill the tub since my Ma died."

His walk was a heavy walk and Margo could even hear him as he crossed the grassy field between the blacksmith's shop and the granary where she and Matt were eating. The grass, weeds, and twigs snapped in protest beneath the weight of his great body.

"Where's my girl?" he asked in a loud voice. "Sorry I'm late, sweetheart," he said gently to Margo, "but if things don't change, I'm going to kill every last jack male child in your generation. Know what I've been doing, Matt? Instead of getting the upstairs rooms cleaned up for my new boarder, I've been pussyfooting around all morning catching up on my regular duties since I had to waste all yesterday afternoon fixing tires for Doc. Phillips' Ford. All six flat; punched full of nails by those damn kids."

"Give me a ride, Ward, Margo interjected in a soft voice.

"I tell you, these kids of this up and coming generation are just no good. Full of tricks and still four months to go 'till Halloween."

"You're getting old, Ward."

"Matthew thinks everybody's old," Margo said.

"Now what would have happened if Doc. had a baby to deliver?" Ward went on with his tirade as he picked Margo up and put her on his shoulders. "I think if the old willow stick were to be used across some hind ends more often, including yours, you grain-bagger, it might change the pace. Where to, sweetheart? Shall we make it around the lot and then up in the cottonwood tree?"

Margo gave her consent with a squeeze of his hairy shoulders. She liked the feel of the soft red hair on Ward's chest against her bare legs. In fact, she liked almost everything about Ward; even the little bald spot on the top of his head so she could see when he put her high up in the air and it made the world seem so small.

"Would you mind if we kept this ride down to a slow, slow trot? Your horse is a mite tired after pulling all those nails the whole morning long. You know, I could have shod a dozen horses in less time."

Margo and her red chestnut charger took off at a comfortably slow pace while Matt leaned back against the grass and closed his eyes. If Ward didn't stop "horsing" around they wouldn't have time to get in their Indian wrestling, he thought.

"That funny Uncle Bruce telling Margo that the engine's trim was gold. What a guy. What a liar. But who can really get right down mad at him? Just like this morning, when he made that noise about Ellie. Ellie! Maybe she'll be at Coolie's Drug Store again. Maybe we can have another soda together after I get the wagon unloaded. Yeah, that Ellie sure would make a good wife."

Mrs. Cross was watering her geraniums when Cyrus P. Dodson crossed the street on his way home for lunch. She listened intently to the click of his precise steps; and the tap, tap tapping of his cane. "Such a marvelous man, that Mr. Dodson," she thought. "So handsome; wonder what he would look like with a moustache: gray to match his hair; so handsome. That Myrtle Wilkins doesn't deserve him. If only Gilbert were more dignified, more of Mr. Dodson's stature instead of digging outhouse foundations." She leaned far over the railing, "Yoo hoo, Mr. Dodson. Lovely day."

"Yes, isn't it that, Dame Margaret?" he said, stifling an urge to laugh.

"Oh, yes, so lovely. How is Myrtle, today?"

This usual reply also caused a tickle in Dodson's stiff-collared neck. He thoroughly enjoyed this guise of interest when he knew his wife and Margaret Cross hated one another.

"In remarkably excellent health, as of this morn at breakfast," he replied to the question as he always replied, even when Myrtle was feigning one of her famous heart attacks or indulging herself in one of her conversation building hot or cold flashes.

"And how do we find your good health, Dame Margaret? I trust you are well." He continued on with his pace only pausing for a second to watch the expression in her eyes; then suddenly he spun on his heels facing her directly, "Oh yes, tell Gilbert I'll have some work for him Saturday morning."

Since no one in Crescent was supposed to know that Gilbert spent his evenings with her, Mrs. Cross turned white with surprise. The moment of silence gave Cyrus the added touch of satisfaction he had hoped his remark would give him.

"I'll...I'll have him...I'll tell him...I'll tell him when he comes to do the chores," she finally said in a flat voice.

"Fine," Cyrus said.

Cyrus pulled his watch instinctively from his pocket to see if his conversation with Margaret, had thrown him off schedule; then quickened his pace a few steps to compensate for the frittered time.

As he turned the corner onto Burnett Street, he could see Agatha put down her knitting on the step of the porch and run into the house to warn her mother that "Daddy Dodson" was home for dinner. That would be the cue for action in the kitchen and the ladling of the split-pea soup into the large ironstone tureen.

Agatha's sudden look of fear, which touched the realm of panic every time he came into her line of sight, somehow gave Cyrus a reserve of subconscious satisfaction. However, this feeling came nowhere near the overt delight he acquired from playing mental chess with Margaret Cross or his wife. For in spite of his feeling of self-importance in the face of weakness, when Agatha's pale blue eyes cowered before him, there was the urge to sympathize, almost to caress: a tenderness, he always managed to deny.

He deliberately let the screen door slam with such force that the Belleek set up a faint chorus of varied chimes where it was displayed in the oval-shaped china case in the corner. He listened to hurrying footsteps in the pantry and kitchen; then straightened his black string tie as he looked into the large mirror of the hall coat rack. He hung his black derby on the highest hook and laid his cane on the waxed surface of the oak seat; careful not to scratch it's silver handle. These contrived little luxuries of exactness he allowed himself each day at noon. Then he seated himself at the head of the already set table, his hands resting profoundly on the carved lion headed arms of the chair.

The door to the pantry swung wide, held open by the heel of his red-faced, perspiring wife. Like wooden soldiers, four young women followed her into the room, each carrying her assigned serving dish. Myrtle Wilkins Dodson moved her foot, letting the door swing free and came forward with the huge soup tureen in her hands. She straightened herself up to her full stature, taking a deep breath to counteract the effect of the little trickle of sweat which had found its way from her graying hair over her broad forehead and now delighted itself by slowly coursing along the bridge of her rather pug nose. Signaling action, the tureen was placed in front of Cyrus on the white damask cloth. Silence was master as Alfreda, the oldest, put down the platter of fried parsnips; Cynthia, next, the bowl of wilted lettuce steaming from its bath of hot cider vinegar; Peggy, the veal steak; and last, Agatha. She banged the bowl of Brussels sprouts into her water goblet with a loud clank. Cyrus, in an act of generosity, looked the other way, his heart suddenly pained with empathy for Agatha.

He rose from his chair, his head bowed.

"Biscuits," someone whispered. "Aggie, the biscuits!"

Agatha started for the kitchen, knocking her chair into Cynthia's; holding back a tear, which had pocketed itself in the corner of her eye.

The swinging pantry door accented her departure and her return with the napkin-covered basket. She took her place behind her chair as the others had done and waited, wringing the hem of her apron while her mother went to the end of the table facing Cyrus.

"Father, thy blessings we ask, thy wisdom we seek," Cyrus started his prayer. Though his eyes were closed, he could see was Agatha's frightened eyes and a lump seemed to be forming in his throat. He paused, placed his hands on the soft tablecloth and continued, "Thy understanding we need, thy love we crave. These divine gifts we pray for in the name of thy son, Jesus Christ, Amen."

Five pair of eyes looked to his. He nodded consent and his wife and stepdaughters sat down.

"Where's Gloria?" he asked as he lifted the lid from the tureen and started ladling the thick green soup into a bowl.

All the girls glanced first at the vacant chair next to Peggy, then to their mother, then back to their silverware. Cyrus passed the bowl of soup to Alfreda on his on his right, who passed it to Peggy, who in turn reached over and placed it in front of her mother.

"She's on the committee for the function tomorrow," Myrtle answered as she sprinkled croutons on her soup.

"I asked where she was."

"Cyrus, one doesn't go around questioning every move a woman makes. Not when she's nearly twenty-eight," Myrtle interjected quietly.

"As long as she lives in this house, she'll do as she's told. And dinner is served at twelve twenty in this house," he snapped.

"Having lived all her life in this house and for nearly five years with you, I'm certain she is aware of the time, Cyrus," her tone had a sharpened edge ready for battle.

"Myrtle Dodson, I'll have no arguments at the table. Just notify Gloria of the serving times," he said in finality taking up his ladling of soup again. "Where are you going, Cynthia?" he asked.

"Mother's shawl, Father: she's having a chill," she answered quietly. Thinking to herself, how much she hated, her step-father.

Cyrus looked down the table at his wife, her face pale and yellowed. He finished serving the soup and sat down. He fed his lips the savory liquid. "Needs more ham," he was thinking when Cynthia came back with the gray knitted shawl and put it around her mother's shoulders with a gentle, reassuring pat.

As Cynthia seated herself again, Cyrus was thinking of Gloria. He missed her today. He enjoyed looking over at her when she was at the table. He thought to himself that she was by far the prettiest of his stepdaughters; he liked her long auburn hair, it excited him when it glistened in the sun or reflected a candle's flame. Lately her clothes seemed more revealing; she must be wearing her corset tighter. Cyrus even thought he could sense the delicate touch of toilet water in the air when she was near.

"Soup is delicious today, Mother," he said.

His wife gave no recognition of the compliment; but it didn't matter to Cyrus. He was picturing Gloria; as she was the night she knocked on his door. When he was reading Whitman; and she sat on the edge of his bed. Putting his book aside, the page marked with a leather bookmark, he asked, "What's the matter Gloria; have a bad dream?"

"Just lonely," she said, pulling the fullness of her batiste nightgown around her. "Today Willard Helms was reported killed in France; and Cynthia won't even talk to me about it."

He wanted to ask how Willard was killed; but didn't feel inclined to open up a discussion of the morbid subject, even if he had once expected Willard Helms to be his step-son-in-law and married to Cynthia. Everyone was trying to act as if the war wasn't taking place, when in reality it had altered every aspect of life, even in Crescent.

"That won't do, will it?" he heard himself saying. Her hand held his much as a child's seeking comfort. "Your mother awake?"

"I don't know; I don't care," her head now rested on his chest. Even through the nightshirt he could feel the warmth of her body.

"Guess I'm not much good to talk to, Gloria. Mother and your sisters seem afraid of me."

"Hold me," Gloria said holding his hand a little tighter. Soft auburn hair spilled over him as he held her closely; her lips were moist and inviting as they came close to his.

"Hold me," she said as she lay in his arms.

Relaxed, she fell asleep. For long, long moments she lay there. Then he found his hand accidentally touching her breast through the thin white gown, and he suddenly pulled himself together.

"Gloria, Gloria, time to go to bed, dear."

Her sleep was real and it took what seemed hours to waken her from her slumber. Finally she was awake, her eyes now soft and quite contented.

"Guess I'm a baby," she said kissing him on the cheek, "but all of this killing frightens me; when it gets so close; even Willard."

His softness surprised him as he patted her head, almost as if she really were a small child.

"Thank you, Father."

Whitman's "Leaves of Grass" didn't hold its reader that night.

Suddenly jarred out of his reverie, Cyrus looked past the row of static, silent, eating women; except for the mental touch of Gloria's, he was alone.

In the way of a peace offering, Cyrus cleared his throat and attempted to mend the breach, which separated him from the others.

"New boy's working out fine," he started, then took the last two spoonfuls of soup, wiped his lips with the napkin and pushed the empty bowl to the side. "Pass the steak, Peggy. This new boy's the kind you like to work with, give guidance to, show the road to success."

He received the platter of veal but no one said anything to encourage his monologue.

"Name's Matthew Harwood...excellent at taking orders, steady."

"Mother, you ready for meat?" Cynthia asked.

"I believe his father is a traveling man from Alice Chalmers. Machinery for farming, you know," Cyrus continued.

"Parsnips, Father?" Alfreda asked in her maternal tone; a tone so practiced, yet void of understanding even with thirty-one years of use.

"Thank you, Alfreda. He's a good-looking boy from a family of ten. Top of his class when he graduated this year." Cyrus waited to see if there was going to be any trace of cooperation with his conciliation offer. None came. Cynthia pushed the wilted lettuce bowl into his reach; everybody breathed, chewed, swallowed and gulped. Myrtle's knife screeched across her plate as she cut through her steak; then silence.

Cyrus reached for the lettuce bowl, looked at the five eating women and for a second bit his lip; then he spoke again, this time with more force expecting no answer. "Agatha needs a husband, someone who can look after her," he now had attention again. "This new boy looks a likely son-in-law; right age, right caliber. So tomorrow night at the function I'll make a proper introduction."

Agatha dropped her spoon into her half-full soup bowl, splashing stains down the front of her apron and onto the tablecloth.

"Myrtle, a portion of the Brussels sprouts, please," he said quietly.

Quickly the bowl passed from hand to hand down the table to him.

"And, Agatha, are you going to eat all of the biscuits by yourself?" he added.

Agatha put her hands to her mouth and bowed her head as if to cry.

Cynthia passed the biscuits. Cyrus looked at the clock in the corner, and then ate faster and without further comment. He had told Matt he would be back before one o'clock, and this boy must be given a good example. Pushing his chair back from the table, he rose to his feet. The five women followed his action. He could feel the tension as he left the room and went into the hall for his hat and cane. Agatha followed him, and bursting into tears ran up the stairs to her room. His eyes traced her flight and in them there were tears present but not seen. Once more, he straightened his tie.

Back in the dining room Myrtle and the girls were again seated. Cyrus stood in the archway, cane in hand, watching them.

"Myrtle, please inform Gloria that dinner is served at twelve-twenty in the Dodson home."

"Yes, Cyrus," she said.

The screen door slammed, and he paused, looking down at the half-finished yellow sweater Agatha had been knitting on the porch. Her sobs were audible from the window upstairs. Out of habit, a hand reached along the gold chain toward the watch pocket, then withdrew, clenching itself into a tight fist until the nails bit deep into the palm.

Chapter 2

Flintville was different from Crescent. It had a town square with tall trees and a bandstand painted apple green with white trim on the latticework around its base. Matt carefully backed the wagon up the alley to the rear entrance of Case's General Store. This was the one part of the trip he was not quite sure he would ever master.

"Hey, boy, if you're having such a hard time working that team back-wise, why don't you use your head?" It was Mr. Case's muscle-bound clerk, Morgan; hands on hips, his canvas apron still unsoiled from the morning's work. "Don't cost no more to use your head; than your rear end. Why don't you just run your wagon in front wise?"

"'Cause in this dead-end alley, I'd only have to back it out when I'm through."

Morgan gave a look of amazement and shook his head. "Never thought of that," he said almost to himself as he released the tailgate of the wagon so Matt could unload the sacks of grain.

Reaching over the side, Matt pulled the wagon brake on and locked it. Cyrus had warned him the first trip, "A mare is a bit independent, just like a woman. You shouldn't give her too much rein, the proverbial barn door open, or the wagon brake off: she'll take to her own pleasures, the stallion along with her, leaving a man without a cart to ride."

Matt jumped down from the seat, nearly knocking Morgan over as he swung around to balance the first sack on his shoulder.

"Think you was being paid by the number a bags you loaded the way you're always in such a damn hurry;" Morgan snapped.

Matt looked at the clerk's sable colored hair, straight and plastered tight to his skull--not one strand free to stray from its binding of grease.

"Say, boy, you're from Crescent ain't you?"

"Yes, I'm from Crescent and you know it," Matt said in disgust.

"Just thought I'd ask. You know, boy, I've had more good tail from those Crescent girls than any town in six counties."

"Why don't you keep your mouth shut?"

"Only trying to give you a tip. Maybe you are missing somethin', 'cause it's true. I've taken on dozens of 'em from Crescent, all damn good. Say, boy, you got any sisters?" Morgan started to laugh but Matt ignored him.

"You're green, sure green, boy, don't you know you never put it where it'll get wet?" Morgan paused to clean his fingernails with a long pearl-handled knife while Matt waited for instructions. "Put it in the loft, boy."

The only deterrent between Matt's fist and Morgan's finely cut chin at that moment was the mental image of Cyrus Dodson. It was fast becoming a constant companion. He could remember Cyrus say "Never mix business with pleasure. People have been saying that for a dozen generations, but most have never had sense enough to heed their own words."

Morgan leaned against the loading dock and watched Matt unload the sacks. At one point when Matt was struggling to balance one of them on his shoulder, he heard a loud thud and he looked around to see Morgan's knife buried in the side of the wagon seat, its blade still vibrating, not more than six inches from Matt's head.

Matt glowered at Morgan; but remembered Mr. Dodson's admonitions.

"Just for practice," Morgan grinned, "just for practice," he said reaching over to pull the blade out of the wagon seat. He laughed again as he folded the knife and put it in his pants pocket.

When he finished unloading the grain, Matt had Morgan sign the delivery slip, pulled the wagon out of the alley and tied the team to the watering trough in front of the Post Office. He would pick up the mailbags for Crescent at five thirty. That gave him exactly one hour and forty-five minutes to wait and see Ellie, he thought to himself as he cut across the street to Coolie's Drug Store. He was excited inside, numb in the stomach, just the same as when he was on the verge of a fight. "Now why? She ain't no different than any girl. No different than Margo or any of Mom's girls, except for one thing: I'm going to marry her."

His finger sought out the top button of his shirt and the collar tightened itself into a constraining noose one size too small. Looking around the store, he found it empty of customers except for a large woman sitting at the counter eating a banana split. Matt joined her, leaning on the cold white slab of marble, waiting for Coolie to finish filling prescriptions so he could order a root beer... a sorry consolation for all his dreams. The woman finished; Coolie excused himself to go down in the basement and start the compressor to the fountain, and Matt was deserted, even robbed of his numbness: she wasn't going to be there. After all, he hadn't even asked her; hadn't even said, "See you tomorrow." The spring on the screen door groaned and the hinges squeaked as they opened and closed. Matt turned to see who had broken his solitude. It was Ellie. They were alone. The numbness was back; and he felt awkward as he slid off the wire-legged stool to face her.

"Hello, I thought you had forgotten," he whispered.

"I didn't, you see."

"I'm glad."

"So am I; but you know something?" Her skirt brushed against him as she sat on the next stool.

"What?"

"You're funny. Don't get mad; I like you, but you're funny."

"Why?"

"You didn't tell me you'd be coming back into town today."

"Yes I did."

"No, no!" She shook her head. "You made me guess. You are funny. Then you say, 'I thought you had forgotten'."

"Well, I thought you had."

"Forgotten what?"

"Why, I, I, I don't know. Except I'm not the only funny one."

"You're just fighting back."

"No, I'm not," his elbows propped themselves on the counter. "You are funny...and don't you get mad; because I like you, too. In fact, I think I love you."

"Really?"

"I mean it; and don't ever say I didn't tell you."

Coolie, back from the basement, stood listening to the inane conversation. "You two want a soda or something; or are you just taking up stool space?"

"Strawberry," she said taking off her straw sailor hat.

"Didn't you hear what I told you?"

"Uh huh," her eyes teased as she combed her hair.

"And what for you, son?"

"Root beer."

They drank their sodas almost without comment. Matt paid the twenty cents and they started to leave just as Morgan from Case's opened the screen door.

There was a long whistle. "Now I can see why you're such a hurrying fool when it comes to doing your grain loading chores, Boy; so you can loaf the day away courtin' Flintsville's social set," Morgan said condescendingly.

Matt swung around facing Morgan, his fists clenched; but he felt Ellie's firm hand on his arm.

"Go on Ellie, let him start something," Morgan chided. "He might just as well learn right now: we don't like Crescent trash talkin' to our women."

"Please, Matthew, please," Ellie said quietly.

They left, but Matt could hear Morgan's sneering, voice as the screen door slammed: "Please, Matthew, please," he mimicked, "Ha, ha, ha."

"Let's go over to the bandstand," she said as they crossed the street toward the square. "This time of day nobody is ever there."

They were now in the park and she kicked her shoes off and picked them up. "Race you to the stand," she laughed.

He let her win the race, and she slid down on the bench leaning against the white latticework.

"You know, I told you I loved you and you didn't even smile, laugh or even hear me."

"You didn't say you loved me. You said you thought you loved me."

"Well, I do love you. Someday I'm going to marry you."

"You sound like a little boy when you say that."

"Guess I do; but I mean it."

"Takes two to love, Matthew; that is, for love that's good enough for marriage."

"Then you don't love me?"

"I told you I liked you," she moved the hat and shoes from between them and placed them on the end of the bench. "Let's not be so serious." Her hand touched his.

"I can't help it; I feel all choked up inside; and I don't know why."

"You're a man and I'm a girl, that's all."

"And I want to kiss you," he said pulling her into his arm.

"No, no," she laughed, freeing herself from his arms and held his hand, "even if we weren't sitting in the middle of the square in the middle of Friday afternoon."

"I'm sorry," he said quickly to cover up his embarrassment.

"Don't say something you don't mean."

"But I am sorry."

"No, you're not; I'd be insulted if I thought you were."

"Then why?" he heard himself ask.

"Because even love doesn't give you the right to something that doesn't belong to you. Love starts with giving, not taking.

He reached up and touched her hair, "What did you study in high school?" he finally asked.

"Same things anyone studies, I guess."

"No, you didn't, cause you don't sound or act like the others."

"Of course I do," she said holding his hand tighter.

"You go to Flintville?"

"No; St. Joseph's Academy, in Boston."

"Boston; what kind of school is that?" he asked.

"It's a girl's school. Father's sister is the Mother Superior."

Matt shook his head, "See I told you were different. I could tell by the way you talk."

"I'm not different. What do I have to do to show you I'm not different?"

"Kiss me."

"No, uh...No!"

"Is that a church school, that academy? Is that why you won't let me fall in love with you?"

"Of course not; I thought I explained. Love is a most important word. We've only met. Just introduced by a couple of sodas and Mr. Coolie; hold my hand Matthew, but don't ask for more and spoil everything."

They started back across the lawn. "Want to race again?" she laughed.

"Hell no," he had the courage to say, quietly. "You want to hold hands and we'll take our time doing it."

"Tomorrow night at the dance?" she asked, "Do I get first and last dance?"

"Sure, tomorrow night at the Grange Hall."

"You know something? I'll have to admit, you're not nearly as funny as I thought you were."

"Thanks, Ellie; but do you know something? You've got me thinking you're about ten times as funny as I thought YOU were."

"I've got to hurry; Father will be wondering why I've been gone so long. Remember, first and last dance." And she was out of sight before Matt could collect his thoughts.

He stood there on the edge of the square, kicking the grass wondering why he had talked so silly in front of her, the words, "Hold my hand, Matt," running around in a little sing-song ditty in his ears, "Hold my hand, Matthew."

"Oh hell," he said and crossed over to the Post Office.

Chapter 3

The trumpet blew, the cymbals clanged and the base drum boomed away; while the loudest of the whole ensemble was the trombone Luke Mason had never learned to play.

"Nope, I never learned to play, just kind of picked it up this way." And very few in Crescent ever thought to doubt Luke's words one bit, for he was "leader of the band."

"Old Missouri Waltz, a one, and a two," he tapped his foot.

"This ain't Missouri, Luke," chided Cliff with a bang of cymbals.

"A one, and a two," he glared back, the gold braid on his borrowed uniform swinging with the beat.

Old Missouri stood up quite well under the onslaught, while the crowd gathered around the platform and spilled over onto the fire station lawn waiting for the speeches, the eats, and the tapping of the keg.

Gloria Dodson tacked the last row of tri-colored bunting in place and smiled a signal of completion to Bruce McHenry, who was seating the guests of honor on the stand according to their relative importance in the life of Bruce McHenry and that of Crescent's new "mechanized" fire department.

Even though she was taller than average, Gloria found herself standing on tiptoe looking for her father. "Cyrus mustn't be late, not for today," she found herself thinking. "Not for today, it is so important." Suddenly she spotted the derby and the gray ascot tie and made her way through the crowd to his side.

"Father," she said, putting her arm through his as she came up behind him, "the Missouri Waltz is in your honor." She squeezed his arm with pride.

"And who told them I was from Missouri?" he asked, trying to keep from smiling.

Gloria swung from Cyrus to her youngest sister. "Aggie, honey, you look like a new girl, a new woman. Cynthia, didn't I tell you yellow was Aggie's color, didn't I? Aggie, I'm so proud."

Agatha felt uncomfortable in her new role, her self-consciousness compounded by Gloria's remarks. Tears again were beginning to form in her eyes. Gloria sensed their nearness and changed the subject.

"I've saved a row of chairs down front for you and the girls, Mother; where it's shady."

"Have you seen the Harwood boy?" Cyrus asked Gloria as his wife and other daughters went ahead of them.

"You mean Matthew? No. And Father, don't tell me you're going to make him go back to work when the whole town is celebrating."

"Of course I'm not; besides, I have to have an audience when I speak. I just think this would be a very good time to make him acquainted with Agatha."

"Father, you're not a very good matchmaker, you know."

"Why, he's an excellent boy, and Agatha needs a husband!'" Cyrus said.

"That's not what I mean. You'll have her in tears. Better let me introduce them." She patted his arm as she led him toward the platform.

"More respect," Cyrus said half aloud.

Gloria looked around at him questioningly.

"I said sometimes a little more respect would be good," he repeated.

"From me?" Gloria asked.

"Yes, from you."

"Yes, Father, and shall I make the introduction?" her amusement was unconcealed.

"If you like," he said as he tipped his hat to Margaret Cross and two of her widowed friends who had just waved to him.

"I'd love to, Father."

"Good afternoon, Mrs. Cross; lovely day for a fire engine party, wouldn't you say?"

They had reached the steps of the platform. Cyrus felt for his watch and Gloria's mood changed for a second.

"Good luck, Father," she said with calm excitement. Matt and one of the other volunteer firemen lifted a large keg to its place of honor on the two bunting-draped sawhorse.

"I'll bet they guzzle all five of these before the moon gets to tree top tonight," Bruce said.

"You wouldn't be making all of Crescent into a drunken saloon would you, Uncle," laughed Matt.

"What in hell are you doing at this here shindig? Thought you were going to some hick dance at the Grange."

"Changed my mind."

"Nope, that one don't hold even a pint of beer, let alone make sense. 'Changed my mind'. That is not a sensible answer when a woman's involved."

"Well, I did; just like that, I changed my mind. Besides it's going to rain."

"What did she do, kick you in the compost pit for getting fresh?"

"No."

"All kidding aside, Matt; what's the matter?"

"Nothing, I guess; except what in hell good is a girl that comes up saying, 'Hold my hand, Matt. Don't ask for more, Matthew. Don't spoil things, Matthew.' Just tell me what on earth's a girl like that good for?"

Bruce pushed his fire chief's cap back on his head and wiped his brow. "Sounds to me, Matt, as if this hand-holding SHE has got this marriage business carrying a mighty heavy load on her mind."

"Then why wouldn't she let me kiss her?"

The Election

"You wouldn't believe me if I told you," Bruce said with a smile. "But I'll be generous enough to tell you one thing. You're a hell of a lot better off eating hot dogs and getting sick on green brew than out baying at the moon like a hard-up coyote about to trip a trap."

"You know, your uncle talks in riddles," the volunteer fireman said as he helped Matt lift the second keg.

"Yes, he sure does," Matt, agreed.

"By-the-by, Matthew," Bruce yelled back at him, "Miss Gloria Dodson's been asking for you. Better keep a lookout. Probably wants to put you to work."

Why would she be looking for him? Matt tried to recall what Miss Gloria Dodson looked like. She was the only one of Mr. Dodson's daughters he had been introduced to. She had been in the feed store one day to talk to her father. He could remember that she was tall because it seemed she looked right into his eyes when they said "Hello". Outside of that Matt knew he wouldn't recognize her. That was silly, he thought to himself. In Crescent you should be on speaking terms with everybody.

At that moment, a heavy hand slapped Matt across the back, knocking the wind out of him; it was Ward Kessler expressing his friendship.

"Get ready, on your mark. We're going to wrestle for the folks," Ward said. "Just because you flipped me a couple times out behind the granary it is no sign you've taken the championship medal where the crowd's concerned."

"Where you been, Ward? Looked all over for you."

"On your mark, get set, go!!"

"Who's the girl, Ward?"

"Oops, kind of forgot my manners," Ward apologized. The girl beside him beamed. "Mitzie, I'd like to have you meet Matthew Harwood; he's kind of what you might call a friend of mine. But I'm still going to toss him."

"Pleased to meet you, Mr. Harwood," she said in a rather husky voice. Her hand was extended and held his for a more than usual length of time. Matt could feel a slight tingle go up his arm as he stood there next to her. The perfume was strong; and he found that it was hard for him not to notice how low cut her blouse was, or how full-grown her breasts were. She squeezed his hand tighter.

"Mr. Harwood; how do you like all this proper talk?" Ward snickered. "This Mitzie's a real lady. She's different: won't read newspapers because it's bad luck, but she's always scribbling fancy words and poetry on every scrap of paper she gets a hold of. I used to know her when she was a little kid in Pennsylvania. Grown up a bit though. Going to rent the space over my shop."

"How do you do; Mitzie. My name is 'Matt'. Mitzie, you know, I like your name; kind of different. Like they didn't dig it out of the Bible."

"Now, Miss Mitzie, if you'll let go of Mr. Harwood's dainty pink hand, and you folks will clear a spot on the grass, the contest will begin," Ward broke in, laughing at them.

"I'll hold your coat, Matthew," Mitzie said softly.

The two men sprawled side by side on their backs and the bout began. First their legs straight in the air, ankles locked and grunts and groans of exertion to give added zest to the performance. In the effort, Ward popped the top two buttons of his tight fitting shirt showing the thick mat of red hair. The crowd laughed as Ward went head over with Matt the victor of the first fall.

As the two got to their feet, Margaret Cross, standing in the front of the group reached out and touched Ward's arm. "Hello, Ward. May I talk to you?" Her voice was soft and hesitatingly inviting. He ignored her gesture.

"Make it two out of three," he laughed, rubbing his game left leg, "any fool can be lucky the first time."

Though a little slower and with more sound of struggle, the second fall was merely a copy of the first.

"Tell you what, Ward, why don't we make it six out of ten?" someone in the crowd yelled above the laughter.

"Gad, now there's a man wants to make it tough on Mr. Harwood," Ward countered, "But a sporting man such as myself is always game, if Mr. Harwood can muster enough mustard for the contest."

Fall three was also awarded to Matt. This time Ward called for time out while he took his shirt off. "Must be the shirt is holding back the flesh." His complete torso covered with hair that stopped only at the neck and wrist lines, Ward flexed his muscles and pounded his chest in mock anger as he towered over Matt.

In quick succession the next five times at battle Ward flipped Matt's leg down to the ground with seeming ease and was in the process of winning the required six out of ten falls when Gloria Dodson found them.

She looked down at the sweating men with a smile of near disdain on her lips. Every time she saw Ward, his hairy body both repulsed and attracted her. It left her with a feeling of guilt for having wondered how it would be to be loved by him, forced into submission by his strength, nearly smothered by his weight, crushed into ecstasy by his brute force. Her thought left her with an edge of excitement that was hard to deny. She could feel her cheeks getting flushed.

"Mr. Matthew Harwood, when you are finished with this circus act, Father would like you to meet his family." Her tone was firm but friendly.

"I'm sorry, Miss Dodson," Ward said jumping quickly to his feet, "I'm afraid this whole animal show is my fault."

"Not going to let a woman break up the championship contest are you, Ward?" a heckler yelled.

Ward ignored the remark and helped Matt to his feet.

"You see, the festivities were a bit slow getting started and I couldn't resist putting on a show. You'll forgive us, Miss Dodson?" Ward asked courteously as he put his shirt back on.

"Certainly, Mr. Kessler; but I'm afraid, as a woman, I sometimes do not fully understand the acts of men."

"You know, ma'am," Matt said catching his breath as Mitzie helped him on with his coat, "as men, sometimes we have a hard time understanding ourselves." They all laughed.

"But we have a hell of a lot harder time trying to figure out women," the heckler added at the top of his voice.

Ward's hand touched Gloria's arm as he pushed back the crowd to make room for her to lead the way. It made her catch her breath for a moment because she imagined their bodies close together. She looked up at him, seeking his eyes, but he was busy looking to see if Matt and Mitzie were following. When they reached the row where Myrtle Dodson and her daughters were seated, Ward and Mitzie stepped back while Matt went forward to do the honors of proper introduction. Gloria was most deliberate in her task.

"Mother, I thought you and the girls might like to meet father's new employee, Mr. Harwood. Chief McHenry is his uncle."

"How do you do, Mr. Harwood?"

"Hello, Mrs. Dodson."

"My daughters, Cynthia, Alfreda, Agatha, and Peggy... and of course, you've met Gloria."

"How do you do," Matt said awkwardly, not quite knowing what next to say to six women. Then he saw Ward out of the corner of his eye and his problem was solved at least for a moment. "I want you to meet my friend, Ward Kessler, and Mitzie."

"Mitzie Kowalski; Polish," Mitzie came to the rescue. "Mrs. Dodson," Matt went on.

Ward again accidentally brushed against Gloria as he clumsily went down the row of women shaking hands with each. Her reaction repeated itself and she was ashamed of the feeling. Agatha, who a moment before was on the verge of tears when Matt had been introduced, now even smiled at the town blacksmith as he shook her hand gently and was completely diverted from her sense of self-consciousness by Mitzie's smile and strong perfume.

"Mr. Dodson is a very fortunate man," Ward said. "So many charming women to call his own."

"Won't you please sit with us," Cynthia said.

Myrtle Dodson was at first distressed by her daughter's suggestion; but Ward's last remark had softened the blow.

As Bruce McHenry stood up, Luke gave the signal for the fanfare and the trumpet blared wildly.

"Ladies, gentlemen...and that rather strange group of personages I revel in calling friends," Bruce started, and then paused for a drink of water. "Every last jack of you has been the opinion that this gathering was concocted to dedicate this red and gold gas buggy as the official fire extinguisher of this fair city of Crescent. How far wrong can three thousand, six hundred and thirty-one people be? Even got my favorite nephew sitting down there in the audience balanced on his thumb and scared out of his boyhood 'cause he thinks he's going to be called upon to spout for five minutes on the heroic deeds of that distinguished group of dauntless beer hounds: the volunteers, our sparkling counterpart of the D.A.R. But he can save his wind because the only one who will have the honor of verbosity this cloudy afternoon is one Bruce McHenry who, in his most eloquent style, has a hell of a lot to say." Bruce took another drink of water as Luke struck up the band once more and one of the volunteers clanged the fire engine bell, while another wound up the siren to its full pitch. When the noise had subsided, Bruce smiled and continued: "Now I'm damn glad you got that exhibition off your chest. Like to see you having such a good time one and all; but the next one of you touches that siren or bell except when going to a fire, you're off the force for good and we'll pour the beer down the cesspool before you get a drop."

Everybody laughed except the volunteers.

"All kidding aside, there is something mighty important about to take place here today. Ever since I took my first vacation three years ago and my volunteers let the firehouse burn down while they played pinochle in the back room of Mayor Kirk's office, I have been acutely aware of the ability of some men to get things done and the ability of other men to place the inertia of their pompous souls right dab in the path of anything that looks like it might move. It's a most remarkable study that the whole damn lot of you should take up now and then. One group of men paved your main street, built this new fire station that even the volunteers will have a hell of a hard time burning down, and had the foresight to build some storage reservoirs so you'll at least have water to drink during dry spells such as this when all we get is sun and more sun. These are our progressive men." He took another drink and waited for the crowd to settle down. "You just take a look at the men on this platform...to my left, our beloved Mayor Kirk; Reverend Pritchard, that illustrious master of the pulpit; Sheriff Clay; Mr. Martin; Ted Aldrich and Welby Saunders all members of our town council."

Applause accompanied each introduction and Bruce capitalized on each for dramatic appeal. "Of course you should know a hell of a lot about these men. God knows you run into them every day; but I want you to know what I am about to say in their behalf is not said because they earned better grades in high school than Bruce McHenry, or earned more money than Bruce McHenry; but rather that through their untiring efforts, they've earned more notoriety than Bruce McHenry." The crowd clapped. "Yes, I am certain you know, as I do, these of our town fathers aren't as marked by achievement as our first-mentioned group of men!"

Not understanding the intent of Bruce's words, the crowd applauded and cheered.

"Solidity is their byword, righteousness their plea. Gentlemen, Crescent salutes you for your valor in battling the daily rigors of government and those shadows of experience which haunt us all."

Cliff accidentally let his cymbals bump together and the sheriff found it an opportune time to blow his nose.

"Enough for the past. You are all acquainted with your own aches and pains, therefore, you must know Dr. Phillips, the man who went in hock to build you a hospital. That's him with the smirk on his face. Just delivered triplets this afternoon out at the Willis' farm." The crowd applauded and cheered. "Yes sir, he couldn't have been more helpful to a more deserving man of God than old Carl Willis, who's been bragging about this going to make an even dozen. What variety are the newcomers, Doc.?"

"Two to one in favor of the feminine side of life," Dr. Phillips said, looking up at Bruce through his bifocals.

Bruce McHenry joked with the crowd and the men on the platform for another ten minutes, before he held his hand up as a signal for order.

"Two men I haven't introduced; one you have only read about, the other you know. The one is former Governor of this great state, the other, though he himself at this very moment does not know it,

The Election

is destined to be the center of much controversy and name-calling. At this time, I'd like to introduce Governor Clarence Calder."

The ex-Governor was a wiry little man with thick brows, which contributed as much to his expression as did his unruly black hair. Clarence Calder stood up, walked to the center of the platform and began, "Came down here, one hundred ninety six miles today, to look for an honest man, and I wouldn't want you to think I was talking about my old friend Bruce when I made that remark because I wouldn't want to ruin his spotless record for never taking his tongue out of his cheek." This time even the siren and fire bell clanged for all they are worth in complete approval. "Been in politics a long time and never yet found such a man; but this time I think we've found him. Followed his career since he acted as state senator from this county six years ago. Not flashy, not a 'know it all', not a crackpot; but an honest man who can see fifty years ahead without trying to crawl back under his mother's apron for protection. That sounds like we might be asking for a second coming of the Savior and maybe we are; but as I said, I believe we've found him. Now, knowing this man, as I believe I do, I have neglected to mention my purpose here in Crescent today until this moment; because I was afraid he would refuse, out of modesty, what the people of this state are about to ask of him. So instead of asking his approval, here at the very grass roots, I am going to ask your approval, your backing, and your hard work to make this name known across the state: Cyrus P. Dodson, our next Governor!"

There was silence for what seemed an eternity. Cyrus had tears welling up in his eyes and his hand found the large railroad watch but he could not see the face to tell the time.

Myrtle Dodson was so busy trying to get Cynthia's attention so she would put the shawl around her shoulders that she missed the last sentence of the Governor's remark. She sat shivering in a cold, damp chill wondering why Cynthia was so slow. Gloria felt the lump she knew was going to be there swell in her throat, and her entire body became alive. Suddenly she could hear the roar of the crowd rising to join the pounding of her own heart.

Chapter 4

Ominous black clouds had been pushing themselves up over the southeast horizon all afternoon until now, in the early hours of night, they were starting to form a dome of darkness; even to the point of threatening the moon, as it swung high in an arc, trying its best to skirt the path of the persistent intruders.

Ward had teased Matthew about being afraid to go to the Grange Dance because of a girl "who liked to hold hands." Finally Matt had given in and joined Ward and Mitzie in the ride to Flintville in Ward's surrey. Conversation was sparse.

"Going to rain, Matt; but isn't that what you're looking for: a romantic setting with rain a-pattering on the roof?"

"I hope to hell it's a cloud burst and you get stuck up to your axle in that damn river mud," Matt said.

Silence held the three captive. Finally Ward said, "Should have borrowed Doc. Phillip's automobile; could have made it in a third the time."

"Yeah, with nails sticking out of all the tires," Matt laughed.

"Every time I think of those kids doing that, I get so mad inside that my stomach just stops digesting and does nothing but pump bile up into my mouth," Ward snapped.

Mitzie cuddled closer to Matt as the moon was finally devoured. She let her hand rest on his knee.

"You two always sound as if you're mad at each other," she said. "But I don't really care, gives me two men and I think you're both very nice."

"Mitzie, you've only got one man at this moment, that's me," Ward said; "because all this boy can think of doing is holding hands, isn't it, Matthew?"

"That I don't believe," Mitzie said with a husky giggle.

"That, I don't believe," Matt chided.

The conversation ended again and Ward urged the horse to greater speed with the sting of the rein. Matt couldn't keep his thoughts from the image of Ellie. She would wonder why he was late.

"Click, click, click" Ward clacked his tongue at the horse and slapped the rein once more against its flank.

The silent moments were at first awkward, then disquieting. Mitzie could feel the emptiness of melancholy sapping the warmth from her body. Even between two men, she was alone with the memories of Pennsylvania to taunt her. She was thirteen when they brought her father out of the mine shaft, crushed but alive enough to hold her hand and whisper, "Where's your mother, Mitzie? I love her...God, Mitz, tell her...tell her, tell her...I..." and he was gone.

Then there was the curly black hair of Kurt who had married her mother a few months after that. "I can't stand him trying to take Daddy's place," she said over and over in her pillow at night, and once she had even said it to Kurt himself. She remembered her stepbrothers, three of them who had tied her to the bed the afternoon Kurt and her mother had left on their three-day honeymoon. She had fought at first, then cried, and exhausted, collapsed.

"Hell, Mitch, look, she was a virgin; blood on the mattress, all over hell."

"Maybe so; but it's the best fourteen-year-old I ever had."

"Untie her, Mitch, she's broke now, might cry, but she won't bite no more."

They let her go and she had hidden in the tool shed behind the house. The tears dried and left parched river beds down her cheeks and her lower lip had begun to swell where one of her new brothers had sunk his teeth into it.

There was an echoing rumble of wheels when the surrey crossed the new bridge and the first salvo of thunder split the sky as the clouds began warring in the heavens. Mitzie was jolted back to the present and she realized she was holding Matt's hand tighter than she should.

"See, they haven't torn the old bridge down," Ward said.

"Just sitting over there like a ghost," Matt added.

"Be a darn wet ghost if the river gets as high as that storm in April."

"Yeah, it'll wash it out sure as hell one day," Matt said. "All the planks missing in the middle from last time."

The tap, tap, pattering of the first few drops of rain played on the top of the surrey just as Ward pulled up in front of the Grange Hall.

Tall, graceless windows framed the flood of light which spilled into the yard and over onto the cars and carriages of the dancers inside.

"Well, at least it waited till we got here," Ward said.

"You two get out and I'll drive around and park the rig and Chestnut in Marvin Crater's barn just in case the storm gets too bad.'

"Look at the automobiles, Ward, just like Philadelphia." Mitzie said.

"Yeah, kind of makes us old-fashioned, with this hay-burning engine of ours," Ward commented.

"Seven of them," Matt observed as he helped Mitzie down from the seat.

"Still, there's a lot more buggies and wagons than cars," Ward said as if in self-defense.

Another bolt of lightning lighted the sky and for an instant exposed the building in an aura of blue-white brilliance; Gothic facade complete with fake arches, towers and scrolled cornicing, all classically styled in clapboard and proudly labeled in block letters, "Walker County Grange."

Inside, a caller was whipping the dancers into a frenzied reel while a four piece orchestra strained to keep in pace with a wild and happy fiddler.

Matt paid the seventy-five cents for the three of them and told the ticket-taker that Ward would be coming in a few minutes.

"You can't miss him, red hair, you can't miss him."

"I know him; big blacksmith from Crescent. Yea, that's Ward: a blacksmith all the way. I know him, I'll let him in."

Matt was busy looking for Ellie when he realized Mitzie was holding his hand.

"Dance?" she asked.

"Sure, guess that's kind of what we came for."

The next three dances were rounds and Mitzie proved herself to be 'all woman' as she pushed herself close to Matt. His response was not cold, but he couldn't help wondering about Ellie. Then he saw her; she was dancing with Morgan from Case's store. Morgan was dressed in his finest clothes, complete with spats and checkered vest. "Lord, he's got his hair plastered down," Matt thought to himself. It was obvious that Morgan had been drinking as Matt purposefully danced Mitzie over close to them. Ellie's expression was one of surprise at first, then one of desperation with her present partner.

"Matthew Harwood," she said. "I thought we had first dance."

Morgan stopped dancing and glared. "Well, if it ain't the boy who delivers the chicken feed to the store."

"We were late;" Matt said. He could feel himself about ready to say something silly just as he had done in Flintsville's square when he had been alone with Ellie the first time. "Maybe next dance, if it isn't a square?" he asked.

"Still trying to crash the upper crust, huh, boy?" Morgan butted in. "Why don't you stay in your own class with the girls from Crescent; like the slut you're with, perfume and all."

Matt's fist shot out, but Morgan stepped to one side and grabbed him by the coat collar as he threw himself off balance.

"Careful, little boy, you just might get hurt," Morgan said in contempt.

"Matthew," Ellie said as she danced Morgan off into the crowd.

"I'm sorry that happened," Matt said to Mitzie as he straightened his coat.

"Don't worry, I'm used to men," she said. "But don't you listen to him, if she's the girl you want."

"I'd like to kill him," Matt said.

"There's nothing he could say that's that important."

"I know, but..."

"She doesn't care for a man like that," Mitzie said, holding his hand. "I can tell you that without even knowing her name; just by her eyes when she looks at you."

"Gad, it's a regular cloud burst out there." Ward was right behind them. "Let me get through to that stove; hope they've got it going, because I'm damn near soaked. Even tried using that piece of tarp to keep dry."

The three of them pushed their way to the corner and the pot-bellied stove; which had been lit to take the chill off the evening air.

"We'll never get back to Crescent tonight," Ward said.

"Where we going to stay?" Matt half-asked himself.

"Ah, that's no worry; Crater's barn is as dry as they come. Plenty high and dry, and since he's away there's four stalls with no horses. One stall for each of us and one for old Chestnut"

While Mitzie stayed with Ward by the stove, Matt found Ellie and they danced.

They talked in quiet whispers.

"I'm glad you finally got here, in spite of the storm, my brother and I have been here since eight." Ellie said.

"I wasn't going to come; kept asking myself, 'What's the use, just what in hell is the use?' But then I changed my mind."

"What do you mean, 'what's the use'?"

"Just that: it's you. I tell you I love you and you laugh at me."

"I didn't do that."

"Yes you did; said, 'Takes two to love. I like you Matthew.' If that isn't laughing, I don't know what is."

"Matthew, that's just honesty. I can't love you, not the way you think of love."

"Of course you can."

"You don't understand. There are many things that make us different, and we each have a life that we live that no one else will ever understand."

"You're not making sense. What's that got to do with not being able to love me?"

"Matthew, if I could ever love anybody, it would probably be you. I've never known anyone who made me feel the way you do. But I can't."

The dance was over, and as they started walking from the center of the floor they realized they were being, slowly circled by Morgan and three of his friends.

"Don't fight with him, Matthew. He's dangerous."

"I'll kill him," Matt heard himself say.

"Matthew, don't fight with him or I'll never be able to see you again."

"Don't be silly; someone has to give him a lesson."

"All right, boy; we think it's time you left the dance and went back to Crescent," Morgan said grabbing Matt's arm firmly above the elbow.

"Who cares what you think," Matt said.

"Come on, little boy, before we have to throw you out."

Matt's fist this time did not miss its target; Morgan went spinning to the floor.

"Matthew, please, please," Ellie kept saying over and over.

Morgan's three friends moved in fast: two grabbed at Matt's arms, the third ready to repay him for the first blow. He, too, went crashing to the floor from Matt's fist. The other two now held his arms firmly behind him.

"Warned you, social climber," Morgan said as he lunged forward. "Warned you." And he let his fist bury itself deep in Matt's midriff and the next blow crashed to the side of his head. "Now you're going to get the licking that's coming to you."

As Ellie screamed, "Stop, stop, stop!" the fist hit Matt's stomach again and again and again. Matt's knees started to give way when Morgan suddenly backed away as he looked up, seeing Ward's big frame looming up behind Matt. "Crack!" Together went the heads of the two who held Matt's arms. One of them started to cry, the other lay on the floor holding his head.

"Matthew, oh, Matthew, please don't spoil everything" sobbed Ellie.

But Matt could not hold back. He surged forward at Morgan who kept in a crouched position, circling clockwise around his pursuer.

"I'll kill you," Matt kept saying.

Then he saw it for the first time: in Morgan's left hand, the knife, its pearl handle and polished blade both glistening in the light.

Matt could not stop; he lunged and felt the blade slash across his right forearm. He kept pushing forward and again on the next lunge the knife found its mark, this time on his shoulder. Anger took complete control and Matt no longer could see Morgan's face or the knife; everything was a blur and he struck out wildly with his fists and his feet. Once more the knife bit the flesh of Matt's arm before the fight ended with Matt's foot square in Morgan's groin. All was quiet for a long moment as the color drained from Morgan's face. He doubled over on the floor, then rose to his knees and began to vomit.

Ward held Matt back as he started to kick at the crumpled Morgan.

"Oh, I hate you!" Ellie cried. "Hate you!"

Matt could hear the words in the background; but he was too weak to even lift his head. He could vaguely remember the rain pouring down over his face and body, then Mitzie opening the barn door and lighting the lantern. He lay on the straw where she had put him. He felt her place the horse blanket over him; but all he could do was shiver; he was so dizzy he couldn't even open his eyes. Finally sleep overtook him and only the rain pounding on the barn roof disturbed the night.

When Matt opened his eyes, Mitzie was lying beside him, her eyes closed. He stirred and she sat upright, looking down at him.

"You all right?" she asked.

"Think so," he answered, fingering the bandages on his right arm.

"Just part of my petticoat," she said. "He didn't cut you very bad; took a long time to stop bleeding though." She caressed his head; her cool fingers pushing his hair back from his face.

"We were soaked," she continued "put our clothes over the stall. Hope they dry by morning."

"Still raining?" he managed to ask.

"Yes, it just keeps pouring."

"Where's Ward?"

"Stayed down at the dance to be sure none of them followed us. You sure can fight, Matt."

"Morgan, hurt?"

"Not too bad; but I'll bet he'll have a stomach ache for a few days."

"I guess I will too;" Matt added holding his side, realizing for the first time that he was lying there in only his underwear.

"You know, Matt, you should watch your temper. In a way you're just like Ward used to be. When I was young, I saw him when he got violent. It was frightening. He completely changed. He was almost insane."

Matt sat upright. "Ward? You're fooling me. Ward wouldn't hurt anyone."

"I'm not fooling you; I wish I were. That's why Ward left Pennsylvania. He had to leave Whalen where we lived. It doesn't matter at all. I just want you to watch your temper, Matt."

"What did he do?"

"Nothing."

"Tell me."

"Let's not talk about it."

He wondered if she were lying. Looking into her eyes, he knew, that she must have been telling the truth. How could Ward do anything bad enough that he was forced to leave town? Ward wouldn't hurt anyone; he wouldn't even try to win an Indian wrestle except in fun.

"Lay down," she said, pushing him back against the straw; "you need your rest." She bent over him and kissed him gently on the cheek. He looked up at her. In the flickering of the lantern she looked very soft, even with her hair straggly from the rain.

"You know, you are very pretty."

The lantern wick sputtered a few times and they were in complete darkness. Ward's horse, Chestnut, snorted once or twice and stomped his hind foot in the soft earth to register disapproval of the change.

Mitzie slid under the blanket next to Matt and they lay there silently and Matt slept for a few minutes. Then he woke up.

"Tell me about Ward," he said, startling her.

"Go back to sleep," she said.

"No, I want to know about Ward."

"Matt, I'm not going to say any more. Ward is the only friend I have, anywhere."

"Tell me."

Mitzie could feel the tears welling up inside her. Was she going to have to relive that day this time even to the point of putting the whole horrible thing into words? "No, it doesn't matter, anymore; it's all over and I want to forget it, Matt. Ward is just like my big brother, the only brother I had until Dad was killed."

"What do you mean?"

"After my mother married again I had step-brothers, that's all."

"Tell me what happened with Ward."

She started to sob softly. "I'm sorry," she said, "But I don't want to talk about it, not any more. Ward's my only friend."

Matt moved closer to her and kissed her. "I'm sorry. I didn't have sense enough to stop asking questions; seems I've a lot to learn."

He started to move away again but she took his hand and put it on her breast. He was tingling all over. Their thighs were warm when they touched.

"You're nice," he heard himself saying; "you're so nice."

"I wish I were. Do me a favor, Matt."

"What?"

"Take me. I want to forget, forget everything. Slow: and easy. I want to forget."

Chapter 5

"Cyrus P. Dodson; our next Governor!"

"A dark horse headed for the capitol building."

"Imagine, nominated by the people rather than the party. Straight from the grass roots."

"Cyrus Dodson, right here from Crescent; always knew he was a-going places."

Crescent had hummed with opinions all afternoon and evening. The comments still rang in Cyrus's ears.

"It's the biggest thing to hit this town since the fire," Bruce jested as he, ex-Governor Calder, and Cyrus sat at dinner. Cyrus by now had grown used to the idea of at least the words, "Cyrus Dodson for Governor," but inside there was still excitement he disguised. Outwardly he was the calmest person in town, including Governor Calder who kept talking of all the people they would have to line up on their side to get the independents organized strong enough for victory.

"I'd like to go to church with you in the morning," the Governor went on; "if we're seen there, maybe we can start the Gold Star mothers working for Dodson. Older women are a natural, just a perfect natural."

Would you like more wine, Governor?" Gloria asked as she came around with the decanter.

"And there is another thing, Cyrus," the ex-governor added, putting his arm around Gloria's waist as she stood next to him. Gloria started to pull away, repulsed by his touch, but then thought better of it.

"This little suffragette of yours should be put to work." He turned to Gloria, "Don't you agree that women can do a great work and wonder, young lady?"

Gloria filled his glass and forced a smiled. She hated the smell of his strong cigar. Cyrus did not like the way Calder touch her; it caused a chill of resentment to go up his back; he would have to clear that up later with him.

After Gloria had gone back into the kitchen, the governor laughed, "Gentlemen, we will not be able to hold back the tide of this suffrage movement forever. To be brutally honest about it, I can hardly wait until it comes to pass. Can you picture the political power we will control? All that is necessary is to have the right man, such as Cyrus, to be their idol."

Cyrus sat thoughtfully, his hand on his chin; carefully analyzing each word the ex-Governor spoke. Perhaps it was something in the past years that was bothering him; he had never really liked him, and he and Governor Calder had had more than one public difference during Cyrus's term in the State legislature. Why had they chosen him? Why would they come all the way to a little town such as Crescent and seek out a relative unknown to run for such an important public office?

"Of course," the ex-Governor went on, "the biggest thing in our favor at this point is the growing swing to prohibition; every last person you talk to thinks it is nothing short of barbaric that this, of all states, should hold out against the trend. Even the confirmed drunks are beginning to sound like temperance workers. Let the "drys" have their way. The war not even over before they're crying for blood. People always have to build a cause or life seems useless. Here we sit with a state statute that practically bans everything but beer and sarsaparilla and they bawl to have the whole hog: ratification of that damn Eighteenth Amendment. I say, let them have it and right along with it, women's suffrage."

Women's suffrage was one of the subjects that made Cyrus cringe. He found the idea nearly impossible to accept. Of course it was only fair that women should be allowed to express themselves, which it seemed they were doing quite well even under the present laws; but there the conflict began. He thought of Myrtle with her hot and cold flashes and tried to visualize her making the right decision during one of her conflicting attacks. He thought of Agatha who cried from insecurity even when you said "hello" to her. Then there was Margaret Cross, seeking gossipy tidbits from her front porch observatory. He smiled to himself. No, you could place all the arguments you cared to about equal rights and American women being captives, "mere counterparts of the harem girls of Turkey," but what justification could man possibly give to the theory of turning government over to the hands of such incompetence? The right of free men to intelligently choose their representation at the polls was the strength of the nation. To place the cornerstone of democracy in jeopardy was nothing more than treason.

Ward had stayed by the fire to dry out, after the fight; keeping a constant watch on the four beaten Flintville defenders in case they tried to follow Mitzie and Matt. Morgan was brooding in the corner with one of them while the other two went back to their dancing. At twelve thirty the fiddler took up his small megaphone and called the dancers to attention.

"Ladies and gentlemen: this would just about be the last dance, but seeing as the storm kind of got out of hand and the roads are one holy mess, there will be some hot soup served in the kitchen in about half an hour and for those who want to stay right here for the night, plenty of gunny sacks to use as beds when you get tired. For now, let's just plain and fancy dance the night away!"

Everyone cheered the announcement. Ward saw two of Morgan's friends leave the hall and followed them, but when he opened the door to look out, he could not see them. The rain was still coming down and, as he stepped off the porch, he could feel his boots sink deep in the mud. It was almost like a swamp; each step became a little more difficult. The two men had disappeared. Ward strained his eyes to see where they had gone. Then it happened, as he came to the corner of the building. He started to look around the corner and a wagon brake handle came crashing down on his skull. He didn't fall, but was dazed and he wandered aimlessly into the middle of the road before falling face down in the mud.

"You sure as hell clipped him one."

"Tell Morgan we got him and then let's get out of here. God, I could have killed him, you never know."

One of them went inside to get Morgan while the other went to the wagon. Morgan came back to the door with two men beside him.

"I'll take care of him from now on, if he comes back."

"I doubt you will have to worry, Larry; he really got it square on the bean," and the other three started to ride off into the rain, leaving Morgan behind.

Ward had risen to his hands and knees several times but on each attempt his fuzzy mind had given in and he had slowly ebbed back into the mire. Again he tried, and came close to succeeding, but the side of the Flintville bullies' wagon struck him, shoving him back into the oozing cushion of the mud.

"God, you hit something, Don, on the right side."

"That damn big bastard, I'll bet."

"Well, don't stop to find out, for Christ's sake; get the hell out of here."

Ward lifted his head again before he passed into unconsciousness.

"Ward Kessler, you're a bloody mess. Just because your father is a miner, doesn't mean you have to fight every day after school. Now get the tub off the back porch and take a bath." It was his mother. He could smell vegetable soup simmering in the pot; there would be big chunks of meat in it and he would be entitled to one in his bowl. "Better get clean before your father comes home or you'll go to bed with no supper."

"Ma, it's too hot, too hot," he said as the steam from the kettle billowed up around his face.

"Ward, I'm warning you; it's the scrub brush as hard as I can go if you don't shut up."

Ward started to gasp for breath and he pulled his head up only to find himself deep in mud, not a hot tub. The rain poured down upon him, washing the mud from his face in little streams, trickling into his mouth and nose.

His mother's voice was gone and only the sound of the deluge remained. There was a faint odor of vegetable soup coming from the direction of the grange, but everything else was only a memory and in its place the reality of what had happened since he, Matt and Mitzie had come to the dance. He sat up straight, biceps quivering with the surge of adrenalin that coursed his veins. On the front steps of the Grange Hall he could make out a solitary figure. He stood up and made his way toward it. His mind was clear; now anger was all he had to counteract.

He would go into the hall and tell Morgan that if this ever happened again there would be more to pay for than just tonight. Yes, he would warn Morgan never to pick on Matt or anyone again or he would really beat him for all he was worth.

Ward's back pained him where the wheels had cut the flesh. He trudged toward the light of the windows and the open door. The figure standing there moved toward a buggy; which was tied near the window. Suddenly he recognized the person as Morgan and he walked to the side of the carriage.

"Want to talk to you, Morgan, you got something coming."

Morgan whipped the reins hard against his horse's back, but Ward's strong arms pulled him from the seat before the horse had a chance to move.

"Where do you get this business of having me knocked on the head?" he asked.

Morgan didn't answer; but Ward heard the knife click open and his anger mounted. "Better put that thing away," he said, trying once more to control himself. But it was too late; Morgan had lunged at him and the knife found its mark in his left side sending an agonizing pain charging through Ward's body. For a second, Ward winced; then the full force of his huge fist came crashing down on the back of Morgan's neck. Dazed, Morgan braced himself against the carriage, to keep from falling.

Ward slowly pulled the knife from his side; his head whirling from the original blow he had taken to the head. He backed away, trying to get his balance; but Morgan had regained his senses and was rushing toward him again. Ward, the knife clenched tightly in his right hand, instinctively reached out in defense. Morgan let out a dull gasp as the knife caught him in the stomach. Ward released his grip on the knife. He looked down in the near total darkness for a few second, then turned and started to stagger toward the lights of the Grange. Once more Morgan, this time giving a shrill scream lunged at Ward with the knife, catching the huge man in the left side again as he turned to face the attacker. As if they were cast in stone, the two stood motionless for a moment. Suddenly Ward, the knife still in his side, swung around and caught Morgan by the throat and with both hands shook the fight out of him. Finally, Morgan's body became completely limp and slid down into a heap at Ward's feet.

When he realized what had happened, Ward's eyes opened wide. Things still out of focus, Ward, once more looked toward the Grange Hall. No one was in the doorway. Inside the orchestra was playing full blast. The odor of vegetable soup again came wafting across his nostrils. He didn't know how or why; but he picked Morgan up, and put him back into the carriage. Then taking a deep breath, he pulled the knife from his own body with a loud groan. His body still vibrated with strength, but he felt sick. His mouth was dry and his tongue seemed to swell almost choking him.

Walking was difficult but he made his way to Crater's barn. The door was barred.

"Mitzie, Mitzie, let me in, let me in," he half whispered, half shouted, "God, Mitzie, let me in."

Mitzie, who had been asleep, pulled herself from Matt's warm body.

"Honey, it's Ward; I don't want to leave you, but he'll wonder what's happening if I don't let him in." She kissed Matt's lips then his throat, his chest and stomach. Matt continued to sleep.

"Mitzie, let me in, wake up, wake up."

She opened the door and Ward stumbled through and fell onto the soft, dry earthen floor, the knife still in his hand.

The Election

"Mitzie, I think I killed him, Mitzie. I think he's dead," Ward whispered.

She bent over him to see if he was drunk, but there was no heavy odor of liquor. She lit a match and looked down on the mud-soaked blacksmith, her heart welling up in pain for him.

"Ward, Ward, what happened?"

"We have to get out of here, I really think I killed Morgan."

Mitzie looked around the barn by match light and found a lantern that had a little kerosene left. Lighting it she looked down on Ward's beaten body, his clothes torn, his back bleeding.

"I don't know how I did it," he kept saying over and over.

Matt was snoring lightly so Mitzie put on her still wet clothes, took the knife from Ward's hand and went out to find Morgan.

"What'll I do if he's really dead?" Mitzie thought. She held the knife as if she might have to protect herself with it. As she waded toward the lighted Grange Hall, she remembered the old bridge they had passed when they crossed the river and a plan started to form.

Mitzie found the buggy with Morgan's body in the front seat. She shook him but he did not move, she assumed he must really be dead. She couldn't let anyone know Ward had killed him; she would have to get rid of his body. She got in the buggy, pushing Morgan's dead weight over. She placed the knife on the seat and gave the reins a sharp jerk, pulling the horse out of its drenched stupor and heading it down the fork of the road toward the old bridge. When she reached its dark skeleton, she stopped. She was frightened for the first time.

Below, the water roared in its newfound fury. She pulled the reins tight; the horse stopped abruptly. Whipping the horse with the reins, she tried to get the buggy started toward the washed-out section of the bridge, but the horse refused to budge. Finally in desperation Mitzie got out of the seat and led the horse to the middle of the bridge. It was so dark she could not see how close they were, but when she felt the planks to sway, she tied the reins to the seat and moved gently down the deck of the rickety structure. As she carefully slid passed the horse, she slapped its rump with all her strength. The startled animal reared up on its hind legs then bolted forward. Her heart pounding fiercely in her chest, Mitzie listened for some sound to signal the end. The vision of Morgan's body slumped in the buggy seat clearly dominated her thoughts: There was one last whinny as the end planks of the bridge gave way and with a crash the bad dream slipped into the swollen river.

Mitzie waited for a few minutes for the bridge to stop swaying then made her way back past the music-filled Grange to the barn and Ward's prostrate form on the floor. Matt was still sleeping.

She was drenched and chilled, but the tension was eased. Now no one would ever know what had happened. Ward was safe, that was all that counted. She tore more strips from her petticoat for bandaging. When she turned Ward over and found where he had been stabbed, she realized that she should have dressed his wounds first. His blood left a small sticky pool on the floor of the barn. Again she was frightened. She couldn't get him to talk, he was so weak, and there was no strength in his legs. Matt was hard to rouse but she woke him and together they lifted Ward's huge body into the rear seat of the surrey and put the blanket from Chestnut over him. Mitzie covered the blood on the floor with dirt, and then hitched Chestnut in his harness. Matt blew out the wick of the lantern before she opened the barn door.

"Are you all right?" she asked.

"I ache all over," Matt replied, "but guess, I'll make it."

"You had better ride in back with him in case he comes to," Mitzie said as she came near him in the dark and held him close.

"You can't hurt Ward for very long," Matt tried to reassure her. "We'll get him to Doctor Phillips and he'll be as good as any damn blacksmith."

"He's got to be all right, Matt, he just has to be all right."

The rain seemed to be easing in its wrath as they crossed the bridge heading back toward Crescent. Mitzie listened to the swift current of the river beneath them, and the image of the other bridge loomed up in her mind. Morgan and the knife came back to life, she remembered how he flashed it around before he stabbed

Matt with it; and she could sense her breath getting shorter. This would not be an easy ride.

Cyrus looked up, wanting to yawn at the clock hands, now at three in the morning, but ex-Governor Calder reached into his vest pocket for another cigar, then opened the small gold pocketknife on the end of his watch chain and pared the tip of the tightly rolled Havana. Then he took a deep breath and continued his seemingly unending spiel, "This war will be over in no time and then you'll see some changes. The mob will flounder all over the political map trying to find something to cling to. They'll reject everything and anything that had any part in the war. Even Wilson will get the axe," his non-stop monologue continued.

"Governor, I would say that was a bit of a rash statement," Bruce McHenry interrupted with a smile. "Why, Wilson's the most popular man in the world today; he's the one man who tried to keep us out of this mess."

Pulling one of the candelabra toward him, the ex-Governor lit his cigar and let the first big mouthful of smoke curl meaningfully out into the room.

Cyrus put his glass to his lips and took another sip. He thought to himself that the Governor was getting more and more talkative as the night went on. Too much of Myrtle's loganberry wine, perhaps. Behind the governor, Gloria was standing with the decanter, newly filled, ready to help.

Cyrus watched her; she was perhaps not as pretty as Cynthia taken feature for feature, but more beautiful. She was so much in control of the situation. Her ruffled shirtwaist with a black velvet bow at the collar and her dead father's gold cuff links at the wrists gave her a classic touch. She wore her long hair back, tied with another bow of velvet. Their eyes met, hers questioning his, as if to ask, "Is there anything I've overlooked?"

"Perhaps the Governor is tired, Gloria," Cyrus said, hoping his remark was not too obvious. "Is his room ready?"

"Yes, Father," she answered.

They had moved Myrtle into Cynthia's room and Cynthia was asleep on the couch in Cyrus's room in order to give the ex-Governor their best accommodation.

"No, I'm, not the least bit tired. Guess the rain has given me the pep to keep going all night," Calder interrupted, exhaling a cloud of cigar smoke out over the damask tablecloth. Then he continued "Yes, Bruce; Woodrow Wilson, may be your man of the hour; but that hour is damn near over. People don't want peace. It's just resting place to lick their wounds. Peace, in and of itself, is boring. They'll go at it again. First it will be a war of words, something to be against; probably the Bolsheviks. Then they'll get ready for another fight. No, Bruce, not one person in ten thousand can really stand peace; so they'll be after Wilson's scalp. And I say if that's what they want, let them have it."

Cyrus balked inwardly. "Just because they want war, doesn't make it right," he thought. "I don't agree to this giving in to the masses."

The Governor continued, "The only thing is that you have to out guess them. Lead them along, and in turn they give you what you want. It can be a mighty profitable world if you don't let idealism cloud the facts of practical politics."

Bruce McHenry was the first to bow out. "Governor, I have a fire department to run and with ten o'clock my usual bedtime, the hour of three thirty-five has just about taken its toll; besides you and Cyrus have to go to church in the morning."

"That's right, exactly right; and the Gold Star Mothers," the Governor said.

"And of course the older women," Bruce countered. "Oh, yes, the old women, a natural: a perfect natural," Bruce snickered and their laughter echoed through the house as they went into the hall to get Bruce's hat and coat.

"Rain stopped," Bruce said; "But I'm still lucky to be on a paved street. You see, Governor, that's the kind of progress Cyrus P. Dodson brought to Crescent; maybe he'll have a chance to give the state good leadership."

Bruce walked down the street toward the fire station, stepping wide to miss the puddles which reflected the now-freed moon, as it peeked out low in the west at the soaked earth below. There was a muddy-wheeled surrey in front of Dr. Phillips' house and the light was on in the front room. "Three forty-five. Poor old Doc.," Bruce thought; "not a night goes by without something pulling him out of bed. Even when he's through at the hospital, they catch him at home."

"Been some day," he said aloud, to himself; "We really got the job done." Cyrus was going to make it. Together they would put Crescent on the map.

Mitzie had helped Dr. Phillips dress Ward and Matt's wounds. When they were through, he asked her to help him in the kitchen while he made some coffee. "I didn't want to say anything in the other room, but what happened tonight? Ward is really all cut to hell. He should be in the hospital."

"Doctor, he can't go to the hospital; nobody must know about what happened."

"Well, young lady, they sure as be-Jesus aren't going to find out from me because I don't know what happened myself. I'm waiting for you to tell me."

"There was a fight at the dance over at Flintville; Matt got cut up because the other fellow had a knife."

"And how about Ward? He looks as if a railway train had run over him."

"I don't know except when he came in the barn where I took Matt to bandage him and Ward was bleeding and beat up. He said he had killed Morgan."

"Who's Morgan?"

"He's the one who stabbed Matt; I guess he stabbed Ward as well."

"What a lovely picnic!"

"Ward said he killed him; I went to see and he was dead in his buggy."

"And then you brought them here?"

"Doctor, I did something terrible."

"By bringing them here?"

"No, I led the horse and buggy off the old bridge into the river."

"What in hell for?"

"His body was in it."

The doctor looked at her in disbelief. "For Christ's sake, don't you know that is against the law? It's almost worse than killing him in the first place."

"I didn't know."

"That's not important; why did you do it?"

"I guess, so nobody would know that Ward had killed him."

"I'd say you had really botched things, now."

"I couldn't help it," she said as she put the coffee pot on the stove. Little beads of water sputtered and rolled across the hot metal.

"Young lady, I don't understand what went on in your mind."

"We can't let anyone find out that Ward has killed someone, again."

Dr. Phillips turned her around facing him. "What do you mean 'killed someone, 'again'?"

"Nobody knows I let that man's body go in the river; nobody but you. Matt and Ward don't know. You mustn't tell anyone."

"About Ward killing someone; what did you mean by that?"

"Please, Doctor, will you promise never to tell; please?"

"Yes! Now tell me what you mean. Ward wouldn't kill anyone."

"He did tonight and he has before."

"Before, as in the war?"

"Yes; but before that in Whalen, where I lived. My stepbrothers took some money from one of the mine foremen, so that he could have me for a night. They threatened to beat me if I didn't go to his house, so I went. But I wouldn't do anything so he beat me, instead. My stepbrothers got drunk on the money and they bragged about what they had done and Ward overheard. Mr. Acton was beating me when Ward broke in the door. And then he took him by the neck and killed him. Killed him; I guess like he did tonight."

"You mean the police want Ward?"

"No, I was only fifteen and they didn't want to involve the company in a scandal. After a quiet investigation, they made an announcement that Mr. Acton had been killed in a fall in the mine; and they asked Ward to leave town. So Ward left Pennsylvania. But it got into the newspapers anyway. And my step-father beat his own sons 'till they bled."

"Nice, friendly little town," the doctor said, reaching for the coffee pot.

"You see, now; nobody must ever know about this, or they'll bring up the past and make Ward out to be something he really isn't."

For a long time, the doctor sat looking at the design in the oilcloth tablecloth, taking a gulp of the coffee every now and then. Breaking the silence: he finally gave sigh and said, "Don't worry. I'll think of something. But don't you ever talk or I'll lose my license to practice, and you'll end up in prison, sure as hell."

"You won't put him in the hospital?"

"No, on that you can rely; but you'll have to nurse him closely, because I'll have him under heavy sedation for a few days. Heavy people heal slowly, and Ward will be an impossible patient at best."

"Thank you, Dr. Phillips."

"Don't thank me. It scares the hell out of me to think how far into trouble you have gotten the two of us tonight, young lady. It scares it right out of me."

Chapter 6

A week had passed since her step-father was made the center of the town's attention and Agatha could now again sit on the front porch and knit without feeling that everyone who passed was staring at her. She missed Cyrus, though. Dinner was so different without him being there. Her mother had fixed nothing but potato soup three days in a row, and without Gloria in the house there seemed no one to talk to. She wondered what Cyrus and Gloria would be doing now at the State Capitol. Lucky Gloria; the ex-governor had practically insisted that she go along.

"Man's best political asset is a pretty daughter to stand by his side when he makes a speech."

Agatha looked out over the honeysuckle bushes, the wrought iron picket fence and at four small boys playing ball in the street. The one with the bat was yelling, "I'm going to be Ty Cobb!" But he struck out and the next took his turn at swinging the axe handle at the homemade baseball.

She watched them so intently that she had to undo half a row of her knitting and start over. When she looked up again, the game had been abandoned; and in its place were four young infantrymen fighting the battles of Sergeant York.

"Father doesn't want you to play on the fence," she called to them timidly. When they continued using the fence as an imaginary machine gun, running a stick along the pickets, Agatha could stand the challenge no longer and went inside to get a drink of water. When the firing had stopped, however, she ventured again to the steps with her needles and ball of yarn.

"That's a beautiful shade of yellow," the words intruded upon Agatha's concentration. It was Mitzie on the sidewalk. "I certainly wish I could knit."

Agatha looked at her intently, trying to remember where she had seen her before, then she remembered Mitzie's smile. "Gloria, that's my sister, picked it out," she said. She wanted to add, "Won't you come in and talk?" but the words wouldn't form themselves. She felt helpless. Then, as if reading her mind, Mitzie pushed the gate open and came up the walk to the steps, stopped, looking up at the Dodson home.

"My, this is a big house," she said in wonderment. "And it's where the next Governor will live, I guess."

"Oh no," Agatha was quick to correct her. "If Father is made Governor, he'll have an even bigger house than this. Besides this is really my mother's house. My grandfather built it; and left it to me and my sisters."

"Mind if I sit down?" Mitzie asked.

Agatha nodded her head. She was silently delighted by the intrusion.

"I'm Mitzie. You're Agatha, aren't you? I remember your eyes: soft powder blue. They're beautiful. There was so much confusion that day at the dedication. When Ward introduced us, I could hardly keep all the names straight."

Agatha was deeply touched by the compliment. "I'd invite you inside but Mother is not feeling well. It's so nice to have someone to talk to. Cynthia, one of my other sisters, baked me oatmeal cookies this morning, would you like one? We could make some tea."

"Wonderful, I'd love to. You know, I'll have to tell you something. This is the first time I've ever been invited to have a cup of tea. All the other times tea has been my medicine."

"Oh, it's not like medicine when you put milk in it," Agatha reassured her, trying at the same time to bolster her own confidence for this new role of hostess. "You see, you can put sugar in it; we even have lump sugar for our tea. I guess that's the fanciest thing we have in our home, lump sugar."

"Wasn't I lucky to pass your house today?" Mitzie said. "Imagine, real lump sugar."

"Rationed, too," Agatha added. "But you can take some home with you if you like."

Agatha had so many questions she wanted answered. Finally she braced herself and asked, "Where do you live?"

Mitzie pulled her long gingham skirt to one side as she sat on the steps beside the girl with the yellow knitting.

"I live over the blacksmith shop; you know Ward Kessler that you met at the celebration? His blacksmith shop and garage?"

"Are you married to him?" Agatha asked in a staccato tone.

"No, I live alone." Mitzie looked at Agatha's questioning eyes. "It's really very nice; I like it that way. Don't you like to be alone sometimes? Well, this way, I can be alone whenever I like."

"It would be nice when, when..."

"When people seem to be making you nervous, making you feel that you can't be the way you want to?" Mitzie completed Agatha's thought.

"How did you know what I was thinking?" she asked.

"I guess because there have been so many times that I have thought the same thing."

Agatha relaxed, her words came easily. "I like your short hair. Father would die if any of us even suggested doing it (having it cut) but I like it."

"It's cool in the summer," Mitzie explained.

"Do you wear paint?" Agatha asked, squinting to look closer.

"A little bit," Mitzie admitted, "especially when I've got the curse or don't feel well. I use some rouge."

"We still have to pinch our cheeks to try and make the color," Agatha sighed, "but it never does much good."

"I even use perfume," Mitzie interjected. "Guess some people would say that's being cheap."

"Oh, no," Agatha came to her defense, "even Mother uses toilet water. I didn't mean to pry."

The Election

"I know you didn't, Agatha; it's just that I'm on the verge of crying at times and I guess I pick fights with myself." Her hand patted Agatha's and they looked into one another's eyes.

"We're going to be friends, aren't we?" Agatha asked."

"I'm certain of that. We can have tea parties, just the two of us at my place. There's a kitchen downstairs. You can bring the sugar lumps."

"Come in," Agatha said, jumping up excitedly. As she opened the screen door, she took Mitzie's hand and led her into the hallway. "Mother will be asleep and we can have our tea in the kitchen where it's cool. We'll use the Belleek, Mother will never know."

His bifocals tipped far down on his long bony nose, Dr. Phillips emitted an exaggerated cough while he unwound the bulky bandage from around Ward's middle. His gnarled fingers probed the wound with a firm gentleness that the delivery of over five hundred and thirty Walker County infants had made second nature. Ward winced, closing his eyes and gritting his teeth at each motion of suggested pressure.

Dr. Phillips and Ward had a personal system of communication; which comforted them both in their bachelor loneliness. Except for the year Ward had been away in the service, the two made an afternoon ritual of their cups of strong coffee. Ward drank his black while the doctor filled his cup half full with cream before adding the thickly boiled brew.

"That will sour your stomach as well as the cream," Ward would say, and the doctor would look over his glasses and grunt.

"At least it'll give more nourishment than that mug of turpentine you're drinking."

Neither would smile, but inwardly they were pleased that neither had broken the pattern.

"Take it easy, that side's sore."

"Why do you think I'd be here wasting my time, if it weren't for the obvious fact that it's sore. Now hold still while I put another sponge of iodine and alcohol on it for good measure."

"You should be a veterinarian."

"When I doctor the likes of you, I am a veterinarian. Drink your coffee so I can put a new bandage on without all of this talk."

Ward gulped his coffee; and Dr. Phillips worked on his oversized patient. When he had completed the task, he looked into Ward's eyes and made a single, flat-toned statement, "They found the body of that Morgan fellow from Flintville; two counties downstream where the Smith River cuts in."

"That's too bad," Ward said, filling his cup from the pot that sat on the stove next to the table. "Another cup?"

"No. My stomach is a bit edgy this afternoon; one too many of Mrs. Everett's hot scones for breakfast."

There was a pause for silent conversation, which Ward broke to explain that he had to get back to work. Everything would be in a mess if he didn't.

"That's too bad. You're lucky to be alive with all the blood you lost that night. With all that's happened to you this last year, you're mighty damn lucky. So you just take it easy for another few weeks."

"No reason why I can't just get some of those horses shod."

"I've done quite well," the doctor explained, "and it's mighty nice of Mrs. Cross to have Gilbert come over and fill in. He did all right by your shop while you were away. Can't rightfully say he's a fast one, because that would be a lie. He listens more than he talks and rests more than he works."

"There won't be a horse in Crescent that can trot in another week; besides, what will people think?" Ward asked, showing concern for the first time.

"Who cares," the doctor said, putting his things back in his bag. "If it's Margaret Cross you're worrying about, I explained to her and to everyone else, as we agreed, that you had broken your ribs. Whoever heard of a man with broken ribs bending iron and shoeing horses?"

"You're not leaving?" Ward asked.

"I think I've spent enough time with this charity case," the doctor said, pulling the stethoscope from around his neck and tucking it into the top of his bag. "Now do what you're told, stay put and read your mail. That young lady, upstairs, can fix your meals."

"You know it isn't natural to sit and do nothing," Ward protested.

"And it isn't natural for a man to have his gizzard stabbed with a knife; so you keep your butt in that bed. If we're lucky that cut will heal over the old scar; then if anyone ever says anything you can claim it's your war injury."

Doctor Phillips slammed the door and crossed the dirt floor of the shop. For a moment he stopped and watched Gilbert slowly pounding out a hot piece of metal on the anvil. Amusement lighted his eyes. At the wide, open front door, he shook his head and burped, feeling the acid bite into his sides and up into his throat. "Bicarb; need some soda", he said to himself as he crossed the street to his Model T.

Ward shifted back and forth restlessly in his bed as he listened to the slow clanging at the anvil; then, when he could stand it no longer, he poured another cup of coffee and picked up the single letter, which the doctor had ceremoniously brought him. He had intended to wait for a few days to open the letter. It was a silly method of accepting his mail from Binny Wilcox, he knew, but that way he could make it last longer, knowing that someone would take the time to write to him.

"I guess that's the one good thing that came from going off 'half-cocked' and joining the Army. Never in my life got a letter before that. Good to have someone write to you, even if it's no one but a skinny little corporal with false teeth and cauliflower ears," he said half aloud.

The letter had been opened and marked "Censored" but Ward knew nothing would be blocked out for Binny never wrote about anything but women, food and "Fritzies." Each letter ended about the same way, "Wilson can be as sweet as he wants and call this a war with no hate; but, just like the Indians, the only good 'Fritz' is a dead one! Write soon, Buddy, so the battalion will know what's going on O.T." The "O.T." obviously meant "Over There" in Binny's cryptic language.

He could remember clearly Binny's knotty, stick-like legs bound tight in wool leggings. One of the very first to go into the

Army, Ward had just stepped off the train in Chicago and had stooped over to pick up the remains of the chocolate cake Margaret Cross had given him as going away gift. It lay smashed on the rain soaked platform where he had dropped it; its cream filling oozing out in a yellow gelatinous gob on the wooden planking. It was then, as he looked up, that he first saw those legs in front of his eyes, and he laughed for all he was worth. He laughed until the large foot on the end of one of those comical legs stamped itself in the middle of the crumpled cake, sending a mixture of crumbs, dirty water, and yellow cream filling squirting into Ward's face.

"Snap to, soldier; you join this man's army to fight or play games? Now take your snot rag and shine that shoe," he shouted pointing to his own foot.

"Yes, sir," Ward had answered even before he had looked up into the ugly face.

"Corporal! Corporal Wilcox," the dour mouth barked, "and I hate recruits."

Ward took his handkerchief from his pocket and wiped the cake from Corporal Wilcox's shoe. He then scraped the rest of the splattered pastry up with the lid of the broken cardboard box, in which Margaret had so carefully placed the symbol of her affection. When Ward had finished, he wiped his own face, straightened his wool cap and stood at attention.

Ward's most memorable picture of Binny, however, was of a French bouquet: On July 4th, 1917, much to the dismay of many American officers and observers, one battalion of the ill-fitted 16th Infantry, its ranks swollen with Ward's contemporaries, marched on parade down the Paris streets toward Picpus Cemetery and LaFayette's tomb.

Binny, at the head of his squad, marched proudly to the beat set by the French military band in front of them. There were only a few spectators at first, but the crowd grew as they continued toward the ceremonies. The people marched right along with the troops. An old woman put a wreath around Binny's neck and kissed him on the cheek. He couldn't remove the wreath, and still march, at the same time: so the decoration remained and there were quiet laughs trickling from the troops, until more and more wreaths were placed on other necks. Women with flowers broke into the ranks and cheered, "Zee Ahmerican". Ward had to stoop over to let the petite, blue-eyed brunette kiss him. She skipped alongside of him, throwing flowers into his face. She had put her arm through his, got in step and marched along by his side.

Binny looked like a flower shop window by that time. His rifle, hat, and uniform, had been the object of every French woman who couldn't reach the taller men.

"B...B...B...Binny, Beautiful Binny, he's the only one the g, g, g, girls adore." The singing started from his men; but the tribute to beautiful Katy and to Binny stopped after one sour glance for the marching garland.

"Paulette", the girl tugging at Ward's sleeve, kept saying, pointing to herself. Then she kissed him again. He could remember the strange warm feeling of the tip of her tongue caressing his then suddenly she pushed deep almost into his throat. "Paulette," he had said to himself, "war isn't too bad." but the parade continued and she had disappeared, never to be found again but in the hazy corners of dreams.

After that fateful march, Binny shed his floral mantle, but he could never mute the strains of "B...B...B...Binny, Beautiful Binny", which would echo through the camp every once in a while and fade just as mysteriously when he turned in an attempt to discover its source.

From gas mask and bayonet training to hours spent, sitting around a wooden barrel peeling potatoes on KP, Binny's band of recruits became more adept, but far from polished.

Then one night, just at dusk, they were given the order to move up toward the front. Hurriedly they were issued trench helmets and were loaded along with their full packs onto lorries as blackness closed in on them. Through the night, they jogged over bumpy roads into the unknown with only the sound of the truck engines droning in their ears. Occasionally a motorcycle's higher pitch added an accent as it passed close by carrying an officer or courier in its sidecar. The men, huddled tightly together, chilled by October's descent. Dawn oozed its way in bleakness onto the deserted bricked streets of a village with no name; the men alighted from the rigid planked seats and gathered in small groups waiting to be assembled. A rooster cried out into nothingness and a lonely dog, somewhere, barked; but was unanswered as the empty lorries thundered away through the gray veil and disappeared, heading west.

Muffled were the tones of the sergeants and corporals as they formed the ranks, as if they were afraid their shouted orders might wake the slumbering people in the scattered houses and shops; or wake and alert a German sentry into rigid efficiency.

Later that night they could distinctly make out the grumbling anger of artillery in the northeast. They were in a quiet sector of the Vosges, where action had not disturbed anything but the mind. They gathered around the fire in the huge fireplace of the empty farmhouse they were using as their quarters. They sang and dozed, lulled by the comfort of the warmth.

At twelve midnight, Ward, Binny, and twenty other men, started on their patrol of the darkened trench some five thousand yards out in the wire-strewn field. The men they relieved were cold clear through and welcomed the voices of their replacements. They shook hands, passed expressions of "Good luck," and marched back to the fireplace, which beckoned to them; as would a warm, comforting womb. Binny jotted an entry in his mental journal "November 3, 1917, 12:1O a.m.: as always, all quiet in the Vosges sector."

They would have another six hours of near-sleep searching for a glimpse of enemies one never saw; but they were there. However, at three-thirty, a mortar shell burst halfway between the trenches and the farmhouse. Rattling bursts of German machine guns spit flames into the night and war was real. Still they could not make out their opponents, but Binny, who had never been shot at, suddenly became the hardened soldier.

"Get those G.D. trench helmets on...and hold your fire until I tell you what to do."

Next thing Ward knew shells were coming at them from three sides. He could hear the clomping of boots in the darkness in between explosions and rifle fire.

"Flare, flare," the sergeant screamed and their mortar put one high in an arc over the field in front of them. For a moment daylight was around them and with it the quickly shifting German raiding party.

"Dirty sons-a-bitchin' Huns," someone yelled at the full volume of his heart.

"Shut up, soldier!"

From the right, in quick succession, came ten grenades; each terrifying as it ripped the ground and sent soft earth flying in all directions. Next a mortar hit the farmhouse and its thatched roof started to burn. Behind them they could see the others streaming from the flaming house and crawling toward the trenches. When the next barrage of grenades hit the trench that Ward was in, he crawled over the top toward the house. Binny, too, was out of the trench by this time.

"We're making damn good targets with that fire to back' light us, hit the ground," he rushed at Ward. It was too late. From one of the mounds of dirt the hulky frame of a "Hun" rose ominously behind Binny; and as he turned, the butt of the rifle smashed him across the jaw sending him wilting to the ground. Ward brought his rifle up to fire but the German's quick reflexes were too keenly honed. His next lunge sent his bayonet gashing through the skin, flesh and sinew of Ward's left thigh, the next instant the blade was withdrawn and the rifle butt slapped Ward's right cheek, then swung back, full force to the diaphragm. Next, the hot burning bite of the blade in his left side. Ward could remember his own screams of anger; after that, the sound and recoil of his own gun, but nothing else.

Ward opened his eyes to morning and a French nurse's toothy grin. Not like Paulette, Ward thought. How could you kiss with your tongue such a mouth as this? He could not understand her chatter; then she disappeared, closing the pleated screen behind her.

"Binny, where is Binny?" he demanded loudly. No answer followed, so he yelled the question again.

"Did they kill Binny, those stinkin', lousy Huns?" Once again, he was greeted; by the same tooth-filled mouth. The smile came closer, bringing with it a hand drenched in Lysol, holding a large syringe and needle. She promptly shoved the needle into his buttocks and he slowly relaxed into a calmed slumber.

The accented voice of a French doctor greeted him as he regained consciousness. "Soldier boy, you are not the easiest patient your nurse, Mamselle Plavan, has had to care for. For days you have been fighting zee war right from zees hospital bed. Perhaps, now, zee battle is won, we can all take a rest. Non?"

Following that, the sweet and loving French exterminated Ward's cooties, handed him his cane, and shipped him back to America for his surgeon's certificate of disability and then home to Crescent; still wondering about Binny and the rest of the men in that trench. Later, through the Red Cross, he had received a brief note from Binny: "You saved my life; Thanks!"

"In less time than it takes to whelp a war baby, you're over there, back, and a hero for life, Ward Kessel. This town will never forget what you and the boys did over there, never in a lifetime, Ward," Bruce McHenry gave the homecoming talk from the pulpit Reverend Pritchard had begrudgingly given up for the occasion. Margaret Cross had baked another cream-filled cake. She pawed at his sleeve as she invited him for dinner. He was lucky; he didn't have to refuse her, since the many activities the welcoming committee had planned kept him far too busy to accept. He was Crescent's first hero! Others followed. Gold stars were sewn on flags, candles lit in windows, and now Ward sat in his chair, discontented, an invalid for the second time in less than a year. He fingered Binny's letter again, noticing by the return address that the man who hated recruits was again up on the ladder to the rank of Master Sergeant. "B...B...B...Binny, Beautiful Binny," he sang softly to himself. "No, I'll read it some other day."

(_____**edited to here**)

Chapter 7

Matt picked up the Walker County Journal, which lay face up on Cyrus's desk. There was a feeling of melancholy about the empty office. Without Cyrus's exactness, the routine seemed to lag. Even though he had done his work as usual without his overseeing employer, it was as if everything needed dusting. Only one moving object in the office reminded Matt of Cyrus and that was the pendulum of the clock over Cyrus's desk.

Page one of the newspaper, except for the casualty list, boxed in a heavy black border, in the lower left corner, mentioned nothing of American troops fighting in France and Germany. "Dodson Seeks Governorship' claimed the banner headline, while an editorial entitled "Demon Rum Dumb" and the news of the marriage of a Miss Cornelia Cullpepper, of Marquette, to a Mr. Heber Scoville, of Flintsville, fought for dubious, second-place honors of its readers.

The casualty list, though small, was the first thing that Matt read. However, there was no one on the list that he knew; that is, really knew. Maybe he'd join the army and leave when his brother Oliver did. Sinking down into the hard swivel chair, he saw it, the short article in the right hand corner; "Flintsville Man Drowns". It was not really the news that startled him, for he had been told when he delivered grain to Case's store on Wednesday that Morgan was believed lost in the storm. They had found the horse and the remains of the buggy about a quarter mile below the Grange. Matt could still feel the rain. A chill came over him. Ward and he had not seen one another since that night, even to say "Hello", let alone talk about the fight or Morgan. He had spoken to Mitzie but there was no mention of anything except that Ward was starting feel a bit better.

"You haven't been over to see my apartment", she had said. "I guess I'll never be able to deny you anything you ask from now on, Matt," she went on; but he was certain by the softness of her voice that she was not talking of their hidden guilt.

"It seems logical to assume that in the darkness, Mr. Morgan took the old fork of the Crescent road and rode onto the rotting Gilford Bridge that crosses the Smith River. This paper has, at various times brought to the attention of its readers. It should either be torn down or blocked off so that no more animals, or men, lose their lives."

Matt's arm itched beneath the long-sleeved shirt he was wearing to hide the cuts on his arm. He scratched at the newly formed scabs. He could remember Morgan's face as he knelt on the floor throwing up. He was sorry for him now, even though he had hated him that night.

"Always drank just a little bit too much, Morgan did, but not in the store. I'd lay any kind of sensible odds that he didn't know what road he was on, because he'd be the last one on earth to ever give a horse, or anyone else a free rein, even if he was wrong," Mr. Case went on in the excitement of finding himself the only focal point for the subject being discussed. Morgan had no relatives.

"Too mean for relatives," Mr. Case went on in his display of honest and unemotional concern. "Good thing though, only thing the storm did out of line was get Morgan."

"Too mean for relatives," Matt thought and he wondered if he had really been that way.

There was really no desire to read the article about the governorship campaign. True, the excitement was still a part of him, but it was distant. The words on the page were only words, even the text of Cyrus's speech made before the "Votes for Women" league and a description of the torchlight parade in which Cyrus rode in a Hupmobile touring car with the Mayor. People had cheered the "Crescent Crusader"; a name one of the metropolitan papers had given him, as he sang "Over There" at the Liberty Bond rally.

The Election

Matt reached back into the corner by the desk and pulled out Cyrus's rifle. "You never know when you will be called upon to defend yourself or your country," Cyrus had said to him one day, while he was explaining the workings of the gun and the six-shooter he kept under the ledger in the top drawer of the counter. Matt wondered if his employer ever, used either of them, or had ever fired them. He pulled back the bolt and held the rifle up to the light from the shaded window, inspecting the bore of the barrel.

The front door of the feed store opened, letting a little breeze of summer air filter its way into the dusty stuffiness of the office. Matt turned in the swivel chair half expecting to find Mitzie or his mother standing silhouetted against the bright Saturday sunlight; but there, leaning nonchalantly against the door frame was Bruce McHenry, the look of a knowing parent written all over his face. Matt knew that expression, and he knew what his uncle's first words would be.

"Boss is away and look who in hell's at play," Bruce quipped. "Well at least we can report that the new manager wasn't seen with his feet on the desk and that is one redeeming fact to send back to Governor Dodson!"

If only someone would talk about something else, Matt found himself wishing.

"By the way, just why are you sitting in here with the window blinds down and the door closed? Sick? Asleep?"

"Uncle Bruce, there you go again stretching the truth to win a point; only the front blinds are down and even Mr. Dodson pulls them down on sunny afternoons," Matt said as he put the rifle back in its corner.

"Well, I really didn't come in here to give you a roasting, Matt. Just more or less to find what town news has happened since I went up to the state capital to look around. Anything said by Mayor Kirk or old Welby the day after I painted them as such mud-heads at the dedication?"

"No news at all."

"Don't like the sound of your voice, Matt, you not feeling well?" Bruce pulled the blind down and let it roll up around the top flapping its way to brightness. "Not that girl with the curl from Flintsville again?"

"No, I haven't seen her since the night of the dance when I argued with her and..." Matt stopped. "Well anyway, I don't care about her."

"That's a good bit of news; and I thought you said there wasn't any."

"How's Mr. Dodson?" Matt changed the subject as he put the newspaper in the desk and stood up.

"Fine. He bought a Templar touring automobile for his big campaigning, almost as good looking as the new fire engine, I'd say; and Gloria Dodson's bought herself some new clothes for the campaign. Skirt a full six inches above the shoe line; just a bit suggestive; but good for votes, I'd say. White leather spats for her shoes, and I'll bet she even bought some new corset covers, 'teddy bear' underwear and 'Billie Burke' pajamas."

"When's he coming back?" Matt asked.

"That's really why I'm here. Cyrus will be back a week from today to rest for a couple of days, and at that time he's going to turn the feed store and business over to you for managing right down to each and every last grain of wheat and kernel of corn. He asked me to stand by you in case you had any problems, Matt. He's going to be a busy man with no time to concern himself with pigeon food."

Matt looked and felt nonplused.

"Close your mouth, Matt. You don't look like you got your senses with it open that way." Bruce laughed.

"He can't do that," Matt started to say. How could he do all the things Mr. Dodson did: lining up orders, talking to the mail people about the dray business for the post office, buying grain from the farmers and examining the new government reports Mr. Dodson had been so concerned with before this business of the governorship came along. No, he couldn't do it.

"Cyrus knows you're going to have troubles, Matt; but he's so darn convinced you are the smartest boy about these parts, that he's even talking about you marrying one of his daughters and becoming part of the family."

"He isn't," Matt said flatly.

"You damn bet your life he is; other night at dinner he said it just like that. 'That young Matthew has the makings of a leader: top of the class in school. And Agatha needs a husband who can take care of her.' And old ex-Governor Calder said, 'Smart move, Cyrus, let your gals marry the brainy boys. Good for politics.'"

The words "needs a husband who can take care of her" started to resound in Matt's ears. "Agatha?" he asked.

"Well, Matt, that's the one he mentioned; but he's got five and you can take your choice since not a one of them is married. Of course, if I were doing the picking, which you know by this time, I never intend to do, I'd first, above all the others, ask Miss Gloria."

"Hell, Uncle Bruce, I don't love Agatha. Damn it, I don't even know her."

"Matthew Harwood: man to man, who cares? We're not talking about love, we're plain and simple discussing a possible wedding to the daughter of the next Governor of the State."

"For a man who hates women, Uncle, you certainly let on like you know all there is to know about them."

"It doesn't take too much reading about history, past and present, to know a few of the universal points of weakness in the old theory of love and marriage. Love is for the fun of it, marriage is a business of raising kids and having someone give you the comforts of respectability and take care of you when you're old or sick."

"Why Agatha? I only met her once, don't even know her; and she's too quiet."

"All the better you don't know her; the more you know a girl, the less chance there is of you wanting to marry her. Why do you suppose more brothers and sisters don't marry? Not because their kids will have three heads. Hell, no! Laws don't stop people from doing things they want to do. It's just that brothers and sisters get to know one another too well and know better than to marry someone with all the lousy habits that their kin folks have displayed over the years." Bruce was out of breath and sat down on the edge of the chair.

"I'm sure not going to get married."

"That's what I like to hear," Bruce agreed with him.

"I'm too young."

"I agree with everything you say," Bruce said, blowing his nose. "But just don't express all these sensible thoughts in front of Cyrus; because now you can be done away with. Wait for a couple of years, and then you'll be indispensable to his business. And, Matt, you don't want to be a tractor salesman, like your father, or a second-class fire chief."

"A husband to take care of her," Matt heard the words again in his mind: "Agatha needs a husband." He stiffened his neck and said "No! I'm not going to marry Agatha; I'll pick someone for myself."

"That's just what I was telling you, Matt; get to work on Miss Gloria. Now there's one that can put her petticoats on my bedpost any night of the year."

"Oliver got his green card in the mail yesterday," Matt succeeded in changing the subject.

"I know; the draft board put him on the list at our last meeting; how's your mother taking it?"

"Just like she did with Robert and Willy; kind of proud and scared at the same time."

"I don't suppose there is one boy who leaves for France, Matt, without their mother having that same feeling. Yet, look, we've only got six names on the Gold Star roll. Even old rough and tumble Ward Kessler managed to come home alive."

"I think I'll join up with Oliver," Matt said thoughtfully.

"You will like hell! I'll see to it personally that you stay home as head of that household until your number is drawn like all the other boys."

"You know, Uncle, you really are wound up tight as a clock spring today," Matt said lightly.

"Guess I am; this "Cyrus for Governor" idea has me on edge; but he's going to make it. Imagine, less than one week back there and the papers are quoting everything he says, regardless of what it is. 'The Crescent Crusader', I like that, it fits him. The women, they love him."

"Is he nominated yet?"

"No, but he has filed. Primary's this next week. If one of the parties doesn't pick him up, he'll run Independent. Don't worry, with Governor Calder and his men working, someone will grab him up in a hurry."

"I've got to go down to the post office," Matt said, "Why don't you walk with me?"

"Good," Bruce said, as Matt pulled the window blind down again and opened the door.

Locking the door behind him with the large iron key Cyrus had left him, Matt turned to his uncle with a knowing look in his eyes.

"Uncle, there is just one thing keeps worrying me about you."

"Now what would worry you about me, except that I sometimes snooze in church?"

Matt laughed. "No, I really mean it, how come you know so much about women's underwear?"

"Books have always been my constant and by far greatest sources of information," Bruce said seriously.

"At our house, we have six girls running around from mirror, to basin, to wash tub, to bedroom," Matt said; "so we boys know what goes on in the latest fashions of girls' nightgowns and stuff; but in what book did you read about "Billie Burk's?"

"Oh hell, everybody knows about 'em," Bruce stammered.

"No, Uncle, we just got our first pair of those at our house; blue with elastic and ruffles at their ankles. What color did you see?"

"Pink, no white. Now damn it! That's one secret I'm not goin' to give out until after you've married one of the Dodson girls. You might just want to change your mind and remain a bachelor."

They laughed until they could hardly contain themselves. Only the beating of Mrs. Cross's rugs brought them back to Crescent.

"One thing for damn sure," Bruce laughed, "I'll bet Margaret Cross doesn't wear 'em."

"Good afternoon, Matt, Bruce," Mrs. Cross said with a smile.

"Afternoon," they answered in chorus.

"No, I'll bet she doesn't," Matt snickered when they were out of hearing distance.

Mrs. Cross looked after them, sensing she was part of their joke; hiding her resentment of that knowledge under the rug she continued to beat. She must Bon Ami the windows before it turned dark, for tomorrow was Sunday. Sunday, to Margaret Cross, was a day to be kept holy and peaceful. The Lord created heaven in seven days she often said. "And then, he created women;" her husband use to add: "since, there has been no peace!"

A few minutes later Margaret noticed two young women walking toward the

CHECK AND FILL FROM OTHER VERSION!!!!!!

It had been a long walk to the shop. Heat still radiated from the combination coal and gas stove and Mitzie lifted a lid and poured some more slack in. She turned the damper and gave the grate handle a couple of quick shakes. "It really makes it too hot in here," she explained," but if we don't keep it going, we don't have any hot water for baths."

"Where's the ice box?" Agatha asked

"Oh, it's out on the back porch. We'll have to go through Ward's room to get to it. I'll show you." Her knock was very gentle.

"That you, Mitzie? Come on in."

A huge big toe peeked coyly through the hole in the coarsely knit stocking; it and the bottom of Ward's feet were the first things to greet the girls as they opened the door. Ward quickly swung his legs down from the back of the kitchen chair and sat upright in his own.

"Oh, for gosh sakes," he sputtered, the pain biting his side, "didn't know I had real company. Good afternoon, Miss Dodson."

Looking around the room, the girls gave each item careful notice; Agatha out of curiosity; Mitzie to be certain her crippled benefactor was well taken care of.

The Election

"Now, I do hope you two aren't here to encourage housecleaning," he smiled. "Because, you know as well as I that would take all the character out of things."

"I didn't know you were hurt, Mr. Kessel," Agatha said, pointing to the bandaged around Ward's chest.

Mitzie's eyes met his with a look of mixed despair and apology.

"Oh, just fell off a wagon and broke a couple of ribs. Be all right in a couple of weeks; in fact, I'd be better tomorrow if the darn doctor would just get off his high horse and let me get back to work, instead of sitting around here day-dreaming about the past," Ward said convincingly. Mitzie turned from him with a silent sigh of relief. They had met their first test together.

"I'm sorry, Mr. Kessel," Agatha said, her tone sincere. "If I can help, I'd like to." Agatha could hardly believe the bold words she had spoken.

"Thank you. You know, outside of Mitzie here, who can't really get out of helping me, me being her landlord, you're the first woman since my mother that ever offered to help Ward Kessel."

Agatha relaxed a bit more and smiled again as she came closer to him. "To be honest I don't know what help I can be, but we did have a sick calf once that I helped tend."

"I've been classed as a bull before, Miss Dodson, but never as a calf," Wart laughed softly.

For a moment their glances met. Ward had to mentally shake himself. A strange desire to touch her forced itself upon him. He knew by the glint of fright in her eyes, that if he even brushed her hand, she would be gone. Somehow she seemed so helpless, so awkward; so innocent.

"The ice box is out here," Mitzie rescued him. She continued her small, personal tour of the premises.

"Heard the boy deliver a new cake of ice not more than half an hour ago," he broke the trance and brought himself back to a subject he could cope with. "He should have left us a full fifty pounds to; enough to carry over through tomorrow. You might check the pan to see if it's full, Mitzie."

"Hard to believe she's one of Cyrus's kin," Ward thought. "So quiet, none of that show that Dodson keeps trying to impress the world with."

When the girls had loaded their arms with the food they needed he watched them go into the kitchen. Mitzie was already at the sink but Agatha paused in the door, her back straightened, her head high, as if to turn. Intently, Ward watched her quandary, tracing his fingers along the arm of the chair. He wanted to speak, but what was there to say? There wasn't even a thread to tie a conversation to. He grabbed the letter from his lap and tore open the envelope.

"Goodbye," Agatha had turned. He looked up clutching the letter.

"I'm sorry I called you a calf; but I could help, maybe," she said.

"Mitzie would have you think that I'm a bed-ridden invalid. Don't believe her. But, I wouldn't mind having you call anytime you'd like to. It does get a mite lonesome here penned up when I should be out there pounding the anvil, getting things done."

"I'd like to."

"And I don't mind this calf-calling part; it's just that no one has ever seen fit to be that kind," he laughed.

"You don't mind?" she asked without smiling.

"No! Goodbye," he heard himself say as the door closed softly behind her.

"What in the devil is the matter with you?" he asked himself. "You're not going to go around thinking about such things. Why, you've seen enough of the messes people get themselves in without getting stupid ideas on your own." He had caught himself getting sentimental, sentimental over a young girl, a girl who was just a family name and a bunch of incomplete sentences that meant nothing. "What in the world we ever talk about?"

Calmness came over him slowly and he shook his head. He started to read Binny's literary efforts on the war, but stopped as his mind wandered. "Ward Kessel, it's just a matter of you being hard up; you'd better take a trip over to the county seat before you go off 'halfcocked'." The words formed themselves on his lips but remained unspoken. He smiled at his silent, unintended pun, and then read his letter, pausing only briefly on the second page to pull the string and turn on the un-shaded light over the table.

Chapter 8

The Royal Hotel's lobby abounded with ferns that softened the militant clicking of the bellboy's heels as they snapped across the marble floors and up the wide staircase to the mezzanine. Condensation was forming on the sides of the ice bucket he carried, and perspiration beaded on his forehead and gathered in his sparse eyebrows. At the door of the "Dodson for Governor" headquarters, he checked the bottle of "Old Grand Dad" bourbon he had tucked under his left arm and entered the room to an odor of leftover cigars.

"In there, in the bedroom," the male secretary said, not stirring from his reclining position on the couch. "Take it on in."

The boy knocked on the door and waited for an answer. When the voice on the other side ignored him, he put the bucket down and opened the door.

"Well, I'd sure as hell say it was about time," someone said through the haze.

"That's fine, Charley," another more controlled said. "Here... here's your tip," Matt MacQuarrie said.

Cyrus, in his shirtsleeves, sat near the window in an overstuffed chair, his black sleeve bands billowing the white broadcloth above the elbows. He was reading a draft of the speech he was to make before the newly formed Civil Employees Union.

"Drink, Mr. Dodson?" MacQuarrie, who had written the speech, asked in a subdued voice, trying to avoid disturbing him, but wanting to do the best possible service to his new employer.

"No, Mac, I believe I'll pass the alcohol by this evening." Cyrus went back to his reading, blocking out the people around him in his concentration.

"This calls for a big one. *The Statesman* paper pledged five thousand to the campaign, and that isn't the half of it: everything we want will be printed and God be graceful with those half-assed Democrats, because when the press gets through with them in print, they might just as well be running Gene Debt or the whole Wobbly gang on their ticket." The donation figures were not new; everyone in the room had heard them several times in the last three days but it seemed to give ex-governor Calder a talking point for another drink every time he came into headquarters for the daily briefing.

"Now you take MacQuarrie over here: write, my God can, he write. Every time it comes out the way we want it to sound; and the way the damn voting public wants it to come out. Right, Mac?" Calder continued, sitting down on the edge of the bed. "Just on the rocks, Mac, no water," he ordered.

Lighting another Havana, the ex-Governor blew the match out dramatically and laughed, "You know, gentlemen, just to give you an insight into the thinking of the times: I love these gently rolled bits of tobacco leaves; well, I caught my boy with a cigarette in his mouth one day and I gave him hell; promised him that if he'd never smoke one of those pimp sticks again, I'd keep him in the best cigars money could buy, and I'll be damned if he doesn't take me up on it. He's been going through three a day, but now they want to kick him out of high school because of it. That's the width of thinking today; narrow, narrow, narrow. Isn't that something? But if that's the way it has to be to get votes; just like I told my boy, give up smoking around the place. Do it after school or when nobody is looking. Thinking right can avoid a lot of trouble."

Cyrus checked his watch and went back to his reading. MacQuarrie hovered over him, perched on the windowsill, waiting to make any alterations "the future governor" might wish to make.

"Take the delightful taste of bourbon, like this. Well, I suppose we can make a sacrifice for the future..." the ex-governor went on into another lengthy meaningless tirade, but Cyrus and MacQuarrie let it fade as they huddled in the corner with the pages of notes.

"Mac, I must leave in ten minutes; I promised my daughter, Gloria, that I would take her to supper. You understand."

"I'll cover with the group."

"I appreciate it. I just need to get away from this."

"Certainly. A lung full or two of fresh air might not do any of us too much harm," Mac winked. "My wife used to like the veal scaloppini at the Parisian Gardens. When she was alive we use to go there whenever we were in town. The chef, Girard, isn't the least bit stingy when it comes to using wine in his cooking."

"What do the ladies wear there?" Cyrus asked.

"Mr. Dodson, you've got me. Women's clothes usually escape me. My wife always liked to dress up though, and wanted to stay to dance; though I dance about like a lopsided centipede." MacQuarrie paused, then pointed to the script in front of them. "Is there anything you want changed?"

"I see a few things, but I can do that myself, as I go along," Cyrus said.

"Sir, may I offer a suggestion? Mr. Calder probably would not agree with me, but if there are any changes made during your talk, please make them ones of omission rather than addition."

This quiet man jolted Cyrus; he looked straight into his eyes. MacQuarrie winked. "Maybe you had better drop by the first thing in the morning so we can talk the changes over in advance," Cyrus said.

"That would certainly eliminate the possibility of offending any of the men you'll be talking to," MacQuarrie said as he screwed the top back on his large fountain pen and put it in his vest pocket.

There was a questioning expression on his face as Cyrus looked into MacQuarrie eyes.

"The men of the labor movement are touchy," MacQuarrie said as if to explain "with a chip on both shoulders, and rightfully so; but unpredictable in their angers, in their decisions, in their interpretations. They take a lot of understanding, but once you've taken their philosophy and looked at the over all goals in complete honesty, you have to admit they're right. It's the methods that sometime cloud the issue. I remember a Jesuit telling me about the Church and its history. He said, 'We believe the end justifies the means.' And with these men, as with any cause that is really worthwhile, this is the case." There was no emotion or change of inflection in Mac's quiet words.

"We'll have breakfast;" Cyrus said, his watch in hand.

"Certainly, Sir. I must have had a couple too many drinks. I've been talking too much," MacQuarrie said. "Forgive me."

"Oh, I didn't mean that," Cyrus was quick to catch his abruptness and try to correct his offense.

"There are many conflicts of opinion," MacQuarrie continued as he help Cyrus on with his coat, "even within our own selves at times; and bringing them out in the open isn't always the most pleasant way of making friends. Forgive me."

Calder was now expounding on national politics: "Let's face it, Wilson is nothing but a damn conscientious objector in president's clothes. If it hadn't been for his office he'd probably be a slacker along with all the other draft dodgers. But he got caught in his own snare. He may be a…"

Cyrus went out by the bedroom door, unnoticed by the orator, until the door had closed.

"Now where in hell is he going?" Calder asked MacQuarrie. "Doesn't he know that we've got work to do?"

MacQuarrie poured another drink. He bit his lip as he turned to face Calder's cigar. "He's gone to do some research for his talk, Monday. Gone to the library to get some facts."

"You're hired to write his stuff. Don't you let him go off on his own and yak about something he doesn't know a damn thing about;" Calder barked exhaling a cloud of anger.

"Governor, you taught me that last campaign, when you disregarded the script. Remember?" MacQuarrie, his back now to Calder, winked at one of the ward workers.

"What do you mean by that?" Calder asked. "Besides, you're a God-damned liar, the library is closed on Saturday." Calder looked at the emotionless MacQuarrie and shrugged his shoulders when it was obvious he wasn't going to answer the challenge.

"I suppose you're going to bring up Felt," he snapped at MacQuarrie. When there was no answer again he continued more calmly, "It's really an unmitigated shame that sanctimonious Senator Felt had to turn out so damn un-sanctimonious in the bedroom of his secretary's wife."

Somebody laughed.

"That's not funny!"

"No, I agree, that is not funny, as the Governor says," MacQuarrie interjected "But, it is rather amusing. Can't you just see the picture: The Senator, fresh from a lecture on morals and the evils of Demon Run; Fredericks, a smart but quite impressionable young man with a future in mind; and sweet little Millie, a gentle nymph from the age of five, now craving the fatherly affection of some more mature man; all stopped at the Frederick's flat to gather nuts in May. Here we go gathering nuts in May, nuts in May..."

"Oh, for Christ's sake, MacQuarrie!" the ex-Governor was flushed with anger.

"That's how it happened, Governor; you and I and half the inner sanctum of both parties know it. Even in Washington, things aren't so crowded you have to sleep three in a bed. And if you do, it pays to be more discreet than to have the girl's mother living in the same apartment. Especially if Mom; happens to have a slight love of the monetary side of life. Saddest part of the whole story is." MacQuarrie paused and looked over at Calder to see if he were at the breaking point yet. He was close but still held his burst of fire.

"Yes, saddest part of the whole story is that nobody knows how much money Mama was paid to keep her knowledge to herself. Whatever it was, it wasn't enough. And it wasn't until we were down to the wire, silently backing beloved Senator Felt in his bid for the chair, so he can clean up the State's 'iniquity' that it leaks out. The opposition has all the gory details and knows more than we do. No, as the Governor says, it's not funny. Not very!"

"I consider Felt a tragedy," Calder said in a calmer tone.

"If you had added the adjective 'classic' in that sentence, it would have brought tears," MacQuarrie said taking another swallow of his drink.

"He would have made an outstanding governor," Calder went on.

MacQuarrie smiled, "Adjective trouble again, Sir," he coughed. "You mean 'ideal', not 'outstanding'."

"Now damn it, Mac, your stupid comments aren't necessary. Haven't you got sense enough to know how close we came to identifying ourselves with that man? Hell, we could have ruined the whole organization by that one slip. And as far as I'm concerned he would have made a better governor than the one we're pushing now. Maybe not as easy to railroad into office, but he'd have been a lot easier to work with." Calder took out the small pocketknife from his vest pocket and cut off the end of another Havana.

"Your altruism is so varied it dazzles me," MacQuarrie lit a match and held it out to Calder's cigar who reluctantly accepted the gesture.

"Dodson's already starting to get the big head, can't you see that, Mac? You just wait: within a week he'll be telling you how to write speeches. This is a group effort. Hell, any stumblebum can accidentally get elected. But, we are not about to work with that element of doubt. We can't take that gamble; we've got too much at stake this time to let some hick try to take over and run it his way."

"A classic tragedy. The Greeks would have packed the amphitheaters. The only trouble is, Governor, you are trying to wear all the masks; even the part of the clown."

"You're really an arrogant, over-educated ass," Calder finally said in desperation.

"And you, Sir, are greatly improving your adjectives." MacQuarrie's expression didn't change as he gulped the rest of his drink down in one swallow. "Don't go away, gentlemen; I've gone to get another bottle. I'll be back. Don't go away."

"You're fired," Calder yelled.

"That's fine, Governor, you've always been known for your excellent judgment," MacQuarrie smiled, "but don't go away, I'll be back." He left.

"Damn lush; good-for-nothing, liver-bellied lush. A bum; but a good writer I'll have to admit." Calder said quietly after the door had closed.

Gloria Dodson played the brush through her long hair, watching the light from the chandelier reflected in the-auburn strands. Her mind played the field, wondering if her new voile and taffeta dress would be acceptable at the Parisian Gardens; wondering if her mother would be all right without them, while they were away; wondering too, if Cyrus would like her shorter hair. Would he win? Could he win? Of course, he had to. Didn't he have the finest men in the state working for his election? From among the pile of imported flowers she had purchased on sale for only twenty-five cents apiece, she selected a plush orange, rust and yellow chrysanthemum with golden leaves and held it artfully over her left shoulder. Then she danced bare-footed around the room, swirling the full skirt of finely pleated organza that made up her slip. She paused in her waltz to gaze at herself each time she passed the mirror.

"Now this is really a very provocative performance," Cyrus said as he stood in the doorway that connected their rooms.

She ran to him, throwing her arms around his neck and kissing him on the cheek, "I've missed you, Father, but you really shouldn't peek. A women is never enchanting without her complete disguise."

"I'd say that this one is even more so," he answered.

"Father, you stink. Have you been swimming in tobacco juice?"

"Masculine men always smell of tobacco, I'm told," he laughed.

"Is it necessary to be so completely masculine? Couldn't you be more moderate?"

"That's enough;" he said, "remember, when I brought you on this trip you promised to show more respect and act the part of the perfect lady."

"How can I; when you don't smell like a perfect gentlemen?"

"I'll bathe and start the evening a new man. Gloria, I had to do everything but lie today to break away early enough to even

The Election

get back to the room to change clothes. I must be turning into a professional politician."

"Why, because of being a liar or no privacy?" she asked. "When you're ready, I'll send your suit down with the valet to be cleaned and pressed. You wouldn't make a very romantic escort, Father, in that suit."

"Gloria Dodson, what is that, a funeral offering?" he pointed to the floral display on the dresser.

"Oh. Father, look," she started throwing the imitation flowers on the bed. "Flowers, flowers and all of them mine."

"What happened to that hard, practical suffragette that Governor Calder thought we were bringing to the capital to be so much help? Turned into a money-spending female?"

Coyness was feigned. "But, Father, only four dollars for sixteen corsages."

"I don't believe it; but of course I don't really care when you are as happy and beautiful as you are tonight," he kissed her forehead.

Swinging around in front of him, kissing his cheek again while standing on tiptoe, she smiled, "I'm so proud of you, Father, so proud. And being here to see you do the things you want to do is the nicest experience I could ever be a part of. I have a feeling that you are destined to be an important man; more than just a governor, a man whose name will mean ideals and truth and honesty. People that hear that name will feel what I feel in being your daughter."

"You rather embarrass me, Gloria how can any man live up to what you have just said? Now get dressed; I'll be ready long before you are."

"Father, you need a complete change of linen. Your collar is even a bit grimy," she said, not moving from his arm's comfort.

"My, my, you'd just about think you were my wife or mother instead of a loving daughter."

"Your mail is on the desk in your room; and there were several calls that you should answer before we go to dinner. I listed them in the book. Tomorrow after church at the First Presbyterian, you lunch with the Temperance League at the Chalice Tea Garden at

1:30 p.m. sharp. A Mrs. Golightly was most insistent about the time. You will not have to talk; but they have provided enough time for a few remarks if you wish to address them."

"I'd better not. I wouldn't want to say anything that might offend the ladies. Knowing how I feel about this stupid, unconstitutional nonsense, I might really let them know the truth about what they are letting themselves in for," he said from his room while he undressed.

"Your bath is drawn; but you may need to add more hot water," she called back.

"Instead of worrying about me, why in the devil don't you finish dressing?" he asked, amused by her attention.

"If I don't make an impression on you now, when you become President you will never give me a second thought" she laughed.

When they were dressed, Cyrus had made his calls and they started to go out the door, Gloria stopped and turned the light back on. "Oh me; nearly forgot your boutonniere. The florist told me you should be wearing one." From the dresser she picked up the white carnation and pinned it in the lapel of Cyrus's gray shadow striped suit.

"It's real," she said, "and it didn't even cost twenty-five cents. In fact only a dime; so you can wear one every day."

He looked at her and shook his head. "What an unusual, wonderful person," he thought as he turned off the light.

Hundreds of red, yellow and white bulbs formed the brilliant marquee above the Parisian Gardens. Gloria's eyes met and reflected each spot of blinking light, amplifying. The joyful excitement she feared would betray her recently acquired sophistication. The doorman's braided sleeve was offered to help her from the glistening new Templar. An attendant took the driver's seat to park the vehicle and Cyrus joined her on the sidewalk under the canopy.

"Good evening, monsieur," the maitre d' said in an accent not quite French, "you have zee reservation?"

"Dodson; Cyrus P. Dodson."

"Mais oui, monsieur," he bowed deeply after consulting his list. "thees way."

"I'll bet he's from Chicago," Cyrus said as his foot gently nudged hers.

Gloria looked over at Cyrus when they sat down and smiled. "May I call you Cyrus just for tonight without your being angry with me?" Her tone was one of jest, but the words found their mark.

"My dear, why not? I am afraid I usually insist otherwise as a wall of habit. My father was so strict; we were beaten if we forgot our decorum."

"Are you going to beat me?" her eyes flashed playfully. His sudden serious mood had been defeated by a flank attack.

He laughed.

"Oh, Cyrus, I'm so glad you are going to be 'Governor'; we can come often. Can't we?" Gloria's gloved hand touched his across the table.

Across the sparkling stemmed glasses and silver settings, he looked at her. She was radiant. Her lips were still parted from her question. At times like this she almost made him feel like a different person. The gold, diamond crusted locket, her grandmother had left her, now found its perfect setting against the black taffeta bodice of her gown. What a changed picture from that first night when she had interrupted his reading of Whitman.

"We can come, can't we?" she patted his hand gently for reassurance.

"If, is a very important little word in answering your question my dear. You know, I may not even receive the nomination let alone win the election. But the reason we came here tonight was to forget all of that."

"I like you wearing a carnation, Cyrus. Will you dance with me just once, maybe twice?" Her directness disarmed his poise when he least expected it. Without her sudden offensives driving past his line of solidly built defenses, he could comfortably return to a world free from outside interference. His defenses however, were not organized to combat her surprise attacks. He was about to say, "You don't want to dance with an old man," but his reflexes quickly brushed the thought aside before it was even clearly formed in his mind.

"A waltz, perhaps, or two," he said. They laughed and he admitted to himself that he had been defeated once more, in a subtle, unrevealed encounter.

"Are you about to place your order, sir?" the waiter asked spreading a large menu open before Gloria.

"Why don't we have the waiter choose it for us, Cyrus? It's all in French. I wouldn't know what we were ordering, would you?"

"That is a very good idea," he said, wonderingly. "The chef will be flattered," the waiter said in a confidential tone. "So few people ever give him the privilege."

"Imagine, Cyrus, we'll make friends with the chef. Another vote for Dodson," Gloria said.

The waiter's expression was one of confusion.

"For Governor. My father is running for Governor."

From his stiff shirt, to his bow tie, to his plastered down hair, it was obvious he did not believe the "my father" part of her last statement.

"For an aperitif sir, I would suggest an imported chardonnay."

"That would be fine," Cyrus said.

The waiter folded the menus under his arm and started to leave for the kitchen, then paused, turned stiffly on his heels and came back to the table. To Gloria he said in a serious tone: "Ma'am, I hope he wins. We could sure use a change." Again he turned and was gone.

"Cyrus that's the new 'Forget Me Not' waltz they're playing."

"I've never heard it before," he said "but I did promise you one dance."

"It's on the other side of the 'Felicia Waltz'. You must remember that; Cynthia is always playing it on the Victrolla."

Again she was nudging him forward in a playful way that kept him slightly off balance, just a bit unsure of what to expect next. Her gloves remained on the table: another symbol of flexibility, a source of fashionable discomfort, discarded for the time to make room for freedom of expression.

Fingertips brushed with accidental excitement as he reached for her hand and they swung gracefully into the swirl of dancers.

Amazement comforted Cyrus as he found the ease with which he recaptured the art. How well they danced together! At first their manner was formal, but halfway around the floor, his arm had pulled her close, and her hand had made itself an intimate part of his. They danced in near oblivion.

Neither of them broke the trance with words until three waltzes later when the musicians stopped for intermission. Only the pianist continued, providing a mixture of Chopin and Liszt patterns tinkling into the voices and sounds of the otherwise quiet restaurant.

"The wine is compliments of Chef Girard, sir," the waiter said placing the label in front of Cyrus for inspection. To Gloria, he bowed and. said, "A campaign contribution, Ma'am." He poured their wine and left them to their little walled city.

Glasses clinked with the gentle touch of a toast and they sipped in silence. She looked over the crystal rim at Cyrus's attentive face and lowered her glass just enough to reveal the suggestion of a kiss which she formed with her wine moistened lips.

Cyrus wanted to say something except, everything he could possibly think of at that moment seemed so mundane. Instead, he again let his foot touch hers to let her know that he was aware of gesture. Then he took the napkin rapped bottle from the cooler and refilled their glasses.

The waiter's polite cough acted as a call to order and they pulled back in their chairs for the first course: a soup with toasted croutons and cheese garnishing the surface.

"What is it?" Gloria said carefully sipping it. "It is so different."

"Ma'am," he said in a guarded tone, "they call it 'soupe au oignon avec le fromage'. But if the chef will pardon me, it's just bouillon with onions added."

The two of them laughed quietly at his straight-faced comment. And then the serious eating began: course after course with no time in between for dancing or anything but brief debate on the epicurean merits of each dish. More often than not, the waiter would give his abbreviated version of the recipe in amusing but down-to-earth terms.

"It's a rye waltz," Cyrus said, using one of her tactics, "would you like to dance, mademoiselle?"

Between glasses of chardonnay, they danced until there were no more people in the Parisian Gardens except the bus boys, the waiters and the man at the piano.

Cyrus looked at his watch, now a symbol of frivolity rather than frugality, and asked the waiter where they could go for more dancing.

The waiter's smile was one of compassion. "Outside of the Royal Room at the Hotel Madison, Sir, there are really none fitting a Governor."

Even in his new found gaiety, provided by the abundance of wine, Cyrus' precise mind caught the gentle note of caution.

Gloria sensed his mood. "You do have your speech to work on and I'm really getting tired," she said, putting her gloves back on. "Perhaps we can dance next week."

His tip to the waiter was by far the most generous Cyrus had ever given.

"Thank you, sir. Here's a toast and a vote for Dodson," he said lifting a glass of water to his lips. Make that two votes, I forgot about the chef."

At the hotel desk Cyrus picked up a handful of lengthy, urgent messages from Calder requesting his immediate appearance at headquarters for a conference and a brief note penned in MacQuarrie's graceful hand: "From the sleeping Caldron fumes the billowing smoke of Hell.

So, breathe deep the heavens 'till dawn awakes the smell. Breakfast at eight! Mac."

Cyrus chuckled to himself at Mac's advice to go to bed and sleep tight. Everywhere he turned, he suddenly found strangers interested in his well being, making sure that he didn't say the wrong thing, or go to the wrong places. He wasn't certain he liked the new fenced-in feeling, but there seemed nothing he could do about the net which closed in tighter and tighter to "protect" his future.

In their adjoining rooms, Gloria busied herself getting ready for bed, while Cyrus read over his notes on the talk.

He sat in his darkened room with only the small goose-necked reading lamp bent low to light his study. Awareness of Gloria's presence came from the stillness as she stood there in the doorway waiting to say "good night". Turning in his chair, he sat looking at her for minutes, watching her silhouette in semi bas-relief against the light of her room, the thin batiste of her gown forming a hazy halo around her shapely body. He said nothing and she walked slowly toward him. "I don't want to disturb your work, Cyrus; but you'd better go to bed, as Mr. MacQuarrie suggested."

"It was you, my dear, who was so tired."

"I'm not now," she said quietly, her hand softly stroking his hair," not at all. It was like another world; I could have danced forever." Leaning gently against him as she stood next to him, her long cool fingers played through his hair and a wisp of her gown touched the lobe of his left ear, sending a playful chill running down his body.

"We'll dance again," he said, patting her hand and turning back to the desk and the yellowed circle that spotlighted the pages.

"Did I tell you I'd made an appointment for you with the barber for Monday? And remember the poetry 'Breathe deep the heavens till the dawn awakes. Breakfast at eight...Mac!'"

"I'll remember, if you will," he said sensing his strength ebbing away; "now go to bed."

"I'll go but I don't want to," she said. "I really don't."

He kissed her hand as she leaned over him to read the speech. When she stood up her breast accidentally brushed against his cheek and they paused, searching one another's shadowed faces for understanding.

"I'm afraid the wine is making me too sleepy to do any more work," he said. "I'll have the bellboy wake me at six."

"We both need our sleep. Good night, Cyrus," she said.

Leaving his chair and her closeness, he went into the bathroom and poured cold water over his face and arms. And when there were no strangers, he thought, there was always the past probing the present with the gnarled and bony fingers of memories. The towel, soft and warm, took the edge off the cold water, but his mind was now clear.

"Good night, Gloria," he said through the half-opened door and turned his lamp into darkness.

Chapter 9

From the world of tractors, bailers and combines, Matt's father had returned home leaving his ventures in selling implements to renew acquaintances with the clan he called with affection his "bratty heritage." His full head of snowy hair gave him a halo of dignity; which instinctively called his children to order when he sat among them, and quietly churned the blood of his wife with a desire for evening and the bed she had kept waiting these weeks without him.

Soon there would be no babies playing blocks at has feet, none to ride "horseback" on his crossed legs. Even now there were no lines sagging with the weight of diapers and small-sized clothes fresh from Ann's scrub board. This lady in his life had shared with him the experience of having one son leave for France; two more take their metal suit cases, packed for cantonment: and a fourth, the youngest and admittedly closest to his father's heart, keyed up for the veiled adventure of rowdy patriotism.

This was his only record of the exciting lantern show he had lived: his children spanning the better part of thirty years; each a mystery, each an education, each a part of Ann.

Matt watched his father dressing in the bedroom. He must talk to him. There was no one else he could talk to. Maybe he would understand about Wart and the fight and Morgan being killed. He could remember years before, he had been crying because of a fight with the Behmis boy who had lived two doors away.

"A little beat up, huh, Matthew? Well it doesn't really matter," his father had said, inspecting the cut on one side of his face and the bruised eye which was soon to turn black. "It doesn't matter too much, as long as you did the best you could."

He guessed just about every father had said about the same thing to his son, because no one loves a coward, even one who is only seven years old. His mother had washed the cut with boric acid and streaked it with burning iodine. The eye would just have to take its course. Then to get his mind off of his troubles, his father had invited him to the garden to help weed the vegetables.

Though his father understood fighting, he wouldn't understand killing. He couldn't even talk to his father about that night. He turned to leave, but there was no turning back.

"Something on your mind, Son?"

"Nope, not much."

"But something important?"

"No, just thinking about Mr. Dodson running for Governor."

Well, Matt, that shouldn't cause much thought; Cyrus Dodson has been running for public office since before you were born," his father said, stretching his neck to fasten his collar button. Karl Harwood dressed as a salesman even when he wasn't selling.

"Didn't it even shock you a bit about such a big job?"

"Afraid not. Some people are just born politicians."

"Mr. Dodson isn't a politician, Dad; not really. He's too honest."

"My God, Matt, what are you mumbling about? It sounds to me as if you are spending too much time playing fire chief with your uncle. Honesty is a lot more than not stealing or not telling lies. When used by politicians it usually infers that the word 'honesty' insures good judgment, selflessness, generosity and complete impartiality in dealing with others. Understand that?"

"Of course; but Mr. Dodson is honest."

"Let's put it this way: Cyrus thinks he is all of these things and maybe those who vote for think so; but those who are actually putting him up for office are betting that he isn't. They know that to be a politician you can't be honest; you have to put self before everyone and everything and you have to be ruthless in eliminating all your enemies on the way to the top. If you don't, you'll fail as a politician."

"I can't believe that; I just can't. I know he isn't bad."

"Son," his father paused in tying his tie, "there is nothing wrong or bad about being a politician; now remember that. Nothing wrong with being a politician as long as the politician and others realize that is just what he is and nothing more. I talked to Bruce for a moment yesterday and, as always, your uncle is prone to wrap every one of his causes in red, white and blue bunting and sing the 'Star Spangled Banner' in order to carry others along with his enthusiasm. Bruce McHenry doesn't know what life is all about!"

"Doesn't know what life is all about" always seemed to be Matt's father's final note of contempt when putting people in their place.

"He's a nice, loud-mouthed, know-nothing who basks in the glory of name-dropping and sweet-sounding platitudes."

"Platitudes?" Matt asked, not understanding exactly what the word meant.

"Shall we say your uncle is a pleasant, likeable, phony that wouldn't do anything to hurt anyone intentionally; but he is a small town nut who doesn't really, know as much about this world as he thinks he does. Even though we all sort of love him. He's a great guy and I get a kick out of him."

"I still don't believe Mr. Dodson is a politician."

"Son, you could be right."

Matt looked over as his father put on his vest and suit coat. He didn't know his father too well. There was an intense longing in Matt when he watched him but it was as if there was an invisible barrier between them when it came to talking the last few years. How could he tell him about the fight, when he couldn't even mention Mr. Dodson without getting a sermon?

"Rather hot to be wearing that long-sleeved sweater isn't it?" his father changed the subject.

"Keeps the dust out when I bag the grain." Matt's excuse even satisfied himself, though he didn't know where it had come from. It would serve as an answer to everyone until the wounds healed.

"You'll have to pardon me, Matt, if I don't sound too impressed with politicians. You see, I've been taken a couple of times by some of these carnival barkers and their games. Even lost some money."

There was a rattling of cuff links in the ornate metal jewelry box on the dresser as his father searched to find the pair with small imitation rubies in the corners, that his wife had given him as a wedding gift. He never wore them on his trips for fear of losing them; saving them to please Ann when in Crescent.

"In fact, hundreds of innocent but greedy people of the states around here, and that includes your father, clipped by one of these hustlers, who later became governor of our state and at this time goes around looking for an 'honest man' to run for office. Does that sound familiar?"

"Governor Calder?"

"I'd say that was a fairly good shot; right on target."

"Do you think Mr. Dodson knows about him?"

"I'm not sure he does. Not very many people do. They just know their money disappeared, not who was behind the scheme that swindled them. You know, Matt, we're all a bit on the cowardly side. I don't suppose I lost more than five hundred dollars, all told; but I was so embarrassed that I didn't tell a soul when I got back in town that I had been a sucker. Main reason was I didn't want your mother to find out. I was just too proud."

"Didn't you get any of your money back? None at all?"

"Nope!"

"How about the police?"

"Son, it is a closed issue; someday I'll show you the stock certificates of the New Liberty Holdings and a few more pieces of useless paper from other such venture your greedy father has lost money on." His father smiled a big grin and put his arm around Matt's shoulders," Now that I've slipped and told you of one of my weaker sides, what say we get back to serious things?"

"Dad, this is important," Matt broke in. "If Mr. Dodson doesn't know about this he should be told so he can watch out for Governor Calder."

"Matt, calm down. I'm certain Cyrus will find out soon enough what Clarence Calder and his boys are. Anyway, on this particular swindle, he wouldn't stand much chance of proving anything."

"Why don't we try?"

Karl Harwood stopped brushing his hair for a moment and smiled. "Nothing wrong with being a crusader either; but it has some of the same pitfalls that you find along the path of the politician."

"All I said was 'why don't we try to prove it if it's true?'"

"It's true. Son, I have a trunk full of old stock certificate from my adventures that you can look at, and a string of news paper clippings about the formation and dissolution of New Liberty Holdings."

"Then let's try."

"Doing this to save Cyrus from Calder; that what you want, son; or just for the adventure; or to be a hero?"

"For everyone."

"No, Matt. Now let us look at the picture with our glasses on. As I said 'nothing wrong with being a crusader', as long as you recognize the fact that you're really doing it to bolster your own self rather than the cause you are fighting for. Just as the politician does when he runs for office to 'clean up corruption and bring honesty to government'."

"You're making fun of me."

They both laughed.

"Nope. Not really, because what I'm saying is true and one of these days you'll see. Everyone finds that out sooner or later if they live long enough."

"I'd still like to try."

"Then do it. I don't think for a moment you'll be able to find any evidence to prove anything in court but you might prove something to yourself; and that is really what you are after anyway. Tonight after supper, we'll go upstairs and raid that trunk. Now,

Matt, what's really on your mind, some girl? Or are you letting this war get to you?"

"Oh, once in a while I think about how I'm missing out on going 'over there'. Besides, Uncle Bruce has given me three or four talks about how I must stay here and as he says 'to keep the home fires burning.'"

"That's, not a bit like, our 'flag-waving chief'. Do you suppose when it gets close to home his patriotism wears thin?"

"He's not really so bad."

"He's beautiful; he's so predictably human that he is beautiful."

"And wrong?"

"God no, Matt. He's right; there is no need for you to go off to war until they call you. Don't rush fate. Bruce just gives the wrong reasons for being right. Son, your mother is fully capable of running the show without the weak protective efforts of any ineffectual male. Your mother and the girls are plenty self-sufficient."

"Uncle Bruce knows more than you'd think he'd know about women," Matt said with confidence.

"Son, I'd be the last to rob Bruce of any of his sparkle. I rather like him, too, but though he is quite conversant on the opposite sex, I doubt his understanding of the more subtle aspects of the subject. What knowledge Bruce has amassed about women can probably be purchased at a most reasonable sum."

"You don't give him much credit."

"Of course I do. Bruce knows what I've just said is true. He just can't bear the thought of having his favorite nephew leave. I have the same feelings, Matt. Bruce and I are both selfish; we're more concerned with our own loss than with your danger."

Usually his father could make Matt forget anything that seemed too serious; but now, even his making light of Bruce did not bury the taint of Morgan's death.

"Well, Matthew, we've covered the war, the election and the art of higher finance. Now, what's on your mind? Your forehead has as many wrinkles as old Doctor Phillips. You in love?"

"There is a girl, Dad."

"Suppose he tried to talk you out of that, too."

Matt laughed, "Well, he did, a little."

"He tried the same thing with your mother and me. I suspect he's met his match," his father chuckled as they started down the stairs; "that's one force his red, white and blue won't alter much."

For the moment Matt had forgotten the pressure exerted on his conscience by Morgan's death.

In the kitchen Karl kissed Anne on the neck, sending that usual pleasant little chill down her back; and then sat down to breakfast.

Later at the granary Matt checked Mr. Dodson's invoices and then went back to shovel wheat. The shed was hot and very stuffy so he opened the big side doors; then pulled the thick sweater over his head. His chest welcomed the flow of fresh air; and as he propped open the two doors with a couple of rocks, he sucked in the coolness until it filled his lungs. Turning back to the semi-darkness of the warehouse he stopped abruptly as a pair of soft cool hands caressed his back.

"Nice, your muscles feel so hard; and strong," Mitzie whispered.

"Oh for hell's sake, Mitz; you scared the crap out of me."

"That's descriptive."

"Sorry. Where were you hiding? I didn't see you."

"I watched you come in. Was going to knock when I heard you unlatching the door and so I went around front and peeked while you took your clothes off and beat your chest." She giggled.

"You make me sound silly."

"Never. I just miss you, Matt. You haven't been over, once; you don't even know what my room looks like."

"Busy."

"Just a few minutes, or a word, or a smile?" Her hand was on his left arm touching the scars. He felt as if he wanted to run away from her.

"Mitzie, I'm really busy; really. Got to get all of this loaded and over to Flintsville."

"When you get back? Then?"

"Maybe; but I can't promise."

"I need your friendship, Matt. I thought we would be tied very close now, especially. But there seems to be nothing on your part. Have I done something wrong?"

"No, Mitz. I told you I'm just busy;" he said turning back to his shovel.

"Tonight then? See you," she said in a light tone.

When he turned she was gone. She had vanished as quickly as she had appeared. Now that she had left he had a strange empty feeling and wished that she were still there in the barn talking to him. If she just wouldn't push and make him feel guilty. Someday he would tell her how much he loved Ellie and then maybe they could be more comfortable with each other.

When the wagon crossed the river on the way to Flintsville, Matt looked straight ahead doing his best not to notice the workmen busy dismantling the skeleton remains of the washed-out bridge; but its image pulsed in his mind until he was beyond the sound of the river. The steady thump of the horses' hooves beating the thick dust of the road relaxed his attention and he dozed off. When the reins slackened and the horses' pace began to increase, he awoke with a start, pulling the reins so hard and fast that the team nearly stopped.

Flintsville was unchanged, except Morgan was not there to goad him into anger. In Morgan's place was a large pimply-faced boy with tousled black hair.

"You taking Morgan's job?"

"Yeah," the boy said lifting one of the grain bags to his shoulder and starting up the ramp.

"I'm Matt Harwood from Crescent Grain."

"I know," the boy said over his shoulder and disappeared into the store.

Matt followed him with his own load and they met face to face again at the top of the loft stairs.

"Seen you before, somewhere," Matt puffed as he put his bag on the stack. The boy didn't answer, but started to brush past Matt.

"What's your name?" Matt said in a puzzled tone, putting his hand on the boy's arm.

He pulled away quickly, "Look I don't want to fight. Leave me alone, I don't want to fight."

"What do you mean 'you don't want to fight'?"

"I was drunk."

"What are you talking about? Make sense, will you?"

"The Grange; I was drunk."

"I don't remember you there."

"I know; I was holding your arms."

"You mean when Morgan and I?"

"We'd been drinking. I'm sorry."

Matt felt suddenly sick to his stomach. His fists clenched tight and his mouth became very dry.

"I don't want to fight," the boy said once more and ran down the stairs.

Matt stood at the top of the stairs for several minutes, then, slowly followed him. The boy was at the tailgate of the wagon about to pick up another bag.

"What's your name?" Matt asked again.

"Paul; Paul Crawford."

"Hi."

They finished unloading the wagon and Paul signed the delivery notice. "I am sorry. That was a terrible, screwed up night," Paul said.

"Sure was." Matt pulled himself up into the seat of the wagon and slapped the reins gently against the fly-laden horses. Again Matt had run into an emotional brick wall. He couldn't even talk to Paul Crawford about something they had both been a part of because Paul obviously didn't know the truth about Morgan's death.

He stopped by Coolie's drug store for a soda hoping that Ellie might be there. She wasn't and Coolie was too busy listening to the advantages of a new line of corn plasters to spend any time joking with Matt. The salesman went from plasters to liniments while

Matt sucked the dregs from the glass, making a sudden disturbing noise that caused the peddler to turn around. Matt smiled at him. The salesman coughed and went on with a description of ailments that could be comforted by the potions.

"See you Saturday, Mr. Coolie."

"Bye, Matt,"

"Do you know how to get to the Fitzgerald's house?" Matt asked.

"White place, corner Center and Maple."

Matt nodded his thanks and let the screen door slam shut behind him.

Ellie's home sat well back among the trees behind a semi-circular drive that made entrance on both streets. Matt tied the team to one of the three gargoyle metal hitching posts at the curb and walked self-consciously through the ornate metal gate. His feet seemed to make more noise than usual as he slowly scuffed his way toward the white-pillared porch. Ivy clung tightly to the pillars and the red brick wall; here and there partially covering some of the black shutters which bracketed each of the many windows.

He let the shield and crest of the doorknocker bang a loud, unexpected clank that seemed to ring down into the soles of his feet. Minutes magnified themselves while he waited. No one answered, so he knocked again. This time the door opened slowly and a small, puckered face in a dowdy, black uniform poked itself out at him.

Matt could hardly tell if the person in front of him was a man or woman until a high- pitched voice asked him what he wanted.

"Miss Fitzgerald; does she live here?"

"No, she's not here."

"Isn't this the Fitzgerald's?"

"Yes; but she's gone."

"Gone? Where?"

"Convent; back East."

"When will she be back?"

"Won't. They don't when they're nuns."

Matt was deflated, but he regained his composure. "Is her brother here?"

"No, gone back to school, Boston."

Then, in her established brevity, the housekeeper closed the door in his face, much as death, without further useless conversation.

Matt picked up the mail sacks from the post office and started back to Crescent still not sure if the woman at Fitzgerald's was telling him the truth or not. She must be lying he reasoned; but he knew inside that Ellie was gone forever from his life. He felt empty and wanted to cry, but slapped the reins against the horses instead.

It was nearly six-thirty when Matt reached the granary. He should go home for dinner but he wasn't hungry and didn't want to talk, or be asked questions about where he had been over the supper his mother would keep warm for him. He wanted to be alone, so he sat in Cyrus's swivel chair in a sort of trance, not thinking, unaware of the darkness that took over, until suddenly a light switched on in one of the windows of Mitzie's room.

He shook himself back to consciousness as if he had momentarily fallen asleep in church. He saw a shadow cut the beam of light that fell across the office floor. It must be Mitzie. He had told her he might come over and see her if he wasn't busy. He would like to touch her again even though it made him feel uncomfortable to think about it.

Quietly he climbed the stairs and knocked on her door. Before he had an opportunity to knock a second time she was there and the door opened. She stood looking up at him as if she were going to cry.

"Oh, Matt I'm so glad."

"I hope I didn't scare you."

"No. I just knew you'd come tonight, I just knew."

"Can't stay long. Haven't been home for dinner."

"If you're hungry, I'll fix you something," she said as she walked to the side window and pulled the green window blind down.

"I'm not; not really."

"Sit down, Matt," she said, pointing to one of the wicker chairs. "Or maybe you'd rather sit on the bed. It's more comfortable."

He chose the bed and moments later laid back across it, relaxed.

"Want to take your shoes off?" she asked.

"Uh huh" he answered, responding to the suggestion.

"I watched you when you put the wagon away; and when you stayed too long, I knew you would come see me, Matt."

"How did you know that?"

"Been thinking about you all day; just as if you were thinking about me, too."

Matt was tender for a moment; he didn't tell her the truth. He watched in silence as she lowered the blinds of the windows facing Elm Avenue and felt for the first time since the night in the barn the excitement Mitzie stirred in him when they were alone.

She primped for a few moments, in front of the oval mirror over the dresser. "I washed my hair today so I'd be fresh for you;" she said as if there were no question that they would belong to one another as they had before.

"Take your sweater off so you can get cool"

He obeyed her, throwing the sweater on the foot of the bed. It slid over the brass bedstead to the floor. Mitzie picked it up and put it over one of the chairs by the window, then went to the dresser and poured some water from the white ironstone pitcher into the large washbowl. He listened as she wrung a washcloth out and came close to him. He kept his eyes closed as she put the cool, damp cloth to his forehead, then washed his face, then his neck and arms. He relaxed completely. Next, he felt the coolness and the touch of her fingers as they gently worked down over his chest to his waist. When her tongue touched his chest, he opened his eyes and pulled her to him and kissed her, her hands fumbling with his belt buckle.

"Oh, God, Mitz."

"Just a minute, Dear," she whispered and was gone. He closed his eyes again and heard the chain switch on the lamp snap back as she turned the light off. The rustling of her clothes as she undressed excited him even more and he could hardly wait until he felt her next to him again, her hands caressing him. Slowly she let him take command as they lost themselves in a whirl of writhing, pulsing, beating madness that spun them in wild-spinning circles until they were without breath or consciousness. Finally, in a burst of throbbing convulsions, they clung to one another in a complete calm; then in exhaustion fell asleep as one.

Matt woke to the coolness of the washcloth. The lamp was on and Mitzie was bathing his entire body.

"Sorry to wake you. It's almost eleven. Your folks will probably wonder where you are."

He could hardly pull himself up, he felt so tired and relaxed.

"I don't want you to go, Matt. I have a feeling you'll never come back again."

"I will," he said, struggling with his clothes.

"Do, Matt. You drive me insane when you don't."

"I will, tomorrow."

"You drive me crazy when you don't come and you drive more insane when you do; but I like it."

They kissed good night several times before Matt finally started down the stairs, bumping his head on the low beam.

"Going to kill myself. Where'd that come from?"

"Sorry, forgot to tell you. Want me to kiss it better?"

"Nope; I'll never get home if you do."

Mitzie turned the light off as she heard the door close in the hall below, then pulled the window blind and let it fly to the top on its spring roller. She watched the outline of Matt's figure under the streetlights; until he disappeared. He had left her again, but this time his warmth was still a part of her.

She slipped her bathrobe on and sat at the desk in the dark for a few minutes before she turned on the lamp. Its light lit the few books she had there and the warm wood surface of the secretary. She picked up the page of paper she had been writing on that afternoon. She had intended to read it to Matt and she had planned that they would talk about things if he came to see her, so he wouldn't be embarrassed. If they read from Emerson or discussed

Hawthorn or Poe he would relax and then she might be able to keep his interest. Of course, she would have to give him more than just love; she wanted to give him everything. Matt was no ordinary boy; he would need much more than love, even if that was all she could think of, when she was near him or thought about him. And her poem, she had forgotten to read it to him, because it was for him and was about him. Reading it over to herself silently:

> "You merry me, churn my subtleties,
> Cut all the calmer breath I own.
> Oh, God, if I could only have more of you
> to engulf, to nourish all my parts that are not fed;
> For I am hungry,
> I make no pretense to my wantings:
> Let somehow there be three more of you,
> Instead of the others
> Whose crackling dryness burn my craving nature.
> If only your color could always bathe
> The absorbers of my eyes,
> Your form, half nude, be there to lull upon,
> I would hold all other wish in check.
> Why winter, spring and summer
> ever had to be, I'll never know,
> When there is you to love, autumn."

She was glad, now, that she hadn't read it to Matt. She had deleted, added and rewritten until brave enough to say what she felt, then disguised it and turned it into sort of a funny pun. Mitzie knew better than to let others read what she had written but writing her thoughts down and having no one to hear them was lonely, empty, sometimes like being dead; and yet safe, because people couldn't hurt you if they didn't know what you thought or who you were. With Matt, however, she had given without her poems, spoken or written, and now he knew who she was and he hadn't hurt her. She was warm with love and tensed her muscles inside to remember his being there. She dropped the bathrobe to the floor and slipped between the cool sheets and went to sleep.

The next day Karl Harwood salved his conscience in the attic as he showed Matt the remains of his ventures into speculation. The round-topped trunk had only one key and that was snugly fastened to the key ring at the end of Karl's watch chain where in its small brassy way it formed an ideal anchor and reminder of past folly.

They took the stack of yellowing stock certificates and newspaper clippings to the library and closed the door. Spreading the papers out on the round oak table, they sorted and placed all of the New Liberty Holding Company information together.

"Five cents a share! Now, Matt who could go wrong on a nickel a share, especially when they guaranteed you a ten-for-one bonus in stock if you invested in the private trust before the public company was formed?"

"I don't know what that means."

"Well, I thought that I did. Look at them: one hundred and ten of them, each for a thousand shares; worth nothing."

"Looks as if it should be worth lots."

"Greedy people hear only what they want to hear; and believe me, I was greedy: 'Class A, Preferred Voting Shares'. See it printed right there, Matt? That's what makes them so valuable, the 'Preferred'. They just had to be worth more than the 'common' stock which Milton Calder and his friends were going to sell to the public. 'Preferred,' meant you would get a two percent dividend out of all profits before any of public got anything from their 'common' shares. Just how could you lose?" Karl smiled and shook his head as he flipped through the clippings.

"Can you imagine a confirmed Democrat getting sucked in by a bunch of Republicans? They made their stock split just as they said they would. Count them there, one hundred and ten thousand shares and all it cost your silver-haired father was five hundred dollars. Even better than that, the organizers agreed to take their options for 'common' shares, leaving the 'preferred' for the people who put up the original capital before it was sold to the public.

Why? Because it would give the preferred share-holders a reason to support their company, knowing they were going to get rich before the public received any profit from their 'common' shares which cost twenty-five cents a share."

"I'm lost, Dad: I don't understand. All these shares worth a nickel each and you say they cheated you."

"Wrong. I didn't say they cheated me. They really helped me cheat myself. All of these clippings: they were saved to be a part of my scrapbook to show how I made my fortune, certainly not to prove anybody was cheating me. Karl Harwood was going to be put into business by these people; they were even going to start an equipment company that I would be president of someday. They started the company all right and many other companies, each to be headed 'someday' by people who held 'Preferred' stock. Calder and his friends were only interested in guiding the main company, New Liberty Holdings, which they did."

"And Governor Calder was president of that company?" Matt asked, beginning to feel the things his father was telling him made sense.

"No: that was another important thing. As far as I can tell, Calder has never held an office in New Liberty Holdings, not even on the board of directors, and probably didn't have one share of stock with his name on it. But, I'll bet he controlled every move the board of directors and officers made; and I'll bet he owned a controlling interest in the total company because of the options he or his friends had."

"I don't follow you."

"They didn't intend anybody to understand, Matt." A look of exasperation came over his face. "I find myself getting carried away with trying to explain to you, getting off on all sorts of side tracks. The whole trick was that the 'preferred' shares were what they call 'assessable', meaning that those shareholders had to make up any losses the company might have, if they 'were to keep their stock; while the 'common' stock was 'non-assessable', meaning they couldn't be forced to pay any losses of the company. And believe me, New Liberty Holdings had many losses for which preferred stock-holders paid assessments until finally they couldn't afford to hold on any longer and found their stock worthless."

"You, too?" Matt asked.

Matt's father looked down at the certificate he held in his hand, smiled a weak smile and said quietly "Yes, me, too. I didn't mention that, did I?"

After a couple of minutes, he seemed to regain his composure and went on, "The strange thing, Matt, is that many of the companies owned by New Liberty actually made money. And, if anyone checked the books of the companies that lost money, they would probably find that they probably paid higher prices for things by dealing with companies that Clarence Calder controlled. It was a mess, a sticky mess."

"I'd sure like to find out and tell Mr. Dodson, so they don't make a fool out of him, too," Matt said with a touch of excitement in his voice.

"Now, wait a minute. What's this 'too' business? Are you casting aspersions on your own father? As I said before, Son, nobody so far has been able to pick a hole in that wall; and those that could are either too ashamed or too afraid to speak out."

"Mr. Dodson's awfully smart, Dad; he really is."

"Now there you go contradicting yourself again," his father said in an attempt to cover up his irritation over Matt's idolization of Cyrus. "First you say he's honest and then you turn around and brag about his brains. I hate to say this, but I believe you'd make a good Republican."

They laughed and his father sat down in the chair next to the fireplace and leaned his head against the leather padded back.

"It's funny how fast it all disappeared. First New Liberty went into receivership; next thing Governor Calder called a special committee to investigate some charges of fraud. Nothing was found except too many cooks, maybe crooks, in the broth. The management admitted that their plan of allowing 'preferred' stockholders was a weak link in their chain because such stockholders felt they should have a voice in management and most of them did not have the business background to make proper investment decisions. After that most assets were sold to outside companies at a few pennies on the dollar and both the remaining preferred stock and common stock ended up useless."

"If Mr. Dodson gets to be Governor, then he could have his own investigation," Matt said, but his father wasn't listening.

"Dozens of companies and in days they all disappeared into thin air except for a foundry and a small dairy. Joke, if there ever was such a thing among the stockholders as a joke, it was 'they've milked us dry!' Ha, ha: 'milked us dry'."

"Then we should tell Mr. Dodson, right away."

"Calm down, Matt. Let me think. I know that if Cyrus Dodson ever finds out the truth about New Liberty, it will be because Calder either slips or one of his insiders turns on him. I have a friend in Springfield, Norman Gardom, he's a lawyer, good one."

"Can you write him?"

"I have a better idea: Bruce says Cyrus is coming back to Crescent next Wednesday for a rest and some local campaigning. While he's resting, we'll ask him to give you a day or so off and I'll send you on a trip to the capital of that decadent State to the east and have you talk to Norman. Maybe he can guide you in looking for information. You know, Matt, I know very well you won't find anything that will help a political campaign, or Cyrus Dodson: but you've got my interest up and I'd like to know just what did happen to my money. Any little piece of information might just make me feel a bit less sorry for myself."

"I wouldn't have to mention it to Mr. Dodson unless I found something," Matt added.

"Much more important than going off to war," his father laughed. "Just think, you might be helping the people of the State elect an 'honest man', right, Matt?"

"Want to make a bet?" Matt countered.

"On what? That Calder is a crook? Cyrus an honest man, or that the price of wheat is going up next year?"

Dodson quietly returned to Crescent with MacQuarrie a day early to avoid the commotion of a hero's reception. He was pleased with Matt's handling of the granary and at Gloria's suggestion offered him the rest of the week as a short holiday for the job well done without Matt's even asking for time.

Matt was excited about his trip to Springfield. He packed a few clothes in a worn and crushed Gladstone bag that had once belonged to his father. Carefully wrapped in one of his mother's prized bath towels were a bar of soap, the new straight razor his father had given him as a graduation present, his toothbrush and a comb.

His mother accepted with pride the explanation that he was going on business for Mr. Dodson. His father went along with the deceit. His mother had packed him three sandwiches in a paper sack and his father had secretly given him twenty-five dollars for the trip.

Karl's final words in private to him were direct and explicit: "Go to the Secretary of State's office at the Statehouse. They will have the incorporation papers and charter for New Liberty. Copy as many of those papers as you can. After that take the newspaper clippings to Norman with this letter. He's a criminal lawyer, not a corporation attorney, but he'll know if there is any thing to all this and where to start. And good luck, Son."

At the Statehouse there were marbled hallways that echoed the snap of leather heels, counters tall and ugly with worn and dusty ledgers and record books stacked and scattered on top of their scarred surfaces. Slow, de-energized clerks, professional civil servants, shuffled back and forth avoiding contact with anyone or anything, which might require action. These Matt found himself in the midst of on Thursday morning. Though Springville was larger than he had expected, it definitely was not very exciting; and he started to feel silly for being there. He could even understand his father's initial reluctance to get involved.

"Here we are, young man: June to December, 1911. You just kinda thumb your way through here and see if you don't find what you're looking for."

The little man peeked out from under his green visor for a second and then as a tortoise, pulled himself back into his shell and disappeared among the stacks.

Matt found the page with the New Liberty Holdings Company incorporation papers and copied all the original officers and incorporators' names down. Clarence Calder's name was not among them, nor was his name to be found on the lists of any of the many other companies mentioned in the newspaper articles. There were, however, many names that cropped up again and again. Matt copied page after page on a yellow pad of paper the clerk had given him. His fingers ached and his forearm throbbed, but he did not leave until the little man had taken off his visor, hung it on the coat rack, turned the lights off and started to lock the office door.

The next morning he called Norman Gardom and told him why he was in town. Gardom's voice was gruff and questioning. "Your father is a goddamn dreamer; what in hell is he sending you up here on such a flat-assed, stupid run-around as that? You can go to the newspapers and see what they have in their files, if you want to. Try the Gazette; it's best. You can call me later this afternoon. I'll be out of court around three thirty."

Matt followed the girl from the information desk through the Gazette's editorial office to the library. She seated him at a long table and brought week after week of cardboard-bound newspapers to him; then she checked the index for articles on New Liberty. Most of the articles held little news, except the ones about the liquidation of the company. He wrote down all of the names of the companies and individuals who purchased the company's assets after it had gone bankrupt. Then he had an idea: he would go back to the Statehouse and check on the records of the companies he had added to his list.

There the man with the visor welcomed him back with the same enthusiasm he had displayed the day before. It was easier this time, however, finding the charters of the companies. And when he started to copy the new names, it was almost as if he had gained his second wind. Suddenly he stopped at a name on the board of directors of Malcomb Investments, one of New Liberty's companies: "Norman A. Gardom, Attorney at Law, Director." It had to be a coincidence, so he skipped over it and worked on another company and another and another with some duplication of names but not Gardom's. On the fourth, however, it did appear again and also on the fifth. No wonder his father's friend didn't want him snooping around. Matt carefully erased the name from the list.

Matt felt sick inside. He didn't call Norman Gardom back, but went straight to the depot. He had never met Norman Gardom. He didn't like his voice or his words; but in finding his name on those papers he felt completely disillusioned, as if someone close had let him down. Maybe he wasn't meant to be a crusader. It even frightened him to know that his father's friend was a part of something sinister and crooked; if that was what it was.

Saturday when he arrived home, he showed the lists he had copied to his father.

"Mr. Gardom was in court and couldn't see me; but he told me which newspaper to go to."

"Well, it's a bit disappointing, Matt; but then on the other hand, if you had found anything important that would send Calder to jail, I might not look as wise as I pretend to be. Isn't that right?"

"Good thing I didn't bet you."

"Good thing, Matt. I wouldn't want you to turn into a gambler anyway. One in the family is enough."

Chapter 10

MacQuarrie leaned back in the chair and laughed at Gloria's graphic interpretations of Crescent's more important personalities. "I have seen them before," he said; "a hundred times in every town under ten thousand between Atlantic City to Chicago!' He started to unwrap one of the cigars he had confiscated from Governor Calder's ample supply before leaving for this weeklong vigil in Crescent; then he looked at Gloria and could see an expression of disapproval. He put it back in vest pocket.

"And, Glory Be, let me tell you something that might surprise you: these people, though 'un-citified', are probably about the most honest and lovable individuals you will ever have the honor of meeting."

"Nobody here thinks they are so lovable." Gloria said. "Some of them are very serious problems."

"Do you think so?"

"I'm certain Father does. He can't stand crude people, men or women."

"They sound colorful," he said.

"When you meet them, you'll have to admit they are crude. Cyrus says people cannot progress unless they lift themselves above the vulgar level. Some of them really upset him with their lack of manners. Why, the mention of our blacksmith's name sends him into a rage."

MacQuarrie watched Gloria in thoughtful amusement. Three times in five minutes she had mentioned Ward Kessel without saying his name. "Obviously," he thought, "there must be more to her ridicule of this man than she was aware of." He would like to meet Mr. Kessel and see just what it was about him that disturbed the womanhood in Gloria so much.

"Say something," she finally said; "don't just look at me."

"I was thinking."

"You were laughing at me."

"Oh, no."

"Then you weren't listening. Were you?"

"Very much. Just concerned with your father," he said trying to skirt around the subject.

"Why?"

"Simply because he's human and he doesn't know it. Your father is about to change before your very eyes, Glory. The next six months will leave him a marked man."

"You think he's going to lose, don't you?"

"I think he's going to win; but win or lose he is marked."

Gloria shook her head in a mixture of disbelief and disgust. "How can you say that? If the people elect him it will be an honor. And to be an honored man certainly doesn't make him a 'marked man', does it?" she asked.

"In all honesty, I have to say he has been very fortunate. So far in life, he's been able to live on ideals and work. From now on he's is going to be faced with emotion and reality; and let's say 'with the true stench of humanity'. Damn good speech," he said with a chuckle, "I wish I could remember where I read it."

She smiled but her eyes were defiant. "You don't think much of God's children, really, do you?" she asked.

"On the contrary," he said with a new seriousness. Perhaps I doubt that Man is the misguided offspring of some omnipotent deity; but I think a lot of Man. Getting close to people is an exciting experience. Even the most rotten have some noble features."

"When it's all added up, you don't think Father understands people like Ward Kessel. Isn't that about all you are trying to say?"

MacQuarrie's eyes sparkled. He was tempted to drive the question of Ward out into the open and watch her in action, fighting the ghost of something she must consider so far beneath her dignity. To restrain the urge, he gazed out of the window at the mounting evidence of a storm.

"Isn't, that what you think about all of us here in Crescent?" Gloria went on.

"Glory, suddenly you worry about what people think about you. Why? There was no evidence of a shrinking violet in you that would give all this inner thought to the opinions of others until just today, Gloria."

She sighed and looked away from him.

"I'm sorry, it's just that I have always felt that what people think of a someone else's thoughts, actions or words is one part in the scheme of things that means absolutely nothing. Don't ever base your life on the desire to be liked or looked up to."

He could not help but noticed the completely bored look on her face.

"The trouble with me, Glory, is I never know when I'm writing a speech or talking to a friend. And. the result is sometimes: no friends."

Gloria finally smiled and stood up. "I'm not a very good hostess sometimes either, and my results: no guests."

They laughed.

"May I fix you a cup of tea?"

"No; but a glass of that wine you served last night at dinner would more than earn you a friend at this moment." He noted her poise as she walked into the dining room to get the decanter and glass for him. There was a rhythm to her body that sensually caressed his imagination.

"The moment you shattered my classic soliloquy into a billion bits, I was about to tell you that your Mr. Kessel, the blacksmith, has no bearing at all on the tragedy of your father's life. I sincerely admire your father; but his understanding is that of universal laws and principals, not the knowledge of man-to-man exceptions to those laws."

Gloria's indifference was not to blame for the next interruption of MacQuarrie's monologue. This time the creeping awareness of

Agatha's presence filled the room. She stood there, her hat askew, her hair mussed by the dust-laden wind that whipped skirt, shrub and dignity into frustration. Her lower lip quivering visibly to MacQuarrie, Agatha glared at Gloria.

"What about Mr. Kessel? Just what do you know about him? You shouldn't be so free to talk about someone you've only met once. No, you shouldn't, Gloria."

Without defense from the sudden fury, Gloria remained seated, stunned by her sister's unusual outburst.

Tears streamed down Agatha's face as she now turned on MacQuarrie.

"You mustn't believe anything Gloria, or any one else, says about Mr. Kessel. Ward Kessel is the most wonderful man. You just mustn't listen to her, you mustn't."

Gloria put her arm around her sister and the two of them slowly went up the stairs.

"Tears," MacQuarrie thought. What weapon of war could man devise that would win as many battles? He examined the skewered, half-knitted gray sock that Agatha had dropped, needles and all, with her hat, on the library table. "Under the spreading chestnut tree, the village smithy stands," he said aloud, chuckling as he wondered at the immense size of the sock. "And some men die bachelors," he went amusing himself with his mental capers. Longfellow would have been happy with this one: a model blacksmith that any poet would be proud to call his own. A protector of the village maids."

MacQuarrie was suddenly ashamed of his enjoyment of someone else's misfortune. "Either you are becoming a jaded malcontent, or you're a panic-stricken ape afraid of the unknown powers of emotion," he chided himself. One thing was very clear to him, however: Ward Kessel, contrary to prior opinion, probably carried more weight around the Cyrus Dodson household than the town of Crescent would ever suspect. The decanter was more than half full; MacQuarrie would find solace in it. He might even go for a walk and, while outside, smoke another of Milton Calder's missing cigars.

Gloria pulled the window blind up, letting the gray light of the stormy day wake Agatha's bedroom to the somber mood. On the bed next to her many hand-me-down dolls, which had no successor's line to follow, Agatha lay, face down, crying into the designs on her embroidered pillow sham.

The tears themselves were nothing new; it was the cause of them and the overt violence that jarred Gloria. Communication between them would be difficult for hours after the last sob had racked Agatha's body and she had escaped reality through sleep.

What could have brought such sharp words from so quiet a person, Gloria pondered? She must question Cynthia and find out who Agatha had been seeing. She couldn't have been visiting Ward Kessel, she just couldn't have! But of course he was a friend of the Harwood boy, and Agatha had met Kessel when she was at the rally and dedication of the fire engine.

Rain now mixed with dust embroidered weird lace patterns on the windows. The storm must have its way. Violence and the wind blended strange colors of thought. Gloria could remember vividly the desire she had felt as she watched Ward and Matt. There had been a compulsion to touch Ward and to be held close to him was a feeling that through her sense of self-respect she had quickly overcome, but continued to wonder about and relive with calmer passions long after. She and Agatha were different, though; Agatha would never sense the force in men or desire them in the same way.

A couple of automobiles, their curtains lowered against the weather, were racing down the street, splashing huge sprays of muddy water over the sidewalks. Gloria watched as one of them hit another puddle sending a deluge over a lone pedestrian. The man shook himself off; then braced himself into the wind.

"Gloria, Gloria, I'm sorry about downstairs," Agatha said as her sobs faded. She sat on the edge of the bed, kicking her shoes off.

"There's nothing to be sorry about, honey. Are you all right now?"

"I guess so; but I couldn't help myself, Gloria, I just couldn't. Every time I think about him I want to cry. And when I thought you were saying something mean about him, I just couldn't help saying what I said."

Gloria's arm was around her sister and they sat in silence for a moment. Gloria tried to appraise Agatha's words, not wanting to believe what she was hearing.

"Gloria, you just don't know how sweet and wonderful Ward Kessel is until you have been with him day after day."

The hush continued; Gloria trying to appraise Agatha's words, not wanting to believe what she was hearing. Gloria held herself back. She wanted to swing Agatha around and shake her to make her tell in clear, uncluttered words what she was trying to say, fearing all the time what she might be about to tell.

"He's been so sick; but it's not hard to tell what he will be like when he's well and can get around again. He's so understanding, Gloria, so quiet. And he teases me and makes me laugh."

There was no containing the questioning further; Gloria took Agatha's hand in hers. "Has he touched you? Tell me, has he?"

"Oh, Gloria. Of course not! Not even to hold my hands."

"Then what have you been doing alone with him? Agatha, you haven't been making a fool of yourself have you, honey?"

"I've been helping Mitzie Kawalski take care of him, that's all; because he's sick. His ribs are broken. That's all but it's been so much fun. And, Gloria, I feel so important when I'm there."

Gloria looked at the still moist eyes, at the pleading expression she had seen so many times. The thought chewed at Gloria's mind that perhaps Ward Kessel might be an answer to Agatha's need. The prospect of such a thing, however, sickened her.

"I even wonder if he might love me," Agatha said winsomely.

"Aggie, that's silly! What could he have possibly said that would give you that ridiculous idea?" Gloria's dismay at her sister's innocence showed in her face and she felt her body become tense all over, again, at what Agatha was saying.

"There don't have to be words. Besides, I didn't really mean that he loves me. That would be expecting too much; what I meant to say was that I would like to have him love me, because he makes me feel like I belong to him."

"I hope you'll be careful not to get hurt when you find that he doesn't love you, and you will," Gloria said softly, almost to herself, disturbed that Agatha should be so misled. She looked over at the dolls on the bed. An eerie sense of foreboding seemed to be closing in on her.

Agatha, not hearing, her continued on, "Isn't it strange, Gloria? Some find love everywhere they turn, others only once or twice, some never in their lives."

In spite of her fear, caution and apprehension at the possible affair, Gloria, in some inexplicable way, was excited by the realization that Agatha was experiencing something she had never really known herself.

"Love," Agatha said, her pupils dilated with anticipation. "Oh Gloria, could I be? Do you really think so; just like that?

"I don't think so; but then what would I know," Gloria answered, not knowing what else to say. When she saw the disappointed look in her sister's eyes, she continued, "Men, I understand are cowards, they are funny that way, they are easily frightened and run."

Encouraged by Gloria's vague comment, Agatha sprang from the bed and paced the length of the room. At the window she looked out at the storm. "I knew you would understand, I just knew."

"Agatha, there will be a lot of people who would not understand. Mother, I'm certain will just die at the notion of you talking about loving an older man."

"Oh, he's not old, Gloria. What ever made you think that? He's the kind of man a girl couldn't help liking; and as you say maybe even loving."

"Anyway, honey; let's keep your secret so the whole family and town doesn't jump on you and turn your dream into a nightmare. People do that sometimes when they think they are protecting you from your own mistakes. It ends up that everyone is hurt, especially the one they've been trying to help."

"The only one I want to know is Mr. Kessel. I don't care if anyone other than you ever knows the way I feel about him. He is a very nice person; the nicest person I've ever known."

"Probably the only man you've ever been alone with. That could be why," Gloria said as she smiled in half disbelief at what they were saying.

"We haven't been alone. You're making fun of me, Gloria; I don't blame you, but you are. I'm serious, even if you and I know I'm silly, and maybe not very bright, and not grown up. I can't help how I feel."

"I'm not really, honey, just nervous, I guess. You know, it is rather hard to get used to the little girl whose diapers you changed telling you she is in love with a man, when you, yourself haven't found one; and the house is teaming with older sisters, each dreaming of the altar and aching inside," Gloria went on as she hugged Agatha with all her might. It was the first time in her life that she had so openly talked of her frustration at being unmarried.

They stood in the middle of the room for a long time. Inside was the resentment which she had jokingly put into words, but Gloria could not distinguish it from the fear of Cyrus's possible reaction and her mother's certain disapproval of Agatha's involvement. Sisters lined up as bridesmaids, passed up by a sobbing little girl: as Gloria constructed a fantasy wedding, in her mind, the bitterness faded and the two of them started down the stairs.

MacQuarrie let the hot coffee roll around in his mouth as he sat looking at the latest edition of the Walker County Journal. It was a poor substitute for a newspaper, he thought, as he skipped over the front-page local news, and searched lackadaisically for some sign of national coverage in the pages of the second section.

"More coffee, Mac?" Cyrus asked as he filled his own cup once more and went back to cataloging his latest foreign postage stamps, a diversion from the campaign.

"Thank you, Governor, I believe I'll just have to call it quits after these six cups; but I'll be the first to say this really is gracious living: coffee served in the library after breakfast."

"It isn't actually the library; just Gloria's idea that the parlor would make a good place for me to get out of everyone else's way by calling it my study: books, guns and all," Cyrus chuckled, pointing towards the glass case along one wall which held his prize collection of antique hand guns and rifles.

MacQuarrie tried to show excitement as he looked toward the glass cabinet. In reality, he was not much interested in guns of any kind; not since he was a child and Rich Webber, his favorite cousin on his mother's side, had died on Christmas morning with a bullet in his skull from the new 22 caliber rifle "Santa Clause" had brought to the Webber household the night before.

"Some of them handed down over three generations," Cyrus continued, "rotten family, but we had the right tradition when it came to guns, second amendment, all the way. Give your rights up and you're dead from the start."

After the brief explanation, Cyrus went back to concentrating on his stamps. MacQuarrie was amused by the solitude with which Cyrus surrounded himself. For a moment he reflected on the fact that in his whole life he had never as much as touched a gun, let alone fired one; was there something he was missing? Did it give one a sense of power or achievement, he wondered, as he stepped closer to the case: to look at the collection. "Ever use them?" he asked.

Cyrus looked up at his guest "No, not actually; but all of them are operable. I sometimes target practiced, though; with my father, when I was young, it was a requirement. You know, everyone should know how to defend themselves. I have insisted that my step daughter learn to become good shots: use the barn out back for target practice once a week. I even keep a couple at the granary for that reason."

The stamps again regained Cyrus's attention.

Mac carefully opened the unlocked case and took a closer look at the guns; carefully closing it when he was through. It was obvious that Cyrus was back in his concentration mode. After a few minutes, MacQuarrie excused himself and went for a walk.

There was no better time than a Sunday when a town was closed for worship, to line up a couple of good campaign men for the candidate. They needed men who could reach the feminine side of the ledger who, in turn, could influence their voting husbands. MacQuarrie wondered how many votes were really cast, even in secret ballot, that didn't have the mark of a woman's influence. Why all of these cries for suffrage? The morning was wet with the violent scrubbing it had received the night before. MacQuarrie inhaled deeply the clear, moist air as he walked at a more relaxed pace than usual, observing each of Crescent's landmarks and symbols of normalcy. It was hard at this very moment to imagine a war raging on the battlefields of France.

He tipped his hat to Mrs. Cross when he noticed this prototype of American spinsterhood studying him with undue skepticism. She was on her way to visit Reverend Pritchard before services started. MacQuarrie stepped graciously aside as he opened the gate, allowing her to proceed ahead of him before he stepped back on the sidewalk to continue his easygoing stroll.

He grinned as he watched Margaret Cross's haughty, yet self-conscious walk. She must be wearing a bustle, out-dated or not, he reasoned. He wondered for a second if she had ever experienced, other than vicariously, the torrential outpourings of a man's passion. Quickly he slammed the door closed on the fleeting thought, realizing that even if he were in the mood for such easy prey, he would have to decline, having long grown tired of sobbing purity and ignorant chastity. "However," his wit echoed faintly within the walls of his resting mind, "what more active in the world than forty or fifty years of stored-up energy, just waiting for a release? And what if she's the deceptive mother of six? No, she must be the victim of self-denial."

He quickened his pace as he passed the fire station. This was one spot of Crescent he would avoid until called upon to make an appearance. He had met Bruce McHenry when they first decided Cyrus P. Dodson was the man to push. For three days he heard stories of Bruce's great feats as fire chief of Crescent and how he personally was going to see to it that Cyrus was the next occupant of the Governor's Mansion. No, as little as there was to do in Crescent, MacQuarrie could not stand another session with the perpetual dinning of "I, I, I, I, I, I," pounding in his ears. Lord, did he hate small town politicians!

The feed store was just as MacQuarrie would have it, as ideal a cradle for a political career as a man could find these days, with log cabins getting scarcer by the year. Written words would have a "heyday" with this humble beginning; it was only too bad that Cyrus couldn't boast a complete lack of formal education, MacQuarrie mused, gathering the threads of his plot tighter by the moment.

In front of the blacksmith shop he stopped. This was it: a destination for business, curiosity and pleasure, for certainly this Mr. Kessel would answer all three, or MacQuarrie would lose his bet on human nature. He knocked on the wide front doors; which he found locked. There was no answer. He knocked again. Then after a long wait, the latch was lifted and one of the doors creaked open a bit. Through the slit of the door he could see the brightness of a yellow dress and he looked into Agatha's surprised yet beautiful eyes. MacQuarrie found himself without words. She was dressed for church, complete with bonnet.

"Is Mr. Kessel at home?" he heard himself ask hesitantly.

"Yes, Mr. MacQuarrie, he is. He's in bed, but I'm certain he'll enjoy the company. I just dropped by before church to see that he was all right."

MacQuarrie's active mind started to question, but he held back. The tears of the day before were still vivid in his memory. He did not want to unleash the flood, but he was both shocked and puzzled by her appearance at the door.

"People usually use the rear door, then they don't have to go through the shop," she said escorting him past the furnace and the bellows;" but unless you had been here before you wouldn't know that."

He was not certain whether he was being reprimanded, or just informed, in Agatha's child-like way, that she felt he was intruding in her domain.

"Next time, I'll know better," he laughed, trying to relieve his own embarrassment. A young woman alone in an apartment with a blacksmith, even in the sanctity of Sunday sunlight, was not the accepted behavior for America's rural society. The thought of such an affair reinforced his devoted belief that amorality would in the end break the world's shackles of needless inhibition. More power to them, he chided himself. But, at the same time, this was a political campaign, even if no one else in Crescent knew it. He must not let the impetuous awakenings of puberty derail the insane, though organized, lust for power. "You'd make a lousy chaperone," he said to himself as Agatha opened the door to Ward's apartment.

Ward was propped up in a sitting position on his bed. Beside him was his breakfast plate, now empty. MacQuarrie stood, his mouth perhaps open just a bit too wide, displaying his astonished dismay. It was not the hairy-chested blacksmith who had taken him back, but the realization that he had been misjudging people again.

"I'd like you to meet Miss Kowalski, Mr. Kessel, and Mr. Harwood," Agatha said in her calmest voice." This is Mr. MacQuarrie, who is a friend of Daddy Cyrus. And now, I must go before I'm late for church; I'm to sing a solo today."

Agatha was not the same girl MacQuarrie had seen the night before; the new composure, though maybe forced, was an improvement, he thought.

"How do you do," Mitzie said, "I hope you will forgive Agatha and me if we leave."

He studied the complementing contrast of the two young women; then catching himself, said "Certainly," and smiled as he shook hands with Matt and Ward. From Agatha's expression he could tell she meant to say, "Now, you'll see that what I told you about Mr. Kessel is true."

"I work for Mr. Dodson," Matt said as the two girls started for the door.

MacQuarrie was still disturbed by the room full of unexpected new faces.

"See you this afternoon, Matt?" Mitzie said before MacQuarrie could respond to Matt's reference to Cyrus.

"I guess so," Matt said reluctantly.

Mitzie's expression was one of urgency.

"Sit down, Mr.," Ward hesitated.

"MacQuarrie. Thanks."

When the door closed there was an almost audible sigh of relief from the three men.

"I don't know just why," Ward finally said, "but the two of them were making me as nervous as a filly about to foal."

"Did I hear you say you work for Mr. Dodson, Mr. Harwood?"

"Don't know what Mr., Dodson would say about it," Matt said, "but I like to say I work for him; at the Granary next door."

"Most of the time lately Matt's just been running up and down these stairs to my rent paying lady acquaintance, Mitzie."

"Just what every red-blooded American male should be doing," MacQuarrie jibed, being careful to keep his comment vague enough to be above the usual level of thought.

"Mr. MacQuarrie, Ward Kessel has one hell of a big imagination. Besides, Ward, she spends all her time with you and now she's got religion."

"That last statement could be true; it could be true," Ward said. "You see, Mac...may I call you Mac?"

MacQuarrie nodded consent.

"With a name like that it would be a shame to call you anything else in this world. Well, this morning is probably one of the few times Mitzie has ever gone to church."

"All of God's "chillum" must fall sometime," MacQuarrie mimicked, and the three of them laughed.

"Mitzie's a nice girl," Ward said, "I guess if I knew what the world was all about, I'd marry her; except I don't think she'd accept my offer; and I wouldn't want to make her miserable if she did."

"Miss Agatha's sure got an influence on people in her quiet way," Matt said.

MacQuarrie thought to himself the words were well selected: "in her quiet way", but he never would have stated that she had an influence on people.

"I suppose you would like to know why I'm here, Mr. Kessel," MacQuarrie said.

"I'd be surprised at anybody who had anything to do with Cyrus P. Dodson at this particular time, who didn't have this politicking business on his mind. Why, even Matt, my long-time friend, can talk of nothing else but going off on trips to Springville to try and dig up dirt on some holding company stock scam; just to make sure his honored employer stays honest in office. No, if you came to talk anything but politics; I'd get up and dance a jig."

MacQuarrie laughed at Ward's colorful dissertation, but it was the talk of the stock scam and holding company that interested him. He must be running from shadows to assume that it was a reference to New Liberty. Besides, the whole thing was so well worked out, that even the people involved didn't know what they were being used for. No. The odds were too great for a boy from Crescent catching onto the intricate devices that were used to make the group as powerful as it had been.

"Well, Sir, isn't that what you came to talk about?"

"Mr. Kessel, you are so right."

"You are about as formal as Cyrus's daughter with that 'Mr. Kessel' line; it's a lot easier for me to know who you are talking to if you just say 'Ward'."

"How was your trip to Springville?" MacQuarrie asked, turning to Matt.

The expression on Matt's face was one of dismay; he hadn't wanted Ward to mention the trip to anyone.

"Just fine, just fine. Met a couple of real interesting people."

"I used to edit a newspaper not too far from Springville," MacQuarrie said, catching the quandary of the young boy; he parried to put him at ease and at the same time continue the probing.

"It's a beautiful city. I was surprised at how big it was. How clean, too. I always thought big cities were supposed to be dirty."

MacQuarrie smiled at his bait being taken so easily. "Not quite as clean as it might seem. In fact, I'd say the capital of that State had about as much corruption as this one has had, from time to time; and their Statehouse is damn near as full of thieves as any in the Union." He was tempted to say, "What we need is an honest politician like, say, Mr. Dodson," but the words stopped short in his throat. No, he couldn't stand to hear himself echo the script he had written for Calder: "Looking for an honest man."

MacQuarrie's visit to Ward's shop was a success, he told himself as he said goodbye. He had added three more cups of coffee to his already upset stomach, but he had won concessions. Ward had agreed to campaign for Cyrus's election, even though he said Dodson was a "pompous ass": who thought he was too good for anyone else in town. Matt had in detail spelled out his failure at sleuthing the activities of the holding corporation. The boy's naive comments had convinced MacQuarrie that he had found no clue of how the clique really worked. It was a relief to know Matt would not, have to be "bought off", not even in a roundabout way, like a bright young newspaper editor up near Springville once had been when his editorials came a bit too close to the mark for Calder's comfort.

Reverend Pritchard's services had just ended as MacQuarrie passed the fire station. Margaret Cross was walking just ahead of him. Again he studied her walk from the rear. "Well, Mac, you're out on the town; why not?" he said to himself. He quickened his pace until he was walking by her side, "How do you do," he used his politest tone as he tipped his hat to match the attitude of his intended victim, "I'm Rex MacQuarrie, from the state capital, managing Mr. Cyrus Dodson's campaign for Governor; I wonder if I could talk to you, I know so little about your wonderful town and its people and...."

But MacQuarrie's speech had no need to continue. Margaret Cross responded faster than he had expected. "I'm Margaret Cross, a very dear friend of both Cyrus and Myrtle and his lovely daughters."

At the gate to Margaret Cross's house, his hand touched hers as he opened the gate for her, He watched her reaction and felt a surge of guilt mixed with nausea whirl inside him, but it soon passed.

"The parlor is nice and cool, Mr. MacQuarrie, and I could serve you a glass of cold milk and some cookies I baked last night."

"A game nearly forgotten...and usually played on a much better field," MacQuarrie thought as he sat on the mocha colored plush of the settee, "but milk was better than more coffee."

Margaret Cross broke a glass in the kitchen in her excitement as she prepared to serve her visitor. She reminded herself, as she swept the scattered pieces up into the dustpan, that Gilbert would be working at the Nesland farm for the rest of the week. She straightened her apron and arranged a couple of hairpins that had worked their way loose in the bun at the back of her head.

While talking of the campaign issues, even using the Calder line of "honesty", MacQuarrie mentally undid the bun on the back of Margaret' s neck and let her hair flow long around her waist. It made her more desirable; it softened her slightly squared chin; it even made the milk taste fair; not quite as good as Dodson's wine or Calder's bourbon, but certainly palatable.

Next his conversation turned to the piano, which was rosewood and obviously polished daily. Margaret played "Liebestraum" through twice to demonstrate her cultural side, and Mac was pleased at only being jarred once with a note that could find neither reason nor place in the score. "Such a lovely home. Impeccable taste," he remarked, silently congratulating himself on the selection of the word 'impeccable'.

"Would you like to see the rest of the house?" led to a tour, including the front upstairs bedroom with the gossamer lace curtains at the front windows. The candlewick spread on the bed which had invited and drawn tears from Margaret more and more times lately, was next. The tour stopped there in its natural course, without tears, protests or indignation. Perhaps the playing field was better than expected, MacQuarrie thought as he noticed for the first time how neatly their clothes were folded on the needle-worked chair next to the bed.

How wrong could a man's judgment be? Maybe even without Calder's booze, Crescent would not be such a bad place to plan and write a political campaign. He relaxed back against the soft, clean pillow. What forgotten calmness there must have been: even the bedspread was folded back. The hairpins he himself had taken from the bun were carefully placed in the Dresden candy dish on the marble-topped bed table. Silence comforted strangers who were not strangers, but with nothing more than names to converse on, they stayed on in silence while Sunday afternoon started its pious course.

Chapter 11

Mitzie and Matt had taken the lunch basket out to the buggy. Ward smiled at Agatha, "Now you just get yourself out there and have fun with those two on their picnic."

"Mr. Kessel," she scolded, "I sometimes think you are unaware of love when you see it."

"I probably am just about as blind as you say; but how can you be sure it's love you see?"

"Can't you tell when you see them together, and the way they look at each other even when they try not to?"

"That could be just plain darn foolishness, you know, or as my pa once tried to tell me: 'A flower has a little thing inside of it covered with soft, velvety fuzz and when a bee or a wind comes by that soft fuzzy stuff gets itself carried off into the air and next thing you know it gets all mixed up and lights on another flower and from then on there is a union and that is how flowers is born. Now, Son, does that make good sense to you, or does it sound like plain darn foolishness?' That's what he tried to tell me." They both laughed.

"I couldn't tell if they were in love, Agatha."

"When people are in love, Mr. Kessel, nothing else seems to matter, and everything is beautiful and sad."

There was a long, slightly awkward pause as both Agatha and Ward realized that this was the first time they had been together without someone else in the room. There had been many times when both of them had wondered if this was ever going to happen and now they were really alone.

"And so they go on picnics?" Ward broke the obvious lull in the conversation.

"And so, they leave the world to itself and..."

"I wish you'd go out and break up their picnic," Ward jested, "It would be too bad if our two friends took to all that foolishness Pa talked of. You best be off in that buggy."

"When nothing else seems to matter, I'd best stay right here," she said, softly placing her cool hand on his forehead.

For the first time their eyes paused long enough to ask questions of one another. The sound of the buggy's neglected wheels squeaked a protest as they broke inertia's binding grip. Agatha and Ward were unaware of its departure as it carried Matt and Mitzie on toward the willow-rimmed spot near the river,

"Besides," Agatha said, "it's too cold for a picnic; I'd rather stay right here."

The bright yellow dress pressed closer to Ward, then Agatha slid to the floor and leaned her head on the bed next to him. Their breathing quickened. He timidly let his mental fingers trace her features: her eyelids, her chin then her cheeks. Her lips, at first dry, were now moist, waiting impatiently for their turn. Then, for a second he put his hand on her chin and lifted her face upward.

"Miss Agatha Dodson, I feel I must tell you something important."

As if he had suddenly lost courage, he dropped his hand and remained silent. She looked down at the floor. Agatha could feel her heart starting to pound slightly; but she did not look up into his face again.

"You are going to either leave or become a blacksmith's wife."

She kissed the hand that had so cautiously touched her, said nothing.

"Did you hear me?"

Again she kissed his hand and touched his arm gently.

He sat up straight in bed, "Do you know what that means, Miss Dodson?"

"I'm not sure," she said her voice nearly muffled.

Ward touched her head again, to reassure himself before he spoke again, "It means I have feelings, important feelings," he said in a stifled voice that ended in a gasp of achievement.

"I'm so glad you know...so glad," her voice trailed away to a breathy whisper.

"It means I want you to be my wife."

"Nothing else matters, Mr. Kessel,"

He slid back down in bed and looked up at the ceiling.

"That's what it means, and I won't let myself even kiss you till we get married," he said with a sigh.

They waited quietly for energy to find its way back into their bodies.

"We'll have Matt send for Reverend Pritchard when he comes back from his picnic."

It was almost as if they had said the same words before; but they hadn't.

"Mitzie can be the bridesmaid," she said.

"And you'll be Mrs. Kessel."

"Sounds wonderful: 'Mrs. Kessel'. Isn't it funny, Mr. Kessel, how words can mean so many things; especially a name: Mrs. Kessel."

Then Ward became uneasy as he thought of Cyrus for the first time.

"Maybe we'd better get married in Flintsville and keep it a secret until after your father is elected."

"I don't mind, Mr. Kessel, if you'll kiss me the minute I say 'I do'."

She kissed his hand once more. "Tomorrow, Mr. Kessel."

Her sudden confidence amazed him.

"If the sun's is shining and you still love me in the morning," he said.

However, she leaned over him once more, folding softly beside him and into his arms where she had ached to belong.

There were thoughts of kisses and she whispered over and over again a word new to her lips: "Ward, Ward, Ward, Ward."

In spite of the maturing experience forced upon them, they parted slowly, reluctantly, in a haze of regret; saving the peak, the complete belonging, for another day.

Matt lay on his back, his head in Mitzie's lap. They had made love as soon as they had arrived, as if in desperation. Now, sheltered from the wind and warmed by the sun they needed only the caress of thought to keep the excitement tingling pleasantly through them.

Mitzie giggled, breaking the mood, as she held a sandwich over his mouth, then playfully pulled it out of reach when he stretched for it.

"Mitzie, I've been thinking." He turned over facing her, "I've been thinking about this friend of Mr. Dodson's, this Mr. MacQuarrie. I've been..."

Suddenly she pushed the sandwich into his half-open mouth. Her laughter this time was louder and she threw her head back in a gesture of uncontrolled mirth at the sight of him stuffed with homemade bread from Mr. Schmidt's bakery.

"Damn," he said chewing away, "if you're not just like Margo and all the rest at our house, just another damn girl."

She ruffled his hair playfully, and he pushed her over in the still, dewy grass, wrestling with her. Their bodies touching, she whispered into his ear.

"Please, please."

"Just another damn girl who doesn't know what life's all about."

Mitzie took his hand and placed it in her unbuttoned blouse, "Please."

"No, Mitz, I'm serious, really. That MacQuarrie bothers me. He looks right through you, as if he knows what you're thinking. As if he's too smart for Crescent; even for Mr. Dodson."

"Why Matt, you only met him today, and you said Ward did all the talking."

"Do you suppose he's one of the governor Calder's men?"

"Aren't they all? After all, they're the ones who wanted Mr. Dodson to be the next governor."

Matt caught himself before he said more. Mitzie's hand was touching his bare chest. He kissed her to stop the conversation he had started and pulled her close to him. "Now?" he said.

"Now!" she whispered, but the horse's neigh brought them both to a sitting position, then to their feet, as another horse nickered back not too far away, followed by voices through the trees. Mitzie immediately pulled her hair back into place and Matt put his shirt on. They were picking up the picnic basket and blanket when Matt pointed to Mitzie's open blouse. She blushed and buttoned it.

"Guess we might as well be married," she said out off breath. "I feel so much a part of you, I never notice whether I'm dressed or not."

Suddenly there was a variety of laughter as a buggy with several couples rounded the clump of tall willow trees.

"Well if it isn't a private picnic ground," one said.

"Hello, Matt. Kinda crowded around here, huh," a tall boy with a pimply face said, almost apologetically.

"Yeah," Matt grumbled, "how are you, Fred?"

"Fine, just fine; we didn't think anybody would be all the way down this road."

The girls in the buggy giggled as if someone were playing with their corset strings. Mitzie busied herself picking up the remains of their afternoon together.

"Just thought we'd take the girls for a ride down by the river."

"We like to pet by the river too," one of the girls chirped in.

"Aw, for Christ's sake shut up, Wilma; sometimes you're as bad as a broken gramophone," her companion said.

"Well, I do, Henry, 'specially with you."

"I don't," said another girl. "I want to see where the murder was."

"See ya, Matt," Fred said, giving his horse a nudge with the reins. See ya."

"Nah, you won't see the murder spot along here, it was way down the river they found him, maybe five or ten miles."

"I wanna pet," Wilma said again; "at least, first, I wanna pet: then we can talk about all the murders you want. You can even commit a murder if you want."

"I might just do that," he said.

The buggy and the intruders were gone. The sun, though still above, seemed to have lost some of its warmth. Mitzie and Matt avoided looking at one another. Then she leaned over and kissed his cheek. He did not respond.

"I guess we'd better go," he said.

"I guess we had," she answered as he helped her up into the seat.

They just sat there looking straight ahead, not moving. The horse continued to grub away at a worn clump of river grass.

"We might as well stop trying to forget it, Mitz. Every time I go to sleep, I see Morgan's face, just like he was on his knees after I kicked him."

"You've got to stop thinking about things that are past."

"You know, it's funny; I don't see him as dead, just as he was when I kicked him and he started to heave. I can't run away from seeing him like that any more than I could run away from fighting him that night."

Mitzie took his arm firmly, "Matt, let's go home now, please." As she looked up into his suddenly tired face she wanted to caress him, to make him forget Morgan. But to caress him again so soon would not do. If only she could, it might help, but there swelled up in her a complete sense of helplessness. When she couldn't reach him on just everyday matters, how could she expect him to understand her need for him: a need that went so much further than just daytime. But, she told herself, she was so happy that she and Matt had strangely joined in a melancholy union; that he had become even a small part of her life. Even if she could never have him completely, there were moments when there seemed nothing but the pounding of his heart and the warmth of his breath. Dreams of Pennsylvania, her brothers and Kurt were now replaced with these sketches of things that mystically made up Matt. She touched his hand and thought how it would be to have his children.

"Geddup, geddup", she heard Matt say softly and the horse reluctantly obeyed. The only trouble with Matt was that so many times he would leave her alone with her thoughts, closing the door between them. It had happened even when they were in bed together, or when she talked to him about herself. Suddenly he would be gone, his eyes focused somewhere beyond the walls of the room. It was then she felt complete loneliness. It gave her a faint chill as if there were a draft and even her voice seemed to echo in the room as if she were in a vacuum. She could sense this would be one of those times, so her lips pressed themselves tightly together to avoid the pain.

The wagon tipped suddenly as one of the front wheels went over a large rock. Mitzie held tight to the seat to steady herself then looked over at Matt, his jaw locked with determination. She was stupid to feel this way about someone who didn't love her. Her father had always talked and looked as if there were no other woman in the world but her mother: even in death. She could remember his words and feel the grime of the coal dust as he held her hand and said "tell her I loved her, tell her." It was so unfair to love someone who couldn't love you; perhaps even more unfair to the one who wasn't in love. Somewhere Mitzie had heard it said that it was easier to give than to receive, easier to love, than to be loved. She wondered if this were not the truth.

As Matt turned the horse and buggy onto the main road, Mitzie straightened her skirt and sat taller in the wagon in an unconscious reach for unseen dignity.

Maybe that was why people wanted children, as a means of breaching the gap between acting the part of loving and honestly feeling the need to love something or someone. Children could make this demand on a person and still leave them free to live their own thoughts and dreams. Suddenly Mitzie took a deep breath and thought to herself that she must be crazy to think such ridiculous things. After all, you did live the life that was intended for you. If you fought it, it only made it worse and harder to live. Maybe she would just sit back and wait for Matt to learn that even one-sided love was better than nothing, maybe she wouldn't.

"Hell, Mitz, I wish I weren't so damn moody. I didn't used to be, not until that night."

Think it so and it might come true, she told herself at his seeming understanding of her silence.

"I wish I knew what Ellie was doing," he said "You don't suppose a girl...a girl like that would actually spend a whole lifetime locked up like that do you, Mitz?"

"They've been doing it, I guess ever since the nuns were taken into the Catholic Church," Mitzie said, thinking that if the girl didn't love Matt, then she shouldn't have him. Convent walls were right for people who were so foolish.

"I wonder what would make a person do that."

"A belief, Matt; they believe it or they wouldn't do it,"

"I can't understand it; not as much as I try, will I ever be able to figure it out."

At that moment, it was Mitzie who left Matt; what use was there in making talk about something you couldn't explain, about something that meant nothing but hate in your heart when you thought of the waste. Even with the joggling of the buggy, Mitzie was aware of a tightening in her stomach and this, in turn, made her notice the tenderness of her breasts and a slight ache deep at the base of her back. Tomorrow it would mean the usual, and the cramps that would turn her almost green with pain for several hours. She should welcome the sign that all was well; but now she caught herself wishing it were not.

"I wonder how those damn people get so tied up over religion."

Mitzie didn't hear him; she was thinking of how she would have to tear up one of her old petticoats; to make a pad as soon as they got home.

Mitzie took a deep breath. Matt had better hurry, she wouldn't have as much time as she expected; the cramp was beginning to start early and soon she would be sick to her stomach. If there was one thing she didn't want, it was to have Matt or any man for that matter ever see her in that condition. Men always thought of women as weak anyway. When one really considered it however, there seemed to be some question as to which traits were those of strength and which were those of little boy cowardice. Words meant nothing, but they destroyed more in the world than any other force, even the men who used and misused them. Next, after words, were women when it came to destruction. To be able to talk to Matt of personal, now important things would be so comforting, but there would be no chance of that. She would have to hide the pain, the nausea and her love, all at once and jog along on the hard, uncomfortable buggy seat without asking him to make the horse gallop faster. At moments such as this, Mitzie knew again what loneliness truly was. There was no one in the world she could turn to, even in thought; no solace, except in silence itself.

Unconsciously Matt whipped the horse as if in response to her unspoken request and Chestnut responded. "Yep, Mitzie, I must surely be in love with Ellie, to feel the way I do," Matt went on to prove the shallowness of his empathy. "Most people never know what love is all about," he said. "Guess I'm just lucky even with all the sadness."

Mitzie had an urge to push him right off the seat; but restrained herself as she fought back the pain by tying her handkerchief in knots instead. "Matt, I wish you would stop talking about her, you're about to make me sick," she finally said.

Matt looked over at her amazed. Women were one thing you could never understand in the world; just as Uncle Bruce had said so many times, "You'll never be able to trust 'em or understand 'em. Best to love 'em and leave 'em before they make your life miserable." Yes, sir, old Bruce really did know what he was talking about. But then, he also said, "You got to learn for yourself because that's the only kind of knowledge that sticks in the human mind." He was an odd nut, but he was so right about women being a "damn strange lot."

Chapter 12

Cyrus had completed his stamp cataloging for the day and now sat in the comfort of his own dignity wondering inwardly where the girls were. His routine had been so completely shattered by this political campaign that it came close to unnerving him with such unanswered questions.

He pulled his watch out and checked it with the clock on the mantle. The clock was running slow, probably Myrtle had forgotten to wind it this last week; he must speak to her about it. And he noticed there was dust on the mantle as he reset and wound the gold-faced clock. He let his finger rub across the thin layer, tempted to write: "dust in this room". The temptation brought back the memory of his own father's crime of like sorts and his mother's fury. His father had gone without clean underwear for a whole week after that and had been forced to sleep in the barn because his wife would not tolerate a man who smelled of sweat and cows between her clean sheets; but the parlor was always dusted from that day forward. His mother had seen to that because it was added to Cyrus's growing list of everyday chores. Cyrus seldom afforded himself the pleasure of reminiscence unless he could draw a moral from the experience. This time he failed to find any plausible excuse so he brushed the incident aside. He managed to sidetrack the urge for the dusty note and decided to tell Myrtle in person. Besides with company in the house, he did not want to cause a scene. This he could not stand, especially with MacQuarrie. MacQuarrie was an unknown quantity with an almost insatiable desire to champion the underdog. That much Cyrus had figured out about his new aid. That meant he must have radical tendencies. He would have to watch him carefully. It must be the result of his newspaper experience, Cyrus pondered as he opened the study door.

There the pleasantness of Myrtle's cooking filled the air, changing his mood and his thoughts. He had reset the clock to the correct time but had completely failed to notice that it was two-thirty. Sunday dinner was served promptly at three. His routine was being destroyed by the helter-skelter pattern MacQuarrie and the rest had forced upon his habits in the last few weeks. He must make a concerted effort to rectify this trend.

In the kitchen Myrtle had put aside her hot and cold flashes for the time it took to prepare the meal. Three of her daughters were helping her. The four of them worked quickly and efficiently, avoiding one another around the crowded stove as if guided by unseen hands.

"Where's Gloria?" Cyrus asked, "She should be helping." "She's upstairs cleaning," Myrtle said quietly as she poured the water off the potatoes.

"This is Sunday; she should be observing the Sabbath," he snapped.

Myrtle paused, noting the obvious hypocrisy of he complaint. "True," she said, "this is the Sabbath, Cyrus, but we have a guest and I do not believe it proper to ask him to make his own bed."

"There's dust in the library and the clock hasn't been wound," he added.

"Those two chores would have been attended to, Cyrus Dodson, if you had let us know you were returning and that it was permissible to go into your beloved sanctuary."

"Myrtle, I will not have people talk back to me."

Myrtle grunted a laugh. "If you are to be Governor, Cyrus, you will have to get used to people talking back to you."

"Myrtle, I want that room dusted!"

"It is on Gloria's list for today, Sunday or no Sunday, as long as she's home," she said, working the potato masher over the soft lumps, fluffing them into heaps of creamy white clouds as she added the hot milk and huge lumps of butter.

"And Agatha? Don't tell me she's in her room crying?" he changed the subject, aware of the complete indifference the three girls seemed to have of his presence in the room. He thought, for a second, that he should shout at the lot of them to get their attention, but decided restraint was a better tool.

Myrtle did not answer.

"Where is Agatha?"

"Where you should be. At the church house."

"Church at two-thirty in the afternoon? I always knew the reverend was long winded, but that is a ridiculous excuse. Where is Agatha? Is she in her room crying?"

"She hasn't cried since you've been away, Cyrus, because there is no one here who wants to make her cry, but you."

"Where in the hell is Agatha, Myrtle? Do I have to get angry?"

"She and some of the women of the church are knitting stockings for the troops on Sunday afternoons. The war doesn't stop for Sunday, even if you want it to."

Cyrus could tell that he was outclassed. He was stripped of his weapons and all he had left was his dignity. In the enemy camp, the general was no match for the sentry. He would retire, even if he lost face in withdrawing. Besides, his stomach told him that hunger was not far away and he could not stand burned meat for Sunday dinner. How could a woman who ran only second best to a medicine bottle and continually whined about her poor health, rise to such moments of powerful resistance? He was losing control in his own home; something must be done about it.

As he came out of the pantry door, Agatha darted through the front door and up the stairs. He started to ask her where she had been, but he could not do it in a quiet tone and still be heard. By the time he had reached the bottom of the stairs, Agatha and her whirl of yellow skirts had disappeared into the dark of the upper hall. It was unlike Agatha. Maybe what Myrtle had said about her not crying was true. If no one else knew it, God knew that he didn't want to have Agatha cry. It tore at him inside to see her unhappy.

Then he noticed Agatha's knitting bag on the window seat in the dining room. He went over to it. Not wanting to open it up and cause further dissention, but unable to restrain himself, he slid the folds of the tied knit bag apart. Inside were assorted colored balls of yarn, needles, and a pair of gray socks not quite finished. He thought back. That bag had been on the window seat when he went into the kitchen. His anger was building up, his collar tightening around his neck. He would make Agatha face up to this ruse when she came downstairs for dinner, tears or no tears, Myrtle's accusations or not. He would not have people lie to him; there was no excuse for falsehood in a home that was based on truth and under the direction of Cyrus Dodson. He clenched his fists and sat on the padded chintz of the window seat.

Upstairs Agatha had found Gloria making the bed in Mac's room. She closed the door behind her and grabbed Gloria around the waist, twirling her around until the two of them almost lost their balance.

"Glory, it's happened; it's happened and you'll never believe it."

Gloria looked at the flushed cheeks and the ecstasy in her sister's eyes; and a lump caught her in the stomach and throat at the same time.

"Glory, I just know you'll never believe it."

Knowing she must not spoil anything of beauty and wonder, but at the same time afraid to ask what Agatha's secret was, Gloria sat on the newly made bed, holding one of the pillows in her lap.

"Glory, we're going to be married. I knew you wouldn't believe me, Glory, but I'm going to be Mrs. Ward J. Kessel."

Gloria hugged Agatha close to her and kissed her on the cheek. Suddenly she was aware of the intense heat of Agatha's face. It frightened her, but she held back the question she wanted to ask.

"Course we'll do it secretly, until after Daddy Cyrus is made Governor. Ward says it wouldn't be good to upset him when he should have his mind busy on being elected. Glory, will you be my bridesmaid, will you?"

"How did one keep from crying in a situation like this?" Gloria asked herself.

"Of course, Aggie; and how wonderful. How wonderful."

"We'll get married in Flintsville, I guess, as soon as Daddy goes back to the capital again. And then we'll let everyone know as soon as the election is over 'cause Ward says Daddy will want to kill everybody the minute he finds out."

"I think your Ward is probably right," is all Gloria could say and still smile. It was too bad to have misgiving about someone else's happiness, but she did.

"I have to get my hair combed. Be back in a minute, Glory; almost late for dinner," Agatha said closing the door behind her.

Ward Kessel visited the room then. And with only the two of them there, Gloria held the pillow tight to her body and rolled over and over on the bed, quivering as she bit her lip and tried to weep but couldn't find the tears.

Cyrus was at the bottom of the stairs when Agatha and Gloria came down. His hand gripped the banister post in an attempt to control his temper.

"Agatha, where have you been this afternoon?" he asked bluntly.

"At church, Daddy Cyrus," she answered, looking right into his eyes.

"Knitting stockings for the Army boys? Grey socks?"

"Yes."

"Agatha, that's a damn lie and you know it," his voice was quiet but hard. He looked at her, expecting her to either run or cry; but she just stood there with a fierce defiance in every part of her body. "Agatha, I said you are a liar, did you hear me?"

She did not answer, but continued to stare at him.

Suddenly he could hold back no longer and he slapped her across her face with such force that she fell against the wall, knocking one of the small oil paintings off its nail. It crashed to the stairs, bouncing down the law two steps to the hall floor.

"I'll not tolerate any insolence or lying in this house as long as I am the master of it, do you understand? Do you understand, Agatha? Or do I have to beat it into your head?"

"Father," Gloria started to interrupt.

"And, Gloria, you keep out of this, I've had enough. Agatha, where have you been?" He raised his hand once more to slap her, but felt his arm firmly pulled backward.

"She was with me most of the afternoon, Cyrus." It was MacQuarrie. "I'm sorry to upset you so much, but I asked Agatha not to tell you because I didn't think you'd want her out soiling her good name delving into politics. We have to campaign for you, even here in Crescent."

Cyrus was about to speak, but almost as if he had read his mind, MacQuarrie stopped him.

"Even on Sunday, Cyrus," MacQuarrie smiled wisely; "love, politics, death and truth, even on Sunday."

Cyrus lowered his arm. There was a great surge of guilt that pushed itself upon him. He should apologize, but there was still too much anger in him and besides, Agatha was still standing there with only defiance in her eyes, not tears. There was an urge to slap her again; then he calmed himself.

"Dinner is about ready," he said taking a deep breath.

"Yes, dinner is about ready," Gloria echoed.

After her father and sister had gone into the dining room, Agatha looked up into MacQuarrie's eyes. He winked.

"Thank you," she said, and started to cry.

"You are certainly welcome," he said, taking the handkerchief from his pocket and handing it to her. She dried her eyes and gave it back. He watched her as she went in to join the others.

"What elements go into courage," he thought, and what in a woman's makeup can in a second turn her from a spitting, clawing cat or a knowing owl to a soft tender pet? "How can a girl, who is such a child, confound me so completely?" He shook his head and followed her to the table.

Sitting next to Gloria, MacQuarrie looked over at Cyrus. He felt sorry for the man he had been hired to make the next governor of the state. However, he reasoned, it sometimes can be as wearing on those around him as it is on the man himself. As Cynthia opened the door to the pantry, he took the soft linen napkin and spread it carefully on his lap. It was a shame to soil anything so glistening white but few ever came through a meal without a few gravy spots and wrinkles. Even when protected and disguised in the roll of a napkin ring, one could be almost certain of a few stains insides."

Myrtle and the girls waited to be signaled, as MacQuarrie stood in shallow gallantry that they might be seated first. Then he readjusted his napkin and waited for Cyrus's blessing on the food.

"Christ bless this food," was all he could say in this, his day of many defeats.

But Cyrus was hungry, and soon the sting was dulled by good food and soothed by the fact that Myrtle in her womanly way seemed to sense the situation and held back any further stands of independence. MacQuarrie talked of success in local politics and Gloria managed, as always, to remind Cyrus of her loyalty by touching his leg with hers several times during the meal. Only Agatha's dry eyes remained to cut the wound. But even that was more of a puzzle than a hurt. He found himself watching her closely. He would tell her he was sorry for his mistake after dinner or sometime when they were alone and it wouldn't embarrass her.

In the library afterward, he and MacQuarrie had their coffee alone and talked while Myrtle and the girls did the dishes and dressed to go to evening meeting at the church.

"You know, Cyrus, as a man's perimeter expands, he can afford less and less time for details and trivial matters. There is more and more area to be covered and less and less time to cover it. I sometimes marvel that any man can grow enough to meet the challenge. And that is where the paradox really hits me, right up here in the head. I know damn good and well as a sensible agnostic that there has never been and never can be a personal God; certainly not the kind your wife and daughters are going to church to pray to tonight. Yet, inside I know that it takes more than a man within himself to rise above the mediocrity of humanity itself. So there has to be a God for men to try and pattern themselves after if they are to be nourished enough to grow into more than animals." MacQuarrie paused to light a cigar.

Cyrus sipped his coffee for a second, then rose and poured two glasses of wine from the bottle on the mantle. A toast would make him feel foolish, for he knew he was being verbally spanked with the hand of his God; by a man who didn't believe that God even existed. He pushed one glass to Mac, and sat down in silence. How could he calm the turmoil inside him? Things were closing in on him; things that, just as MacQuarrie said, he must ignore.

"Every man has his maximum level..." MacQuarrie went on, but Cyrus closed out the words and soon blinked on the edge of sleep. Perhaps he would get ready and go to evening church services with Myrtle; but before his decision had crystallized, his lids had closed.

A long monologue was eloquently nearing its climax when MacQuarrie noticed his audience had cleared the hall. He smiled understandingly, stood and poured himself another glass of wine.

"Even on Sunday", he toasted his slumbering host.

Chapter 13

MacQuarrie unlocked the door of the dingy hotel room and turned on the light. There was something about rooms in rural hotels that brought potato cellars to his mind the minute he entered one. There was a stuffy, unused odor, even in this room: "the best in the house". He yawned, shook his head and wiped the tears that formed in the corners of his eyes.

"Well, Governor," he said, fingering the cut glass water pitcher on the washstand, "I wouldn't go so far as to say we had convinced them tonight."

Cyrus was tired. Weeks, busy weeks with traveling, talking, scheming and arguing had gone on with no respite. But there was always an excitement about it that kept them both going, drawing on energy they didn't know they had. In the last few days though, they had received nothing but silent opposition from every committee and every group of voters they had met. He took off his hat and laid it carefully on the dresser. Perhaps he was disappointing MacQuarrie; but he couldn't help it; he didn't think he could go on this way, too much longer. Then he realized there wouldn't be too much more time to the whole campaign. As he removed his stickpin he noticed his tie was wrinkled and there was a spot on it, right in the middle of one of the light gray strips where it would show.

"It could be you picked the wrong candidate," he said, testing MacQuarrie. He put the tiepin in the small leather jewel box in the pocket of his Gladstone bag and threw the tie in the wastebasket.

MacQuarrie's answer was slow in coming, as if he were carefully planning his attack. There was no attack. "Pardon me, Cyrus, I guess it has us both a bit edgy. They didn't pick the wrong candidate. I just picked the wrong battleground and the wrong weapon. One doesn't come out into these southern counties with a well-dressed gentleman and present him as an 'honest man' when the hicks down here will not go for any stranger, I don't give a damn if he happened to be Abraham Lincoln. The only stranger who could ever win votes for you down here would be someone who looked as if he had horse manure caked an inch thick on the bottom of his shoes and was dressed in homespun cotton. Besides, these god damn farmers can't win the election for you, although they might lose it for you."

Cyrus started to undress; it embarrassed him to have to be in the same room with someone when he undressed, even MacQuarrie, to whom he should have gotten accustomed by this time.

"Do you want a drink?" MacQuarrie asked, pulling a bottle of bourbon from his bag.

Cyrus shook his head and MacQuarrie pulled the cork and poured half a glass for himself. He took a quick gulp. "If I were to stay in small towns very long, I am damned certain the weaknesses of my mind and body would carry me away on an alcoholic cloud into oblivion." He went on, "It took me years of careful study to figure out just what it was about places like this that made me feel 'closed in'. 'Sunflower', Now there a name for a hamlet that shows great foresight. Obviously the founding fathers could see that, as a community, it had potential growth, almost as much as their imagination; so they looked around them and found the most plentiful crop growing in their fields that hot August day, and they named this ghost town of tomorrow 'Sunflower'. You know, that's damn near as original as 'Sunset'. I'll bet there's a 'Sunset' in every county of every state in the whole country. The end of the day, the end of the world and the second coming of Christ every hick in the world thinks in his own little conceited way he is going to be called upon to share."

"Mac, you are hedging with me. What's the truth? What has gone wrong? I don't want you to protect me; but if I am to continue in this campaign, I must know what is taking place. I must have the truth," Cyrus's eyes narrowed in his concern.

MacQuarrie took another gulp from the glass and put it down on the washstand. "Cyrus, when the day comes that I hide important things from you, we will shake hands and leave acquaintances, if not friends. We've bit a pocket of resistance. What we've done wrong, I believe I know how to correct it, but I am not certain. The only way to find out is to play with ideas; ideas, which might seem at first to have nothing at all to do with what we are worried about. You know what it is in small towns; that chokes you to death, Cyrus? It is the closed, selfish, tight little minds of the people."

"You are forgetting that Sunflower is three times as large as Crescent and nearly twice as large as Flintsville," Cyrus said as he looked out through the dirty lace curtains to the street.

"I'm afraid to offend you, Governor, but neither comparison does much to improve the stature of Sunflower; besides, in naming those burgs, one at least had to know something about far east literature and geological terms, while even a parrot knows what a sunflower seed is."

"What has all this have to do with this campaign?" Cyrus said sharply.

"Not a thing, except those tight little minds. Must find a way to pry them open if only long enough to insert a grain of sand," MacQuarrie smiled for the first time in days. "You know, Cyrus, it could be us; maybe it isn't Sunflower at all. Yes, it could be us. You better have a drink," he finished the glass. "It may not solve the problem but it certainly makes it more pleasant to look at."

Even MacQuarrie's jesting failed at this time to do much toward improving Cyrus's humor. At times it seemed to him that MacQuarrie was a fool. He talked in silly riddles and never gave you a direct answer to a question. It was as if he hadn't grown up. He was certainly not the type of person Cyrus would want to hire as an employee. And he always seemed to be looking through you;

whenever you turned around there was Mac looking at you as if you were a newspaper or a politician. Cyrus then smiled inwardly for a fleeting second. Yes, MacQuarrie looked at you as if you were politician. Cyrus took off his trousers and hung them carefully on the hanger, checking the creases to see that they would be presentable for tomorrow's talk at the ladies' county literary club. Mac had made a joke of "county literary", but added, there for certain Cyrus would shine even if he didn't make any impression on the husbands. He noted that of all the wives who might have some influence on their husbands' voting habits, those of Sunflower and Savannah County would come last place on the list.

"We've had enough of one another for a while," MacQuarrie said as he poured another glass of bourbon and rolled the first gulp around in his mouth as if about to gargle with it, "and when I smoke Governor Calder's cigars, I'm like the man who couldn't stand to sit in his own pew in church. I think I'll go for a walk so I won't have to breath my own stale tobacco smoke all night."

He finished his drink and started toward the door; then he stopped and, turned around. As he watched Cyrus put on his nightshirt, the cynicism softened in the lines of his face. The tiredness in Cyrus's shoulders shouted his despair and discouragement even under the folds of flannel. "The first fight's always the hardest," he said to himself. "Let's hope it isn't the last. Damn small towns: so hard to figure the norm. You never know what dusty prejudices are stored away in those rigid, tight minds."

"Cyrus, I'm serious, a glass of whiskey would help you sleep better."

Cyrus turned as if to protest. They both smiled.

"Nothing more stupid than a Don Quixote. Unless it's two of them fighting one another," MacQuarrie said softly. "And if it will help your opinion of me any, Cyrus, I wasn't really trying to ignore your question about the truth. It is just that there isn't an answer. There is only one place you can find that: 'the Spirit of truth will guide you unto all truth'. A quote as you might suspect. You can read it for yourself, St. John 16-13. You might even find a Gideon in the top drawer of the dresser."

By the time Cyrus looked up again, MacQuarrie was gone and all he had to look at was the closed door with the faded card of hotel rules tacked to the top panel. He poured himself a drink of the warm whiskey but did not look to see if there was a Bible in the drawer of the dresser.

MacQuarrie went down the dimly lit hall, his eyes following the circular floral design of the mauve and apple green wallpaper. Even in the near dark it stood out clearly. If nothing else in the hotel was new, at least the crack covering wallpaper was. It matched nothing, from the once crimson strip of carpeting that frayed down the center of the floor to the ornate gas light fixtures that now bulged like pregnant ground hogs, their stomachs full of modern twenty-watt globes.

The lobby stood begging for attention. As lonely as a politician, MacQuarrie thought as he paused for a minute at the desk to look at his surroundings. Perhaps there was a clue to his problem in this musty place. His nostrils quivered as he sniffed to identify the mixed odor of mothballs and freshly boiled cabbage. As Irish as his father was, he was suddenly happy that traditional corned beef dish had never been one of his favorites.

It was all MacQuarrie's hands could do to maintain decorum and not pound a repeated series of clangs on the desk bell to see if life really did exist. What an ideal location for a funeral parlor. All that was missing were the floral sprays, smelling salts and the acrid tinge of formaldehyde in the air. He finally could contain himself no longer and he coughed loudly to attract attention. All the disturbance did was to create a hollow, mocking laughter of itself that echoed back and forth across the room.

"Depressing," he thought. "Main Street" was probably the only real street, the only street with lights and recognizable as such. All the rest were dusty country roads cutting in at any crazy angle that the farmers might choose to bring their cows home, from pasture.

At the general store he stopped, hoping to buy some pipe tobacco. It would be a change from cigars. The doors were locked, but through the windows he could see several men in overalls, their feet propped up on the black, fireless, pot-bellied stove, watching a checker game being played by two of the older citizens.

MacQuarrie pounded on the door. For a long time no one seemed to notice him. He knocked longer and louder, as if the silence, the isolation the town of Sunflower was inflicting upon him was causing him to panic. Finally one of them looked up, furrowing his brow, straining his eyes to see who was causing the intrusion. MacQuarrie pressed his face close to the window and motioned to his empty pipe, pantomiming filling it and smoking it. The farmer scratched his head, said "Closed" and turned back to the checkers. MacQuarrie couldn't hear the word but he could read the tight, thin lips. Once again he knocked long. The contest had now become a challenge. When no recognition came, he nearly shook the doors from their hinges. The same man once more looked up with the same expression of wonder. MacQuarrie repeated his acting job, even adding the touch of a lighted match to make it more realistic. "Closed. Store's Closed," the soundless words came back. But MacQuarrie would not be denied, and pounded on. Finally the man looked up again and endured another of MacQuarrie's performances before he shook his head in disgust and stood up. MacQuarrie watched with satisfaction as the man stretched himself and slowly walked toward the door. Then he stopped, pulled out his own corncob pipe, filled it from a worn leather pouch, returned the pouch to the hip pocket of his overalls, balanced himself on one leg long enough to strike a match on the sole of his boot, light his pipe and methodically grind the match into charcoal with his heel before he continued to the door. MacQuarrie was patient; he waited with no further commotion.

He had won. At last they were face-to-face through the glass and MacQuarrie put his hand on the knob to open the door. The farmer took a deep puff on his pipe and let the smoke curl out the corners of his mouth, nearly hiding his face in a swirling haze. Then with ceremony he pulled both the green shades down over the windows, leaving MacQuarrie facing the night alone.

"Shit!" MacQuarrie said in disgust. Nothing more eloquent could form itself into words at that moment. He turned to leave, but stopped and was amazed at the number of wagons, buggies and horses tied up in front of the store. Almost like a Jack London novel he thought, just like the true and wild west. He continued further up the street. Horses, horses, horses: he thought they must be getting ready to run the Kentucky Derby.

At the corner he paused under a light post to read the names listed on the Gold Star memorial to Sunflower's war dead. The list was long, many of them newly lettered. MacQuarrie scanned the list, as if from habit, to see if any of the names were familiar. At times he could not hold back the questions he knew he should ask himself, but there would be no answers, for why should he fight a war when he couldn't tell the reason for it's existence? In all history there had never been a war recorded as anything but useless after it had been fought; each merely a monumental tribute to man's weaknesses. Fury over mind, passion over pain, and pride, enviable, heroic pride over life itself. The mores and creeds of men and their ritualistic solutions were all so pat, so futile, so undignified in the last analysis. True, he hadn't been called, but that was more a credit to Governor Calder's unspoken exemption notice than to any honest attempt on MacQuarrie's Irish fighting spirit. It might be a good escape though. What better breeding ground for malcontents than the rank and file of those shorn of initiative?

He laughed out loud, "Probably poor old Cyrus Dodson would like, at this very moment, to join the ranks and sneak off into the darkness of France's Argonne plains, with no more speeches, politics or loving daughters to fog his mind." Yes, he and Cyrus both would make good targets for a recruiter tonight; but not because of heroics, a cause or even a national defense, just escape.

He gestured a salute to Sunflower's departed sons as he continued his tour. "Sheer waste of good farm hands; might even have been a brain or 'an honest man' hidden somewhere among the lot."

Next came the dark movie house with next Saturday's feature posted. He was tempted to light a match and read what it was, but quenched the desire; they wouldn't even be in Sunflower after tomorrow night if he could help it.

The drug store corner was different; MacQuarrie was nearly knocked into the street by a group of girls in middy blouses and pleated skirts, swaying back and forth, spread arm in arm, across the walk. They were singing "Mademoiselle from Armentieres" and MacQuarrie listened to the words, marveling at the ingenious rhyme patterns they used to avoid the obvious and tabooed lyrics the troops had created out of boredom. On the corner itself the next generation of Savannah County's leadership oozed itself from the drug store soda fountain into little groups of manly nothingness. Some were in uniform, some dressed as if for a Saturday night ball and smelling of toilet water and hair oil; others still evidencing their day's work among the animals; laughing, joking, noisy and boisterous young men ready for the slaughter themselves. MacQuarrie pushed past one of them in the narrow door. He must be either drunk or intoxicated by the bands, the bond drives and the Victory girls. Pure logic would prove their uproar nothing more than a moral hoax conjured up by the greedy and the emotional and intellectually immature. He bought his tobacco and left the only brightly lit corner in Sunflower.

As he passed the general store again, he rattled the doors once more for spite. With the blinds down, they would have to pull them back up to see who was knocking. It would disturb their game. It would serve them right.

He patted one of the horses tied to the porch railing, and as he stood there scratching behind the animal's ear and wishing he had a lump of sugar, the key to opening Sunflower's locked doors, hearts and minds fell softly at his feet. He mentally stooped and picked it up. He examined it. There was no question that it would work. Maybe not too honest, but "finder's keepers" and it would work even if it wouldn't answer Cyrus's plea for the "truth". That, he would have to find within himself because he was certain semantics would block their agreement on what the term encompassed.

In the hotel lobby he was greeted by the sullen stare of the desk clerk, disturbed in the middle of the engrossing task of picking strings of stubborn corned beef from between his yellow and irregular teeth.

"How many automobiles do you have in Sunflower?" MacQuarrie asked.

"Quite a few", the clerk answered, pausing long enough to take the toothpick from his mouth; "I'd say pretty close to seven or eight. You know, Sunflower's got most of the new things in life. Going to form a water system next year."

"How many blacksmiths?"

"Stranger, we've got a lot of 'em, a hell of a lot; if you're looking for a job as a blacksmith, you might just as well join the cavalry. But we've got a lot of them 'cause they do most of the work for all the folks of Savannah County, Burksfield north."

"Do you know how many, right here in town?" MacQuarrie pressed the question.

"Nope. It's a pretty big town, you know. But I can find out for you in a mighty big hurry," he said with pride, turning to the telephone on the wall next to the desk. He turned the crank with intense efficiency; "Can sure tell you in no time at all." The desk clerk and the lobby were both coming to life for the first time as the bell of the phone and the importance of the statistic came to the fore. But there the action stopped, and the clerk's face graphically displayed his error. "Line's busy. Supposed to listen first. Mrs. Oggelsby is mad as the devil. Old biddy. 'Course she has her reasons. Just lost her second son and still one more of them overseas in England waiting to go to France."

MacQuarrie hated to leave his new found acquaintance, especially since for the first time, someone in Sunflower had volunteered to be friendly; but the key had been found and now he must put the plan into action. If it would work in Savannah County, it would work in every rural area in the state. He'd send Cyrus on to the capitol tomorrow morning. No, even something as unimportant as the ladies luncheon must not be cancelled. He was forgetting a prime rule of good politics. Tomorrow's evening train from Weston would have to do.

As he bounded up the stairs to tell Cyrus the news, he wondered at his own blindness. What possibly could have been the matter with his thinking? Actually they hadn't needed Cyrus out in the "boonies". If they had used the correct plan of attack from the start they could probably have won without sacrificing him on the altar. But now they certainly couldn't change candidates; anyway it would be good for Clarence Calder and the others to feel the sting of their own boomerang when "the honest man" ignored all of the fancy promises they had so carefully put into his mouth. He would put Cyrus in the larger cities for the rest of the campaign; he was indoctrinated enough now to be aware of the trends in thinking there and he made the perfect public figure for those people, even the laboring class. Most of them didn't trust their own kind but always aimed higher at an idealized image when it came to politics. The grass roots of the rest of the state he would supervise under his new plan. The two should compliment one another and could, possibly, make an unbeatable combination.

Mac shook his head once more as he caught his breath at the door of the room. "Compose yourself, Mac, old man, calm down and get it straight." he said, almost out loud; "in words Cyrus can understand." It had been right there in his hands all the time. When he was in the blacksmith shop that Sunday morning, he should have recognize it: a U.S. war hero (one of the first the Germans had provided), common man, in love with Cyrus's daughter, and in sympathy with the cause. Wart was a natural. Even the clods at the general store would think it over before they pulled the window blinds down in his face. Wart had even agreed to do anything he could to help, but Rex MacQuarrie, the master mind of the Calder machine, had passed it off as a minor fight instead of a whole new direction. Middy bloused girls and soldier-boys-to-be would talk of him and ogle over him, while he talked plain facts to men who shod horses and fixed fences.

Cyrus was asleep for the first ten seconds MacQuarrie was in the room. From then on he sat there blinded by the overhead globe, his mind trying to cut through the barrier between awareness and sleep, straining to comprehend what MacQuarrie was talking about. "Key", "New Plan", "Hero Makes Demands", "Better Life For Men Coming Home From Battle"- "You can even use it in town when you talk to the elite; we'll dig you up a couple of heroes for the rest of your talks and meetings; you'll sound the part of a retired general with nothing on his mind but to bring democracy, true democracy, home where it belongs."

MacQuarrie paused, completely out of breath. He sat down on the edge of his bed and looked at Cyrus, for a long time, breathing heavily as he fought to regain control of his voice.

"No more crooked city politics, Cyrus, in fact we can even campaign to 'give the farmers a break'. Do you hear me? You and the boys from 'over there' will not allow this state to be bamboozled into subservience by the hairy hand of corruption. And while you are working the cities, Cyrus, we've got the perfect campaigner for the rest of the state: Wart Kessel, Crescent's first war hero. A man of the soil who knows what farmers think, how they talk and how to get them riled up in the right direction. Yes, sir, Cyrus, just standing down there on the main street of Sunflower, of all places and there it was: A red velvet carpet rolled out straight from the cow pasture to the statehouse, four hundred and sixteen and two tenths miles. And up that path of glory you are going to strut on inauguration day with all the farmers and their soldier-boy sons right behind you because Wart Kessel is on your side. Yes, Cyrus, a red velvet carpet supported by sixty thousand cow pies and horse biscuits."

Cyrus was awake now. The name Wart Kessel had stung him hard. He rose to his feet and walked over to MacQuarrie. His face flushed with anger, he clenched his fist and pounded it on the dresser. "This is my campaign, and I will not have vulgarity become a part of it. I will not have second-class scum led by a blacksmith represent my good name, and I will not be told what to say any longer. Those things I will not have, MacQuarrie, do you understand me?"

Mac was not surprised by the rejection. In fact, though a calculated risk, it was the first step in making Cyrus see the light. It would also let MacQuarrie know if Cyrus was hungry enough for power to make the plan work. He studied his candidate's face, took a deep breath and pointed his finger at Cyrus.

"There is one more thing you will not have, Cyrus. You failed to mention it, but there is one thing more you will not have," MacQuarrie's voice reached a softness that caused Cyrus to be ashamed of his loud retort.

"What?" he asked, avoiding recognition of MacQuarrie's obvious remark.

"The governorship of this state. No, Cyrus, you will not be the next Governor or anything but a short-sighted, arrogant ass, who hasn't the brains to accept the advice and experience of those who are killing themselves trying to elect him."

"Don't talk back to me, Mac. I'm the one who's running for Governor, not you. Remember that; and I'll run this campaign my way, just as I'll run this state when I'm elected."

MacQuarrie made certain he paused just long enough before cutting Cyrus short. It was like the initial steps in breaking a bronco; give him just enough head then pull the reins up tight and dig the spurs in full shank. Let him know who's boss.

"Cyrus, a couple of hours ago you asked for the truth. You made a plea for honesty, to be told what could be done. Now you just sit back down on that bed and listen to me. I'm not in this damn stew to play a game of tiddlywinks. How do you like that for a mixed metaphor?"

He poured a full glass of whiskey and put it out for Cyrus. "You had better drink this because before I get through, you are going to know what makes this business tick and who makes it run. Go ahead and drink the damn stuff before I walk out of this room and leave you to fall flat on your face in the middle of some farmer's cesspool. Cyrus, if you want to be Governor, you have to go into politics, and if you are going to go into politics you have to be politician. That doesn't mean you have to be a 'crook', or an outright dishonest man, but you have to grow up and realize you are going into business and you've got to run it as a business. In business you are an opportunist, in politics you are an opportunist; and you do business with any man who comes into your establishment and offers to do business with you and help you earn a profit. Now I don't give a damn if that man happens to be Wart Kessel or the president of some hick bank; you give the best treatment to the man with the order that will make you the most profit. That is just what we are talking about at this moment: profit, political profit, the governorship of this damn state; and believe me it isn't a very big margin of profit, but it has to be more than your competition is making or you're out of business.

"Now if you and I are to stay in business as partners that's fine. You stick to your job of bookkeeping and being the figurehead and I'll get out and sell the product to whomever I see fit. You don't, for one minute, believe that the voters down inside think that you are any more honest than any other man in the race, do you? Of course you may be that dumb, but that is about as stupid as telling your customer that your grain is a better quality than your competitor's when he knows good and well that it came from the same fields of the same farmer. Don't underestimate their intelligence, but have brains enough not to limit the unlimited capacity of their emotions. To some people dignity is the spark that instills this emotion; in others the spark is war heroes and blacksmiths. Or would you prefer to say vulgarity fires them up with the zeal of emotionalism.

"It will probably deflate you, Cyrus, but that dirty smelling blacksmith is a bona fide war hero and therefore is a lot more valuable to the voters than you are. We know they are wrong, but they think he's done a hell of a lot more for the people of this state than you possibly ever could.

"Now, Cyrus, my job is to get you up on that platform to take the oath of office. Your job is to take my directions at least until I get you there. That's what Calder and his backers picked you for and that is what they hired me for. Now if you don't want those services, I'll damn sure not waste them. It's my living; I'll make them work for someone else next time around and put them up there in that seat where you think you can get by dreaming and quibbling over the blemishes on each grain of wheat you buy."

MacQuarrie was out of breath, even though he had not raised his voice during all the time he was lecturing Cyrus. He poured himself a glass of whiskey to match the one he had handed to Cyrus, but which was not touched; then he walked to the window, pushed it open and stood blindly looking out into the night. His anger had taken over part of the task of working over Cyrus's ego; the rest had been a carefully calculated variation on a theme he had used before on other candidates for exalted public offices. There was a slight breeze now, carrying further evidence that Sunflower still depended primarily on farms for its economic wellbeing.

There was silence between them. Cyrus felt drained, completely shocked, at the sudden brutality he had unleashed against himself by crossing MacQuarrie. There had been no indication that the rage was coming, nor that this man was capable of such anger, of such directness, of such plain cutting words that left one "bleeding from all pores." Finally he took a deep breath and mustered enough will to look up. He watched MacQuarrie and wondered whether or not what he said was absolute and true. There was really no doubt that there were exceptions to his own standards; and it had not seemed to be bitterness that MacQuarrie displayed, but outright disgust at Cyrus's lack of experience.

MacQuarrie looked back from the window, finished his drink, turned off the light and undressed for bed.

In the darkness, Cyrus sat listening as MacQuarrie untied his shoes and let them drop to the floor. He should say something. Perhaps he should apologize to Mac. Maybe even apologize, mentally, to Wart Kessel; but he couldn't, the idea made him ill. He couldn't. He slid down between the sheets and looked up at the ceiling until about the time the cows became restless and their masters stirred, knowing that soon they would have to start the day. Then he fell asleep, still weak from the stormy onslaught.

A trip to Flintsville in the middle of the week was unheard of in the Dodson house, but Myrtle would never question anything Gloria said was important.

"Such a pleasant day, Cynthia," she said as she pulled her shawl tighter around her. "Fall is the nicest time of the year. More so than spring don't you think, Cynthia?"

"Why do you suppose Gloria is taking Agatha to Flintsville, Mother?" Cynthia asked as she sat in the swing mending one of the bed sheets that had suddenly decided it was time to become shreds.

"Shopping," Myrtle said flatly and breathed deeply to enjoy as much of the air as possible. Myrtle Dodson had felt less angry with her husband since he had been gone. She was tired, and when Cynthia brought her mirror each morning, she saw much more grey in her hair and the wrinkles in her face were noticeably growing deeper and more plentiful. For so many years, Myrtle had fought the idea of getting old, but today she accepted it with less resistance, almost embracing the knowledge that youth had passed.

"Even in the girls," she thought as she observed Cynthia's matronly posture, It was too bad none of her daughters had married. Cynthia could have, should have. Myrtle knew, inside, why Cynthia had returned Willard Helm's ring. Cynthia had said it was that he was "not worthy", but Myrtle knew it was because Cynthia thought her mother needed her. The other girls certainly were not as attentive, and she had become more and more dependent on the considerations Cynthia showed every day. Cynthia would marry some day, though, someone who deserved a person as understanding and giving as Cynthia.

Now Gloria of course would marry as soon as someone with money and position asked her. Gloria was that way. She looked younger, spent more time grooming herself. Though she had never said so, Myrtle could tell that Gloria knew just what sort of man she wanted to build a home for.

Of course Peggy was entirely different. All her girls were different. Alfreda, Myrtle sensed, would die without having known a man as more than someone to speak to; but in this she would be happier than if the crudeness, the suffering and the constant, silent giving of a married woman's life had been thrust upon her. Myrtle doubted whether Alfreda could stand labor panes, let alone what went on before. Agatha, on the other hand, she felt would adjust to life if Cyrus would just leave her alone.

"If it were only shopping, why didn't she invite the rest of us to go along?" Cynthia asked without looking up from her thread and needle.

"They are very close," Myrtle offered. "Yes, they are very close, Agatha and Gloria. It's good of Gloria to take the time with her."

"They shouldn't be traveling alone; Father wouldn't like them to do that," Cynthia persisted.

"But they're not; and Cyrus would be very pleased if he knew Agatha and Gloria were riding together in the wagon with Matthew, the boy from the store, because he has said so many tines that he would have Agatha consider him as a possible husband. Cyrus has made plans to leave the entire grain business in Matthew Harwood's hands to manage when he's elected," Myrtle was showing pride in Cyrus's achievement for the first time since he had been nominated. She picked up a copy of Liberty Magazine and thumbed through the pages, looking at she wood engravings of the war scenes. It would be so nice if they had prettier pictures, she thought.

"You sound as if you thought Father had already won the election. You shouldn't, you know. It's very, very bad luck to talk that way."

Myrtle looked at her daughter in dismay. She was sounding as old as she looked, and this in turn made Myrtle feel even older than she had a few minutes before.

"Mother, I have the strangest feeling, a nervous feeling about then going: I just know Father wouldn't want Agatha and Gloria to go to Flintsville."

"Your father wouldn't want Agatha to go anywhere except to the bathroom and church, and there are eyen times he wouldn't allow that if he thought for a minute that forbidding it would make her cry. Why won't people leave Agatha alone? I get so tired of her tears and seeing her look sad." Myrtle put the magazine down and nervously started the swing going gradually back and forth, back and forth.

"Mother, I'm sewing; please don't swing while I'm sewing. They shouldn't go," Cynthia went on.

"Your father is in the Capital and will be there for the next three weeks. Who's going to start him making a scene if he doesn't know? Cynthia, you are making me upset. When Cyrus is away from this house let's enjoy the peace and quiet, shall we?"

Myrtle remembered her first husband easy going ways and wondered once in a while what had gone wrong in her life: Cyrus, too, had seemed to possess that nature when he courted her. Then, almost immediately, after the wedding he had started to become more and more demanding. Lately it was almost becoming more than she could live with.

Cynthia opened her mouth to give her next objection, but stopped as she gulped a large mouthful of air. Gloria and Agatha were standing in the doorway, just opening the screen, Gloria had obviously heard Cynthia's last remark, but chose to make nothing of it. Cynthia, knowing this, flushed slightly as she concentrated on her sewing.

"We are on our way to spend Papa's money on finery," Gloria said gaily.

"My, we do look nice, just as pretty, so pretty. Don't they, Cynthia, look pretty?" Myrtle said in a cheerful tone.

Agatha gave a twirl so her mother could look.

"I told you your petticoat wasn't showing just two minutes ago," Gloria laughed.

"Is it, Mother; showing?"

"No, Agatha; but you should always wear yellow. Don't you agree, Gloria?"

"It's the nicest dress she's made," Gloria said.

"Cynthia?" Myrtle went on.

Cynthia looked up as if wondering what the question was.

"Agatha's dress, isn't it pretty? The yellow I mean."

"I like it," Cynthia said, putting her sewing down. "What are you going to shop for, Gloria?"

"For one thing," her mother interrupted, "the newest copy of Liberty from the drug store. The Emporium refuses to even buy the good publications."

"Some patterns and some materials and we don't know what else."

As the two of them went out of the front gate, Myrtle was proud of them. Agatha seemed so young; again it compensated for other things and for a second she forgot her own age. "Be sure and be extra nice to Mr. Harwood," she was about to say, but put her hand to her lips for fear she might be heard and spoil the entire day.

Wart and Mitzie had left earlier in his surrey. Gloria and Agatha had to wait while Matt finished loading the wagon, before they could start. Finally he put the note on the front window and locked the door. They had Agatha sit in the middle as if to protect her from some unseen danger, and the three of them bounced over the rough road to Flintsville without saying a word.

Matt felt as though he himself were being married. He wondered how it would be to be married to Agatha as Wart would soon be; how it would be to have Ellie whenever he wanted her, not laughing every time he told her he loved her. He hadn't even kissed her and yet he loved her. And Mitzie he had kissed so many times he could no longer keep track; kisses that lasted and lasted and her voice low and different always saying, "Matt, I love you, love, love, love you." And yet Ellie was the one. Why?

Agatha shifted in the seat and he looked over at her.

What made Wart, the best Indian wrestler in the whole county, the best blacksmith, war hero...suddenly his mental catalogue of qualities stopped for they were crossing the bridge. Wart Kessel and Mr. Dodson's daughter just didn't match, especially Agatha. Gloria, yes, Matt could imagine her in the barn, just as Mitzie was, making loved in the rain. Gloria had that deep look in her eyes, soft full lips that looked as if they knew what kissing was all about. But Agatha looked almost as innocent as Margo; of course she was much older but she didn't act it or sound it, or at times, look it. He suddenly hated himself as he asked himself, "Would Wart kill for Agatha, as he had for him?" He mauled the word "kill" over with his tongue even though his lips would not let it escape. He felt for just that instant that he resented Agatha; but perhaps she, too, would get to know Wart as he and Mitzie did. It wasn't fair; she hadn't been a part of that night; wouldn't, couldn't understand how the three of them felt at the time it happened and what it meant to them: the excitement, the terror, the fear, the hurt. He didn't want to share Wart with Agatha. Mitzie was different; they were a threesome, but Agatha was an intruder. Would Wart kill for her as he had for him and Mitzie? His head was getting hotter and he looked over at Agatha once more. She smiled back at him, her stomach whirling with the unknown of what was soon to be hers. Then Matt laughed to himself. What was the matter with him? Maybe Wart would feel the same about him when he got married someday.

Gloria strained her eyes for a sign of Flintsville; the steeple on the church would be the first thing to appear. And even that would make it harder for her to accept. She was a conspirator against Cyrus. How could she ever explain it to him; he would never forgive her. But Agatha and Wart would marry whether he had given his consent and blessing or not. She would just have to tell him the truth. At least they had never done anything together. Agatha was being married a virgin. How many women in the world could ever in their hearts say: "married a virgin", even in mind? This Agatha could, even if when she lost it would be to a blacksmith that had thick red hair all over his body.

She stopped herself. How did she know he had hair all over his body? So many times since she had met him, she had visualized touching it, even dreaming of caressing it and being loved by him. How could she? He was so crude; and yet Agatha was the purest thing Gloria could think of, especially, she thought, in that yellow dress. In that yellow dress, the thought again, wanting to change places with her; but knowing that years before she had lost that chance, in the back row of the choir seats in Reverend Pritchard's church after choir practice. When Willard Helms ran his hand along the inside of her thigh, even through the organdy dress and petticoats, the excitement had electrified her. Later, in his buggy, she had completely forgotten who she was.

"What will Cynthia do, Willard? It would kill her to know," she had asked him afterwards.

"She'll never know, not unless you tell her. Besides, Gloria, Cynthia's not a real person like you; she's not warm."

His hands had worked fast and frantically. He had taken her and left her sitting on the front steps of the house all alone, still waiting to know what love meant; aching inside, tense, tight, wanting to scream out loud for someone to touch her and ease the pain. And then Cynthia was asking why she was crying. "Gloria, you never cry, never." After that, Willard decided he didn't have time to be in the choir. He didn't even speak when they met on the street. And even though Gloria didn't tell Cynthia, and by the guilt in his face, she could tell that Willard hadn't, she suspected that Cynthia knew. Willard's ring was taken off and put back in its purple velvet box and left with his mother one Monday afternoon when Willard was working. Willard was dead now, just another gold star. As a memory though, it seemed he had just left her there on the steps minutes before, and she ached inside as she looked over at Agatha: scared, uncertain Agatha, who would be married a virgin in a homemade yellow dress of organza trimmed in satin. Gloria winced as the buggy crossed the bump at the far end of the bridge. She had betrayed Cynthia and now Cyrus and still there was nothing else she could do.

Agatha picked at her nails as she sat waiting for the clerk to complete the papers. Wart stood next to the bench, his hand resting on the hard oak back. She leaned back touching him and a burst of happiness and calm came over her. She looked up. They smiled. He was so big, so very big and yet she felt so safe around him. No one, no one would ever make her feel like running away again. This Agatha knew just strongly as she knew she was going to be Mrs. Walter J. Kessel. And whether Daddy Cyrus approved or not, it would just have to be, for she was sure God had planned it this way. Anything that made a person so quiet inside and so nervous just waiting for it to happen must be just as it should be.

"I wish they would hurry," she said softly. "Don't you?"

"He says about five minutes; until the clerk gets back to put the seal on it. That makes it legal," Wart explained.

It was almost like waiting at the dentist's for the first time, she thought, as she gently touched Wart's hand, sure that he would make the pain go away, and yet not knowing just what to expect.

"There's a minister in town here, Agatha. Would you rather have him marry us than the Justice of the Peace?"

"You mean in a church?" she asked with excitement. "I'll bet he has this happen every day with kids getting ready to go off to war."

"It would make it seem so much more real," she said. "Then we'll do it that way, Miss Dodson; we'll have a church wedding that will make the King of England wish he could attend."

Agatha laughed softly at his joke and reached over and pressed his, hand firmly to tell him just how proud she was to be the future Mrs. Kessel.

Gloria, Mitzie and Matt waited in the wagon.

"I must remember to get a few dress patterns and some cotton yardage before we go back, Matt," Gloria explained. "Mother is expecting this to be a shopping trip."

Matt laughed, for the first time, suddenly starting to enjoying the intrigue. But Gloria's expression told him she did not think anything about the trip very funny. He wondered just why she had agreed to come in the first place if she had any misgivings about Agatha and Wart getting married. Perhaps she thought that Wart wasn't good enough for Agatha. Well, she had to remember that none of them were Cyrus's daughters, just his stepdaughters. His blood didn't really belong to them, even if he became Governor. And Wart Kessel was a man no one told what to do. He fought his own way and made his own living and everyone thought the best of him. Gloria should be glad that Agatha could get any man, let alone someone who was as important as Wart. The funniest one in the family and the only girl to get married; Matt thought it was quite a strange turn of events. He wondered if all the other old maid sisters, sitting home with their sick mother, would be jealous too. Gloria and the rest of them should be proud of the match, instead of looking down their noses at Wart.

At the chapel, they waited in the foyer while Wart went in to see the minister. The two of then talked quietly in the study for a few minutes, then led the way to the altar.

"Until in death God do you part, I pronounce you..." There was no ring. In their excitement and upset, all of them had forgotten. Wart and Agatha would pick one out after the ceremony was finished.

"Something bound to go wrong when people are in a hurry," Gloria said to herself. "But we were very lucky to get the bride here in one piece."

Mitzie bit the nail of her left index finger as she wondered and tried to remember if a 'forgotten wedding ring' wasn't one of a long list of Polish omens of bad fortune her grandmother had given her to avoid for a long and happy life.

But Matt chuckled under his breath, for Wart Kessel had lost another point of battle in the chess game of jest. Now Matt would be able to tease him before every Indian wrestle they had; or would this moment of silence, he wondered, end that?

Agatha and Wart kissed.

"Just a child," Gloria thought as she dabbed at her eyes with the small orchid-trimmed handkerchief Cyrus had bought for her their first day in the capital. "How fast they grow up and leave you."

After the wedding MacQuarrie settled Wart down to a routine of daily speech drills in which he tried to get the feel of Wart's natural speech patterns as much as to get him to enunciate. At the end of the first week MacQuarrie felt as if he were working on a production of George Bernard Shaw's newest play, Pygmailion, however, "Wart," he chuckled to himself, "must be the world's strangest flower girl."

Gloria, Mitzie and MacQuarrie all took turns making excuses to Cyrus and Myrtle so Agatha could visit Wart, and acting as body guards for the newlyweds so they could be alone every afternoon.

"If this isn't the silliest bunch of shenanigans," Wart said at the peak of his frustration. "Agatha's my own wife and we go around hiding like we were criminals or something."

"As if we were criminals," MacQuarrie countered.

"Have it your way; as if; but it doesn't make sense. What difference does it make? We're married!"

"Simple: Agatha and I both need your help to get Cyrus elected."

"Now you know that doesn't add up. Cyrus can handle his own campaign. He'd tell you himself that he doesn't need a blacksmith to speak for him."

"That, I am prepared to accept as a valid statement; in fact that is exactly why you have to keep this secret until after the election. That really would kill his chances. I know what I'm talking about, Wart. Cyrus is so damn proud he'd destroy everything."

"I think it's ridiculous. Agatha and I have decided..."

"I don't give a damn what you have decided. We made an agreement and I expect you to live up to what you promised." MacQuarrie had reminded Wart of his promise time and time again, until it was almost as painful to Wart as being away from Agatha.

Gloria helped ease the tension, however, by talking her mother and Cyrus into letting Alfreda and Agatha go on some of the rural campaign trips with Wart and MacQuarrie. Governor Calder had pointed out that it would be good for votes; and, of course, Alfreda had all of the qualities of an excellent chaperone. MacQuarrie added the final touch in his arranging for the hotel rooms: making certain that he and Wart shared a room, and the girls were in separate rooms, Agatha's adjoining Wart's whenever possible. Alfreda made things even easier by demanding a private room, just as she had at home.

"Thank God, for middle age," Gloria giggled to MacQuarrie.

"You might say the single-minded make the best chaperones, Glory Be. They're so busy seeing evil in everything that isn't, they miss everything that is," MacQuarrie said with a straight face.

The first three days of Wart's campaigning were very satisfying to Mac. Wart relaxed and became part of every group he talked to, but after each encounter with the public Mac gave him new pointers and re-wrote parts of the script. Saturday would be the first real test, however, in Sunflower, where Cyrus had been so stiff and coldly received.

"War Hero, Blacksmith to speak at Torchlight Rally!" the posters and handbills blared, and MacQuarrie made sure that every post office box in Sunflower and every rural delivery mail box in the area received one of the yellow handouts. MacQuarrie's theory of motivating farmers was about to be tested. The results were astounding.

The wagon was completely surrounded and the crowd pressed closer as Wart spoke. Enthusiasm mounted to a crescendo. Transformed from blacksmith to actor, Wart paused and dramatically lifted his hand. The audience sensed that he was asking for silence, but not immediate silence, and obliged his direction. He displayed his pleasure at the continued noisy response, and with a calm he had never been able to clothe himself in before; as armor, he dominated the crowd around him, and only when there was complete attention did he continue to speak.

"And I say to HELL with all this bunk about putting an honest man in the Governor's Mansion. We've been doing that for generations and what good has it done us? No damn good at all! The rural voters, (that's you and me) have been voting into office every 'honest' Tom, Dick and Harry the city politicians served up to us term after term after term. And has it really helped us out here in the sticks? Are the roads any better with this present government than the last? And how about the schools; have they improved since Governor Simpson took over from Governor Calder? Have they built that new high school here as they promised? When it rains have you noticed any better flood control on Chipaho river over there, or when there's too long a dry spell, is the state aid for irrigation much improved in the last four years? NO! 'We're at war'. Of course we are at war. That's as good a reason as any for not doing anything. But if we win the war, is it going to make it any better for you and your farms? Or will you still have to get down on your hands and knees and beg for everything you need and then be turned down in the end?"

"Ya know, I'll be go to hell if that crawdad ain't a damned good man," one of the torchbearers near the wagon said.

"Sure is," said another as he spit his tobacco wad on the fading leaves of the lilac bush next to him. "At first I thought he looked like a damn hick though."

"When your crops fail do they help you? When they steal your harvest for pennies on the market do they protect you? When do you think they'll ever get around to putting power lines out to your farms so you can have electricity and make some money?"

Wart's voice had trailed off into a throaty whisper and the long silence that followed pressed in heavily on those who strained to hear him. He waited, letting each one in his audience listen to their own breath and heartbeat until they felt the air would shatter into a million brittle splinters of pent-up sounds. Then he lifted his head slowly and screamed at the top of his voice: "NEVER, I say NEVER until we realize that there is more than one war. We have to admit that Kaiser Bill isn't the only enemy we have to lick; we have to fight the big city machines if we ever want to reap the benefits of all the taxes we pay. You sure as HELL don't think Sunflower is getting its fair share, do you? Right now we are being taxed without representation, but it is our fault, because we don't stick together. The farmers and the people of Sunflower and other farm towns had better start thinking about the farmers and the farms instead of 'honest' and 'qualified' and 'experienced' politicians. We'd better vote for someone who knows our problems and will fight to help us solve those problems instead of selling us a load of manure about 'Honesty in Government.'" In other words, we'd better vote for Cyrus Dodson. Now I don't know for one damn minute if Cyrus Dodos is honest or not, but I do know that Cyrus Dodson is a farm bred business man who knows where this state's bread is buttered, right here in the farm country, not in some dirty city street. I know that Cyrus Dodson will fight for the farmer, and THAT is what we need now: someone who will do the things we need done; not ten, twenty or a hundred years from now, but now!

"If we want honesty, we'd better start by being honest with ourselves. We'd better get up off our wagon seats and start things rolling for Dodson. We'd better make sure the Grange votes go to Dodson and a victory for our side, not only on the battlefield but here at home as well. Unless we are willing to do that we might as well all say to HELL with all this bunk about putting an honest man in the Governor's Mansion; because we'll never get one unless we do."

He had barely finished his last sentence before the crowd broke loose in spontaneous cheering. MacQuarrie, sitting on the wagon seat, sighed. He noticed his own hands were trembling slightly. "Bourbon's the only medicine for the shakes," he thought, but it would be a long wait before they got back to the hotel. They must keep their guise of complete sobriety, as a silent symbol of sincerity and honesty for the women who controlled the votes.

Wart had climbed down from the wagon tailgate and was shaking hands with each man in the group surrounding him. His bare chest showed from between the strained buttons of his shirt as he graciously bowed in gentlemanly recognition of each female spectator who was introduced to him.

"What a perfect student," MacQuarrie mused to himself as he watched the reflected festive mood around him in the excited expressions of Agatha and Alfreda's eyes.

Cyrus and Calder would be turned into either pouting children or raving maniacs at the things he had given Wart to say; but then who was writing this play anyway? Who was the author, director and prop boy all wrapped up in one? He was. Maybe if his new protégé kept growing at this pace, he'd cast him in the lead instead of just a supporting role when it came time for the next production.

He should be more pleased by the ovation his masterpiece had received; but the puppeteer was tired, exhausted. He needed bourbon, sleep, and perhaps the faint, lyrical sound of hairpins dropping into a Dresden candy dish.

Though they were tired, Wart and Agatha caressed gently in the darkness of her room, and for the first time reached far out beyond consciousness to a point of infinite focus together. Wart felt her body writhe, tremble and then fold limply beneath him. For a long time they lay drugged by their exhaustion.

"Am I too heavy?"

"Never, never, never."

"I love you, Mrs. Kessel."

"And, oh, Wart Kessel, I love you."

"You are a marvelous lover."

"Only because I have you for a teacher and because I love you, Wart Kessel, even more than I thought I did."

Their predictable, carnal conversation rarely varied. They laughed and slowly rolled over and she fell asleep in his arms. He watched her calmed body through the darkness and kissed her cheeks and eyelids with his breath. A silent, wordless completeness filled every corner and subtle shadow in the room.

There would be a time to tell all Crescent, all Flintsville, all of Walker County of their love between November and the fall of snow. When the election was over, he and Agatha would tell everyone about the child they both wanted so much and hoped had been conceived.

He watched the shadows lighten and stretch themselves across the room and rose to go tack to MacQuarrie's room, leaving Agatha to her dreams and a bed now half vacant.

MacQuarrie's snoring roused him into awareness as he closed the door between their rooms and snapped the lock. There would be no use trying to go back to sleep, he told himself as he yawned and scratched the thick matt of auburn hair on his chest. He turned on the light over the dresser. MacQuarrie snorted a couple of times but turned over with a resounding thump and squawk of bed springs, resuming his snoring, but with a tone one octave higher.

Wart's fingers grasped a glass and he poured himself a drink of lukewarm water from the pitcher on the washstand. He yawned again and gathered the scattered pages MacQuarrie had dropped on the floor as he finished scribbling the words Wart would utter in his next speech. It would be hard to decipher the latter parts of these for the sum of whiskey, ink and MacQuarrie's mind added up to more than sense and less than reality and the writing trickled off into unsolved forms. But day-by-day, speech-by-speech, Wart found the struggle lessen and the code more easily broken. Until now he had felt free to take liberties with the script and change words that didn't fit his mouth; switching his simple bluntness for a poet's devious paths into semantics. Many times he thought MacQuarrie was more in love with his own words than with the meanings they might have for those hearing them. But it was Mac who insisted he learn to say "hell" and "damn" convincingly.

Silently he read the speech; noting how he would gesture and pause with each statement. He could practice the words out loud between the time he and Mac ate breakfast and started on their wagon trip to the various farms. In the late afternoon he would have an opportunity for a final rehearsal in front of the mirror and Mac before curtain time on the stage of the high school auditorium at Caxton.

Chapter 14

In the following weeks, MacQuarrie divided his time between Cyrus and Wart, traveling back and forth from the capital to the rural areas. Cyrus seemed smoother and more assured in the delivery of his speeches and in discussions and meetings with the party workers every time MacQuarrie saw him; just as every trip back to Crescent proved Wart more solid and earthy in his give and take with the terse questions and suspicious minds of the farm constituents. He felt at times as if he had outlived his usefulness with both of them; and yet he knew their flaws, and constantly watched that neither Cyrus's pedantic strut nor Wart's raw frankness interfered with his plans. Clarence Calder was the most upsetting force of all because he required actual physical exertion to shout down his arguments.

"You're giving Dodson too much rope; God, he's got the big head. Nobody can tell him a damn thing anymore."

"As long as he doesn't have your neck in the noose, don't worry," MacQuarrie jokingly sparred.

"Not funny; not funny in the least. You watch him; he'll go down in defeat. He's going off making speeches that aren't scheduled. Hell, I can't keep track of him; he bounces around like a son-of-a-bitchin' gadfly. I don't know what the damn bastard is going to say half the time."

"No worry; I think he's doing fairly well. You don't like him, Clarence; but he might just win in spite of us. If he doesn't, it is no skin off yours," MacQuarrie said.

"The hell it isn't. It's my reputation he's playing with."

"Then we don't have to worry about it, do we," MacQuarrie said lifting his empty glass in a toast.

Clarence Calder ignored the remark. "It's my reputation and my campaign and he'd batter damn well understand that I give the orders and no tin-horn with straw coming out of his ears is going to forget it. It's my election."

"Then why aren't you running yourself, Clarence? If your reputation is so outstanding, you could win hands down. You didn't have to go to Walker County to pick a candidate for a job that you, Clarence Calder, could fill so well, and win so easily."

"Drop the vaudeville act, Mac; you're a pain in the ass when you try to be funny."

"Then tell me what is really sticking pins in you? Dodson is not doing such a bad job; even if he is a bit on the schoolteacher, prissy side; but then so is Woodrow Wilson, and he's a hero to the whole world. You knew what Cyrus was like before you even started to use him."

"You said it right there: 'use him'. The punk thinks he is using us. You know, he never reports in at headquarters, never. We have to go to his hotel room, if we can ever catch him. He thinks he's running the show!"

"Sounds as if you are on the way up, Governor."

"MacQuarrie; when this is over you are through," Calder said, sitting down on the edge of the bed.

"You are a bit late; I was through when it started."

"Well, foul this one up and you are through; I'll have you black-balled clear across the country, so help me God."

MacQuarrie had heard the same threat a thousand times. And each time he had swallowed another glass of Calder's whiskey and wished for more than words from the tired and frightened man across from him. Political campaigns and politicians were fed with the stimulant of fear, which disguised itself in many devious ways as it whipped its victims on to exhaustion. After the shouting was over and the counting done, the adrenalin ceased to flow, the fever subsided and left the men older, less hopeful, less knowing and less sure of the issues to which they had been clutching. Even the victorious, as in war, paid a price they couldn't afford.

The whirl of the final days took over and Calder and Mac forgot their differences and the campaigning and concentrated their efforts on the ward workers preparing to get the voters to the polls. Cyrus showed signs of fatigue and spent more time in headquarters. This gave Calder a feeling of greater security as he took control of the workers and knew his instructions were being carried out. And Wart went back to blacksmithing. He had kept his bargain with MacQuarrie.

Telegraph keys tapped Morse-coded returns across the wires while Cyrus and Gloria paced the hotel corridors with MacQuarrie and Calder, and Walker County held its breath in anticipation of victory or defeat. The vote was heavy, especially in the outlying districts and took longer than usual to tabulate and report. The blackboard in Calder's room had lost its luster and now partially hid the ever-changing white figures in the swirls of grey left by many erasures.

Simpson was ahead, not by much, but he had led all the way. Hours added to hours and cheers and boasts turned to doubts and gave in to the ever-present fear of defeat, even when there was an occasional surge in Dodson's total making figures look vaguely promising.

In the end it was a faint win, and a galling loss. Four days later, when finally a wire of concession was sent by the incumbent Governor Simpson, and Cyrus P. Dodson, the dapper symbol of honesty, the unknowing champion of the farmers, was Governor Elect.

Cyrus was patently smug in his acceptance: "The people have spoken." MacQuarrie shook his head and reached for the bottle; even in knowing Dodson he had hoped for something more genuine if not original, it was not Dodson's victory, but Wart Kessel's. His gruff voice had turned the tide and given Cyrus his thin margin.

Gloria hugged the victor; then went to her room to primp. Instead she cried. It was the first time she had ever been so happy that she let tears fill her eyes.

Calder, the veteran, smiled as the deus ex machina. Experience counted in the end. He had picked the right man; right from the beginning when he spent that first night with Cyrus, he knew he'd make Dodson the next governor. He must send a wire to Bruce McHenry; they would need Mac when Calder ran for the U.S. Senate next year. And where Dodson was concerned, Calder knew it was wise to have your own man in the Statehouse when you moved to Washington.

Wart kissed Agatha and then pulled the covers down so they could spend the afternoon in bed. There would be no more hiding; they were man and wife and everything else was unimportant.

Cynthia gently placed the shawl around her mother's shoulders and fixed her a hot toddy to fight the chill while Alfreda and Peggy washed the noonday dishes and sang in the kitchen. Myrtle Dodson hoped Cyrus knew what he was doing. This might mean they would have to move to the capital, but she and Cyrus had never discussed it.

But the rest of Crescent was jubilant. They had won; things were going to be all right in the state and especially in Walker County. Everybody knew what big plans Cyrus P. Dodson had for Walker County.

Bruce McHenry marched the band up and down Elm Avenue for hours with the volunteer firemen acting as a guard of honor. His men had shown "them big city slickers" what it was to really put on a fighting campaign. Single-handed, Cyrus had taken the fight right into their midst and won. Now there would be some changes in the establishment. And most important of all, Crescent was on the map. They would have to erect a monument, next to the firehouse in Cyrus's honor and maybe make his house into a shrine when he moved into the Governor's Mansion.

Matt shoveled grain at Dodson's Feed Store and worried about his employer's fate. Governor Calder had deceived him and now Mr. Dodson was surrounded by crooks. Even worse, Mr. Dodson didn't know how dishonest they were or what they had already done to the people of other states. Matt wondered if his father was right, if Calder and his hoodlums would take over now that

Mr. Dodson had won, or if he would be strong enough to be an effective Governor.

The only thing that marred the day in Crescent was that a barn and a chicken coop had burned to the ground while Bruce sang and the band played Yankee Doodle and drove the new fire engine over to Flintsville to parade the victory in the face of Flintsville's upper class.

Clarence Calder called an afternoon meeting; which Cyrus refused to attend. "We have matters we've got to discuss," Calder said confidently. "I have a string of appointments that have to be made for offices that are going to be vacant after the first of the year. And I've got to outline the program for the bills we want for this coming legislature."

"I'll attend to all official matters when I return from Crescent," was Cyrus's curt answer.

"We have to get things settled today; we've made promises," Calder demanded.

"I haven't made any commitments and I haven't even taken office. So I'm leaving for home."

"Now wait a minute! Where's MacQuarrie, Willard? Where's that drunken bum?"

"Probably drunk, Governor, drunk in his room," Willard said.

"I've had my gut-full of that sloppy lush. I don't ever want to see him again. You tell him that; and this time it's final. Whenever you need him he wipes out drunk. But in the meantime, Cyrus, you're not going any place until I tell you. You be here at three-thirty."

"It's strange, Mr. Calder, but I was of the opinion that it was I who had been elected Governor," Cyrus said in his most controlled voice.

"That's just a figure of speech, Cyrus. You be here at three-thirty; on the dot."

But Cyrus would not be there for the meeting. Instead he walked to the Statehouse and toured the grounds and building. He checked the ornate clock in the rotunda with his own watch to verify its accuracy. It was five minutes slow. That would be corrected.

Though he had been in the building when he served in the State Legislature, it had had no personal relationship to him; it had been awesome but distant. Now it all related to Cyrus P. Dodson and he carefully examined each of the photographs, paintings and framed proclamations displayed on the drab walls of the many dimly lit corridors. A Statehouse should have more light on things; that would be changed.

Turning a corner, he was blocked momentarily by a group of clerks discussing the election, their faces worried by the events of the week, their voices pitched nervously high as they talked of change. He was recognized and a whisper whistled through them. The obstacle melted before him. Too much loitering; that would be changed.

At the door of the governor's office, Cyrus once more took his watch from his pocket: two-fifteen, exactly.

The two female clerks blushed and giggled as the governor's male secretary welcomed Cyrus. Their faces were painted. That, without fail, would be changed. In fact, a governor's office was no place for women at all.

"Governor Simpson is expecting you, Governor Dodson," the secretary said, opening the door to the inner office. "Governor Dodson to see you, Governor." The door closed behind him, leaving the victor and the vanquished to smile and lick their wounds.

"Won't you sit down?"

"Thank you."

The desk was cluttered with documents and a collection of mementoes ranging from Indian headdresses to inscribed, ornate, silver ashtrays and a stand holding more than a dozen of Simpson's prized pipes. Cyrus would have the desk more a symbol of efficiency than of sentimentality; yes, that, too, would change.

"Congratulations."

"Thank you."

"It is very considerate of you to visit so soon. I imagine you'll have a great many questions. We'll answer as many as we can."

"Mainly I really wanted to get acquainted and ask for your recommendations."

"You'll have our cooperation. I'll dictate a status report for you next week and ask each department to do the same."

"Thank you. Would you have them sent to my home in Crescent?"

"Of course. It's rather tiring, isn't it; the fight?"

"I can see you are a man of modest statements," Cyrus said with a smile.

"In defeat, it would be rather ridiculous to say otherwise," Governor Simpson said. "Would you have a glass of sherry with me?"

"Thank you."

From the oak credenza behind the desk, the Governor took a decanter of wine and two glasses and poured. Pushing one of the glasses across the desk between the photographs and stacks of papers, he smiled for the first time.

"You are amazing; you ran your campaign so cleverly that we didn't know what you were doing, until it was too late. You must be a very serious scholar of military tactics. We knew how Calder's machine would operate; we'd beaten them once before. In fact we had counted on Senator Felt as their pawn. We would have torn him to shreds."

They sipped their wine and the Governor lighted a pipe.

"I've never met Senator Felt," Cyrus said.

"A very sad story. David is a very fine man in some ways. It's unfortunate that in public life, even the privacy of our bedrooms is not sacred. In fact it seems to create an enticing target."

"Was he careless?"

"Now you are the one to make modest statements. No, it was unbelievable, almost as if senility had taken over prematurely."

"I dread seeing men on their way down," Cyrus said as he watched the wine swirl in his glass.

"Thank you," the Governor said. "In victory, you can be discrete if not generous."

"I'm sorry; I didn't mean..."

"Lord, I know that; but I couldn't pass it by. Again, on your strategy: brilliant! When you moved to the urban districts, we likened you to Quixote. We laughed, we thought you had abandoned the grain fields as a place of battle and were going to fight us on our own ground. We had you licked; until we woke up and found that we had been ambushed by your second front." The Governor lifted his glass, "A toast to your brilliance, Cyrus Dodson. We had lightly touched the farms, just as you did, in the beginning; we had no idea you would send in reserves with entirely different weapons. "My people tell me it's the first time the rural vote has exceeded the city vote for any one candidate in this state. Two separate campaigns, but unified under one general; what a plan."

"Thank you."

"Thank you for the lesson. Those reports will be in the mail next week."

After the Governor introduced Cyrus to the various department heads and the Secretary of State, they agreed on a time for a second meeting and parted with a handshake that was firm and long in duration. For a moment, Cyrus was almost sorry that Simpson was no longer governor.

On his way down the front steps, Cyrus picked up a crumpled newspaper and noticed how unsightly the marble pillars were where people had written dirty sayings and war slogans. Laxity was a disease; that, too, would soon change.

He walked back to the hotel and dictated a short letter to Calder explaining his plan to return to Crescent for a rest and business and that any correspondence should be forwarded to him there. Other than that, he didn't want to be disturbed. Then he had the desk clerk make reservations for two at the Parisian Gardens restaurant for that evening.

Gloria was quieter than usual, but she laughed and placed the white carnation in his lapel. "Told you that you could wear one of these every day, didn't I? And now you can."

She held his arm tightly going down in the elevator, but became almost distant while they walked through the lobby to their automobile. She came alive, however, and her eyes sparkled as the maitre d' acted out his part: "A great honor, Governor," he said, bowing deeper than necessary, but without the expected imitation French accent. Gloria was less impish and more respectful than usual.

They danced, they drank, they talked, in their private dining room, both aware of the difference that had taken place; they were both saddened that they were not able to recapture the mood of their first night there.

Cyrus was disturbed by the insolence of Calder, and Gloria kept visualizing the scene that would occur when Cyrus heard the news of Agatha's marriage. It had been her first venture into deceit where he was concerned, and though justified, her dishonesty gnawed inside her. The elation of Agatha's happiness had thrilled her into almost intoxication; it was funny, and clever, and humane the way she and MacQuarrie had worked together to help the lovers Cyrus had been robbed of his parental warrant and, when he learned of his sudden loss, would be wounded deeply. He could not stand surprises on his one source of insecurity.

"More champagne, Mamselle?"

"Merci," she said in exaggerated jest. They laughed quietly together.

"That could mean 'non' as well as 'oui'," he said.

"I'll buy a better dictionary."

When the waiter left, she patted Cyrus's hand; he smiled across the table and offered to dance, but she declined and he eased back in the red plush chair and puffed on his cigar.

Calder really believed that he was going to give the instructions on how to run the government. Perhaps Calder was merely provoked by the strain of the election and had lost sight of the situation as it was in fact. Whichever, their relationship would be changed. There would be no question about it in the future and there definitely would be a show of respect; or Clarence Calder would be banned from the governor's office, in fact from all of the Statehouse.

Chapter 15

Though Crescent had been riotous with celebrations throughout the day, Mitzie could stand the silence around her no longer. She whistled a soft, womanly monotone as she dusted the windowsills, stopping once to give a profane curse as she pricked herself with a sharp splinter from the cracked paint. She must have Matt, she must. This thought disturbed her. Usually when this happened, it came only as an undefined unrest, but today the reason itself was foremost in her mind. She must have Matt. Before, she could always at least go downstairs and talk to Wart until a calm settled down upon her as tiredness. Then she would sleep. Today there would be no Wart with his hairy chest to listen to while he discussed his reasons for living, or why Agatha was the most important woman in the world, or why Cyrus was the biggest ass in the whole of the mid-west. Wart and Agatha were together.

The dusting ceased. The whistling stopped. She must talk to someone. The stairs creaked under her weight as she descended toward the cool air outside. Revered Pritchard was briskly sweeping the wooden sidewalk in front of the chapel. He might be the answer to her loneliness. He might talk to her. She stood watching him sweep, his wrinkled black frock much in need of cleaning. He was an ugly man, his mouth filled with a maze of unevenness; widely spaced yellowed tusks for teeth.

"Good evening, Reverend."

"'Tis a mighty fine evening, Miss Kawalski." The Reverend had turned back to his task, terminating the brief exchange.

"I need to I talk to you, Reverend," she countered, suddenly aware of the coyness with which she had charged her voice.

The broom's straws ceased their noise of scratching and the little whirlpool of dust settled itself on the walk.

Mitzie found herself brushing past the man in black. Her own hand was the first to reach the knob, and she could hear his uneven breath as he followed close behind her.

It was even more silent in the chapel than in the apartment. The Reverend, despite all his past eloquent sermons, said nothing, just stared at her. She felt a sudden dryness in her throat. He closed the door and turned back to her. They faced one another for long awkward minutes without words.

She took a deep breath, "Uh, Reverend, I wanted to talk to you."

"Talk, Miss Kowalski? From my observations, it's more than talk you do," he said taking her hand.

She stepped back and he dropped her hand.

He smiled, "Don't be afraid. What I see and hear I cherish and keep for myself. I've watched you and I've watched Matthew Harwood and I know what you have been doing." He grabbed for her wrist, "Don't be afraid; we can talk." She pulled away from him, but his other hand was more accurate and she felt herself thrown in a circular swirl of motion and then pushed with a bruising crash against one of the pews.

"I know people, Miss Kowalski; someday, I knew we'd talk," he said as he pushed his lips toward hers. She turned her cheek but he pulled her face around full and kissed her. Mitzie mustered all of her strength and shoved him away; then ran down between the pews to the other aisle. He started to follow her then stopped and watched her like a cat.

"God damn you, you son of a bitch, you son of a bitch," she panted as she straightened her clothes.

Reverend Pritchard smiled. "A whore should be careful what she says; the citizens of Crescent are very particular."

"You leave me alone," she said, regaining her calm. She took a deep breath and backed slowly down the aisle opposite him, pew by pew toward the door. He didn't stop her or move toward her. When she was outside she ran back to the blacksmith shop.

Mitzie was embarrassed when she barged into Wart and Agatha's room without knocking. She was sick to her stomach and felt intensely lonely and outside of their world. They, too, were awkward until Agatha giggled and then they covered themselves with a blanket.

"Just going to the icebox."

"That's fine," Agatha said "We'll have a cup of tea, later."

"We can celebrate for my father-in-law," Wart laughed.

"I'll come down then."

"Be sure," Wart said. "We'll expect you."

She needed Matt now more than ever. For the first time since she had arrived in Crescent she felt completely alone. Wart and Agatha would want the space over the shop for themselves now that they were living together. She would have to find another room. Without going upstairs for a sweater, she walked through the field to the granary and knocked on the side door.

Matt let her in.

"What do you think of it?" he asked. "It's hard to believe isn't it?"

"What?"

"Mr. Dodson; Governor Dodson. What else is there that's news?"

"It's fine and I'm glad he's Governor."

"Boy, oh boy; are there going to be changes made!"

"You think so? Wart says they are all alike."

"Wart is just being bitter. It's the popular thing to do."

"I wonder."

"You wonder? You know how Wart is when it comes to Mr. Dodson; he just doesn't like him. But you wait and see; Mr. Dodson will clean that mess up. Calder and the whole dammed bunch."

"I don't follow you. Governor Calder and Wart Kessel just helped elect Mr. Dodson Governor. You seem to think everybody is against everybody."

"You don't know what life's all about, Mitzie; you don' t. How could you, someone who's afraid to read newspaper? And don't think that Calder or Wart or anyone else won the election for Mr. Dodson. It was because he had the reputation and the character to give the voters what they wanted in a governor. He did it himself and that's all."

"Matt, I don't want to argue with you; I don't know anything about politics."

"You bet you don't."

"I want to love you. I do love you, Matt. And I want you to love me," she said pushing close to him.

"Mitz, not here. I just can't take the chance."

"Who would know? You could lock the door."

"Don't be silly."

"Well, you could if you wanted."

"Somebody would see you leave; somebody would find out."

"We've done it before," Mitzie said, kissing his cheek.

He pulled away. "Not for a long time."

"I know; but I need you, Matt. Don't you understand that? I need you terribly. Please, Matt, now. Just kiss me, or hold me, Matt. Please."

Matt's arm's held her cautiously and his kiss was only partially there.

"Things are different, Mitz, now that Mr. Dodson is Governor. I can't take the chance."

She cuddled closer to him, as they stood there and she kissed him once more. "I understand that. Don't you know I understand? Tonight then; after supper I'll take a bath and wait for you, then."

"All right; I'll see about it after supper."

She gave him another kiss. "I feel better already."

When she reached the door he called to her. "Mitzie:

about tonight. I won't be there. You'd better get someone else. Things are changed and I can't take the chance. I'm sorry."

She stood there for a minute or two, but she didn't look back at him. She bit her lip to keep it from quivering. Her breath was gone and she felt completely empty, drained of strength. "I love you," she said so softly the words barely left her lips. Mitzie closed the door quietly behind her and walked back to her room. She dragged her suitcases from under the bed and packed her clothes and her dictionary and other books into them. At the desk she put her only completed poem for Matt in an envelope and addressed it to him. It wasn't appropriate and he wouldn't understand it, but it was for him:

> "A touch of Velvet"
> crimsoned
> in its luxurious
> regal plush
> and yet...
> close your eyes
> and the wild
> erratic
> excitement
> of a million
> muted candle flames
> electrified the earth.
> famished they lick
> the icing from the night
> with one
> subtle,
> pliant kiss."

Matt had said he was sorry. She was sorry, too; sorry that only she could feel the velvet.

Her note to Wart and Agatha was more successful: "Have the wanderlust again and have borrowed a horse and the surrey. I'll leave them at the livery stable in Flintsville. Please tell Mr. Schmidt that I have left and wish him the best of luck. I think he kept me on just to be sweet. Thank you all for your kindnesses and love. Love Mitzie. P.S. Please give Matthew the enclosed envelope."

Mitzie placed the letter on her bed and left the door to the room open, then very slowly walked down the stairs, careful not to disturb the Kessels.

The horse whinnied as she put the suitcases up behind the front seat, but she calmed him with a scratch behind the ears and then got into the surrey herself. Riding towards Flintsville she pondered where she would go; perhaps to Chicago. She had heard many things about Chicago. It was big and one could get lost there.

Mitzie arrived in Flintsville late that night. The next morning news came that the war in France had come to an end. The fighting had stopped. November 7th, 1918 would long be remembered, as the world would now know peace. Flintsville was wild with jubilation and the church bells rang most of the day. The boys would be coming home and there would be no more killing.

The morning after, though, gloom descended again; the report was incorrect and the fighting continued. Mitzie felt empty. She missed Matt, but she would never look back. Next time she wouldn't fall in love; next time she would choose an older man who could make up his mind. No, that wasn't it; Matt had made up his mind too fast. He hadn't given her a chance to make him fall in love with her, hadn't given her time to show him how much she loved him. She was alone and when you are alone you never have to look back unless you are afraid. Mitzie wasn't afraid; she was just lonely.

Chapter 16

Sticky with jam and infested with breadcrumbs, the cracked red and white oilcloth on the table in Josh Ferguson's kitchen was piled high with dirty dishes and the remains of the interrupted evening meal. On the drain board by the sink was Friday's mail: a seed catalogue, an un-opened letter and the weekly copy of the Walker County Journal with its news as left over as the food on Josh's table.

"Farm Vote Elects Dodson." Dr. Phillips glanced at the headline as he picked up a chair, which had been up-ended and blocked his way across the dirty green and yellow linoleum-covered floor.

"Bethie, your father will be here in a few minutes. He's following me back from town in his wagon," he said to the ten-year old girl who stood cowering in the corner.

The doctor turned his head instinctively and listened for a moment, then plunked his bag down on top of the newspaper and added, "Better go in and change David while I look after your mom."

The row of small faces that looked up at him as he went down the hallway was familiar to him. All except one he had seen before anyone else had. It was sometimes a wonder to him, how everyone of them matched a name he could recall by the ailments each had had in their brief lives.

Mildred was frightened as usual and had torn the muslin sheet in her terror. She was sobbing softly in between pains.

"Now, Millie, we've been through this lots of times before," he said patting her hand. "The pains---how often?"

"Don't know," she whimpered.

He pulled back the heavy quilt. She was still in her flowered print housedress. Its color, and Mildred's, was faded and forlorn. She had been so attractive and laughing when she was a child and especially when she was in high school, living in town with her folks, next door to his house. Now he only saw her on occasions when she was crying

Suddenly she clawed at his hand and dug her nails deep into his skin. She gasped and then put her other hand over her mouth.

"Let it out, Millie; scream if you want. Go on, yell for all you're worth. No one to hear you but me and the kiddies."

He looked around when he heard a noise. Bethie was leaning against the door frame watching her mother's agony. She had David's diaper changed and was cradling the baby on her hip.

"Bethie, let Martha or Michael hold David then come in and help me get your mom changed into her nightclothes. And close the door."

He placed his hands on Mildred's hard, extended stomach and gently felt for the baby's position.

He had asked Josh to send her to the clinic for checkups when he heard from her mother that Mildred's milk had dried up and she was pregnant again. He had seen Mildred once at the Emporium buying yardage and had told her it was important.

"Joshua doesn't believe in doctors; you know how he is, Doctor Phillips. He doesn't want no man to touch me, not even a doctor."

He had treated Josh since Josh was six years old and his mother brought him into town on their buckboard after he had been kicked in the head by the family plow horse. Josh's father didn't believe in doctors and neither did Josh, unless he was sick or was afraid one of his children was going to die or Millie had started labor and panic closed in on him.

He wasn't sure, but the baby didn't feel as if it were in a normal position.

Mildred was studying his face. "I'm afraid," she said, the tears streaming down her face.

"Millie, every time you're afraid; just as any other woman would be. But there's no reason. You just mind your work and I'll do mine and in no time Josh will have another mouth to feed. You have a name picked out?"

Millie didn't answer, she was crying so hard.

"Bethie, you watch your mom a minute while I wash my hands."

"Doctor Phillips, is it going to be a boy?"

"Can't say, Beth; that will be a surprise. I suspect sometimes that's why people keep having babies: just to find out what they'll turn out to be when they're born."

There was half a kettle of water on the stove in the kitchen. He put a large lump of coal in the stove, shook the grate and placed another bucket and a dishpan full on to heat. No water tank in the place. After hanging his coat over the back of a chair, he rolled up his sleeves and put some boiling water in a wash basin, then rummaged around in his bag for the bottle of Lysol he always brought along when he visited Josh's place. He poured some of the strong disinfectant into the water, took a bar of soap and scrubbed his hands, then emptied the basin into the sink.

Another basin of medicinal smelling water he took into Mildred's bedroom along with his bag.

"Come on, Bethie; we best get your mom undressed and ready."

Together, in spite of the hindrance of Millie's dead weight, they slipped her out of her dress and underclothes.

Millie's pink flannel bloomers had spotting on them, the doctor noticed as he pulled them down her legs and threw them in a crumpled heap in the corner. He looked momentarily up at her pale, almost grayed face. She must be very anemic. He wondered how much she had been bleeding. Millie's once azure blue eyes tearfully looked down at him with apprehension.

He patted her legs as if to say "I won't hurt you, Millie."

But Bethie didn't Move; she just stood there, her mouth half open as if to cry, her eyes spread wide. The doctor looked at her in bewilderment, then ran around the bed. Millie had her fingernails dug into Bethie's arm. He took Millie's hand and slowly pulled it away.

"That's a girl; nothing to be afraid of, relax. Nightgown, Beth."

"Here it is," Beth said, pulling a gown from under some clothes on the chair at the end of the bed.

"Get a clean one," he said as he slipped a towel under Millie's buttocks, spread her thighs apart, and started to wash her stomach and legs. There were times when husbands should help deliver children, he thought, and this was one of them.

They got her nightgown on and laid Millie back on the pillow just as she started another pain and tried to grab Beth's arm again. The Doctor interceded and guided Millie's hand to the brass bedstead.

"Now, Millie, squeeze as hard as you like," he said and she shrieked once and then settled down to a dull moan.

"My mom going to die?" Bethie asked, looking up at him.

"No, Beth, and don't you worry about it," he said as he slid his glasses back up onto the bridge of his nose. "And now that we've got her dressed and bathed, you go out to the kitchen and put some coffee on the stove. When your father comes in tell him to get some more coal and water."

"I can't; he won't. Those are Mamma's chores."

"Bethie, tonight, just tonight, I think maybe your father will do them for her; you tell him I said so."

She seemed reassured and went out to the kitchen. Mildred's pulse was fast but weak and her blood pressure dangerously low. He could feel his own pulse speed up as he realized Millie was probably not strong enough to help much in the delivery.

He examined her cervix again. She had only dilated about a quarter enough. Then he probed internally and found the baby was in the breech position, as he had suspected. His stethoscope did not give any sound of the baby's pulse. Perhaps it was merely weak, too.

He listened again more closely; but all he could hear was his own pounding heart.

"Has it been kicking much, Millie?"

"A little," she whispered.

"That's the way we like it," he reassured; "Now, you try to sleep. Don't wear yourself out because we're not quite ready to go to work. Just doze off and try not to fight it for a while."

The cold, soapy water swished back and forth in the basin as he carried to the kitchen door and emptied it into the back yard. Yes, the dignity of being a doctor was sometimes overpowering, he thought. Dumping his instruments into the basin after he had rinsed it again with boiling water, he sent Beth for her mother's rubbing alcohol and poured part of it over them.

"Where's that father of yours? He shouldn't have been more than ten minutes behind me," he said as he poured a cup of Beth's weak coffee.

"Want some milk for your coffee?" she asked. "There's some out in the cooler."

"Might make me feel more at home, Bethie; better for my touchy stomach."

"I remembered when Michael and Adam had measles, how you like milk. Mom don't use milk. You want something to eat?"

"No thank you, Beth. We'd better get on with your Mom."

Beth went to get the milk, and as she did he saw that she had brought in some coal and two buckets of water and placed them by the stove.

He poured the milk into the already pale coffee.

"You know, Bethie, I think I'll have Mrs. Everett come out tomorrow and help you with the housework. She won't mind; she always liked your mom when she was small. Now, maybe best if you put the kiddies to bed; I'll go sit with Millie."

From the cupboard in the hall he took a stack of towels and carried them back to the bedroom.

"It moved, Doctor, it moved."

"Did it move, Mom?" Beth asked.

"Kids to bed first, Beth," the doctor said shaking his finger playfully.

"Yes, a minute ago, it kicked right here."

"Just what we're waiting for. And the pains?"

"Maybe harder."

He pulled the covers back and examined her again: she was still dilating; but there were more spots of blood on the towel which he didn't like. Her knee hit him in the chest when she reacted to the next pain, and her scream brought Beth back to the room.

She stood watching her mother calmly, almost objectively, until Mildred's body had ceased its spasm and had eased back into the softness of the feather mattress. Then she left to finish her task.

"'Almost halfway there," he said with a smile, but he was wrong. Though the pains continued, the dilation stopped and in the next two hours Millie didn't hold the bedstead as tightly or scream as loudly. Finally her water broke and he and Beth had just started cleaning her up again after changing the bed, when he heard Josh's heavy footsteps on the back stoop.

"What did we get this time?" Josh asked from the kitchen.

Neither of them bothered to answer him. Beth closed the bedroom door and they went on bathing her mother.

"Doctor..." Millie whispered.

He could not understand what she was trying to say and put his head down next to hers.

"Don't want Bethie to know, but I think it's dead." Her lip quivered and she held his hand limply.

"No, just the water, that's all," he assured her.

"Mom, you must had ten gallons in ya." Beth giggled.

"Now, Bethie, that's an awful lot," Mildred said in a soft voice and smiled.

"For such a small young lady she tells some pretty tall stories." The doctor patted Beth's head. "Now, go see that your father is all right."

When she had left Mildred spoke in a weak but clear voice.

"It's not alive, Doctor; I can tell."

"We'll see," he said with not quite as much confidence in his voice as before; and for a long time he listened intently to her stomach. As before there was no pulse from the infant. Even Millie's heartbeat seemed weaker; but then, he was tired. He was probably imagining things, but Mildred's sudden acceptance of the possibility of the worst upset him. His stomach growled; it was sour and protesting the lack of food since morning.

He watched her. She seemed to be sleeping. Only time would tell. Not a thing they could do but wait. Removing his glasses, he sighed and rubbed his eyes, then folded the glasses and put them in his vest pocket.

Josh looked up from the newspaper.

"Where in hell did you go?" the doctor asked.

"Saw you was here by yer car so I finished my evenin' chores."

"Could have used you here."

"Knew everything was goin' all right; besides, had six of Anderson's cows to milk. Curley's over to that big Grange meetin' in Flintsville for couple of days. How's Mildred?"

"Have any bicarb of soda in the cupboard?" he asked Josh.

"Don't know; have to ask the cook," Josh answered.

"We've got some," Beth interrupted, "on the second from top shelf. I'll get it."

"Thank you, Bethie; you are going to make a darn good woman when you grow up. And that won't be long. It doesn't seem very long ago your mom was your age and would crawl under the back fence to visit our house to have some of Mrs. Everett's cookies or hot bread."

"Mom bakes bread."

"Won a blue ribbon at the fair four years ago," Josh added; "knows how to cook a spread when she's in the mood."

"Bethie, you take a cold washcloth and a towel and keep your Mom comfortable," Doctor Phillips said, sitting down across the dirty table from Josh, who had gone back to reading the Journal.

"Should I bath her all over again?"

"Just her forehead. I'll be back in a couple of minutes."

Bethie was gone and only the noisy alarm clock sitting on the windowsill broke the stillness.

"Cyrus Dodson sure showed 'em a thing or two about elections, didn't he," Josh finally said as he turned the page. "People in the city don't know what to think of a farmer takin' over the Statehouse, I'll bet."

"Josh, will you stop reading that damn paper. Millie is in trouble. She may lose her baby."

Josh lowered his newspaper and leaned forward with his elbows on the table. "Then why in hell aren't you in there with her helpin'?"

"Nothing we can do but wait, just now. Her baby will come when it's ready. If it makes it."

"Wait? What do you mean: wait? Jesus Christ, man, if that ain't just like a stupid doctor to say something like that. Get in and help and stop saying 'her baby'."

Lord knows it's as much mine as hers. Get in and help it," Josh shouted as he stood up and pounded the table with his fist.

The doctor watched the dishes shake on the disturbed table; their rattle and ringing making a welcome change from the hushed mood which had preceded the outburst When the racket had subsided he looked up slowly.

Josh was standing; his legs apart, his strong jaw jutted forward, his deep set dark eyes hidden under their bushy brows, his huge hands clenched into hard, desperate fists. He moved as if to strike the table again.

"Joshua, sit down," the doctor said quietly. Josh looked at him with a surprised, almost wounded expression.

"You're a fake," he said and sat down., "you're a no good fake."

"Joshua, Millie's in poor health. I told you last time that she shouldn't have any more children for a couple of years. She needed a rest. And I told you to bring her to the office for a checkup. But you didn't."

"You are a God-damn fake. That's my kid in there in trouble and you sit here doin' nothin' but givin' lectures. No wonder people don't have no damn trust in doctors."

"Millie needed a rest."

"God, other women have children; all the time. What's so damn special? Millie even had one all by herself. Only time we have trouble is when we have a stupid doctor."

"Joshua," the doctor said in a loud voice, "shut up, Millie thinks the baby's dead."

"Mom's crying." It was Beth. Doctor Phillips looked around, wondering how long she had been standing in the doorway.

"She's getting harder pains."

"How in hell does she know it's dead?" Josh demanded. Beth looked into her father's face for a moment, then turned and disappeared down the hallway.

Josh sat with a vacant stare on his face as he realized what he had done; then put his head down on the table.

"Now, you listen, you son of a bitch," the doctor finally said, "because I'm just about through talking. You may not believe in doctors, but you wouldn't be here 'today if I hadn't saved your life twenty-three years ago. Your mother believed in doctors and if she hadn't I wouldn't have to be listening to you blabber like a five year old. And Millie wouldn't be in there in danger of losing her life. Have you got that, Josh? You understand what I mean?"

Josh didn't answer.

"Now there is nothing unusual about a woman having child, Josh. God knows you've got six fine ones. And most times there's no trouble. It's the most natural thing in life. But it takes lots of healthy blood to build a strong child and strength to deliver it. And right now, Millie has neither. If she gets through this, you promise me you'll leave her alone for a couple of years."

"That's none of your damn business," Josh said suddenly, then looked into the doctor's eyes and lowered his head again. "None of your damn business."

Millie had her pains for another three hours; but the cervix slowly closed to near normal. There had been no further movement inside of her, there was increased spotting on the towels, and still no sound of life.

The Election

Beth sat at her mother's side, asleep, still holding the damp cloth on Mildred's brow.

"Knew it was dead," Mildred said calmly. "Just knew it was; knew it was going to happen for months now... strangest feeling."

The doctor lifted his head up from his momentary dozing. He patted her foot. "You sleep now, Millie; sleep as sound as you can."

She lay back against the pillow for a few minutes; then with a scream she started to push down and hard as she could with her muscles, thrashing about in the bed. Immediately the doctor was by her side, feeling her stomach. He checked her cervix. There was no dilation and she was near convulsions.

"Millie, for God's sake, Millie, relax, relax," he said. "Bethie, get my bag quickly."

Beth ran toward the kitchen and he tried to hold Millie's arms down by her side, but she flailed them about and screamed, not seeming to know what she was doing. She writhed herself nearly out of the bed.

Beth brought his bag and he quickly filled a syringe with morphine and tried to hold Millie's arm steady. It was no use: he couldn't hold her still.

"Get your father."

"Father, Father, come; Doctor needs you," she yelled and tried to help hold her down.

Josh was there in seconds and held Millie's arms to her side while the doctor gave her the injection. She fought for a few minutes; then the intensity subsided and she fell asleep.

Josh kissed her hand and started to cry; then got up and left the room wiping his eyes with his shirtsleeve.

Doctor Phillips placed his hand over his own mouth to slow the pace of his breathing down. Millie was right, the baby was dead; now he must give Mildred her chance. The morphine would let her sleep and later labor would start to help her discharge the fetus. She must rest and get some strength.

Beth had gone into the other bedroom; when she came back she brought her own rag doll and put it in her sleeping mother's arms. Then she washed her mother's forehead once more with the cold cloth and dried her with the towel.

Doctor Phillips waited for his examination, until Beth was through. Mildred's pulse was still weakening. Then he pulled the covers down again and there was a small pool of bright red blood on the towel. He felt dizzy and wanted to vomit. The room was very hot and stuffy, and there didn't seem to be enough air to breath. He looked at Mildred's graduation picture on the dresser, then at her, quietly sleeping with Beth's doll in her arms; and then at Beth. He took a deep breath and slipped his glasses back in place. The pool's perimeter spread, slowly out-ward. He was helpless: the afterbirth must have parted from the womb and Mildred was hemorrhaging inside.

Beth was watching him; without emotion she looked into his tired eyes and deeply lined face.

"Bethie," maybe you'd better go out in the other room."

"No, I'll stay, unless you want another cup of coffee," she said, adding "or somethin' to eat."

He didn't urge her; just shook his head.

"Mamma, too?" she asked, as she patted her mother's head.

Again he didn't answer; but stood there without expression.

"You want me to tell Father?" she asked quietly.

"No, Bethie, I'll do it," he said and started toward the kitchen. The difference between the sexes was something he would never understand.

"She'd better not, you butcher, she'd just better not," Josh said as he put his head on his arms and leaned on the table.

"Josh, Millie is hemorrhaging, inside. There is no way to stop it. No do you want to go in and be with her? She's asleep, but I think she'll know you are there."

"No, I'll stay here," he said sitting up straight for a second. I can't go in there; but she'd better not die." He put his head down again.

The doctor watched him for a moment and then turned to the bedroom. Children were conceived in bedrooms; but bedrooms were no place for birth. He was exhausted. Why did it ever have to be this way? When would they find some way to save them? When would he be able to get the people themselves to do what he told them?

Millie continued to get weaker. She stirred once in a while, but never woke from her sleep. Finally at three-twenty she gave a faint gasp and there was a stifling silence in the room. The doctor felt for her pulse; there was none. Beth looked at her mother then at him, then put her arms around him and clung tightly. He caressed Beth's head gently and pulled the blanket up over Mildred's once pretty face.

The lamp sputtered as he turned the wick down to flicker out; then he picked up his bag, took Beth by the hand and closed the door.

Beth, still dry-eyed, followed him into the kitchen.

"Josh, I'm sorry; but it's over," the doctor said.

Josh was sobbing softly, but did not lift his head. The doctor's hand rested on Josh's back. "Just nothing anybody can do when this happens. It leaves us helpless. I'll make arrangements when I get back to town."

"Coffee?" Beth asked in a flat little voice.

"No, Bethie; I must go now. I'll stop by the Anderson's and have her come over; then Mrs. Everett or your grandmother will be out to look after things tomorrow. Thank you for helping, Bethie. You'll be a wonderful woman. You go to bed now and try to sleep."

Hunched over in the cold darkness, cranking his stubborn car, Doctor Phillips could see her still standing in the open doorway looking out into the black farmyard.

When he drove up to the Anderson's, the dogs barked and snarled until an upstairs window lit up and Willa Anderson stuck her head out and yelled at them to be quiet.

"Who is it?" she asked.

"Karl Phillips. Need you to go to the Fergusons. Mildred and the baby; lost them both."

"Poor Mildred; but it doesn't surprise me. Be right down, Doctor," she said closing the window.

The next thing he knew, Willa was standing by the car in her bathrobe.

"I'll tell the girls and we'll take the wagon right on over."

"Maybe you'd better ride over with me."

"That's not necessary, Doctor Phillips. You go home; probably have people lined up in your front room now waiting to see you. How did Joshua take it?"

"As you'd expect, Willa," he answered heavily.

"They've been such good neighbors," she said and started toward the barn.

Doctor Phillips leaned back against the stiff seat; he was almost asleep. He shook his head and sat up straight again, yawned and stretched. Maybe a drink of whiskey would help. What was he going to say to Mildred's mother?

Leaving the engine running, he got out of the car and unlocked the toolbox on the running board. There in one end, wrapped in cotton was a pint he kept for emergencies. He pulled the cork and put the bottle to his lips. It burned all the way down. He started to put it back in the box; then he changed his mind; might need another one before he got back the thirty-odd miles to Crescent. He locked the toolbox and got back into the car, placing the bottle on the seat next to him.

Exhausted both physically and emotionally, he had never felt as drained as he did right then: empty, useless, without purpose. It seemed as if he could hardly lift his arms or move his legs, they were so tired. He rested for a few moments in the car without turning the motor off, then took another long drink and started down the road toward home.

The funeral was on Wednesday attended by what seemed to be most of Walker County's dignitaries and everyone in Crescent and its surrounding farms.

The obituary in the Journal was most generous in its praises of the "life now ended" and the goals it had "epitomized"; however, a news article on page one had hinted in couched terms that the "demon rum" might have caused another accident and taken another life. They had pulled Doctor Phillips' car from the barrow pit where they had found it upside down.

Chapter 17

Monday, November the eleventh, caused the nation and Cyrus Dodson to take a second breath and start celebrating again; the armistice had officially been declared and the war was actually over. It pushed the news of the Dodson victory off the front page; in fact out of the first section of the Statesman. But even Cyrus was too excited to notice the slight bruise to his official pride.

He and Gloria mingled with the crowds on Capitol Boulevard, waving flags and singing victory songs. Then they went to the Parisian Gardens for a bottle of champagne.

"We'll ask the legislature to ratify the Eighteenth Amendment as their first act," Cyrus said, "Calder wants us to get on the band wagon before there are enough states to make it law. That will make it illegal to toast one another with champagne a year from now."

"We'll be hypocrites and drink at home," Gloria laughed, waving her flag in the face of the waiter and kissing him on the cheek as he filled her glass.

"It won't be available," Cyrus said.

"Father, anything people want will be available. And we will have champagne and brandy even it it's against the law and we have to smuggle it in from wherever it comes from."

It was too crowded to dance; but then it wasn't a night to he romantic so they shouted and sang until they were hoarse and tired, then they went back to the hotel and fell asleep.

Cyrus returned to Crescent in time to give the eulogy at Doctor Phillips' funeral.

It was hard for him to believe that the friend he had looked up to for so long was gone. He and Wendell Phillips had worked hard. to make Crescent grow, to bring the town up out of the cow pasture. They had planned to complete the installation of the remainder of the electric streetlights down Elm and along Main and build a new wing, with eight more beds, for the hospital. When the war ended such projects could go ahead.

Cyrus and Dr. Phillips' difference of opinion was on the subject of people. Wendell associated with too many who were beneath him; his constant boast to Cyrus was: "People are all I have in life." And Cyrus could remember clearly the time Wendell Phillips had laughed at him: "Morals, religion and business have nothing to do with birth, sex or death, Cyrus. They are just irritants that are not part of life; they're particles of sand under an oyster's shell. What they create may be attractive to some, but to most are useless and dead. In fact, Cyrus, sometimes your thinking likens you unto a pearl." Cyrus had laughed at Wendell's joke. Though it had been a joke, he had remembered it clearly; but he was certain old Doctor Wendell Phillips had better sense than to believe half of his own rhetorical statements.

The service was effective; not too long, and he was pleased with his remarks. Doctor Phillips' common touch, however, followed him to the grave; Cyrus had noticed that Wart Kessel and two of Crescent's less successful farmers among the pallbearers.

On the morning after the funeral, he had gone to the feed store and talked with Matthew about the business and thanked him for the fine job he had done in his absence.

"I'm going to hire a bookkeeper for the front office, Matthew. That will put you in charge of the entire warehouse, and of course the mail deliveries."

"Thank you, Mr. Dodson."

"More than that; there will be a dollar a week raise, effective the first of next month."

"Gee, thanks," Matt said with excitement.

"You see, boy, as I told you when you started, with hard work you can go where you want to go in this world. And you have the kind of start most young men never achieve until they are in their late twenties."

As Cyrus started to leave, Matt stopped him. "Mr. Dodson, do you trust Governor Calder?"

"Why of course, Matthew; why do you ask?"

"My father thinks he's a crook."

"Matthew, be careful of what you say. Those are slanderous words; every man is responsible not to destroy the character of another man."

"Father says he robbed lots of people over in Springville in a stock fraud. Father has clippings and everything."

"That's only hearsay, I'd wager, Matthew; all men in public life have to put up with such talk. I'd recommend you not worry about it. If there were anything wrong with Governor Calder, I certainly wouldn't be associated with him, would I?"

"I guess not; but I was worried."

"Well, don't be; and don't stoop to saying bad things about other people. Make it a rule: that if you can't say something good about a man, don't say anything."

Cyrus was please with the boy's concern. He would see to it that Matthew progressed, as he should, within the limits of his capabilities.

After that he walked back home thinking about what Matthew had said. It was interesting, if only gossip. He felt restless when he was at the feed store. For some reason, it was no longer important. But, of course, himself, his listlessness resulted not from overwork, but from confusion. Things at the house had become very disorganized in his absence; there was no routine. He had come home for a rest, but there were too many visitors. Bruce McHenry practically lived in his study. He didn't want to offend Bruce, but it was very inconvenient; there was never time to think or be alone.

Suddenly to his surprise, there was a calm when he opened the front door. Bruce was gone; he would not have to listen or talk. Myrtle was in her room resting; he would not have to argue. The girls were in the kitchen going about their tasks; order was returning to its rightful place.

He closed the door to his study, leaned back in his chair, and let the lids of his eyes slowly shut tight. Whether he wanted to admit it or not, he was exhausted. He should use the time to organize his thinking; but he didn't. Soon he was sound asleep, dreaming of the election and Calder and the Statehouse. Cyrus was even snoring when Cynthia woke him to say there was someone to see him. He sat up with a start and cleared his throat. It was Wart Kessel.

"Sit down, Wart, sit down."

"Thank you, Mr. Dodson. Or shall I call you 'Governor'?" Wart said looking around the room uneasily.

"No, I don't believe it's necessary," Cyrus said with a faint smile on his stern face.

Wart sat on the edge of a chair, his hands on his knees.

"What can I do for you, Wart?"

It was the first time Cyrus had seen Wart in a suit.

Wart took a deep breath. "Thought I should come over and congratulate you on the results of the election."

"I accept; but according to Mr. MacQuarrie, I should be congratulating you on all of the speeches you made out on the farms. It gave me time to work on the city vote," Cyrus said stiffly, then smiled. "Would you have a glass of wine with me?" he asked in a tone somewhat lacking in sincerity.

Wart cleared his throat. "I'd probably better not; must get back to the shop."

Cyrus smiled again. "Well, it was most kind of you to come, Wart. If you are ever up in the capital, I hope you'll stop by and talk again."

"I'll do that," Wart said as he stood up. "There is one thing I wanted to talk with you about, now, though."

Cyrus looked at his watch then nodded his consent of time.

"Agatha and I are married."

The half-interested mask Cyrus wore on his face shattered. "What?"

"Agatha and I are married."

"You can't be," Cyrus said standing up suddenly. "You can't," he sputtered, then turned his back on Wart and walked across the room to the window and looked out. "I'll have it annulled."

"I don't think you will. We think she's pregnant."

Cyrus turned back to facing Wart"

"Don't look as if it's a scandal. We've been married several months. It's quite natural; she's just going to have a baby."

"Agatha? Well, I'll have it annulled."

"Stop saying that. Agatha is of age, we're married, and she's going to have my child."

"Well, she's not leaving this house."

"Yes, I am, Father," Agatha said from the doorway. "Of course I am."

"You go to your room and stay there."

"I thought you wanted me to have a husband."

"I never said that; I said you needed one. And I meant one that could support you, give you a decent home; a man who had some ambition and a future."

"I have," she said, putting her arm around Wart.

"You didn't have to sink into the mud. Now get to your room."

"That's enough," Wart said in a booming voice that shook the room. "Go get your clothes, Agatha. You might as well live with it, Mr. Dodson, Governor Dodson, Agatha and I are married and that means for the rest of our lives."

Cyrus was about to shout back, "If she leaves this house, she'll never be welcome here again."

But Peggy broke the spell, "Father, there's a man in the hall to see you."

"I'm busy," he snapped. He was glad that he had not said Agatha was not welcome in his home anymore. If she left it would be true but he was relieved that he had not been allowed to reduce the emotion to words.

"He's from the governor's office," Peggy went on. "Agatha," Wart said, pressing her hand gently, "get your things, dear."

"You're not to leave, Agatha," Cyrus said in a now calm voice. "For the last time, I'm telling you to stay here."

"I have to. Don't you understand? I'm Mrs. Wart Kessel, forever."

"The man's waiting," Peggy went on in a monotone, stunned by what was being said, "He's waiting."

"Send him in," Cyrus said and turned back to the window. In the hall, Agatha and Wart brushed past a man in a bulky overcoat as he picked up his bulging briefcase and followed Peggy into the study. He seemed embarrassed. He must have heard the argument.

"Good morning, Governor. Governor Simpson wanted me to bring the reports down so you could read them. I don't know if you remember me; I'm his secretary."

"Of course; good morning. Would you mind closing the door?"

"Oh, sure. Governor Simpson thought it important you have the budget figures." The door closed, as the secretary started to explain the documents to Cyrus.

"May I help you, Aggie? Cynthia and I will want to help you pack," Peggy said as she put her arms around Agatha and kissed her cheek. "It's so exciting; does Mother know?"

Myrtle knew; she had suspected for weeks by the happiness in Agatha's eyes, so when Cynthia came upstairs to tell her of Wart's visit and announcement it didn't surprise her. She liked Mr. Kessel. Her last born to be her first married; how romantic, she thought. Now some of the things she had been saving could be put to use.

Peggy, Cynthia and Alfreda helped Agatha pack her clothes and the things in her dresser.

"What'll we put the dolls in?" Alfreda asked.

"Maybe they're good luck," said Peggy.

"Instead of a bridal bouquet," Cynthia laughed.

"Wonder who will be next," Peggy giggled.

"You take the quilt and blankets, dearest," Myrtle said, putting her arm around Agatha. "I just know I'm going to cry; 'bawl' as your father would have said if he were living. And when I start to cry I just never stop."

"Where will we put the dolls?" insisted Alfreda again.

"I'll get a box from the attic," said Cynthia.

"Don't. I won't need the dolls."

"Of course you will," Myrtle said.

"I wont, Mother; I really won't. I have a husband; and I'll soon have a doll of my own. I think I'm pregnant."

"You should have waited for a while," Myrtle said, hugging Agatha as tightly as she could. "You should have waited for your husband's sake. Now I know I'm going to bawl; my baby going to have a baby. She doesn't need dolls anymore."

"Aren't you happy, Mother?"

"Of course she's happy," Cynthia said; "and we're all jealous. And so will Gloria be when she gets back."

"Oh, won't she die;" Peggy shrieked, "Gloria will just die."

"It will teach her not to be so uppity and have to do her shopping in Flintsville, Alfreda commented.

"I'll take just one doll," Agatha said smiling.

"I'm sure too, that it will be a girl:" Cynthia said.

"I'm going to bawl," Myrtle said, and she did.

Wart waited downstairs in the hall for a while listening to the giggling and chirping of the high-pitched voices. Finally when the chatter made him nervous, he walked back to the blacksmith shop and harnessed Chestnut.

He went upstairs to Mitzie's vacant room to get boxes from the closet that went back under the eaves. The scent of Mitzie's perfume still seemed to linger. He wondered where she was. He thought about her often, and missed her. She was a strange girl, but she had been so kind to him, even before he had interceded with her brothers and the mine foreman. She was the only sister he'd ever had. He took the cardboard boxes out of the closet, flipped the latch on the small door and started back across the room.

At the foot of the bed he noticed a piece of paper and started to pick it up with his free hand to put it in his pocket. This was going to be his and Agatha's bedroom; he must clean it up. Then he saw that there was writing on one side of the paper and paused to read it. It was in Mitzie's neat hand:

"Springtime
"Silent nun

> does sigh
> and watch the ducks
> make love;
> wondering
> deep within
> if she has wed
> the One."

Mitzie certainly had it in for Matt's dream girl, Ellie. Mitzie just couldn't get it out of her craw.

Chestnut was anxious to be exercised and nudged Wart as he walked by to put the boxes in the surrey.

When Ward pulled up in front of the Dodson's, Agatha and the girls were waiting for him. They quickly loaded the surrey.

"I'll bring the suitcases back later," Agatha said.

"No rush," Myrtle said; "they can wait until you are all settled."

Agatha and her mother embraced, then each of the sisters kissed and hugged her.

"Mr. Kessel, I want you to know that this makes me happy; and it would have made Agatha's real father, Mr. Wilkins, most proud." Myrtle Dodson patted the back of Ward's big hairy hand.

Ward and Agatha slowly traveled the length of Elm Avenue, silently hoping they would be observed by all of Crescent. It would have pleased them if someone had passed them and waved or spoken, but no one did.

The only person in Crescent who noticed them was Margaret Cross. She watched them from her bedroom window. From her years of watching people, the closeness of their bodies in the front seat told her they were newly married.

Ward was no doubt enjoying himself; flaunting Cyrus Dodson's daughter in front of the whole town; showing off that he had caught the governor's daughter. Margaret knew that Wart was just being cruel in parading that girl in front of her house on purpose. Margaret knew he had tried to hurt her personally, just because he knew that she had always liked him. He had been that way since he came back from the army and felt so important in being a hero. Before that they had been friends, they had even gone to a dance at the Grange once. Their relationship could have been more, but when he had returned from France, he ignored her and made excuses every time she tried to be his friend. Now, he obviously felt even more important with his latest conquest: a young girl. There should be laws against child brides. It was sickening, revolting, and immoral.

Cyrus Dodson had even changed; he had certainly let politics lessen his standards. That poor child led astray by that horrible foreign girl Wart had had living with him. She had told Reverend Pritchard about what had been going on over the blacksmith shop, but he had told her it was all her imagination. Now maybe he would believe her. As a man of the cloth he should be concerned with cleaning up sin, not condoning it and making excuses. And now, there was old Wart Kessel; big and dirty and smelly Wart Kessel taking that pretty, innocent, clean girl to live in that dirty place.

Margaret watched the surrey turn the corner and she lost sight of it as the granary blocked her view.

She looked at her bed and was tempted to cry. She didn't, however, because she felt slightly guilty for her feeling about the young couple. Then, too, she had been thinking of Mr. MacQuarrie and the afternoon they had spent together and when she thought of that she could only smile, not cry.

Chapter 18

Kerosene sputtered as Gilbert Henri let the long handled torch slip up into the chimney of the street lamp; teasing the wick into a ball of yellow that mingled with the twilight. In at few minutes, at the other end of Elm Avenue, the ten new electric lights would blaze forth and shame this antiquated other half. "Someday, someday they will end this job," he thought to himself. "Maybe now the war is over there will be wire to complete the lights." As he walked toward the next lamp, he grumbled aloud, "And someday people will not laugh and say 'there's the lamp lighter' as if I'm some kind of freak." It hurt him when people made fun of the lamps. "Good God," they would say, "Crescent's like a drunk; only half lit". And the children loved to taunt in a singsong chant: "We've got a lamplighter, we've got a lamplighter, we've got a lamplighter," when he walked by. Someday, Crescent might be modern like most towns its size.

Gilbert felt ashamed of himself for being so cross with the people of Crescent, but he could not help noticing the feeling of contempt so many people seemed to have for him. Someday, he would not be just the man people called when they wanted odd jobs done. Someday, he might even be a full-time blacksmith. He liked working for Wart. He was at peace with himself there at the anvil, and some people even called him Mr. Henri when they brought their horses in to be shod.

But now that Ward was well and the politics were over, there wasn't even a place for him there. He liked Ward. Ward yelled a lot but he never swore, he never cussed. And Ward Kessel never hung over your shoulder to tell you how to do your job. He told you once what to do and that was it. When you worked for some folks, they stood around and watched you like a hawk, acting as if they thought you were cheating them on time or something. No, Ward Kessel was the kind of person Gilbert liked; even his voice that jarred you clear out of the shop. Even when he was asleep and talking to himself, his voice was voice was big enough so you didn't have to listen too hard to know everything he said; even if what he said didn't make much sense, like when he was having one of those bad dreams he used to have before he got married. Those dreams were one of the secrets Gilbert had kept completely to himself that and Wart's marriage to Miss Agatha. He hadn't even mentioned it to Margaret. Of course Gilbert had many secrets; he didn't talk much to others. He was happy Ward had gotten married.

"You know, Gil, I highly recommend it; I really do," Ward had said and "Miss Agatha", as he still called her, had giggled that little-girl giggle. "You could do worse than getting married, Gil; something to think about," Ward laughed.

Gilbert had thought about it once or twice; but what was the use thinking about it? Who would he marry?

Two more lamps to light and he would be free to go hone for supper at Margaret's kitchen table. He would bathe at her kitchen sink after eating and; then go into the parlor to play solitaire while she read her Bible or crocheted doilies or chair covers.

The reports Governor Simpson's secretary had brought to Crescent took Cyrus a week to examine, during which time he locked himself in his study, allowing no visitors, not even Bruce McHenry. He didn't answer Myrtle or the girls when they knocked on the door and he came out only for meals and late at night when his eyes seemed to give out and he went upstairs to bed.

Not discussing Agatha was a wise move. He didn't want any arguments to disturb him now; and the issue was closed anyway. Agatha had made her choice. It was now a thing of the past and he didn't want her or Wart mentioned in the house again, ever. If they were, he would leave the room. If they had no respect for him, then they had no place in his life or in his mind.

When he felt that he understood the reports and the figures they projected at least enough to discuss them intelligently, he called MacQuarrie on the telephone.

"You're elected now; you sure as hell don't need me!" MacQuarrie said in a flip tone.

"Well, I do or I wouldn't be asking you to work for me, Mac."

"Don't do me too many favors, Cyrus. I am quite content at this moment doing nothing. Being one of the unemployed offers a great many benefits one does not find while drawing a salary; one of which is freedom of speech."

"Please, Mac; do come down and talk to me anyway."

"I'll think about it, Governor. You may see me."

"Have you seen Clarence?" Cyrus asked.

"No, not personally since the day of the final returns; but I understand he is fuming at the mouth at the unappreciative way you turned down his offer of help," MacQuarrie laughed.

"He acted as if he thought he had been re-elected governor himself. I couldn't get him to discuss things intelligently so I left him there by himself."

"Cyrus you are learning. That was a very good move; it will confuse him. Clarence doesn't know what to do when people don't obey his every command."

"Don't tell him I said anything."

"Why not, Governor? Of course it doesn't make any difference because I won't be discussing many innermost thoughts with old 'cigar-face' anyhow. How's Glory Be?"

"She's fine, Mac. I hope you can come down."

It was a very unsatisfactory call. MacQuarrie had obviously been drinking and probably would not show up. Cyrus would wait until he went back to the capital and then try and talk some sense into him.

However, three days later MacQuarrie arrived in Crescent. Cyrus was visiting Bruce McHenry at the fire station when he got there, so there was time for Gloria to tell him about Cyrus's anger over the news of Ward's and Agatha's marriage and the expected child.

"I felt so guilty; I really didn't want to hurt him," she said.

"GloryBe, he's a grown man now and he might as well learn how apples grow on trees. I'm willing to allow him some leeway because of his recent success; but I'd hate to think he had become so self-important that he thought his illusions were actually going to reverse the forces of nature."

Gloria smiled, "It's wonderful having you back with us, Mac. I didn't know how much we had missed you until you came through that door and started to talk."

"A lovely, delicate creature can make a deliberate mockery of a man and his weaknesses and still smile," MacQuarrie chuckled.

"Of course you didn't; just came out perfectly; accidentally," he hugged her and she kissed him on the cheek.

"Anyway, the Governor has not mentioned Agatha since he found out, so I'd suggest we don't bring it up."

"You know, Gloria; I spent years learning the use of the editorial 'we'; but you have mastered it. And don't worry about Cyrus; time will wear the roughness off the wound. Every governor should have a grandson. Cyrus is so convention-bound that he would never want to break that tradition."

Cyrus was elated when he returned and found MacQuarrie and Gloria sitting before the fireplace in the study.

"Peggy said there was another politician waiting to see me," Cyrus laughed.

"I came close to turning around and going to the church to pray. If I had been Catholic I'm sure I would have. They are always open."

"Cyrus, there you go again putting your head in the sand," Mac said lightly.

"I'm certain you and Father will want to discuss things alone," Gloria said, closing the door as she left.

"I didn't really think you would come, Mac."

"You knew I would, Cyrus."

"It will make things easier, I need you to be my advisor, my secretary. For the past week I've been pouring over reports from Governor Simpson."

"I know. You have made quite a dent at the Statehouse. It's the first time a Governor elect has openly asked for advice from an out-going administration. It makes sense; but a lot of the diehards think you should be a candidate for an asylum with a high fence and lots of bars."

"To be honest," Cyrus said, "it just sort of happened, It wasn't planned; and Governor Simpson suggested it without even knowing it was his idea, And I liked it."

"I'd advise not too many spontaneous combustions, Cyrus. You have to make things happen, not let them happen; or the first thing you know all the junior clerks will be taking over. More or less, your dialogue with Simpson is excellent. It will save you more than a year of confusion that you would have had while you learned the ropes. I'd say you had won a few hundred votes for your next campaign with that one move."

"Your insight is reassuring; that's why I need you."

"Cyrus, I've got to turn your offer down. From now on, I have to be a free agent. I used to be, you know; but for too long I've taken the hard way, being tied to other people's projects."

"You would be a free agent. You'd be my advisor. Together we would literally run the state," Cyrus said offering MacQuarrie a cigar; "and I could write the price tag on your salary myself. How much higher do you want to go?"

"You don't sound like Cyrus Dodson. Besides, it isn't as much a matter of height as distance from where I stand now."

"Think it over, Mac."

"All right, but I have stated my case and I don't think there will be any change. I'm going back to the newspaper business."

The two of them sat quietly for a long time watching the smoke rise up from their cigars. Finally MacQuarrie stood up and kicked the log in the fireplace. "Cyrus, you didn't have me come down to this hick town just to ask me to be your secretary. You could have done that on the phone."

"That's right. I need your help."

"What kind of help? You've got reports from every important official in the government right there on this table. I'm certain all the facts are there and you can get clerks to dig them out for you. So to be very honest, I'm sure you don't need me. That's what I told you on the telephone."

Cyrus sat with his chin resting in his hands. At last he stood up and lit the lamp, "I want to get rid of Calder," he said in a flat voice.

"And you want me to help you?"

"Yes."

"I think they are right; you are insane. You not only want to break every rule in sight but you are indiscriminate in who you crush in your tirades," MacQuarrie said.

"He's dangerous: he believes he's going to run things."

"Of course he thinks so. He handpicked you, trained you and put you in your job; and before you even get moved into your new office you are plotting to throw him out. I didn't know you were such an avid Machiavellian scholar."

"You are making too much of this; besides, Calder had very little to do with my being elected. If I give credit to anyone it will be to you. All Clarence Calder did was talk."

MacQuarrie laughed softly and sat back down in his chair, "Cyrus, that is all any of us have done so far: talk."

"Mac, I know that I can't trust him."

"I imagine at this particular moment, he is thinking the same of you. And that is just on the grounds that you're not taking orders. If he knew what you had in mind, he'd have to have an attack of apoplexy."

"He frightens me; I'll admit it. I don't know what he's going to do and it frightens me."

"Cyrus, that is why I said I was going back to the world of type, ink and paper. There, you don't have to deal with frightened people all the time. You may have to write about them, but they don't surround you; they don't crowd in on you and infect you with their sickness."

"I thought you were on my side," Cyrus said, throwing his cigar in the fire.

"I'm not on anyone's side but my own from now on. I seems those were the first words uttered here today. But, Cyrus, if I were your advisor, I would say one thing: if you are honestly afraid of Clarence Calder or anyone else, for God's sake, don't take that oath, Be afraid of the job if you must, but if someone as unimportant as Calder is going to destroy you, or freeze you up with fear, don't leave Crescent."

"That's ridiculous. Of course he's not going to destroy me."

"But you want to destroy him."

"No; I don't want to destroy anyone."

"Weren't the words strung together something like: quote 'I want to get rid of Calder.' unquote?"

"You know exactly what I meant; so don't twist my words and throw them back in my face."

"If I didn't think you would be offended, Cyrus, I would be tempted to make one more quote."

"Go ahead. I suppose I invited you to say what you wanted to say," Cyrus said shaking his head in disgust.

"Just simply that you said I knew exactly what you meant; but I don't. What I do know is that if you want to 'get rid of Calder' you'll have to destroy him. Calder's entire life is tied up in going ahead in politics. If you break the chain and cut his progress to higher steps in this racket, you'll kill him. Clarence Calder is a very commonplace man who happens to have his life caught up in a wild and exciting game that has an important place in our country. And in the league you and Calder are playing in there is an unwritten law: 'Laissez-faire' or live and let live."

"That's ridiculous. By your own words, time and time again, during this campaign you've let slip how hard Calder can be and how many times he has rid himself of men he thought expendable. You are an example of how he dumps people on the junk heap when he's through with them."

"Ouch, I asked for that one."

"I'm sorry," Cyrus said taking a deep breath, "I'm very sorry."

"Don't be. Give and take, you know; live and let live." MacQuarrie laughed, "I always was bad at chess."

"My main concern is that I have heard rumors that Clarence has had some dishonest business ventures."

"That's at least a better argument than fear. Are they reliable? Or are they the rantings of some disgruntled candidate Calder happened to beat at cards?"

"Stop making light of what I'm saying, Mac."

"All right, seriously then; is your source reliable? If not, you will do yourself a great deal of harm even listening to it."

"Well, I think so. I stopped the rumor where it started, but I think it probably has some basis in fact. It involves a stock fraud over in Springville."

"Cyrus, you are rather late. Guilt by association, you know. If you believed Clarence Calder guilty of some monstrous crime, why didn't you make your break with him then at the beginning of the campaign?"

"I didn't know until this week,"

"That has some of the marks of an outright 'white' lie, The Harwood boy was traipsing all over Springville trying to trace Clarence Calder to the New Liberty Holdings fiasco way back before we even hit the road with your first speaking schedule. And who does the Harwood boy, just happen to have as an employer? Cyrus Dodson, Governor Elect."

"You obviously know more about it than I do."

"Only that the boy said he didn't find anything."

"Well, Matthew didn't even mention that he had been trying to investigate anything; he just said that his father thought Calder was involved in a stock scandal in Springville. He also claimed his father had some newspaper clippings to substantiate it."

"If that is your source, you might just as well forget, because..."

"All right, gentlemen, dinner is served," Gloria said in a cheerful voice as she opened the study door. Your politicking can wait until coffee time." She took Cyrus's arm with one hand and MacQuarrie's with the other. "Come on, the voters be damned. Let them eat cake while Father carves the roast."

"As I was saying, when Marie Antoinette broke in," MacQuarrie said, putting his arm around her waste, "You won't have enough to send Calder or anyone else to the guillotine with clippings from Springville papers. I was in Springville most of the time the New Liberty mess was going on and there wasn't a word in the press that pointed to anything stronger than mismanagement and a board of people who thought they had found a golden egg."

"This does sound different," Gloria said, "Now we are talking money instead of votes."

"Sad part of the story is that the golden egg turned out to be a brick and not a gold one at that," MacQuarrie said and they all laughed.

"Mac, you may sit in your usual place next to Gloria," Cyrus said as he stood at the head of the table and started to carve the large standing roast. Myrtle and the girls seated themselves and MacQuarrie sat down, noticing that Agatha's place had not been set.

"Peggy, pass Mr. MacQuarrie the potatoes," Cyrus said without looking up from his carving.

During the meal there was no mention of Agatha or Wart, but the obvious omission reverberated in everyone's silence.

After dinner when the two men had retired to the study once more, Cyrus broached the subject of Governor Calder again.

"Mac, even if Calder is perfectly honest, even if the Springville stock dealings were above board, I cant work with Clarence any longer. You might sit there and smirk and say that I'm politically naive, which I no doubt am; but I am going to run things my way and not his way. He doesn't understand that. You should see some of the demanding letters and telegrams he has sent, At first I answered them in polite terms; finally I decided that ignoring them completely would give more strength to my arguments than all the reasoning I could express in words. And I haven't answered one since. In fact, I haven't even opened the last four."

MacQuarrie sat looking into the fire.

"I'm going to get rid of him before I ever move into the Governor's Mansion, and I mean completely rid of him," Cyrus said.

"You've given me several reasons," MacQuarrie said quietly.

"I believe they are all very rational," Cyrus agreed.

"But reduce it to its lowest common denominator and the problem is that you and. Clarence have a clash of personalities. You hate one another, and as Gloria said: 'let the voters be damned.'"

"Mac, I was sure I could count on you," Cyrus said, disappointed.

"Now you know that you can't: not with those terms of reference. It is evident that you don't recognize it, but I am just as proud as you or Calder. When I do a job, I do it my way. I wasn't born to be a committeeman."

"It's not a matter of being proud; it's being right that counts."

"Cyrus, you are starting to throw the word 'right' around as if it were your exclusive franchise; remember this isn't a monarchy. You've been elected to serve in office for four years, nothing more."

"You know very well that Calder is no good."

"You have to be the world's worst salesman, Cyrus."

"This is as good a time as any to get things cleared up. Who's side you are on?" Cyrus demanded raising his voice to a near shout.

"It sure as hell isn't yours, if you expect me to help you murder someone just because you think it's an ideal political expedient. And another thing, your price is way too low. As a whoremaster, you are far too chintzy, Cyrus."

"Watch your language, Mac: this is my home."

"I'm sorry. Forgot where I was; but then, I've never been propositioned under such conditions before."

"There are times when I can fully understand Calder's attitude toward you when you keep putting on this superiority act," Cyrus said finally and sat down in his chair.

"It's not as you would lie, or have too, Cyrus, this is not too much different than a voter: the more elections he sees and casts his choice in, the greater the odds that he may wake up someday and realize that once or twice he has voted for a man who is less than the promises he offered in the campaign," Matt continued.

"I suppose now that you will report back to Calder that his protégé is ungrateful and plotting his downfall."

"No, Cyrus. As usual you've had your mind turned off; you haven't been listening," MacQuarrie said.

"Haven't been listening?"

"No, you haven't! If I had said what you wanted me to you might have; but as it is, you just sit there thinking up rebuttals to everything I present."

"My God!" Cyrus said in complete disgust.

"Well, you have; face it you've..."

"Maybe both of you had better face the fact that the election is over. Time's up for name-calling," Gloria said, opening the door. She held the silver coffee pot up in front of her, "Your cups are as cold and leftover as your conversation." She proceeded to fill the empty cups, then placed the pot on the table in front of them.

"Your father is a paradox," MacQuarrie said.

"My, it does take you a long time to figure things out, Mr. MacQuarrie," Gloria laughed. "We've known that for years in this house, without the services of a professional people-watcher."

"MacQuarrie, next to you, she's the most disrespectful person I've ever met. You encourage her; and then neither of us wins. She's my main reason for opposing suffrage for women."

"And if that be any man's main reason, which is no reason at all, then 'tis reason enough for woman to deny the reason of man," Gloria said quietly.

"Oh," the two men sighed in unison.

"I may encourage her; but you feed her the lines to make us the pawns."

"And if I'm to be treated with disrespect, I'll send Peggy back with the cream and sugar."

"As your advisor, I recommend we not let Glory be out in public. With that tongue, she'll cut your image to shreds," Mac jested.

"As my advisor?"

"I didn't actually turn down that offer, Cyrus; but that is not what you seem to want: 'an advisor'."

"What should I want?"

"Just that, and after you have heard the advice make your own decisions. I'll give you one year of my hard earned life; one year. And then you are on your own."

"What about Calder?"

"On that you'll have no decision. I'll help you ease Calder out of your way; but if you are not willing to do it my way, the offer is void."

"How can I depend on your getting rid 'of him? How can you do it?"

"It is none of your concern how I do it. You have no guarantee, just my word that Calder will leave you alone if you don't try to get too hard-nosed yourself."

"That's not good enough. I want him out of there before I move into the Statehouse."

"Why don't you learn to walk first?"

"I want Clarence out of there, now."

"Not you, nor anyone else is going to get him out of there, now. And if you try it, Cyrus, he'll make mincemeat of you and you won't even know what happened. Politics is an alternating, reciprocal agreement made between groups of rival civil clerks. You can't possibly fire every civil servant you have on the payroll and still run your government. You don't even know who's who, or who knows who, or who does what. But Calder does; and right now, he's their chief and he'll remain that until he abdicates. I can entice him to make that move, but not until we get you entrenched and the vacuum filled before his people know why or how it came about. By that time it will be too late and those loyal to you will be in control, at least until the next election. From then on, it will be the same old seesaw.

Cyrus took a swallow of his coffee. "All you are saying, is that you want me to keep Calder."

"No! I could do your bidding tomorrow and ruin Clarence and a lot of other people as well. And a lot of the people I would ruin would be innocent, including Clarence. In my files are enough affidavits, letters, depositions, and tampered financial statements to make anyone who had a penny in New Liberty Holdings look either stupid or sinister. Calder lost money on New Liberty; and the whole thing scared him so much they had him in a hospital. His heart was that bad and he was that upset. It would be the easiest thing in the world to discredit him so completely that not one of his party...your party, now, when you come to think of it...would even bother to speak to him again. That includes the perennial civil clerks. Those who bilked New Liberty were gone from the scene a long time before the break-up."

"Thank you, Mac. Now, even if you won't help me, I can see my way." Cyrus said leaning back contentedly in his chair.

MacQuarrie laughed, "You take bait very quickly, Cyrus."

"That's all a lie, then?"

"Every bit the truth and more. There are documents, which, if taken out of context, would convince anyone that Clarence had gone into New Liberty with deliberate malice, knowing that if things went the way they were planned he would a very rich man. But only I have them. Because I stole them and they are safely stored away."

"You stole evidence of a fraud?"

"You are listening now, Cyrus: I'll put it another way: I'll help you put Calder out of your road so you can become an effective governor, but I won't allow you ar anyone else use me as a means to a vendetta against Clarence Calder. Too many innocent people would end up in a public scandal. Fortunately, Cyrus, several of the key affidavits are irreplaceable because those who signed them are now dead; and the same is true of the most damaging deposition, the attorney has passed away. When I started, I was going to uncover the whole mess. When I was through, I could see why the Springville papers and half the people in that city acted as if it had never happened. They will all cooperate in helping you get the surface truth, but there is so much face-saving interest at stake. that even the professional people will sidetrack you."

"I'll have an investigation started."

"You do that. First of all, you don't have any information. Second, your authority does not cross state lines. And third, Calder had a quiet little inquiry of his own to see if anyone in this state was involved and no one was, according to the records. The management of New Liberty was most cooperative, though they didn't have to be: they came down here from Springville and disclosed 'everything of importance'."

"Then you are an accessory."

"Cyrus, don't go legal on me. You asked me a favor, and I gave you my conditions."

"You've let Calder turn you into as much a crook as he is," Cyrus accused.

"Clarence Calder, Governor Clarence Calder is no more a 'crook' than you are, Cyrus; so perhaps my record hasn't been damaged too much." MacQuarrie stood up and stretched. "I'll be going back in the morning," he said after a wide yawn. "It must be the country air; I get sleepy with the chickens."

"I'll have Gloria show you to your room," Cyrus said.

"Thanks. Just don't give them too much hell, too soon, Cyrus."

"Mac, I really need your help."

"I know you do. You also need my advice; but neither would have worked out."

"If I agree to leave Calder to you?"

"Only if you signed the pact in blood." They laughed and the tension seemed eased a bit.

"You know, Cyrus, you have such a built up resentment of that man, that it could destroy you and the rest of us, if someone doesn't hold a strong leash on you."

"You have the leash; but only on the Calder situation."

"I'll sleep on it. You've probably got an advisor for a year."

Cyrus looked relieved, "I hope so. I think that together we can probably do a good job."

"You are learning," MacQuarrie was tempted to say.

Chapter 19

Snow fell all night on the eve of the inauguration and the capitol was buried under nearly two feet of the white fluff. Because of the storm, the ceremony was moved from the steps of the Statehouse to the rotunda inside. A makeshift platform draped in bunting had been constructed and the speakers' rostrum from the State senate chamber had been lifted to the middle of it. Folding wooden chairs were placed six rows deep between the marble pillars of the rotunda, forming a rickety circle except where an aisle had been left opposite the platform for the National Guard detail to enter when they performed the flag ceremony.

Cyrus was nervous and paced the floor of Governor Simpson's office as he read his prepared speech over and over again. If he had more time he would change it in a few more places. MacQuarrie had an aggravating habit of writing expressions bordering on slang and colloquialism. All the talking in the world was not going to curtail Mac's endeavors to turn Cyrus Dodson into a 'man with the common touch'. Since he couldn't get Mac to stop his efforts to change him, he would just make his own corrections without discussing them. After a few times MacQuarrie would understand the style Cyrus wanted to use and the image he wanted to project to the electorate.

It was amusing to Cyrus, however, how effectively MacQuarrie had used Governor Calder to make arrangements for the services, without letting Clarence get the upper hand.

"Don't you believe it best for the machine to keep in the background at least for these public functions, Clarence? Of course the professionals will recognize your subtle hand, but the man in the street will believe you are just another senior statesman guiding a freshman."

The argument hadn't really worked on the first pass. Calder and MacQuarrie had used hard words on one another and Mac had relayed the discussions in detail to Cyrus. Calder, however, himself came to Cyrus and suggested that maybe it would be good if he remained behind the scenes except as a 'senior statesman'.

"I believe it would be wise to have our distinguished U.S. Senator, Patrick Dowding, introduce you. He might be retiring after his present term and therefore this would be his last chance to have the honor of giving such an address."

Cyrus had thought hard and then agreed with Calder, just as MacQuarrie had told him to do.

"Whatever speaking arrangements he wants to make, let him have his way. Main speaker will be Senator Dowding. Calder wants his seat in Washington and he must start greasing the skids. That is one thing about Clarence: he's predictable. We don't have to worry about Dowding, though, he's never written a speech of his own in his sixteen years in Congress. You know who'll put his words to paper for him: your 'advisor'."

Myrtle and the girls had arrived from Crescent with Bruce McHenry and would be seated on the platform along with Governor Simpson, Senator Dowding, Calder, three clergymen and Chief Justice Malcolm Lee of the State Supreme Court, who would administer the oath of office.

MacQuarrie had arranged the seating with the more important guests and newspaper reporters in the front row of chairs and the back seats open to state employees and the public. MacQuarrie, himself, would get lost in the crowd to make everyone feel at home. His handshake and individual personal invitations for party dignitaries and civic leaders to visit Governor Dodson in his office whenever they had questions or problems would precede the remarks Cyrus planned to make about the "Come-see-us-anytime" policy of the new administration.

The third prong of the attack would be when Cyrus came down off the platform and made the circle, shaking hands with every person in the front row, before he finally stood in the formal reception line in his office and greeted the entire audience. Cyrus had objected to this, which he considered a lessening of decorum, but MacQuarrie had laughed and reminded him again that he had only been elected governor.

"You know, Cyrus, you're not really going to sit on the right hand of God up there today. The man in the robes will only be Justice Lee. And if you are going to take over as party chief in this state, you'll have to soil your hands a bit."

On the mezzanine above the platform, MacQuarrie had arranged to have a select group of the Crescent senior high school band members. They would open with the national anthem, give a short concert of military numbers in keeping with the occasion, and close with a rendition of "The Lord's Prayer". It was MacQuarrie's one major mistake. The marble walls and curved dome of the State House formed a mammoth echo chamber in which sour or misplaced tones punctuated the listeners' ears in a dozen harmonics as they bounced back a hundred times to fight the players. MacQuarrie, from his vantage point across the circle from Cyrus, looked up at the pained back of the desperate conductor.

Whereas the rock-hard acoustics had amplified the band numbers, it seemed to hide the voices of the speakers, as if they were talking into the narrow passages of some subterranean cavern. Cyrus was annoyed by the distraction, and the light was not bright enough on the platform. He would speak to MacQuarrie about it afterwards.

MacQuarrie reasoned that if the acoustics detracted from some of the beauty of speeches, it also minimized many of the flaws of the speakers. He arranged to have the band cancel its final number with a note to the relieved conductor.

Cyrus's voice was strong when he accepted the oath. His composure was exceptional and when he came down from the platform he seemed to radiate confidence in meeting people face to face. MacQuarrie was impressed with the way he accepted that challenge after protesting so strongly against the idea.

"Mac, tell Calder we are going to have a meeting at one-thirty right after lunch in my office. I'm going to make some announcements regarding appointments tomorrow morning and want a clear understanding. And, Mac, I want those lights in the hallway changed, they're too weak; and have someone take the chairs up and clean this stand out of here," Cyrus said, grabbing MacQuarrie by the shoulder for a second and then disappearing into the crowd of admiring and congratulating faces.

"Oh shit! Next he'll be telling me to check the rest rooms for toilet paper," MacQuarrie thought to himself. Well, he had only promised Cyrus one year. He could endure that much; after all he had worked with Calder for three campaigns. When the year was over, he would go back to the Monday deadline, Thursday issue, weekly press and start putting down on paper what he thought and wanted to say to the world. No more having to compromise with selfish, climb-to-the top-of-the-world bastards. Then he could deal with little people with their little problems and little flaws. Who ever said, "the bigger the man, the bigger he thinks," had things a bit screwed up. MacQuarrie could write a book or two on the virtues of big men most, of which centered around their own concept of their own importance."

Myrtle Dodson had been concerned about leaving the house empty for the week she and the girls were going to be in the Capitol for Cyrus's inauguration. Especially in view of the heavy snows that had set in, the house should remain heated; her plants might freeze and someone should gather the eggs from the three hens they still kept. One also had to worry about housebreakers. And though Myrtle's thinking was not always in keeping with her husband's, her solution was practical and it would give Agatha and Wart the privilege of staying in a nice home for the time she was away. They should be welcome there anytime. Young lovers could live on love but it didn't hurt to offer them some comforts. It might make up, in some small way, for the un-Christian way Cyrus had acted. Besides, it was her house, not Cyrus's.

Ward and Agatha were pleased to help Myrtle. She had been so considerate and was constantly sending over bedding, dishes, old kitchen utensils and leftovers for their meals, which they suspected weren't leftovers at all. Her concern for their wellbeing was touching, though at times embarrassing. She had even sent Peggy over one afternoon with Agatha's christening dress for the baby.

Since Wart's trade slackened off noticeably when snow fell, they slept late and enjoyed making love in Agatha's old bed. The dolls that Agatha had not taken with her now sat along the wall and watched them with wide-eyed interest.

"Don't they embarrass you?" Agatha asked.

"Which ones?"

"Well, mainly Gertrude, the rag one with the large button eyes."

"No."

"Why?"

"Because she looks as if she might have sat in some other bedroom before," Wart laughed.

"And watched?"

"She doesn't look the kind that would ever turn away."

"You think she's worldly?" Agatha snickered. "If she isn't, she will be."

In silence the puppet students studied and tasted ecstasy vicariously. And while they studied, Margaret Cross washed the breakfast dishes and complained to herself that Gilbert didn't seem to be much help around the house during the holidays. Of course she shouldn't make too much of it, she supposed, because when Gilbert worked other places, he felt that he was contributing to his keep and was therefore happier and even talked to her once in a while. Gilbert was a good man, even if he wasn't interested in companionship. He didn't seem to care what the people of Crescent or the people of the world were doing or thinking or saying. In fact, it was hard to determine just what there was that interested Gilbert besides solitaire and his own thoughts.

The Election

The most Margaret had ever heard Gilbert say about any one person was during his outburst the other evening when he had become drunk and had gone on at such great lengths about Wart and his war experiences and raved so much about how he admired Wart. Margaret had nothing against Wart, really; it was just that there were better influences in the town that Gilbert could pattern himself after. Then of course the age difference between Wart and Agatha still bothered her some. If Wart had waited, she might have consented herself to have become his bride. She would have been better for him than some high school girl. She was sure of that.

Gilbert had gone out to Clyde Smith's place to help in digging the new root cellar under the house. She did hope that Clyde would not give Gilbert any more homemade whiskey. Margaret knew it wasn't wise for women to interfere in the affairs of men; but she hoped that someday the government would step in and help men help themselves by making it illegal to make or drink hard spirits.

Gilbert did most of the chores that she asked; but he never extended himself. Just like with the old papers and magazines on the porch: he had just dumped them in the corner instead of tying them in bundles so that they would be neat when she got around to clipping the recipes. Now many of them would be crumpled and perhaps wet from the snow that had been blown onto the back screened-porch. When she finished her dishes, she thought again about the papers. She would do that little task before lunch and have it done for another year. Margaret didn't get around to using many of the recipes she had been collecting in cigar boxes for the past twenty-five years, but then if she ever needed them they would be there, and whenever the Church had a potluck supper she might try one or two of them. Gilbert was a plain meat-and-potato type and her husband had been the same kind of person.

She puffed as she went back up to the bedroom to get her scissors. There she thought of the time she and Mr. MacQuarrie had been there together. It was a secret she enjoyed many times every day and she was glad that it seemed to grow in importance instead of fade. She wondered if he ever remembered. Of course, now that Cyrus was governor, one never knew when he might come back to Crescent for milk and cookies. She would play the piano again for him.

Margaret stacked the newspapers beside the table and spread out the top paper to browse through. She always saved the magazines until last since they seemed to have the more exciting, fancy, recipes. She imagined how each dish would taste and how it would be to prepare. Sometimes this experience nearly wore her out, but she found it exciting and satisfying.

Then, of course there were the news items that she interesting than the recipes themselves. She hadn't noticed at the time that Roseanne Holbert had remarried. They had gone to school together. E.J. Marx of Quince Town: she didn't know him; the name sounded Jewish. Ted Holbert had been such a wild one in school, it was rumored that Rose Ann had had to get married. But then it was hard to tell since they had never had any children.

Walker County's Gold Star column was always watched with considerable interest it was alarming how many young men were not going to come back to their parents and families Margaret looked for names that touched a memory or a friendship. Sometimes she might even send a note of condolence, even if she didn't know them. "P.F.C., Sherrill E. Fox, Jr., of Terrence, son of Mr. and Mrs. S.E. Fox, Sr., killed in action," she wondered if that was Ella Fox's boy. "Major Elliot Atwood died of wounds sustained in battle." Everyone knew Elliot Atwood; he had gone to school with Margaret. He was a senior when she was a sophomore; president of the class and then opened his own hardware business in Colton. Now the war was over, she would miss this kind of sad news.

Dr. Phillips' death was a tragedy; but everyone knew he was a slave to the bottle and that it was a wonder any of his patients ever lived when he was drunk. He had lost that Ferguson woman and her child that very same night. When would men grow up and behave like men?

With all the excitement of Cyrus's success she had completely overlooked the news that the new County Coroner was Seth Adams. Margaret liked Seth Adams: he was voted the "Boy

Most Likely To Succeed" in high school. You just knew he world amount to something by the serious way he looked at everything. He never laughed; and he had even represented the senior class as valedictorian when recited Gray's Elegy in a Country Churchyard" at graduation.

And how funny: Alf Perkins had been re-elected dogcatcher in Flintsville. Of course, that shouldn't be too surprising. Margaret chuckled to herself, as everybody in town said when he was elected before: "Always knew he was going to the dogs."

It was disturbing to know that the young Michelson boy, Bobby, had been arrested. It must have been a real heartbreak for his father who was such an upstanding man.

"Held A Slacker"

"Suspected of seeking to evade the Selective Military Service Law, Robert Michelson, of Crescent was arrested today by the sheriff. He had a registration card in his possession and explained that he had filed no questionnaire because he had never received one. Trial has been set in County Court for August 30th."

It would be such a shame on the family. How did people face such problems when their children turned sour?

"Flintsville Man Drowns"

"The body of twenty-eight year old Lawrence Morgan, who was previously employed as a clerk at Case's General Store in Flintsville, was recovered from the waters of the Smith River near Nattox in Burley County. His wagon and horse were found on the bank of the river twelve miles upstream where they had become entangled with a large tree.

"Mr. Morgan was last seen alive at the regular Saturday night dance held at the Flintsville Grange. In the darkness, it seems logical to assume that Mr. Morgan took the old fork of the Crescent road and drove his buggy onto the rotting Gilforth Bridge into the Smith River, which this paper has at various times brought to the attention of its readers. It should either be torn down completely or, at least blocked off, so that no more animals or men lose their lives."

Margaret also read Lawrence Morgan's obituary. It must have been a very sad funeral with no relatives present to mourn the deceased. And Catholic services were always so cold and impersonal, anyway, compared with the ones conducted by Reverend Pritchard. Of course there was a difference also in the length of service: not so many speakers and not so many sad points where one might cry. But then why did one go to a funeral except to mourn? If you weren't going to cry, you might just as well sit home and crochet or read about it in the newspaper. Margaret attended all of Crescent's funerals and some of those in Flintsville and Colton if they were for people she knew or knew about. Those she hadn't attended always left a void in her life; she wondered what the flowers were like and if the songs sung were appropriate and how hard the family had been hit by the sadness of the occasion.

Morgan's obituary did not bring any of these questions to her mind. However, there was a discrepancy between it and the news story on page one. The obituary stated that Lawrence Morgan had drowned; another said he had a broken neck and, possibly, other injuries. Why couldn't the people who wrote newspapers be sure of their facts "Morgan", she repeated the name over to herself several times and then said it aloud, "Morgan." It sounded familiar but it brought no face to mind; of course at twenty-eight he was a bit too young for her to have met socially.

"Killed in action," Willard Helms, had been one of her favorites in the church choir; such a magnificent voice. He used to completely dominate the bass section. His memorial service was nice, but since it was not a funeral with casket and all, to her it lacked emotional power. But she was there, doing her duty.

On the other hand, Melvin Northcott's funeral notice was particularly touching to Margaret. It seemed as if it were only last week that she had sat in the second pew, just behind the family. Reverend Pritchard had been so sincere when he talked of how the many friends and close associates gathered there would long remember the contributions Melvin Northcott had made to their lives. Margaret wasn't sure if it had been the large floral piece with its many sweetly perfumed gardenias obviously imported from the city, or Phyllis Weltie's rendition of "Rest, Rest for the Weary", which caused her to motion to the usher for the smelling salts. Lovely service: she had enjoyed it even though she did not know the deceased. The news story that impressed Margaret most of all the ones she saw that morning in the old papers was the one about the Colton Red Cross.

"Auction A Success"

"The people of Colton held a Red Cross Auction Tuesday afternoon and realized more than eight hundred dollars. Everything was donated: bottled fruit, jars of jelly, sacks of potatoes, pigs, calves and sheep, as well as merchandise of all descriptions.

"After the sale, a farewell reception was held for the thirty eight boys from the county who were called through the draft to serve their country. Gathering at the corner of the National Hotel, the Colton Band played several patriotic selections after which speeches were made by County Clerk, Leon Clarke, and Art West, Assistant District Attorney.

"Later, the procession was formed and, headed by the band, marched to the depot to bid the boys good-bye."

How satisfying it had been to participate in sending the boys away to serve their country in the struggle against the "heinous Huns". Too bad it was over. Those young, innocent faces were so determined to face their adversaries in war. "Do or die for the cause of right." They had been dedicating their lives to the saving of the world, not just the United States. It was almost as if they had been leaving for the Holy Crusades with the "cross of Jesus going on before".

However interesting all of the articles were in the papers she had cut to shreds, Margaret was most confused over a small three-line advertisement in the Personal Column, which read: "Madam Warner now permanently residing at 234 East Broadway, Colton." Why did people waste good money to run such silly, nonsensical things in the paper? She had heard of people who always wanted to see their names in the newspapers; probably just because they were lonely and had no company.

Recipes were more exacting work than news stories; they had to be separated into categories and then arranged alphabetically after that. Eighty-three recipes she had counted; of course she would find some near duplications when she did the actual filing, but it wouldn't take long to separate them.

She was so sorry that she hadn't been able to attend the funeral of Nellie Welch, the oldest woman in Walker County: one hundred and two. She had been over to see Nellie not a month before she died. Nellie had laughed and tried to see her, and talk to her; but Margaret was sure Nellie didn't know who she was. The funeral was held at Parktown and was too far for her to go, but she would loved to have been there for Nellie's final hour.

She had attended Katherine Black's wedding that same day, instead, and had cried almost as hard there as she would have at Nellie's service. Everyone in town knew that Katherine was at least four months pregnant.

"Lawrence Morgan": that name was still bothering her. Where had she heard before? It wasn't very often that Margaret Cross forgot the name of someone she had met. It could have been that it was because she had just read about it when it happened. No, more recent than that. She thought, as she sorted through the papers again and found the news item. July twenty first, same issue as the story about Cyrus Dodson going to run for governor. That seemed too long ago for her to remember just a name. She read the story again; and then thought about it for a few minutes longer. It would bother her until she remembered. However, she must get on with her chores. She would remember. She always did, after a while.

Chapter 20

Cyrus's conference with Calder and the party leaders was conducted on amicable terms. All were discretely testing one another, but the appointments made were to Calder's advantage. Of the six men to be offered posts in the new government, five were Calder's recommendations. This was the way MacQuarrie had told Cyrus to "play the game".

"Six months and we'll have him on his way running for the U.S. Senate; and then you can make as many switches as you want. And you know, Cyrus, all of his people won't be that bad; Calder picks those who can do him some good. Some do an excellent job in their posts if they are left alone and not compromised at every turn."

"If they compromise, they compromise, and that does not make for a good public official," Cyrus said with strong conviction in his voice.

"Don't be too quick to judge, Governor, You never know when you might want them to compromise for you."

"Mac, you may not know it, but I'd never ask anyone to do anything I wouldn't do myself."

"Governor, that is the point; people who do the bidding of another is usually doing what the person who wants the compromise asks them to do."

"Mac, we're getting into one of your time-killing disputes over the meanings of words, and I, frankly, don't have the time to waste."

"Fine; but in the next year you are going to hear it over and over again: don't judge other people so harshly, then I'll be gone and you can do what you want."

MacQuarrie was right about the men Calder had chosen: James Hatch, an attorney with a brilliant court record, for Attorney General and P.J. Muir, President of the Federated Bank, for Secretary of State, were both highly respected. If they would accept the offers, Cyrus knew that he would never have to change them for they were known for their integrity.

MacQuarrie was less impressed, "A record isn't a record until it has been made," Mac commented; "time will tell a lot. You may want to get rid of the whole damn bunch, Cyrus. You never know, they may disagree with you once in a while."

The superior smirk in MacQuarrie's words aggravated Cyrus but he ignored him and went on to the secondary appointments for which Calder had offered only recommendations, leaving the final choices to Cyrus.

"That is where the decisions are made; not at the top. These are the men that are important to your political future. They will either make or break you," MacQuarrie said with a broad grin on his face.

"I don't know why you are so pleased with yourself, but it shows," Cyrus finally said, bringing MacQuarrie back to reality. "Not like you to be so transparent. What's so funny?"

"Clarence; he is getting either senile or careless and it doesn't really matter which. You see, he doesn't care which men from this broad list you choose. He feels so certain that you are leaving control with him that he thinks he is fencing you in. He doesn't care for one minute who you put on, or keep off those jobs. If you appoint them, he will take credit; if you reject them, he can claim he did all he could in recommending them to you personally. It was you, Cyrus Dodson, the twenty-sixth governor of the state, that ignored his plea and awarded the plum to someone else."

"Then he has put me in a spot?" Cyrus said, confused by MacQuarrie's reasoning.

"He thinks he has. Clarence was so confident when he left here fifteen minutes ago that you would think he had four aces up his sleeve, He thinks he's won, Nothing to keep him back when he finally calls you."

"Trying to follow your monologue is impossible at times, Mac," Cyrus said.

"Don't always try. You see, Clarence was so happy, that he let us see his hand. He doesn't for one minute suspect that you have a royal flush. That simple list in front of you is of the prime pork-barrel men Clarence Calder is depending on to control you and this government. I can tell some of the key men who are listed. Those are the ones who, in the next six months, will be courted by us. They will be won over to the side of Cyrus P. Dodson."

"I don't understand."

"The hell you don't, Cyrus. And you know as well as I do that it's stupid of me to be giving away trade secrets. Next thing, I'll find you don't need me, either."

"That will never happen, Mac; and I will never settle for just one year. I need you all the way in this job and any other to which the people of the state might call me to dedicate myself."

"I gave you my terms. They still hold."

It always amazed MacQuarrie how quickly the game of politics turned into a cause of dedication. He had long thought that if one could force men who were successful in the power struggle to understand the true nature of the drive that gave them so much momentum, many useful and possibly productive careers in public life might be saved from derailment and catastrophe. He, of course, was a dreamer. The practical side of things was often beyond him.

"Cyrus, you are going to become the personal friend of each and every one of these men; and you are going to learn to smile more. You won't like it and you'll have to hide the clothespin you might want to clamp on your nose when you visit some of them. But nevertheless, you will seek them out and they will know just how much you depend on them; and without actually saying it, you will strongly indicate just how far they can go in the government and how much they can expect to realize from all of the service they give to you and to the party."

"You wear me out with all of your devious enthusiasm."

"That makes at least two of us, Cyrus."

"And what if they don't like me?"

MacQuarrie smiled. There was still hope: Cyrus didn't really think that he was part of the godhead as yet.

"You won an election that no one thought you could win. You did it by confusing the issues, Cyrus; and you'll follow the same format here."

Cyrus snorted. "Come on back to earth, Mac; after you win them to my side, how are you going to 'move Calder over', as you put it?"

"Don't worry about it."

"I do worry about it, Mac, I promised I'd go along, but I expect some plan of action so I can see exactly how to set the timetable."

"No sir, that was the deal; you were going to leave it to me."

"But I have to have some reassurances that it will work."

"It will work, I told you I had enough files on Calder to run him out of the country. I have; but not you nor anybody else is going to get in on that part of the act, I am going to be selfish and watch out for Number One, I will not commit suicide, Cyrus, not even for you."

"You make my loyalty sound rather questionable."

"Governor, it won't work; I just cannot take the chance of anyone having the information. It is there if we need it," MacQuarrie said, "I was going through one of my files this morning, rereading some of the stock option agreements that were assigned to Governor Calder. They would erase him from the political picture in five minutes. I had forgotten just how devastating they sounded. He probably thinks that he is the only one who has a copy. But I had access to the entire company files when they went broke and I borrowed some of them before they burned the records."

"Incriminating evidence, and you withheld it. That is disgusting!"

MacQuarrie walked across the office and closed the door to the reception room and the intense silence of the listening clerks, "Withheld it from what?"

"From the inquiry; from the due process of law."

"There you go back to a bunch of legal jargon that doesn't mean a thing, Cyrus. Nothing was withheld from anyone, Nobody ever asked for these files, because they didn't even know that it existed. And you had better check on the meaning of 'due process'. I believe it is meant to protect the innocent from the miscarriage of justice when law is taken out of context or bypassed. Clarence Calder is innocent, where most of my files taken at face value, seem to indicate he is guilty."

"It must be disconcerting, Mac, to always try to be on both sides of an issue. No wonder you are confused."

"You and Clarence have one great thing in common: life is extremely simple to both of you as long as it fits into your scheme of things and works to your advantage."

"Then answer just one question: if you won't let anyone see your precious files, just what is your secret plan?"

"No secret plan. Clarence Calder wants to be U.S. Senator. We've gone through that. As soon as we have you strongly entrenched in the machine here, we will start him thinking about Congress. The diversion will throw him off guard and he will be working full speed to get Senator Hunter and the rest of the federal politicos to help him. He can't do both at once. Just as I told you; 'we will move him over'."

Cyrus sat looking at Mac in silence; then shook his head in complete disbelief at the ridiculous plan that had been put forward.

"That's not good enough, What if he doesn't want the Senate? What if we don't want him in the Senate? You can't take a man who isn't good enough for a state post and send him to Washington to make the decisions for the whole of the country. And what if he says to you 'MacQuarrie, you are a no-good lush. You tell Dodson I'M running this state, not him'?"

"It won't happen. As to the Washington end of things, he is capable. He was capable when he sat in your chair and don't ever think otherwise. You don't like him, and neither do I particularly. Even if he wants to stay, all I have to do is show him this one small set of documents and he will discretely leave you alone forever. I am prepared to go that far, if I have to, but no further. I won't disgrace him publicly over something that isn't what it seems to be."

"Let me see your files: and I'll be the judge."

"Come on, Cyrus," MacQuarrie said with a smile and a shake of his head, "That might be a slightly biased jury. They are going to stay under lock and key. I made my first mistake by confiding in you and telling you I had them; but the second mistake is something I'll save for another day."

"I'm sorry, Mac; I know that I become rather demanding and pushy at times. Forgive me. You do it your way. I don't know why I should question you. After all, you have done everything you promised so far. When is the legislative outline meeting scheduled?"

Mac studied Cyrus's face for a long time; then, seeming reassured, answered the question.

"The party committee asked that it be put off until tomorrow at ten-thirty so Senators Fletcher and Crosby could attend; also they wanted more of the representatives there, They seem to figure they can line up all the bills they want pushed through this session in about three meetings if they have all the big wheels here at once to gain their support."

MacQuarrie stopped at the office door and looked back: Cyrus had shifted his attention instantly to other work and was flipping through the papers on his desk. Mac was uneasy about the sudden silence, so he said, "They will have the list of names for you this afternoon. Calder will be here at nine a.m. to brief you."

"That's fine. And, Mac, did you get the clock fixed in the rotunda? It is slow."

"Not yet; watchmaker cannot be over until Friday."

"Fine, and the lights in the corridors? They still seem quite dim."

"Largest bulbs the circuits will handle without fear of fire, the electrician informs me."

"Thank you. Will you get word to Gloria that we will be having dinner at the Potter House dining room this evening and for her to be certain her mother and the girls are ready. You'll check the time won't you, Mac?"

MacQuarrie glared harshly at the two girls who were listening intently to the conversation. He closed the door to the governor's office and went to his desk. That picky bastard," he thought. He was glad his term with Cyrus would be short. It was ridiculous to spend time doing things that were neither satisfying nor productive. Working for either Calder or Dodson had both of these drawbacks. He opened the large bottom desk drawer and pulled out his file on Calder's New Liberty stock options. Every time he reread them, it amazed him how misleading the written word could be. Calder would be able to understand the implications of those documents without much coaching, even though in actuality he had probably lost more money than any other single investor in the promotion. MacQuarrie shoved the file folder back into the drawer. As he looked up he noticed the two girls watching; then he dramatically slammed the drawer and locked it with one of the keys on his key chain.

"Hazel, please type eight copies of this list of proposed legislative committee heads. And Nellie, the governor will need a copy of the proceedings from the last legislative session to study this afternoon. Please get one from the Senate Clerk's office, immediately."

He had argued with Cyrus over the place of women in an office. Though you had to give credit where it was due and Cyrus was right: women in this Governor's chambers were entirely out of their element. If Cyrus ever brought it up again, he would let him have his way and transfer them to the Land Office or the Road Commission.

"Nellie, would you please get that report now. Your paint and powder can wait. There's not one male in the Senate Clerk's Department with the exception of Roger Watts. And he retires next year. So get moving."

Nellie's large brown eyes filled with tears and putting her handkerchief to her mouth, she ran out of the office. Hazel busied herself trying to find some carbon paper in order to avoid MacQuarrie's intense look.

He was losing his sense of proportion, he thought; but then they had had it too damn easy for the past four years. If he didn't straighten them out Cyrus would fire them both without the least compunction. He hated crying females; they were so messy and there was no defense against them. They made you feel guilty even when they were the ones at fault.

"Hazel," he said. Hazel looked up, expecting a verbal lashing, "When Nellie comes back, tell her that I'm sorry."

Chapter 21

Willie Clay was a thin man with an Adam's apple that seemed to dominate his long skinny neck. His watery blue eyes matched the small ruffle of white fringe that haloed his baldhead and rested on the large, heavily veined ears that sprouted numerous dark hairs and clusters of blackheads. He was Sheriff of Crescent, and had been for twenty-four and one-half years, ever since Orville Clay, his father, had died of a heart attack the day Crescent had its one and only bank robbery on July 1st, 1892.

Usually one had to look twice to find the tarnished badge, symbol of Willie's authority. It played hide and seek in the folds of his overly large blue denim shirt.

Crescent had been less than eventful. His feet propped upon the makeshift desk, Willie had filled his hours in his small office reading the adventures of the West that Bret Harte had put on paper and the chilling mysteries of Sherlock Holmes.

He kicked shut the door of the red-hot potbellied stove and leaned back in his favorite position. He yawned and looked up at the clock; one-thirty. He had forgotten to wind it and the pendulum hung limply. He considered for a minute whether to get up and re-set it and wind it tight for another eight days, or do it in the morning when he came to work. It would be more practical doing it in the morning on his way back from the post office: save time.

At the post office he collected the circulars on criminals. He always posted the "Wanted" posters and never threw one away, but he had never recognized any of the faces he found on them.

Crescent was "a silly place to be a sheriff", he had told himself that over and over a thousand times, but what could he do about it? Life had you cut out to be what you were to be and you just had to take the breaks as they came, even if they were mighty hard to swallow at times. You just had to adjust and do the best you could in the slot you had been dropped into. His father had told him that, too; so they both agreed. It was strange that they should both end up behind the same desk.

Margaret Cross was out of breath when she opened the door, bringing with her a gust of cold wind into the room. She stood looking at Willie, her mouth half open: her eyes wild with excitement.

He looked at her, then finally took his feet off of the desk, put the book face down to save his place, stood up and walked over to the door and closed it.

Still Margaret said nothing. He went into the nearest of the two empty cells and brought out a straight backed wooden chair and put it down in front of her. She breathed deeply, stomped the snow off of her high-topped shoes and sat down.

Willie Clay cleared his throat and rubbed his chin with his hand.

Margaret looked at him for a moment longer, then, removing her hatpins, she carefully took her hat off and placed it in her lap.

"Murder," she said.

He looked at her, waiting for her to say more.

"Murder?"

He snuffed and hacked into the spittoon along side the desk

"I think its murder."

"Good afternoon, Margaret, You're right, nasty weather. What are you doing out in it?"

"I told you."

He looked confounded.

"Told you I think it is a murder."

Willie Clay, sheriff of Crescent, leaned attentively across the desk. "Yes?"

"Someone has been murdered."

"Murdered in Crescent?"

"No! Flintsville."

"That's what I was afraid of. Knew it couldn't be Crescent. Flintsville's beyond my jurisdiction."

"Murder isn't," Margaret said in desperation.

"No, but Flintsville is, Margaret, and you know it." He paused and a wry smile came over his face, "Normally, it's a trifle beyond your jurisdiction, too, Margaret."

"You'd better take me seriously, Willie Clay."

"Is there a body?"

"Yes, there is."

"Where?"

"Buried."

"Buried? How did you find it?"

"Read it in the newspaper." Margaret dug deep into her large, cross-stitched hand bag and pulled out two clippings from the Journal and clutched them tightly in her left fist.

Willie sat studying her. The interrogation seemed at an end.

"Don't just sit there; someone has been murdered in Flintsville."

He looked at his visitor again in disbelief. He had been married since he was sixteen, to a normal woman who didn't make sense most of the time; so he should try to be understanding: he should know what caused women to act the way they did. Margaret Cross's behavior, however, suddenly reaffirmed his knowledge that man was never intended to figure women out, more than to appreciate as a convenience around the house for the children.

"Who is the victim, Mrs. Cross?" he asked seriously.

"I don't know."

He aimed for the spittoon once more and missed.

"That is, I didn't until Gilbert came home for dinner last night. He sat there playing solitaire and I looked at him and knew there was something I should remember and it bothered me. When I went to bed, I kept turning and tossing; there was something about Gilbert."

"Has Gilbert killed someone?"

"Of course not! You know Gilbert. Of course not! It wasn't until almost morning that I sat up and remembered. That name: 'Morgan'; don't you see Morgan was the one Gilbert was talking about. All the time I knew that I would remember his name and there it was: 'Morgan', the one Gilbert had mentioned."

"Margaret, Margaret; who is Morgan?"

"Dead. He's been buried, Catholic service. It was in the Journal."

Margaret paused and took a deep breath before she started to slowly proceed. "He's the German soldier with the broken neck. I could hardly wait until Gilbert was out of the house to start thinking about it. I didn't know if I should come and talk to you about it or not. You know, Willie, I don't want to cause trouble for anyone. Then, when I lay down for my nap, I realized that I had to talk to someone and that it should be you."

Willie rubbed his hands together nervously. "Of course you should come talk to me, Margaret. Now let's see; a man named Morgan."

"Lawrence Morgan; the paper said 'Lawrence Morgan', twenty-eight years old'. One place it said he had drowned and the other, in the obituary, said he's broken his neck."

"Did the paper say he was murdered?"

"It just said they found his body in the river; they found his horse and buggy, too." Margaret pushed the crumpled clippings forward with a deliberate move.

The sheriff unfolded them and squinted at them, then looked at Margaret's face and its black message of hostility.

"It didn't say 'murdered.'"

"No; but he was."

"How do you know?"

"Because he wasn't a German soldier at all; he was a clerk at Case's store."

"Case's store in Flintsville? And his name was Morgan, Lawrence Morgan, and he was murdered, when he drowned."

"No, a broken neck."

"I'll telephone Flintsville."

"You don't have to telephone; Ward told Gilbert he killed him. You can ask Gilbert."

"Ward who?"

"Kessel, of course. What other 'Ward' do we have in Crescent?"

"Ward Kessel is no more a murderer than Gilbert is. Now I don't know what kind of dreams you have been having; but you had better take a good long look at what you have been saying here. None of it makes any sense, especially the part about Ward Kessel killing someone in Flintsville who was drowned with a broken neck."

"It happened in his dreams; he told Gilbert that he killed him; that his name was Morgan and that he had choked him to death. What more do you want him to say?"

"I don't believe any of it. Now, Mrs. Cross, if you had killed someone would you tell anyone else that you had done it? Of course you wouldn't. Murderers don't do it that way. You read all of those books on that shelf over there and you won't find one of them that has a murderer telling anybody about how he killed anyone; not even in his dreams. And that's another thing that doesn't make sense; 'he told Gilbert in his dreams'. Do Ward and Gilbert sleep together?"

"Listen, Willie, Ward Kessel used to talk in his sleep when Gilbert was working for him. That was when Ward had been hurt, his ribs broken. What he said in his dream was that he killed a man and mentioned Morgan's name. Gilbert overheard him and asked Ward who he killed in his dreams, and Ward said it was a German. Gilbert asked him if his name was Morgan, because that was the name Ward kept screaming out, and he said yes. Then Gilbert asked how and he said he choked him."

"This is farfetched, Margaret; really farfetched. How does what you have told me make you think for one minute that Ward Kessel killed anyone?"

"Because it was just after Morgan's funeral that Ward told Gilbert."

"If that's true, why didn't you tell me then?"

"Gilbert didn't tell me."

Willie cleared his throat once more. It was getting dry. This whole thing was silly. He had known Margaret Cross since she was a little girl. She was always in other people's business; but never in all these years had she gone this far.

"You told me that Gilbert did tell you; now make up your mind."

"Well he did, but not until just the other night when he was drunk."

"Gilbert was drunk and he told you that he heard Ward Kessel kill someone in his dreams and that someone was a man who drowned with a broken neck?"

"You are trying to make me look as if I'm crazy, Willie Clay, but I know that Ward Kessel killed Morgan."

"Did you know this Morgan?"

"Of course I didn't know Morgan, but that has nothing to do with it. You ask Gilbert. Even ask Ward."

"If you want me to, Margaret, I'll ask them. Both of them if you like; but you are going to look mighty damn stupid. Don't be mad; that's the way I see it. And any judge in the country would see it the same way. But it is my job, and I'll ask them for you. You want to come along to hear what they say?"

"No. That is the duty of the law."

Willie Clay wanted to smile; but his didn't. He was getting very annoyed with Margaret's blabbering.

"That's fine. I'll go down to Ward's shop and ask him."

"You won't find him there; he and Agatha Dodson are staying at the Governor's house. I've watched them go in and out of the Dodson house all week."

"You seem to know an awful lot about a lot of people, Margaret. I'll go see him at Governor Dodson's house, then. Now you go on home, and Ill tell you about what he says when I'm through. Then I'll sit down and talk to Gilbert."

Margaret pushed her hat on her head, shoved the pin in place and slammed the door as she left.

Willie was tempted to go back to reading the Study in Scarlet. No, women with busy tongues cause trouble. He would go talk to

Ward and get the thing over with; then he could come back and pick up Doyle's story of Watson and Holmes.

On the way to see Ward, Willie indulged himself by stopping by Schmidt's bakery for his usual afternoon apple turnover and a cup of coffee in the back room.

Every weekday when the ovens gave up their delicious, steaming captives to be glazed by Mr. Schmidt's daughter, Freya, Willie stopped by for his handout and a half hour or so of conversation with the baker.

"Schmidt, the damnedest thing happened today. Margaret Cross came to the jail. I'm not sure, but she could have been mighty under the influence of liquor even though I didn't smell any on her breath."

Schmidt grunted and went on forming the loaves of bread.

"She tells me that she had a dream that Ward Kessel was a murderer."

"Vimen, auch."

"Not only does she believe her dream, but she demands that I go over and ask Ward a bunch of questions about it. I'll sure look silly? Everybody in town laughs about how I never do anything anyway."

"Vard, he von't talk no how."

"Hadn't thought of that; but Ward has always been understanding."

"Ya. Vimen, auch, vimen."

"I will have to admit that it would be nice to have just a little crime around here once in a while. Even a murder, huh?" Willie said, slapping Schmidt on the back as he went out the back door.

Ward was in Myrtle's kitchen painting the cupboards with a new coat of light grey enamel. Agatha showed Willie through the dining room and pantry to where her husband was on his hands and knees trying to reach the back of the bottom shelf, under the sink.

"Ward Mr. Clay to see you, dear.

"Just a minute, Will. Let me get the last bit on this one shelf; then I'll be with you. Aggie, pour Will a cup, will you, Honey."

"Cream?"

"No, Miss Dodson; I mean Mrs. Kessel, just sugar. You know, sometimes it is hard to change your habits. Been calling you Miss Dodson for a mighty long time; mighty long time."

Ward put his brush in a fruit jar and wiped his hands on the turpentine soaked rag. "Now, Will, what can I do for you?"

"Well, Ward, it's a silly thing. Could I talk to you alone?"

"Not going to be women talk? I'll be on my way; have cleaning to do upstairs anyway," Agatha said, "Ward and I have been trying to spruce things up for Mama and the girls when they come back from Daddy Dodson's big ceremony."

When she was gone, Willie continued, "Now, I don't want you to get mad at me or laugh too hard when I tell you what I came for; but I promised Margaret Cross that I would ask you."

"Go ahead, Will. You know, since I've gone into politics, I can give answers with the best of them. May not make sense, but I can give them."

"This whole thing, don't make sense. It's about these articles from the Walker County Journal, Ward."

Ward took the articles and read them slowly. He didn't look up or say anything, just read and reread the same few lines that he had read and reread over in his mind since the night at the Grange. He walked over to the window and looked out at the yard and the field behind the house, then went back to the kitchen table and stood looking down at Willie.

"See, I told you it was kinda silly. I really think Margaret is ready for the nut house. She said you killed this fellow Morgan, choked him to death. You can see by the paper it says he drowned, but Margaret says you choked Morgan to death."

Ward didn't seem to respond to the accusation.

"I could have sworn she was either loony or been tapping Gilbert's corn liquor. Hope you won't make a big fuss. You know, Ward, I don't like misunderstandings and name-calling; especially over something like this. We can just keep it quiet, can't we, Ward? Why, nobody even knows who this Lawrence Morgan was.

Imagine her coming to me like that, without any warning, and saying you broke some guy's neck."

Ward poured himself a cup of coffee and sat down at the kitchen table across from Willie.

"I'm sorry he died, Will. He was a bully with a knife. He stabbed me and I might of killed him, Will."

The two sat in silence. Willie cleared his throat and looked for a spittoon. There was none and he swallowed hard and took another drink of coffee.

"Now, Ward, wish you wouldn't make fun of me. I told you how silly I felt, and I never would have done a stupid thing like this except that Margaret Cross was involved; and, God, you know what a big mouth she's got."

"Will, I'm not making fun of you. I think I might of killed Morgan; killed him because he was trying to kill me after a fight at the County Grange dance at Flintsville. He stabbed me in the side and I might have choked him."

Willy Clay sat confounded; he took a large gulp of coffee and let it trickle down his throat. Ward was joking with him, he liked to do that all the time; so he would go along with him.

"You really did?"

"Yes; believe me, that's how it happened."

By the seriousness of Ward's expression, Willie suddenly believed what was being said.

"How am I going to explain it?" Willie asked.

"I imagine it will be me who will have to explain. Will, don't you worry about it," Ward said as he read the articles once more. "Things happen so fast, and you can't believe it is true when you wake up."

"Are you sure your weren't just dreaming? Margaret says you were talking in your sleep or something."

"No, I wish I had been; I wish I were dreaming right now. What will it do to Agatha? You know, Will, I don't want anything to hurt Agatha. She's going to have a baby and this will be terrible to have to tell her."

"I could have sworn Margaret Cross was drunk. She didn't make sense; she still doesn't. And you don't make sense either."

"Don't say anything to Agatha."

"All depends, Ward. If you killed Morgan, I'll have to arrest you."

"I was just defending myself, Will. You understand that?"

"That doesn't make any difference until after the District Attorney lays a charge, Ward. If you say you killed Morgan, I think I have to take you back with me; if you say you didn't, I won't."

Ward looked at him and shook his head. "Well, I did and. I'm sorry that I did; but I guess if I hadn't someone else would have."

"You better go up and tell your wife," Willie said after what seemed an hour when neither of them spoke further, "No rush; I'll wait for you."

When Ward left the room the stunned sheriff poured another cup of coffee and put two lumps of sugar in it. A murder in Crescent; it was hard to believe. Maybe he was the one who was dreaming; it could be. Ward Kessel was too calm for a man who had killed someone. Nothing made sense; no one acted the way they did in books, least of all the one who claimed to be the murderer. There wasn't any mystery or even excitement.

Willie's stomach ached a little; there was a strange numbness in his groin as he tried to comprehend what Ward had been saying. He waited until it started to get dark, then he went to the telephone and cranked the bell for the operator.

"Ida? This is Sheriff Clay. Anyone call since I've been gone? Oh, fire at Young's. Bruce get it all right? That's good. Would you call Mrs. Clay and tell her I've been held up at the Governor's house and will be late for dinner? Nothing important. Just tell my her not to worry."

He would go and see Gilbert at Margaret Cross's home after he had fed Ward his supper and bedded him down for the night. That was another thing he didn't believe: Gilbert telling Margaret anything about Ward. Gill lived with Margaret sort of on the side, even though everyone in town knew about it. But Ward was Gilbert's employer. He had treated him well; gave him his first full-time job. Gilbert had even sat in the jail office and talked to Willie about how good Ward was to him. The whole thing didn't make much sense.

Willie leaned back in his chair, put his feet up on the table and sat quietly in the dark waiting for Ward. He couldn't hear their voices upstairs, but he knew they would be talking in low, sad, parting tones. He was asleep when Ward turned on the kitchen light and disturbed him.

"Shall we go, Will? Thanks for the time."

"What time is it?" Willie stammered, his eyes opening wide with a start; almost falling off the chair.

"Seven-thirty; I'm sorry for taking so long. It was an awful hard thing to do: tell Agatha the truth about everything. She's worried. And, Will, she's really all alone you know. Cyrus Dodson was none too happy about us getting married, and madder still about her being pregnant."

"Don't worry about the time. I suppose I should get home for supper, though. You ready to go? Got everything you need for a couple of days? We feed you pretty good and there's wash water and inside plumbing."

"Sure, Will, ready as I ever expect to be."

As they passed the staircase, Willie called up to Agatha, "Mrs. Kessel, if you want anything you call me. And I'll take good care of your husband for you; don't you worry!'

Ward was silent and the front door closed quietly behind them.

Chapter 22

MacQuarrie struggled to get his eyes open. Someone was pounding on the door. He rolled over and yawned and closed his eyes again, but whoever it was kept pounding. Finally he sat up in bed and slowly let his feet slide over the side until they touched the cold linoleum floor. Instantly he was awake. He slept naked except when he was on a trip and shared a room with someone, so he slipped on the faded plaid bathrobe that he always kept at the foot of his bed. Its warmth didn't match the comfort of the bed but it cut out some of the chill that surrounded him.

"Mr. MacQuarrie; Mr. MacQuarrie."

"You are pain in the ass," MacQuarrie said as he opened the door. "What is it? Oh, hello, Son, what's the problem?"

"Awful sorry; they said it was most urgent. It's a phone call, downstairs, at the desk."

"Shit! Who would do a thing like that?"

"I know how you feel, Sir. I hate getting up in the middle of the night, myself."

"I'll get some clothes on and be right down."

"Yes, Sir, Mr. MacQuarrie."

MacQuarrie put on a pair of pants and a shirt and slipped his shoes onto his bare feet. His mouth tasted terrible and he had a slight headache. He wondered what time it was and started looking for his watch on the dresser. Its luminous dial pointed to two-fifteen. He didn't have a single living relative, so who would do a thing like this to him?

It was Clarence Calder in one of his gruffest, loudest moods, talking so hard and fast into the phone that MacQuarrie had to hold the receiver half a foot from his ear.

"And not only that, but you better get your drunken butt down here to help clean up this mess."

"Well, Clarence, I haven't heard a thing you have been shouting about; but I'm certain half the town has. Start from the beginning and let me in on what you are saying and why."

"It's Dodson; he just blew his whole administration out of the tub; all my work and money gone in just one night."

MacQuarrie took a deep breath, trying to figure out if he were asleep or awake. "Just calm down," he said trying to break into Calder's tirade.

"Don't tell me to calm down. I should have known better than to give you such a free hand in this damn campaign. You've screwed it up and it could throw the whole damn party out, just like that."

"What has happened? Just tell me, what's happened?"

"Dodson's son turns out to be a killer, that's what!"

Mac shook his head and stood in silence trying to comprehend what Calder was raving on about.

"Cyrus doesn't have a son to begin with, Clarence. Are you drunk?"

"No, I'm not drunk, and you wait until you see the headline in the paper. Want me to read it to you? 'Governor's Son Charged in Murder'. The night desk at the Statesman called to tip me off. It'll be on the streets in an hour, all over the state. By nine this morning, the whole country will know it. We're ruined."

Clarence, calm down; you know you are not supposed to get that excited. Things can't be that bad. 'Governor's Son'. Hell, Clarence, he hasn't got a son, just girls. I was trying to think if I had missed someone but he only has five daughters, all step-kids at that. That's all. It's got to be a mistake."

"Wait a minute and I'll read it."

There was a long pause while Calder read the news item, obviously for the first time. "It's even worse than it sounded at first; it's that damn blacksmith you had campaigning for Cyrus out in the sticks, Ward Kessel. Arrested at the Governor's home in Crescent. That will make us all look not only stupid, but implicated."

"Ward Kessel killed someone; I can't believe it, Clarence. I know that man. Now I know there is a mistake. Ward and I lived together all through the campaign."

"I wish you wouldn't mention that campaign. It's the worst mess I've ever been involved in."

"Is Ward all right?"

"Good God, who cares? Don't you get the picture, Sonny Boy? Some heads are going to roll over this, yours for sure. You get down here and help figure out what we're going to do."

"Where are you?"

"At my hotel. Where'd you think I'd be at this hour of night?"

"I think we'd better meet at the Governor's office. I'll call him and we'll meet over there."

"What do you want to do, Mac, let everyone know just how scared we are? You have a meeting there at this hour and every reporter in the whole damn state will see the lights and create an even greater mess. You come over here right now. I'll call Dodson and have him here when you arrive."

"Clarence, you had better call your editor friend and tell him that if they let just one copy of that paper out with that headline, there is great danger of a libel suit. Let's see what kind of headline they can make out of 'son-in-law'. They will have to reduce the size of type, if nothing else."

"I'll do no such thing. I'm not going to antagonize them any more than they already are."

"Well, if you don't, Calder, I will; and I won't be as diplomat you are."

"You're nuts."

"You'll call him?"

"Yes, I'll call him."

"All right, then, I'll be there in an hour."

"Make it faster than that. Every damn second counts."

"For what?" MacQuarrie asked himself as he started to climb back up the three flights of stairs. Clarence Calder was always going off on a tangent. There had probably been some kind of accident; that is, if there was anything to the report at all. Newspapers, especially the *Statesman*, made a lot of rash statements and misstatements were the rule instead of the exception in the fast pace of the daily deadline race of a two-paper town. He hoped Ward was not hurt. Agatha probably needed someone to be with her. He would call on Gloria as soon as he was through talking with Calder.

When MacQuarrie reached Calder's hotel room, the ex-Governor was even more upset than he had been on the phone. Cyrus had hung up on him after refusing to discuss the Ward Kessel matter.

"You know what that arrogant bastard had the guts to say to me? 'This is a personal matter and has nothing to do with you at all; you just stay away from the newspapers, or you will wish that you had.' That's what he said; then he started ranting on again about him being Governor and I really put that stuffy-assed bastard on his place. I told him he'd better get it through his head that from now on I was going to call the shots in this pool game and he was going to do what I told him to, or else I'd have the party run him out of office. You know I damn well could. That's what I told him. I said 'Cyrus, you are through giving orders. Your son-in-law just put you out of business and there isn't anything that will push that story off the front page'. That's what I told him, and the bastard slammed the phone down. He hung up on me."

Calder paced the room while MacQuarrie telephoned to Crescent to talk to the Sheriff.

"Oh, he seems to have slept mighty little; but then I guess none of the rest of us down here have either. Other than that, Mr. MacQuarrie, I'd say Ward was doing all right!"

"You tell him that I will have legal counsel there sometime today. And, Sheriff Clay, be certain to advise him of his rights."

"That won't be necessary, Mr. MacQuarrie. He had me call that young Keith Hampden from Colton as his lawyer; but I really haven't talked to him too much. Just to tell him what Margaret Cross said."

"What's Margaret Cross got to do with this?"

"Well, Mr. MacQuarrie, a mighty lot, I'd say; since she was the one who reported he'd done it."

"Margaret Cross?"

"Yes, sir; but her friend Gilbert won't talk to me or her or anyone else. He's back to being his old self: not talking. Just sits in her kitchen staring into space."

"I think you've made a big mistake, Sheriff."

"I thought so too, Mr. MacQuarrie, but Ward says she is right. He says he thinks he might of killed this Morgan fellow; choked him. Ward says that himself."

"You keep the press away from him until the lawyer gets there to take this over. You understand? Keep everyone away from Ward Kessel, and I mean everybody."

"Yes, Sir; I'll do that."

"And tell Miss Agatha that her mother and sisters will be coming home today to be with her."

Calder was flushed in the face, and his breathing sounded sporadic. He lay down on the couch and closed his eyes.

"Kessel has confessed," MacQuarrie said. "I don't believe it; but that is what the Sheriff says. I just don't know what to think."

"It doesn't really matter;" Calder said in an odd, subdued tone," Dodson is through. I'll see to that. I'm not going to sacrifice everything I've worked for, believe me. If nothing else I'll protect that Senate seat and my name in this state. And that means only one thing; Cyrus Dodson is going to be thrown to the dogs. He got himself into this mess, with your help, now let's see him get out of it."

MacQuarrie stood looking at the prone figure of Calder; then he straddled the seat of the desk chair and leaned on the back. "Those are fine words of anger, Clarence, but you can't afford to dump Cyrus. First of all there is a chance that Ward Kessel will be found 'not guilty'. In fact, there is a very great possibility of that. If that is the case and you have started open warfare on Cyrus, the fence-sitters and the anti-Calder boys will join him and really split your machine wide open. They will dismantle it bolt by bolt until there is nothing left of it but a pile of scrap. Then you will never get to the Senate. It will take a well-oiled buggy to get you to congress anyway. Secondly, Cyrus can overcome this bad publicity. The courts and the jurors will take the pressure off his head. Law will take its prescribed course. In the meantime, the appointees you have put in around Cyrus will run the government according to your bidding. The less disturbance, the better for your quiet move to Washington."

"Don't try to talk me out of this, Mac; he's just too much trouble to keep in line."

"Is he?"

"Of course he is, and you know it."

"Looks to me as if he's letting you run the whole show; appointments to posts, scheduling of meetings, legislative calendar, bills and the whole lot."

"Well, yes; but then look at the way he refuses to come to meetings. And the pretentious bastard is rude. Then this!"

"The public thinks he has a mind of his own. So does he; but you, as you said, are 'calling all the shots'. What more do you want?"

"I really had better get rid of him."

"That's fine: but this is not the right time for such a move. Most important thing for you to do right this minute is to call the doctor and have him check you over. Clarence, you can't take a chance with your heart. All the votes in the country won't put you in Washington if you are dead."

"Think I'll go back and sleep for an hour or two."

"I'll have the doctor come up before noon," MacQuarrie said at the open door. And I think I'll go to Crescent for a day or so to be sure only the truth gets put in the papers and to insure that Ward gets a fair trial."

At the Governor's Mansion, Gloria opened the door for MacQuarrie. They stood in the marble hallway with its two sweeping curved staircases and its huge cut crystal chandelier. Their voices echoed even though they spoke in whispers.

"Father will be down for breakfast in a few minutes."

"How is he?"

"Quiet now; but at first it scared me, Mac. When Governor Calder called him he turned white and his lips were almost blue, he was so angry. He slammed the door on me and went into the library and wouldn't talk. I felt completely helpless. I don't believe he's been to sleep all night."

"I feel so personally responsible for this."

"Don't be silly, Mac; if Ward killed anyone it wasn't your doing."

"How much did Calder tell him about it?"

"I guess Governor Calder didn't say much except rave about how he was going to take over and run the state. Won't you come into the dining room and have a cup of coffee while we wait Father?"

"Thank you, Glory Be; the only nourishment I've had so far today has been the verbal kind Calder gives out when he's on the verge of a tantrum."

"I'm taking Mother back to Crescent. We should be with Agatha."

"I told the Sheriff to tell Agatha that you would. I may be going myself today; if the Governor approves."

"Why?"

"The best place to control what goes into newspapers is at the source of the problem."

She held his arm as they walked slowly toward the large dining room.

"I feel so protected when you are around, Mac."

"Careful, Glory; you might unlock the male pride in me and set me off thinking I'm greater than I am; which, today, isn't much."

They laughed together and went into the long window walled room.

"Isn't this house something?" Gloria asked, avoiding the mention of the seeming oppression that in essence hung over both of their moods.

"It would make you feel rather insignificant."

"It was willed to the state by Raymond Marchant. All the marble and glass are from Italy. I guess it was just too much for a private family to keep up."

"I've always said it was too much for an individual to own in the first place. But it is good to see that you are doing your homework. Sometimes, if you like, I will give you a tour of your new home. I once had to write some articles for the paper about it."

"Mac, you take all the fun out of being bright."

"Raymond Marchant was the founder of the paper I worked for," Mac explained, "so the family wanted to get as much good publicity out of his gift as they could. The result was my drawn-out series of articles telling of all the art treasures built into this monstrosity."

They sat at the one end of the long table after Gloria poured their coffee from the silver service on the sideboard.

"Gloria, what lies ahead, for you?" MacQuarrie asked as he stirred his coffee.

"I'm going to be at Cyrus's side and help him, if he'll let me."

"If he will let you?"

"Yes, I suppose I should be happy that he fits well into his new responsibilities and is so self-sufficient; but since the election, he doesn't seem to want any of us around, not even me."

"Do you speak as a mother or a wife, Glory Be?"

She put her cup down and looked at him.

"You don't sound as if you are acting the part of a daughter; that's what I mean."

"I know what you meant, Mac. And it isn't very complementary."

"Just asking."

"If you're asking if we are lovers; I guess I really am in love with him."

"Sorry to be so blunt. One of my better failings."

"You are right, though. I've known for a long time that I would love to be his wife."

"Well, Gloria, let me tell you..." Mac started to say, then stop as he noticed the Governor standing in the doorway.

"Good Morning, Mac. I'm glad you came so early," Cyrus said as he walked over to the table and sat down. "It is a shame to disturb such an intimate gathering."

Cyrus seemed almost placid.

"I would have been here sooner, Governor, but Calder was all excited and ranting on in his usual crisis attitude."

"That's fine, Mac, I understand. He was trying to read the riot act to me at one-thirty in the morning, telling me that he was going to have me impeached and thrown out of office. I hung up on him. I wouldn't listen to all of that blabbering."

"I brought the paper with me. It's in the hall; I'll get it."

"I'll bring it," Gloria said as she got up to leave the room.

"The new edition just came out, delayed because the first ones had Ward listed as your son. We told them they better think it over because if any incorrect ones hit the street, we would sue; it would cost them their newspaper, presses and all."

"I guess this does make me look very silly in the eyes of the public; a man campaigning for me turning out to be a murderer."

"Cyrus, they can't very well blame you for something that was my doing. And what is worst of all is that he's married to Agatha. That is the point they'll play up. I'm very sorry that the whole strategy blew up in our faces, Cyrus. I really am sorry; but there is nothing to do now but tame the newspaper coverage down. One thing I am certain of and that is that, Ward is no murderer."

"I wouldn't count on that, Mac. Kessel is just the kind of trash one might expect to find mixed up in the middle of something like this. Personally, I could kill him with my bare hands for dragging Agatha and the rest of us down with him."

Mac interceded, "I think that it would be wise if I went to Crescent to see what is taking place and to make certain the reporters get their facts straight. We can't stand too many false accusations. I can go down and take Mrs. Dodson and the girls back with me if you like."

Cyrus sat down at the end of the table and looked at the paper, which Gloria had placed before him.

"Newspapers never print the truth," he finally said.

"I didn't think the write-up was that bad, except that any such publicity can't do us anything but harm," Mac said in an attempt to put the best face possible on the situation.

"You mean can't do 'Me' anything but harm."

"Governor, I can't get over the habit of thinking there is more than one person in the world. Anyway, I will be going to Crescent after the legislative committee meeting. That is unless you want me to postpone the meeting until next week so that you can get your breath."

"No, I don't think that will be necessary. Time is of the essence and I can't be self-indulgent in this matter."

Gloria poured a cup of coffee for her father and put two lumps of sugar in it. He stirred it as she poured the cream. When it was his desired mixture, he nodded and she stopped pouring.

"Gloria, will you tell the cook that I'd like to be served now."

"Calder got himself so worked up this morning that I thought he was going to have a heart attack; but before I left he was back down to earth. I doubt that he will be at the meeting, however," MacQuarrie said as a maid placed a plate of scrambled eggs and ham in front of him.

"I was just thinking; you go ahead to Crescent. I'm certain that Gloria and her mother can have the girls ready to go with you by noon and you can catch the four-thirty train to Colton. I'll be able to handle the matter of the legislative committee. You won't have to be there at all today; but call me when you... Pamela, I would prefer whole-wheat toast, if you don't mind...Mac, call me as soon as you talk to Sheriff Clay. It would be more help to me today if you looked after these personal matters for me."

"You are sure you won't need any help at the Statehouse?"

"Mac, stop worrying; I'm not about to make any rash statements to the committee. In fact, I will have someone suggest they adjourn early, and if Calder does show up, I promise not to argue with him."

"Of course," MacQuarrie said. "Glory Be, if you will have your luggage ready, I'll be around about three."

Cyrus was entirely too calm. It worried MacQuarrie, but he reasoned, as Gloria had said, they must accept the fact that Cyrus was taking command of the situation.

After breakfast, he and Gloria left Cyrus alone.

"I'll go see what kind of accommodations I can arrange. With the troops using all the railway cars we may get nothing but a chair car if I don't make a scene on behalf of the Governor."

"Thank you, Mac, for being around when we need you."

"Gloria, it might just be that I need you and that is why I show up at times such as these. Think it over."

She helped him on with his coat.

"That is what I mean; I need your help," he said kissing her on the cheek.

The traffic manager of the railroad ordered a special private car placed on the afternoon train to Colton for Myrtle and the girls.

"We are pleased to be of assistance in times of crisis," he said.

MacQuarrie cleared his throat and smiled, "I am certain the Governor will remember your kindness, Mr. Ellant. It will make the trip more endurable."

Later MacQuarrie had lunch alone in the dining room of Calder's hotel. Calder had been given a sedative by his doctor and was resting. Then he went back to his own hotel, packed his grip and slept until two-thirty. It would be a tiring ride to Colton and this would probably be the last good sleep he would have until he returned from Crescent. When the bellboy knocked, MacQuarrie again found it hard to wake up. It seemed only a few minutes before that he had been roused by Calder's call.

"Mr. MacQuarrie, time to get up. You said you had a train to catch."

"Brought the first afternoon edition of the paper for you. Something about the Governor in it."

"Fine, Timmy. Leave it by the door. I'll get your tip to you when I come down."

MacQuarrie felt his face with both hands. He needed a shave, but he would wait until he arrived in Crescent. The cold water in the hotel room was miserable to shave with and the chance of getting into the one bathroom on the floor was out of the question, even in the middle of the afternoon. He poured some of the chilly water into the basin from the pitcher, however, and washed his face and arms before getting dressed.

They would hold the train until he arrived with the governor's family; but he hated to ever arrive late, giving Cyrus an opportunity to pull his famous watch-checking trick.

As he combed his hair, MacQuarrie noticed several greying strands at the temples. At least he wasn't going bald; nothing worse than going bald, when you wanted to look the part of Mark Twain with a full mane of silver to create a lasting image. He remembered when Hilliard, a bald reporter at the paper, once explained "The human male only has a set number of hormones allotted to its development, and if some men want to waste them on hair, let them go ahead, as for me, I'll take 'bald'." Mack chuckled for a moment, then turned from his mental primping; besides graying or not, he was stuck with a full head of the stuff.

He slipped his overcoat on, grabbed his grip from the foot of the bed and opened the door. His key was still on the dresser and he had to go back and get it. As he locked the door and started to leave, he noticed the newspaper folded by the side of the door. He stooped and picked it up. Six hours on a train with five women and nothing to read would be like solitary confinement in a madhouse.

At the desk he rang the bell and waited for Timmy to arrive so he could throw him a quarter and have him call a taxicab. He might as well go first class all the way, especially since he was going to have his first ride in a private railway car. He could see through the window to the restaurant that Timmy was drinking a cup of coffee at the counter, so he spread the paper out on the desk to read while he waited.

MacQuarrie's face drained of color and he dropped his grip to the tiled floor.

"The dirty son-of-a-bitch," he said aloud, as he looked in disbelief at the headlines: "Dodson Charges Calder in Fraud" He closed his eyes for a second and then took another look. The type had not changed its form. How could he? He didn't have any evidence.

"At a special Statehouse press conference at 11:00 am today, following the Governor's Legislative Committee meeting, Governor Cyrus P. Dodson charged former Governor Clarence Calder with implication in the infamous New Liberty Holdings Corporation scandal of over five years ago. The Governor said a warrant for Calder's arrest had been issued and was being served on the former governor today.

"Governor Dodson circulated copies of a stock option agreement issued to Calder by New Liberty Holdings which would have made over a half million dollars of profit for the former Governor without any investment on his part if the stock had risen to the five dollar price at which it was supposedly conservatively estimated by the company's officers in 1909, the year the company went into receivership.

"The warrant for the arrest of Clarence Calder was the first of many measures the new governor promised in his projected campaign to bring honesty to state government.

"Though the headquarters for the New Liberty Holdings was in Springfield at the time of the alleged fraud, the transactions took place in several cities and crossed state lines.

"'Corruption does not have a place in my administration, neither in my advisors nor my officials, and any who are suspected of any misconduct in their required duties either by commission or omission will be prosecuted to the fullest, Governor Dodson stated."

"The dirty no-good son-of-a-bitch," MacQuarrie said, again, his hands trembling with anger. He scanned the first page: not one word about Wart Kessel and the murder story of the morning paper. Finally, on page one of the second section he found the item buried in between a story on the Red Cross's need for volunteer women to greet homeward bound service men and an item on a party given for wounded men at St. Joseph's hospital.

MacQuarrie clutched the phone, asked for the operator and had her ring Calder's hotel; but it was too late; the state police had served the warrant to Governor Calder at two o'clock and his doctor was with him now. He was taking no calls.

Mac crumpled the newspaper into a ball and threw it across the Lobby. It didn't matter how Cyrus gotten into that desk drawer and found the file on Calder. He had done it, and that was all that counted. Cyrus knew full well what it would do to Clarence Calder and that the name of MacQuarrie would be synonymous with Judas.

Should he go directly to the Statehouse and confront Cyrus with the treachery he had committed or do what he knew he should have done when Dodson first asked him to work for him? How could he be so careless as to leave that damn file in that desk? And why did he ever tip his hand and tell Cyrus any of the details in the first place?

Cyrus P. Dodson was the sum of a million little traits that all pointed to what he was capable of. What made a punk, small-town newspaperman think he could compete with a punk, small town Benedict Arnold? MacQuarrie had convinced himself that he could control Dodson, just as he had controlled Calder. But he should have known better; Cyrus was an enigma, a "deceiving, unmitigated, amoral prick."

Maybe he would challenge Cyrus when he went back to pick up Gloria and her mother, if he was back at the mansion. No; he simply would not see Cyrus again; not ever. He would make him wonder what was going to happen next. And no one would ever get the rest of the files; he would burn them first. He would go to Crescent and see if he could help Ward Kessel clear himself of whatever mess he was in. Cyrus P. Dodson could go to hell. He hoped that retribution would do its part in time. Maybe he could think of something to help speed up the process.

Clarence Calder was dead before the train arrived in Colton. The conductor brought a wire to their private car when they pulled into Grantsville.

"Station Master said you had left word to be informed of any change."

"Thank you."

"You know, I voted for Calder twice; always thought he was a fair Governor."

"He was," Mac said as a verbal epitaph.

Clarence Calder gone. MacQuarrie leaned back on the musty-smelling green plush of the seat and tried to sleep. It was the hardest day he could remember in all of his life. He was tired of fighting people and ideas and arbitrating the vanities of insecure, self-centered men. Cyrus had said that he couldn't afford the time for self-indulgence. Cyrus didn't know the extent of his own appetites; all MacQuarrie could hope for was that time would be the determining factor in stopping him, for it seemed no man was able to satisfy the Governor's desires for power.

A morbid thought slowly crept over Mac's conscience: he couldn't even show up at Calder's funeral to express his grief. No one would understand. He was a marked man. As a centralist, his own balancing act and hypocrisy had caught up with him.

Chapter 23

Ira Calder was a gaunt boy with gangly arms and legs and bony fingers that were long and crooked, all traits inherited from his mother's father. He was overly tall for his fifteen years. His disposition, since his father's death, had changed noticeably from that of a playful youth, teeming with pranks and laughter, to one of brooding sullenness. In those three short weeks he had seemingly turned into a malcontent twice his age.

Ever since his father's funeral, Ira, his younger brother, Robert, and sister, Winifred, now nineteen, had been supervised, on a daily basis, by his mother in packing the family's possessions for the return to the family home in the town of Norman, some seventy miles north of the state capital. Norman was where his father had practiced law. The firm still had his name on the brass plate at the entrance of the town's only three story brick building: "Brooks, Vernon, Calder & Summerhayes, Attorneys at Law."

The first time Ira had seen the sign was on this visit with his mother back to Norman to see if their house, rented all these years had been kept intact and was fit for their return. Somehow "Attorneys at Law" seemed more important to Ira when he look at it, than the sign with the title of "Governor" engraved on it at the gate of Governor's Mansion. It was more lasting, more dignified, and actually a more fitting epitaph for his father than any words that meant "politician".

"You were born here, upstairs, Ira, in the back bedroom," his mother explained as they walked up the wide steps to the broad veranda. We had a wonderful life, here, Ira, before your father started getting so important in politics: becoming Governor and all that stuff," she went on in obvious regret for the turns her life had taken. "It was so peaceful here and friendly; not all the strangers around. It was quiet, but your dad liked the life in the Capitol. I suspect that it was more important to him than this."

As they had walked through the, vacant house, his mother pointing out the various rooms and features, Ira could almost feel his father's presence, though, Ira had no recollection of the first three years of his life, that had been spent there. Most his relationships with his father and his memories took place in the Governor's mansion.

"Law's the place to get started, Son; that's where you learn the basics. From there, you can go anywhere you set your mind to," his father had said, and Ira believed almost everything his dad told him. Late at night, after all the "political types", as his mother called them, had left, Ira usually found his father at his desk either studying or writing letters to various government officials. Ira would creep into the study and sit in one of the large maroon leather chairs in a dark corner and watch his father working. He knew that when his dad finally became aware of his presence they would talk about what was important: his progress in school, his becoming a lawyer someday; his father's plan to become a Senator in Washington. At the end of each of these private, one-on-one sessions, his father would always give Ira something to read: sometimes fiction such as James Fennimore Cooper's 'The Last of the Mohicans' and 'The Deer Slayer', sometimes biography, the Lincoln and Douglas debates, sometimes discussions of laws and what they meant.

Most people thought of Calder as a gruff, loud, little man and he cussed a lot; but Ira knew a different man. He could be very quiet and understanding when Ira came to him with problems at school or his fights with other boys.

"Never want to lose the desire to stand up for what you believe. Knock down what you are against, or you might just as well be dead, Ira. Just don't let it look as if you are the one who starts it," he would say and laugh a laugh that started in the pit of his stomach as a frail, distant rumble, way down in his throat, and work its way up into a hilarious roar, as he would lean his head back and let his humor burst forth to fill the room. Ira could remember many such incidents; and now, they kept coming back in his dreams and in his mind when he was trying to study, or at the dinner table when he was just "picking at his food," not hungry.

"Stop dawdling, Ira," get on with your eating so Teresa can clear the table," his mother would reprimand nearly every evening.

Things were greatly different now than when the family had lived in the Governor's mansion for those eight years. Ira could remember all of the servant s from the time he was three until he was eleven. His father and mother acted as if all the help were members of the family; and all of them from the butler, to the chef, to the maids, loved him. As a result they spoiled Ira and his sister and fussed over them. They had played games in the back hallways and secret staircases, ridden on the dumb waiter that traveled from the off the kitchen downstairs to the butler's pantry on the second floor next to the family dining room and study; he had the run of the mansion when he was young; and had even gone back several times when Governor Simpson lived there and twice since Governor Dodson had moved in, just to visit Nancy, who was his favorite of all of all the staff.

These last four years, however, the Calders had lived in a large rented house in Claymore, a small town thirty miles from the city. There, whenever his father wasn't staying in town at his hotel, where he lived most of the time, during the Dodson campaign, his father talked and lived politics, smoked far too many cigars, spent endless hours complaining about President Wilson, and explaining what he was going to do when he became a United States Senator. No one even questioned that Governor Calder, as they still called him, would run and be elected to that prestigious office. He would have run and won in this recent election, except for what his father called "a fluke of human nature". He had selected the wrong man to replace himself as Governor and his party had lost the election to Simpson and the "damn Democrats".

Now, Ira sulked inside and out, whenever he thought of his father's death and his father's lost goal: the U.S. Senate. There had even been talk of his father eventually becoming President; but he had been robbed of that dream by Governor Dodson, another man he had personally picked to run for the governorship and this time had succeeded in getting elected. Ira felt as if there was no way to express his own loss. There was no way to right the wrong that had been done to his father.

Governor Calder had been told many times by Doctor Taylor not to get "overly excited." That was much the same as telling him not to breath, because his "give them hell" nature was one of his strong points: he used it to get things done. He did, however, carry nitroglycerin tablets at all times, but sometimes when he was upset, he was so distracted that he forgot to take them. All the men around him understood this and tried to protect him from himself.

Ira watched his mother taking his father's clothes from the closet and packing them into boxes to send to the Salvation Army. She showed no emotion. He had not seen her cry once since the word came of his father's death.

"Ira, would you clean out your father's desk for me? Put everything in one of the apple boxes in the dining room when you are through," Elizabeth Calder, instructed in a detached tone, almost as if she had not even uttered the words. "Go ahead, Ira; I must finish going through the dresses and pack the trunks."

"Mom, do you think the Governor did that to Father on purpose," he asked.

Elizabeth stopped her packing, looked at him sadly for a moment, put the suits she had in her arms down on his father's bed.

"Ira, Ira, who knows, I don't think the men who play at you father's game know what they are doing most of the time," she said after awhile.

He could make no sense of what his mother was saying, so he stood there waiting for her to say more. She didn't. Instead, she put her arms around him, pulled his head down to her level and kissed his cheek. The embrace lasted for a long time; then silently she went back to the packing, and finally left the room.

The desk was covered with untidy stacks of papers, books, magazines, newspapers from all over the state and the nation. A family picture, a silver gavel mounted on a wooden base to commemorate his chairmanship of the State Republican Committee, several pictures of politicians who worked with him, a brass humidor of his father's cigars, three ash trays (two still with ashes in them, since his father preferred people not cleaning off his desk). Ira opened the top middle, drawer and fumbled through a strange assortment of fountain pens, bottles of ink, blotting paper and pencils.

He examined a magnifying reading glass, a key ring with two small keys on it, two pairs of spectacles, an engraved silver letter opener, some rubber bands, a handful of paper clips and a small bottle of his father's heart medication. There was not very much for him to remember of his father. He sat down in the big swivel chair and twisted back and forth a few times before he started to open the other drawers.

The bottom side drawer was filled with files of letters and some more pictures of politicians. The top left side drawer was locked; however, one of the small keys on the key ring worked, and Ira unlocked it. What was inside was not much more interesting than the other drawers, just stacks of papers. Ira pull a large handful out and placed them on top of another stack on top of the desk, then another handful. "How would he ever know what to throw away and what to save," he thought.

Then he noticed a black object peeking out between the folders left in the drawer and he reached for it. It was cold, hard and metal. He flipped back the pages of paper to reveal his father's prized forty-five pistol next to it a full box of cartridges. He picked it up cautiously and examined it. It was heavy and he could remember that he had seen it once before.

"Never point a gun at anyone you don't intend to kill" he could hear his father say when he had once showed him the gun. "Only reason on God's earth for a gun is to kill; believe me that is a gun's only purpose."

And now, Ira had a gun in his hand, gently at first, then with more confidence. Abruptly, he put it down on a small empty space on the crowded desktop, as if it had frightened him just to touch it. Perhaps it had scared him because of what his father had said; but then his father was no longer his father. His father had been killed; by Governor Dodson and now Ira was alone. Even though his mother had kissed his cheek and put her arms around him, he was alone and he would never be able to talk to his father again. He thought about that fact as he took the rest of the papers out of the drawers of the desk.

Suddenly he looked up and saw his own image in the mirror over the small bookcase opposite his father's desk. He looked at himself in the half-light of the study. He looked so different than he had remembered seeing himself before. His eyes seemed to be a dark, deep green; like his mother's. He had never noticed them before. Looking down at the gun again. He could remember his father's warning "never point a gun at anyone you don't intend to kill." Ira picked up the gun in his left hand, examined it again, then pointed it at himself in the mirror. A chill ran up his spine and he started to squeeze the trigger.

"Ira, have you started to clean Dad's desk out?" his mother's voice prodded gently from the downstairs hall.

Ira slid the gun under the stack of papers. "Yes, Mom, I'm doing it now," he said as he continued to watch himself in the mirror.

"Tomorrow," it was his mother's voice again intruding on his forlorn, private thoughts, "is Saturday so we will have to go into the city and collect your father's things from the hotel and his campaign office. I'll need your help," she was saying; but Ira was not listening.

He pulled the gun out again and pointed it at his mirror image and squeezed the trigger. There was no sound. He practiced holding it steady over and over and over again, pulling the trigger after each careful aim at the mirror.

Winifred drove the car the next morning to the Capital, her mother in the back seat, Ira sitting up front next to her. After they had loaded the car with her father's possessions to take to the Salvation Army, and they had lunch at the Palmer House, Winifred and her mother would go shopping and let Ira go off at the movie house for part of the afternoon. Ira was so restless when there was shopping to do, so it would be a relief to have him out of the way while the two of them took their time looking for the latest fashions, and the best prices. Shopping, because of the war, was skimpy these days, but in Norman it would be practically impossible. It would be the only negative factor, in Elizabeth's mind, that the move back home to Norman would cause.

After lunch and the ceremony of parking the car was completed the two women started off the visit the shops and Ira went off in the direction of the Star Theater. He watched in the window of Cornwall's Men's Wear as his mother and sister crossed the street toward the Emporium. When they had gone inside, he quickly walked back to the car, opened the tool box on the running board and took out the paper sack he had hidden there the night before; then started walking toward the Governor's Mansion. He cut through a couple of back lanes, and into the stable of the mansion. The Governor's car was parked there, so Ira knew that he was probably home, maybe working in his study as his father had done so often when he was Governor.

Nancy, Pamela, Fred, Madge and the chef were eating their lunch at the table by the window in the far corner of the servants' lounge, when Ira slipped quietly down the hall that ran along the full length of the kitchen and pantry area. Through the windows of the swinging door into small side room where the dishes were washed, he could see their profiles and hear their muffled voices, laughter, and the clatter of their dishes. He stood watching the people he knew as his friends and protectors for a few seconds, and then, just as when he had played hide-and-seek with them when he was a child, tip-toed to the other end of the hall and silently inched the far door open far enough for him to slither his way through into the butler's main serving area with its stacks of dishes and ever polished silver serving pieces. From there, he went up the narrow back stairs unnoticed.

When he reached the small butler's pantry on the second floor, he cautiously looked through the small windows of the door into the main hall. From there he could see the door of the Governor's study. It was open slightly and Ira could perceive it move and he stepped back from the window just in time to escape being seen by one of the maids Ira had never seen before, bringing a tray of empty dishes, probably from Governor Dodson's finished meal. She headed directly to the butler's pantry and pushed the door open with her free hand as Ira stepped behind the swinging door. He held his breath and closed his eyes as if that would save him from being discovered. The maid noisily slid the tray into the dumb waiter, and went back out into the hall, the door swinging shut behind her.

Ira breathed again and watched her go down the hall toward the family living quarters and into one of the anterooms off the bedrooms. He waited, still trying to get his breath back into to an even rhythm, as he watched to see if there were any other staff members moving around. When none were obvious, after a minute or two, he took the gun out of the sack, threw the rolled up paper bag into a wastebasket under the small counter, and slid the gun into his left pocket.

He walked casually toward the open door of the study, and quickly walked into the heavily carpet room. The Governor was sitting in front on the fireplace, in his big swivel chair, his back to the door. Ira could hear his breathing and an occasional grunt, as he stood there studying him: Dodson was asleep.

Ira took a deep gulp of air into his lungs, pulled the gun out of his pocket and felt the tension of the trigger increase as he started to squeeze it. Then he heard a door slam down the hall and maid's voices talking to one another coming closer. He stepped quickly behind the study door, his left hand and the gun almost resting on the ornate brass knob. The voices faded, and Ira raised the gun again to take aim, when he felt the door start to move and he instinctively moved back away from it.

"Governor, I just came up to see if you had decided whether you wanted any desert or not," Nancy said coming into the room.

The Election

The Cyrus woke up with a grunt, "Oh, no, no, Nancy; I think I will forego it this afternoon,"

"Very well, Sir," she said and closed the door as she left.

Ira felt the same chill come over his body that he had experienced the day before when he pointed the gun at himself in the mirror. Now, the clamminess even intensified as he listened to the Governor's breathing and looked around the familiar room, the room he had spent so many hours with watching and listening to his father. There was still the faint odor of his father's cigars; and Nancy's voice saying nothing more than "Very well, Sir" in the same tone he had heard her use over and over again.

He wondered what Nancy would say now; what his father would have thought; how his mother would be able to live with the knowledge and would he ever go to law school, as his father had wanted. The gun's weight was becoming more than Ira could endure and he slowly lowered it. At that point he realized he was not going to use it; not today.

Cyrus was now snoring, in gentle sleep. The thought came to Ira that someone would see him with the gun; he had left the sack in the pantry. Suddenly he felt awkward with his father's gun in his hand. He looked around for a moment at the books on the shelves and finally, without a sound, hid it behind the huge unabridged Webster's dictionary. No one would find it there; Governors, not even his father, ever used the dictionary, they had clerks and secretaries to look up words.

While Cyrus slept, Ira opened the door and left; going down the hall to the main stairway, the grand foyer, with its portraits of Clarence Calder and all the other Governors, and the front steps of the Governor's Mansion on his way back to the automobile and the long wait for his mother and sister. Maybe there would be another day, and place, to vent his anger.

Chapter 24

Victor E. Burton, Attorney At Law, sat alone at lunch in the dining room of Colton's National Hotel. His soft-boiled eggs were too soft; they were runny. He had complained; and a large waitress with mounds of frowzy blond hair had just brought a second order of eggs to the table. Now his toast was cold. He checked the dish to be certain none of her hair had found its way into the gelatinous swirls of the yolk. He wondered if the eggs were fresh.

"Is everything satisfactory, Sir?"

"I would like some more butter and a glass of milk."

"You said coffee."

"I said coffee. You are right; but I would like to have a glass of milk as well."

"A glass of milk."

As she walked away from the table he thought to himself how important cleanliness was in women. With men it didn't seem to matter as much. He abhorred the idea of women serving him. Waiters were so much more efficient. He picked up a piece of the dry toast with his long bony fingers and crunched it between his small, even teeth.

She returned with the butter and he cut a large hunk of it off with his spoon and let it melt against the edge of the warm egg dish.

Burton slowly ate his drab, tasteless lunch and thought how well the case was going; just as he had outlined it in his mind. He would win and the Governor would have to pay off as he had promised with the appointment to the appellate court.

Poor Hampden: in his attempt to prove self-defense for Kessel, had proven himself a poor craftsman. It had been a fiasco. Keith, and all other akin to him, it seemed, always treated their cases as if they were somehow personally involved and thus expended emotion they couldn't afford. When an attorney got himself mixed up in the private lives of his clients he was asking for disaster. His judgment went soft and precedents and common sense methods of handling facts were sacrificed. In the translation into legal action, important facts became so much emotional hogwash. Keith Hampden was a victim of his own philosophy of law. Facts in their proper order could defeat any emotional display; and what was worse in this particular instance, was that the defense really had nothing but emotion to play upon. It was pathetic; and yet, they were probably congratulating one another on their brilliant presentation of Kessel's defense; gloating over the way the prosecution had seemingly sat back and let them have their own way.

But it was all according to plan. Burton felt sympathy for someone who was going to lose a case. But then every lawyer, of necessity, must have a few defeats to make a better practitioner of him. Keith would benefit by this experience. It least he would learn that the war was over and war heroes were no longer exempt from the law just because they were "heroes. They became just ordinary "killers" as far as a jury was concerned, if you played your cards right. Next time Keith would probably do a more credible job on his homework, and be harsher on his client. If you ever, for a minute, let a client run a case, or let him hold back on you when there was important evidence to be had, you were doing a disservice to your client and running the risk of damaging your own career. Imagine an attorney so naive that he thought he could win a case on patriotism alone; especially in a situation such as this where the public was convinced that everone had been deceived by a hero. Keith Hampden had been so confident of victory that he was almost arrogant. Perfect, perfect, it had been so perfect that Burton hadn't challenged one juror. It always caused resentment when you were forced to challenge potential jurors, even among those who were finally selected for the panel.

His witnesses for the prosecution had been few. Two were concise in their testimony: Margaret Cross, and the coroner who had examined Morgan's body. Of course, the reluctant Gilbert Henri would not answer one question and succeeded in infuriating the judge and probably convincing the jury that he was hiding some heinous crime from them. Gilbert, still silent, was charged and would serve thirty days for contempt of court. It was the first time Burton, in all his years before the bar had ever seen such a serene witness, nor such a recalcitrant one.

Burton had used nothing but facts; no drama, and an opening statement that plainly pointed out that no man, not even a war hero, should be afforded the luxury of taking another man's life without paying the ultimate penalty.

His closing summation, however, would be brutal and demanding and he would bring in questions that the defense wouldn't dream he would project; well placed comments that the judge might pound his gavel at and demand stricken from the record. But they would be planted firmly enough in the minds of those in the jury box. The law rightfully gave its latitudes and it was up to the attorney to know the reasons for and the limits of those tolerances.

"You want your coffee now?"

Burton looked up, annoyed at the intrusion upon his mental privacy.

"Oh, yes; you can bring it now, if you please."

She returned with a cup three-quarters full; the rest was in the saucer. He looked at her and she looked down at the sloppy service. She grunted and picked up the cup, poured the coffee from the saucer into it and put it back on the saucer.

"Long way from the kitchen," she explained lamely.

He didn't answer.

You may not like people, he thought, for they were unnerving and not to be trusted too often, but you couldn't afford not to understand them. You must accurately predict what they would say, think and do in any given situation. People were actually the prime tools a lawyer had to work with in his trade. They were even more basic than the dry, logical exercises one indulged in arriving at any set of legal decisions or in interpreting the sacred guiding laws.

After the noon recess, Victor Burton was busy at his counsel table before anyone else entered the small courtroom. Wart Kessel had been the defense's last witness before the break and now it would be Burton's turn to cross-examine him. When Matthew Harwood was on the stand for the defense, Burton had dramatically said "No questions", to the surprise of Keith Hampden and Judge Chenoweth. But with Wart Kessel he would not disappoint his audience.

As Hampden and Kessel entered the room, Burton studied them with cold eyes and an expressionless face. Never let them know what you are thinking and they will reveal what they are; it was a simple little rule he used in situations such as this.

"Mr. Kessel, will you take the stand again," Judge Chenoweth said and the voices in the crowded room faded out.

Ward's face was drawn and he looked tired as he sat on the straight chair, cramped by the lack of space.

Burton stood up and started asking his first question as he came around the table.

"Mr. Kessel, you said in your testimony that there was a fight in the Dance Hall and that you were involved. Is that right?"

"In the Grange, yes."

"Did you fight with Mr. Morgan at that time."

"Yes. Well, yes and no."

"Mr. Kessel, either you did or you did not. Which was it?"

"No; I fought with some of Morgan's friends; pushed them around."

"Mr. Kessel; how do you know the men you here fighting with were Mr. Morgan's friends?"

"Because they were fighting on his side."

"I thought you said that you were not fighting Mr. Morgan."

"I wasn't."

"Then Mr. Kessel, what do you mean when you say they were fighting with him?"

"Four of them were fighting with my friend, Matt Harwood. Two were holding his hands behind him. I broke it up; then Morgan and my friend, Matt, fought."

"What happened then, Mr. Kessel?"

"Morgan got kicked in the guts and he stopped fighting."

"Now, you said that after that you went outside and were hit on the head. Is that correct?"

"Yes, I was hit on the head."

"What were you hit on the head with?"

"I don't know."

"You have no idea?"

"No."

"Mr. Kessel, is there a chance that you night have just bumped into something; a wagon, the building, an automobile? Or perhaps you just fell and hit your head on a rock?"

"No."

"Had you been drinking?"

"No."

"Are you sure, Mr. Kessel?"

"I said I was sure."

"What had you been doing before the dance?"

"Driving to the dance."

"Where were you earlier?"

"In Crescent; at the dedication of the new fire engine."

"Very interesting, Mr. Kessel. According to the Walker County Journal news article on the celebration that day, there were several kegs of beer served at the dedication. Was there any beer served, as it says?"

"Yes."

"Did you partake of any of that refreshment?"

"Only a couple."

"Then you had been drinking."

"Yes."

"Then when you said that you had not been drinking, you were lying, right?"

"No! I mean..."

"Do you tell lies very often, Mr. Kessel?"

"Objection!" Keith Hampden yelled, as if suddenly shocked into action.

"Sustained. Mr. Burton, I believe you know why," the judge said shaking his head.

Burton walked away from the witness box and as he turned away from the judge, he smiled broadly at the jury.

"I withdraw the question, Your Honor."

The audience reacted with complete silence and Burton let them sustain the hush before he continued with his next question.

"Where was Matt Harwood at the time you were hit?"

"He had left the dance,"

"Who hit you?"

"Morgan's friends."

"Now, Mr. Kessel, how do you know that they hit you?"

"Because I saw them leave the Grange. I thought they were after Matt and I went to follow them."

"Did you see them when you followed them out of the Dance Hall?"

"No, it was dark; but it was them."

"You couldn't see them, Mr. Kessel. How do you know who it was that did it?"

"It had to be. Because they had left the dance."

"So had your friend left the dance, Mr. Kessel; and I submit to you that, if you were actually hit at all, it could have been your friend Matthew Harwood who hit you just as easily as it could have been Mr. Morgan's associates.

"Now, Mr. Kessel; you stated in your testimony that you were run over by a wagon driven by Mr. Morgan's friends. Is that correct?"

"Yes."

"Again, was it still dark?"

"Of course it was dark."

"Did you see the faces of the people in the carriage that hit you?"

"It wasn't a carriage, it was a wagon; and no, I didn't see them."

"How do you know it was a wagon instead of a carriage?"
"Because of its weight."
"How much did it weight, Mr. Kessel?"
"Objection."
"Sustained."
"I withdraw the question, Your Honor."

Works just like a broken phonograph record, Burton thought: as this part of the game was almost routine, get them flustered.

"And you could tell the identity of the people in the wagon by their weight, too, Mr. Kessel?"
"No!"

Burton smiled again at the jury, and turned almost as if he were going back to his seat, then he whirled around toward the bench and said quietly "That I believe is an honest statement; one of the few I have heard."

"I object, Your Honor," Keith said, standing up in defiance."
"Objection sustained."

"Mr. Kessel, do you know if anyone else saw you run over by the carriage?"
"I didn't see anyone."
"I guess not; it was dark, wasn't it, Mr. Kessel?"
"Yes."
"Then how did you identify those who attacked you and supposedly ran over you?"
"I heard their voices."
"When?"
"When the wagon ran over me."
"What did they say?"
""One of them said a name: 'Don'; and then he said: 'We hit that big bastard', and the other one said 'Let's get out of here'."
"And that is all they said?"
"Yes."
"Could that name have been 'John' instead of 'Don'?"
"No, I told you it was 'Don'!"
"Had you heard any of them call one another 'Don' or 'John' before?"

"No."

"Then how did you know it was one of Mr. Morgan's friends that spoke, if it was dark and if you didn't know their names?"

"I don't know."

"Now, Mr. Kessel; back to when someone supposedly hit you over the head. You don't know what they hit you with?"

"I said I didn't know."

"Did you see their faces?"

"No."

"Did they speak then?"

"I don't know."

"Could you tell by their weight who they were?"

"I object."

"Objection sustained."

"I'll rephrase the question, Mr. Kessel. Since you didn't see your assailants and they didn't speak and you don't know what weapon you were attacked with, was there any other reason for you to suspect who attacked you?"

"No."

"Then, Mr. Kessel; wouldn't you say that your plea of self-defense had rather flimsy proof to back it up?"

"No! It was just like I said it was."

Ward felt the tip of his tongue search the back of his front teeth. Dry, hot air, his breath, parched his palate, his gums and his nostrils. His tongue again stretched full length against the roof of his mouth, now tracing the outline of each tooth. It seemed to give moisture, create saliva and cool the storm of dryness. He relaxed back against the hard chair, allowing the content of his lungs to escape.

Burton paused long enough in his endless questioning to take a drink of water.

"Mr. Kessel; since I have many more questions to ask, would you, too, desire a drink?"

"Yes, thank you."

Burton held the pitcher far from the glass, causing the pouring water to be heard throughout the courtroom; then dramatically picked the glass up from the counsel table and slowly carried it to Ward. Ward had to reach out over the railing of the witness box to grasp the glass.

"Thank you," Ward said again.

"Very much my pleasure, Mr. Kessel," he said and waited for Ward to finish the water.

"'What strong-looking hands, Mr. Kessel. Are they the weapon you killed Mr. Morgan with?"

"I object."

"Your Honor, Mr. Kessel has already admitted to choking Mr. Morgan. I merely wanted to identify the weapon used in the attack."

"Sustained, Mr. Burton," the judge said in disgust.

When Ward handed him back the glass, the prosecutor slowly walked back to the table and put the empty glass by the pitcher.

Ward self-consciously looked at his own hands and lowered them to his lap.

"As I recall in your testimony, Mr. Kessel, you stated that after you had been run over, you went back to the Grange hall and killed Mr. Morgan."

"I object, Your Honor."

"Objection sustained."

"You had a discussion with Mr. Morgan. Is that right?"

"Yes."

"And he pulled a knife and stabbed you with it?"

"Yes."

"Did you see the knife?"

"Yes."

"What kind of knife was it?"

"It had a pearl handle and..."

"Mr. Kessel, pardon me, but did this happen in broad daylight?"

"I object, Your Honor, Mr. Burton is badgering the witness."

"Objection sustained."

"I'm very sorry, Mr. Kessel. Was it dark?"

"Yes!"

"Could you really tell that it had a pearl handle; in the dark?"
"No; but..."
"That is all the answer I need, Mr. Kessel."
Ward looked desperately at the judge, "Your Honor, I saw the knife in the Grange and in the barn after it happened."
The judge motioned for Ward to address Burton
"Do you know where that alleged knife is now?" Burton, pleased with himself, asked.
"No."
"Have you seen it since that night?"
"No."
"Mr. Kessel; you testified earlier that you choked Lawrence Morgan after he had stabbed you and that the knife was still sticking in your side after you put Mr. Morgan back in his buggy. Is that correct?"
"Yes."
"Mr. Kessel, didn't you, in reality, guide that horse and buggy with Mr. Morgan's body in it right into the river, yourself?"
"No."
"I object to this line of questioning, Your Honor; the prosecution is trying to cloud the issue and the witness's mind."
"Your Honor, I am merely trying to establish a very primary point: that Mr. Morgan's horse would not very likely have wandered into that raging river by itself, especially since Mr. Morgan was not in a condition to drive the buggy himself."
"That is circumstantial and does not prove a single point at issue."
"Objection sustained. Please strike that question and answer from the record."
Burton seemed unperturbed by the minor setback. He smiled and took another drink of water.
"Mr. Kessel; you did say that Morgan's knife was still lodged in your side after you had placed Mr. Morgan in the buggy?"
"Yes."
"Then what did you do with the knife? If there was a knife."

"There was a knife and I don't know what happened to it, but my side was all cut up there are still scars."

"Where did you say Mr. Morgan stabbed you?"

"The left side."

"The left." Burton walked over to his counsel table and picked up a large manila envelope and brought it back to the bench.

"Your Honor, I request this exhibit be accepted by the court as evidence. It is a transcript of Mr. Kessel's army service records including those of Mr. Kessel's stay in a French hospital."

"I object, Your Honor; such information is irrelevant to this case."

"Your Honor, I intend to prove that this record of Mr. Kessel's war injury is of major importance."

"Objection overruled; you may submit your exhibit, Mr. Burton."

"Thank you, your Honor. Now, Mr. Kessel, I am not a medical doctor; but I would like to read one page from this record: 'Multiple abrasions and lacerations about the head with two penetrating bayonet wounds below the rib cage on the left side of the abdominal cavity, just above and to the left of the spleen. The patient also sustained from the rear a bayonet wound in the left latissimus- dorsi muscle and one presumed bayonet wound in the upper left thigh. A total of sixty stitches were required for the abdominal wounds, thirty-five for the back wound and twenty-four for the thigh injury. Because of the severity of the injuries and possible irritation of resultant scar tissue, a medical discharge has been recommended as further military action might impair the safety of others depending on the patient for support should the present wounds cause acute disablement in battle.'"

Burton looked to the judge for a moment and then at the members of the jury to see how the medical report had "played in their minds" and then continued.

"Would you say that was a correct description of your war injuries and of the remaining scars resulting from those injuries, Mr. Kessel?"

"Yes."

"Do these wounds still bother you from time to time?"

"I'm not certain."

"Now, Mr. Kessel, you certainly would know whether a wound hurt or disturbed you, wouldn't you?"

"Yes."

"But you don't know if these serious war injuries still bother you."

"No."

"I hate to sound insistent, but why don't you know?"

"Because that is the same place that Morgan stabbed me."

"In the left side?"

"Yes."

"Right where the bayonet wound was?"

"Yes."

"How strangely convenient. Wouldn't you say that was miraculously convenient? Perhaps supernatural, a case of divine intervention."

"I object."

"Objection sustained."

"Are you occasionally disturbed by the wound you say was inflicted by Mr. Morgan?"

"Your Honor, I object, the attorney for the prosecution is deliberately trying to upset the witness."

"Your Honor, I'll be damned if I am trying to upset the witness. Counsel for the defense must think that we are having an old maid's tea. There is a first degree murder charge against this man and I am trying to establish the facts; and that is all."

"Mr. Burton, shut up." the judge said looking down over his glasses, "Objection overruled."

"Mr. Kessel, are you ever distressed by the wound in your left side?"

"Yes."

"Who treats you when you have trouble with it?"

Ward looked at him with a puzzled expression.

"Do you go to a doctor?" Burton asked.

"Yes."

"Which doctor, Mr. Kessel?"

"Dr. Phillips in Crescent."

"You are sure of his name?"

"Yes," Ward said with a disgusted grunt.

"And he is the doctor you claim you went to on the night you say Mr. Morgan stabbed you, right?"

"Yes, but he's dead now."

"How convenient. Mr. Kessel, just what did Doctor Phillips do for you the night you had him treat you?"

"He washed out the wound, put some antiseptic on it, sewed it up and bandaged it. Then he gave me a shot."

"Going back a bit, Mr. Kessel. On the night of the alleged stabbing and Mr. Morgan's death, how did you get to the doctor's office to be treated?"

"In my surrey."

"And you were bleeding heavily all the time?"

"Yes."

"How long did it take to ride from the Walker County Grange to Doctor Phillips?"

"I guess about an hour or an hour and a half."

"And you drove your horse and surrey back to Crescent by yourself and had Dr. Phillips dress your wound."

"No. Mitzie Kawalski drove the surrey back to Crescent."

"Miss Kawalski, the conveniently missing witness you mentioned in your previous testimony?"

"Yes."

"How old was Mitzie Kawalski?"

"I don't really know; about twenty-two or three. I think."

"Did you know Mitzie Kawalski before you came to live in Crescent?"

"Yes."

"How strong was Mitzie Kawalski?"

"I don't know."

"But strong enough to drive a wagon back through the storm?"

"Yes."

"And Matthew Harwood?"

"He was injured, too."

"Now, Mr. Kessel; once more, just for clarity, I'm going to paint a word picture and when I'm through I want you to tell me if it is correct. You put Morgan in his buggy; then you pulled the knife from your bleeding side. Mind you, according to your testimony, you thought you were about to die and the wound was serious enough to keep you in bed for six and a half weeks. Then Mitzie Kawalski drove you, in that weakened, and bleeding condition, in one of the worst storm this county has witnessed in the past fifteen years. An hour and a half trip to Dr. Phillips', where he washed this gaping wound, sewed it up and bandaged it. Is that correct?"

"Yes."

"Your Honor, I have another piece of evidence that I would like to have entered at this time," Burton said as he went back to his table and picked up a green cloth-bound ledger book and placed it before the judge. "That is, Your Honor, if the defense does not care to object to proper evidence. It is the record book of the late Doctor Phillips."

"Does the defense have any objections?" the judge asked.

"No, Your Honor."

"On page two twenty-one there is an entry for two forty-five a.m. on July fourteenth, nineteen eighteen, the night of the fight, which reads: 'Mathew Harwood treated for knife lacerations on the forearms, right shoulder and several severe bruises on the stomach and face.' There is no mention of your visit, Mr. Kessel, whatsoever. The only mention of your name comes a day later when Doctor Phillips recorded a visit to your blacksmith shop when he wrote: 'treated Ward Kessel for two broken ribs on the right side'. Mr. Kessel, can you think of any reason why the doctor would want to omit any mention of treatment to a man who had been bludgeoned in the head, run over by a heavy wagon and left with gaping abdominal wounds bleeding all over the place, when he made a detailed listing of minor injuries that same night where another man was concerned?"

Ward looked at his attorney in despair.

"I object."

"On what grounds, Counselor?"

"This line of questioning is irrelevant to this case."

"Objection overruled. Will the witness answer the question."

"I don't know what the question was, Sir."

"Would counsel repeat the question?"

"Yes, Your Honor. Can you think of any reason, Mr. Kessel, why Dr. Phillips did not mention the treatment of your supposed knife wounds?"

"To protect me."

"From what, Mr. Kessel? You said you didn't know Morgan was dead until you read it in the newspaper the following Thursday."

"I don't know."

"'Well then, perhaps I can add a few points of interest; I submit that you were never attacked when you left the dance hall, that you were never run over by the wagon and that Lawrence Morgan, in fact, did not stab you with a knife. I submit in truth, by the evidence before this court, that you followed Mr. Morgan out of the dance hall that night after the fight and in your anger over the brawl inside and jealousy over Mitzie Kawalski, took Morgan by the neck and choked him to death, and that you then put Morgan's body in his buggy and ran it into the river."

"Now, Mr. Kessel, let me paint another picture. After you murdered Morgan...."

"I object."

"Objection sustained."

"After you dumped Morgan in his buggy, you and your girl friend, Mitzie Kawalski helped your injured friend Matthew Harwood into your surrey and drove him to Dr. Phillips for treatment. You were not treated by a doctor until the next day when you were actually kicked by a horse in the routine of your business as a blacksmith and had some ribs broken. Does that picture make sense?"

"I object."

For the first time Burton showed a tinge of aggravation. His cheeks flushed and he noticeably took a deep breath and slowly let it out. To regain his composure, he walked back to his table and looked down at it his notes. There would be time enough in the summation to plant doubt several more times.

"Your Honor, if the counsel for the defense did not want to have the defendant asked questions about this death, then he should not have put him on the witness stand in the first place, where by law he is subject to cross-examination."

"Mr. Burton, perhaps someday you will be on the bench. Until that time, please confine yourself to the role of prosecutor, and refrain from lecturing the court. The court is capable of making its own rulings. Now, Mr. Hampden, your objection?"

"The prosecuting attorney is editorializing and dealing in speculation rather than in the cherished facts."

"I sure as hell am not."

"You sure as hell are."

"Gentlemen, gentlemen, I've had enough."

"I apologize, your Honor," Burton said.

"Objection sustained. Now Mr. Burton, once more: confine the interrogation to proper questions."

"Yes, Your Honor. Mr. Kessel, did Dr. Phillips come to your shop the day following the alleged stabbing and treat you for two broken ribs as is stated in his record book?"

"He didn't?"

"No."

"Then Dr. Phillips was a liar?"

"I object."

"Overruled; continue Mr. Burton."

"I guess so."

"And why would he lie?"

"I don't know, except to protect me."

"I submit that he was telling the truth."

"He fixed the bandages on my wound; the knife wound."

"Mr. Kessel, were you in the courtroom when Mrs. Cross testified that Dr. Phillips told her that a horse had kicked you. It had two broken ribs and that you would have to be kept in bed for a matter of weeks. Gilbert Henri would be needed to work in your blacksmith shop because of those broken ribs?"

"Yes."

"Then she was equivocating under oath; is that what you are saying?"

"I object, Your Honor."

"Objection sustained."

"Mr. Kessel, Dr. Phillips was a respected member of his profession. As such, do you think he would be in the habit of altering the truthfulness of his medical records to accommodate the personal needs, desires or protection of any one of his patients or friends?"

"No."

"I agree with you once more, Mr., Kessel; and that is why I submit that you were never attacked with a knife at all, and that you are merely trying to cover up your murder of Lawrence Morgan by making it appear to be self defense. Mr. Kessel have you ever murdered a man before?

"I object."

"Objection sustained."

Burton shook his head and went back to the table again and shuffled through his stack of papers.

"In that case, Your Honor, I would like to enter one more piece of evidence: an article from a Pennsylvania paper in which there are details of a killing where a man was choked to death during a fight over a young girl by the name of Mitzie Kawalski. The man with the killing hands was Ward Kessel, according to this newspaper and the records of the Hatch County Sheriff."

The defense attorney was on his feet and to the bench before Burton was back from his table.

"Your Honor, I request permission to examine this questionable piece of evidence."

"Granted."

Burton handed the small newspaper clipping to Keith Hampden and he read it.

"I object to this being submitted by the prosecution on grounds that it is prejudicial to this case."

After the judge read the clipping, he shook his head, "Sustained. Mr. Burton, you amaze me with your impertinence. Strike all of this last reference from the records. Now, do you have any further questions for this defendant?"

"Yes, Your Honor. Mr. Kessel, when you read in the paper, as you have stated in your testimony that Morgan was dead and since the act of violence was supposed to have been committed in self defense, why didn't you report the incident?"

"I don't know."

"You don't know, Mr. Kessel? Isn't a man's life important in your mind?"

"I object."

"Overruled."

"I'll rephrase it anyway, Your Honor. Mr. Kessel, did the report of Mr. Morgan's death disturb you?"

"Yes."

"But not enough to disclose the true nature of it to the law."

"I guess not."

"I submit, Mr. Kessel, that if it had been an accident, or self defense as you claim, you would have had no reason to hide it. No further questions."

There was a lengthy pause, while the judge seemed to be re-reading the newspaper article. Finally he looked up, as if embarrassed by his delay of the proceedings. He took out his handkerchief and blew his nose then said in a quiet voice, "The defendant may step down. Court stands adjourned until tomorrow morning at ten a.m."

The following day was mainly filled with the defense summation. Keith Hampden brought tears to the eyes of the women in the audience as he told of Ward being victimized and Agatha expecting a child.

In response, Burton changed his tact and in a statement that took less than three minutes presented his entire case once more and ended with a simple cold sentence.

"If Mr. Kessel is given the right to live after this vicious killing, why not give the same right to every murderer in the land?"

After that the court was adjourned.

Through the bars of the one small window, the tired warmth of the low afternoon sun slashed purple streaks down the bare, whitewashed walls of the cell.

Fuzzy footsteps in the distance magnified themselves into crisp, militant percussion dominating the foreground, then halted with a stomp, the harsh rattling of key in lock and an echoing, metallic clang.

Suddenly fear faded and strength took its place, Ward pushed the straight-backed wooden chair screeching back from the table and stood up. Agatha folded in his arms, oblivious of the guard. Her hands were moist and he held them gently, then kissed her fingers and smiled down at her.

"It was strange," she said. "I thought I would freeze to death."

"It was cold, but has been like being in hell."

"Ward; do you think, even for a minute, that they might...."

"Darling," he said and kissed her long and hard, "it doesn't matter now; we told the truth. If they believed me, I'll be all right. If not, I don't know how I could have told it any differently."

"But that ugly man kept making it sound as if you were lying."

"I know; but I wasn't. And I believe he knows that I was telling the truth. I could tell by the way he looked away when I looked in his eyes; he seemed to avoid me as if he were trying to keep me from seeing inside him."

"It isn't real. It's worse than a dream; and I feel as if I'm going to wake up and it will be all over. But I'm afraid."

"Aggie, Aggie, come on, darling. Things will work out."

She looked up at him for a second, then turned her face away and stared, without focusing, at the floor.

"Hey, we've got a lot to live for; now...."

"I know, Ward; that's why I'm lost. They're trying to take you away from me; I can feel it. That horrible little man is trying to kill you."

He held her closely and felt the defiance in her small body.

"They are just doing what they have to as lawyers."

"They are not, Ward; it's more than that. Matt told me what my father said to him; and if anything happens to you, Ward, I'll spend the rest of my life making Daddy Cyrus pay for what he has done. I will; yes I will."

"Aggie, nothing is going to happen; I have a feeling that everything will be all right."

Again she did not look up at him, but stayed in his arms, silently absorbing the warmth of his embrace; the child of her pregnancy pressed tight against his body. The sunset and the cell became shrouded in a cold, blue grey haze, however the guard did not disturb them until word came from the courtroom.

"Mr. Kessel, Mr. Kessel; the jury has a verdict."

They held their embrace until their strength seemed to ebb from them and then they walked, emptied, into the crowded, noisy room of glaring flash bulbs and anticipating faces.

"It's good news; such a short deliberation," Keith Hampden said."

"Will the prisoner rise and face the court."

Ward stood, feeling as if he were numb and naked.

"Has the jury reached a verdict?"

"Yes, your Honor, we have."

"How do you find?"

"We find the defendant guilty of murder in the first degree, Your Honor."

"Your Honor, Your Honor, Your Honor, Your Honor," echoed back and forth across the room.

"Guilty," Ward said aloud.

Keith Hampden stood up as if to protest, then slowly sat down and put his hands over his face.

"Pronouncement of sentence will take place in this court room tomorrow morning at ten a.m. Court is adjourned."

"What does that mean?" Ward whispered as he leaned toward Hampden.

"Ward, we'll appeal for a commutation of sentence; then we'll try for a retrial, and..."

Ward looked into Hampden's desperate face. It was flushed and worried.

"I don't know: I don't understand how any jury could sit there and come up with that answer," Hampden muttered, half to himself.

"Then they're going to hang me?"

"No! No! No; they're not going to hang you! I'm going to the Governor and have it commuted."

"You believe in miracles?"

"You'll see, Ward; the Governor will change that decision because it's unfair and unlawful."

"They will hang me. I know Cyrus Dodson."

"You may know Cyrus Dodson, but I know the intent of the law. And there is so much reasonable doubt in this case that even he can see it. He'll commute it."

"To what?"

"Life. And then we'll really get to work."

The guard took Ward's arm and led him from the courtroom. Ward didn't even look back at Agatha. He knew she would be crying. But if he had looked, he would have seen her without tears, a fierce, determined fixation in her eyes.

Chapter 25

In the weeks following the trial, Crescent was divided over the news of the verdict. Gilbert moved from Margaret Cross's house without saying good-bye. Agatha hired him to work in the blacksmith shop full time; letting him use Ward's old room to sleep in.

Reverend Pritchard gave a sermon that delved into the divergent paths of human weakness, all of which led to where the cast-out third of the hosts of heaven suffered in eternal damnation. Those who broke the commandments would be judged for their sins on earth or in the millennium, for the commandments said "Thou shall not kill" among other standard texts used as cover ups for the shortcomings of civilized man.

Myrtle Dodson decided against going back to the Governor's Mansion; she was needed more in Crescent. She fit in better in Crescent. Cynthia would stay with her, while Alfreda, Peggy and Gloria would live at the capital. They would enjoy the excitement of the new life, but Myrtle herself had paid much more than a fair price for her second marriage. Making any further adjustments was more than she was prepared to ask of herself, especially now that Cyrus had become the way he was; obsessed, inhumanely obsessed with his own importance. Let him drink his own poison; he would not force it down her throat. The way he had become so calloused over Ward Kessel and Agatha: not one flicker of sympathy, even when the news of the sentence had been received. Even Gloria seemed confused by this attitude.

Bruce McHenry was silent, without opinion on a controversial topic for the first time in his life. He was torn apart by two loyalties and two friendships, neither of which seemed to offer a solution to his dilemma. He didn't know who was right and who was wrong; so, in his newly acquired wisdom, he kept quiet. He thought over and over that things would be different if Dr. Phillips were still alive to help him reason this all out.

Though the war was over, Matt Harwood tried to join the Navy, but would have to wait for a month or so before he could take his physical examination as the training camp facilities were filled and a bog-down in logistics was temporarily holding back the recruiting program in the state. Cyrus had written and offered Matt his job back on a permanent basis, apologizing for "their slight differences of opinion" and noting that it was time for another raise. Matt threw the letter in the wastebasket; it didn't sound the way Mr. Dodson would talk. It was almost as if he were begging for something, and it was not like Mr. Dodson to beg for anything from anybody.

Margaret Cross was proud. She, too, had received a letter from Governor Cyrus Dodson. She had traced her fingers over the embossed State seal on the envelope and letterhead time after time, realizing the importance of the contents. Cyrus Dodson had commended her on her citizenship and on her insistence in seeing that justice was done. He was depending on first-class citizens such as herself to help him make the state a safe place for people to live their lives. He needed help to bring honesty to the people. She would cherish his praise and would keep the letter in the drawer of the small gold and black lacquered jewelry box she kept on her dresser. The prized box was a gift from her husband, Harry, on their fifth wedding anniversary. Gilbert would have obstructed justice if she had not spoken up, even after she had explained to him what had happened. He was wrong; but she missed him. He would change his mind, someday, and would come back to live there.

Willie Clay had been the focal point of attention in Crescent. He had caught a murderer and had calmly gone about his job of taking the criminal to jail. People would look up to him from now on. Willie Clay had been the first law officer in Crescent's history to solve a serious crime. He thought to himself how empty he felt now it was all over. It would be hard to go back to just sitting by the stove reading books. He knew now that he would never feel the same sense of suspense when he read Doyle: fiction and real life just were not cut from the same pattern. The peak of his life had passed, and there would never be another important arrest in his career, probable not even another robbery. The article, the *Journal*, had printed about him, described him as "hard, efficient, businesslike and determined". He had mailed a copy of the paper to his brother, Robert, who had moved to Des Moines, Iowa; and one to Tad, his boy who was in the Navy. His wife had wanted him to mail more copies, but it embarrassed him even to send those. Everyone in Crescent must know inside that Ward Kessel wasn't a murderer and that Willie Clay wasn't a "dedicated officer whose one desire was justice." The printed word could make one sick to one's stomach.

Mr. Schmidt was relieved; Crescent would now be a safe place for his daughter's new son to grow up and live. He hadn't really liked the blacksmith since he had returned from the war and all the speeches made about him; that told how he killed the Germans and was so vicious and dangerous as a soldier. Now, that all the killing had stopped when would people stop telling horrible stories about the Germans? When, when, when would people realize that the Germans had been victims of their leaders and that the German people were not responsible for all the horrible things that were written about them in the newspapers? He was troubled about the war that had left him an outsider in Crescent; and he was satisfied to know that Ward would hang.

Anne Harwood would not believe Ward Kessel had murdered that Flintsville man. He very easily could have killed him, he admitted that; but murder; that was something that took a scheming mind. What she had seen of Ward Kessel and what Matthew had told her about him was enough to convince her that the fight was one of spontaneous anger on the parts of all the men involved. She didn't approve of fighting, but it was part of the male animal, the nature of the male beast. That quality had been so evident in her boys, perhaps not so much in Karl himself, but in her boys; a bit fiery, irrational and impetuous, all of which added up to danger if not released in minor ways on a regular basis. It would be an irreparable tragedy if the sentence were carried out. She would write a letter to Governor Dodson who she had heard talk many times; about "honesty and justice".

Karl Harwood was sorrowed but relieved by the news. He had received a letter from Matt in Colton. He was elated that Matt had not been implicated any more than he had been. It would have been so easy: for some conviction-happy prosecutor to have brought charges against Matt as an accomplice. It left him weak every time he thought about it. Karl felt that the law should take its course and that the verdict of any court should be obeyed. He was glad Matt had been lucky, even though Matt in his letter indicated that he felt guilty at being free of any charge. Crescent would be different without Ward Kessel: and Matthew would no doubt feel the loss of his friend more than anyone. While he grieved over what would take place on the scaffold in the courtyard of the state prison at Grantsville, Karl felt annoyed by an idea that poked its nose out through a small crack in his mind every time he looked in the mirror. He had wanted to start an automobile agency in Crescent. It was certainly the coming thing: "a car in front of every home." Perhaps he would buy the blacksmith shop and start selling auto and farm equipment; as the need for horseshoes faded. It would allow him to put his suitcase in the attic and stay home to enjoy Annie's cooking and love, and it would give the boys a perfect reason for staying in Crescent.

MacQuarrie took hold of the railing, slammed his suitcase up to the vestibule of the railroad car and climbed the steps. When the train got going he'd sneak a drink. His visit to Ward had been barren, void, and impersonal. With a guard within a few feet, all the time during the visit Ward didn't want to talk.

"What's there to say? They are simply going to hang me that's it!"

"Now look, Ward, Keith is one of the best young defense lawyers in the county. In his letter to me, he said he was convinced he could arrange things."

"You know 'who that depending on'; don't you?"

"On the courts, I suppose."

"No, you are wrong; very wrong. He's counting on Cyrus Dodson to give me a stay of execution, as he calls it, and then a commutation of sentence. So I can spend the rest of my life in jail."

"Keith didn't say that."

"I think he believed that damned prosecutor as much as the jury did. I don't want to spend one more day in this place; I've been away from Agatha long enough already. I killed Morgan in self-defense. If I hadn't, he would have killed me."

"Keith Hampden has been..."

"Do YOU believe me?"

"In more court cases than any other attorney in this," MacQuarrie tried to continue.

"Do you believe me?"

"Yes."

"Then stop talking about Hampden. He thinks I'm guilty as much as the rest of them."

"Who should I talk to, who?"

"I don't know; I don't know. There just isn't anyone who can do or say anything to help."

"I'll try anyway."

"Certainly not Cyrus Dodson. If I know him he'll be happy to see me die just so he can make Agatha suffer for marrying me."

"Now come on, Ward; that's a bit much to swallow."

"If you think Cyrus Dodson is so fair and just, why did you leave him?"

"A personal matter."

"What kind of a personal matter?"

MacQuarrie stood up and turned toward the door. "I didn't come all the way down here to talk about myself."

"I know."

"And I really will keep trying."

"Imagine calling your resignation a personal matter. That's a cover up."

MacQuarrie ignored Ward's last remark and called for the guard.

"Mac, I hate to be morbid, but there isn't a chance. Think about it: only sixty-two days."

"I'll still try."

The trial had changed Ward and him. There had been a time when he and Ward could talk for hours and make sense; now they said nothing and got on one another's nerves saying it.

In Colton the following morning, MacQuarrie went to the courthouse and combed the transcript of the trial again. There might just be something there he hadn't seen before; but there wasn't. The only thing that interested him was the testimony of Matthew Harwood. It was similar to Mac's last conversation with Ward: it didn't say anything. Keith's questioning had been directed only at establishing the fight inside the Grange and the visit to Dr. Phillips' home; nothing about the characters of Morgan and the others involved in the brawl. Since Matt was involved he certainly could have elaborated on Morgan. In fact, there wasn't even a mention of the names of any of the other boys in the fight. What was Keith Hampden thinking of? They certainly could have traced the boys somehow.

"Kind of a dull trial, wasn't it?" the County Clerk said as he put the record back in the file. "It sorta; well, kinda made you feel like the guy was, you know, put on greased skids."

"Kind of railroaded?" MacQuarrie asked.

"Well, no; not exactly. I thought Judge Cheneworth's instructions to the jury were kinda fair; almost, you might say, in favor of the guy. But then, that prosecutor, he was something else, he really was. Didn't you think? However, as I said, it was a dull one. The trial, that is."

April was primping and there were tulips and daffodils along the sidewalks in Crescent, and in spite of the rain that was busy washing away all of winter's leftovers, MacQuarrie enjoyed his walk from the Dodson home to Doctor Phillips'. Mrs. Everett opened the door and led him into the small parlor.

"Mrs. Everett, Myrtle Dodson suggested you might be able to help me. I'm trying to get Ward Kessel a retrial."

"Anything I can, I will."

"Dr. Phillips' records?"

"I'm sorry; but you see, the State hasn't returned them."

"None of them?"

"No; of course all they took was the book."

"Any letters or personal notes that I might be able to look at?"

Mrs. Everett thought for a moment, then walked to the china closet in the corner and opened the drawer at the cloths and linen napkins, she pulled out a worn, maroon leather photo album.

"Letter, no; only ones he ever saved were the ones from his sweetheart; she died of diphtheria before I even came to work for Doctor. But photographs; you might like to look at them."

He wasn't interested, but he politely watched while she turned the pages.

"It is so hard to believe a life is over when you look at an early picture of a baby all dribbling and nude, isn't it?"

"Yes." MacQuarrie said, trying to seem attentive."

"Oh, and when he was young, there were more young women. He never talked about them, but you just watch; almost every other picture has young, lovely women holding hands or hugging him, and sometimes, just for fun, kissing."

"Seems most of us are inclined that way."

"You are a philosopher, aren't you," she said and smiled in reminiscence.

"Not really; that is just being rather basic."

"But with Doctor Phillips, I can understand everyone of them. He was still attractive to young women when he died. I know because, even though old, I am a woman."

"Did Dr. Phillips keep any other records; any at all?"

"He wasn't too much for business. Oh, Doctor had a stack of notes he kept to keep track of charging people; but there wouldn't be anything there for Ward."

"Why not?"

"They had a gentlemen's agreement as the doctor called it. Ward fixed the doctor's buggy and horses and then his car when he got that; in turn Ward got free coffee, scones and medical treatment."

"How convenient."

"Ward didn't collect too often; his one injury was the only time I can remember Doctor mentioning."

MacQuarrie sat up straighter in the chair and leaned forward. "Do you remember anything about the night Ward Kessel was hurt?"

"'Fraid not. Doctor kept all hours for fixing people; and a body just can't stay awake all the tine to keep track."

"Wasn't there anything? You said Ward had never been here before, so wasn't there anything you might remember that was different?"

"Oh, Ward Kessel was here before, lots of times. He'd come over and eat hot scones with the doctor. About that night, I was asleep so I couldn't have paid much ado about what Ward Kessel was doing."

"Mrs. Everett, may I look in Doctor Phillips' office?"

"You know, I almost of instinct say 'no' when you ask that, forgetting he's gone. I am certain, however, very certain he wouldn't mind if it would help Ward Kessel keep his life."

Cluttered and musty, the office revealed little except its lack of occupancy and the carefree nature of the man who had once worked there.

"I haven't dusted since it happened. Doctor wasn't too inclined at being tidy; but he was always so gentle, even when he acted tough with some of his patients such as Ward."

In one corner of one room, MacQuarrie noticed a doctor's bag,

. rø white with a faded red cross on its glass door.

"What did the doctor keep in here?"

"His drugs, mainly; some instruments, but mainly just drugs." MacQuarrie tried to open it, but it was locked. "May I look inside?"

"Oh, of course, the key. Let's see, I think he kept it in this vase with the fluted top. She picked it up and rattled it. "There it is." She laid the pencils on the already crowded desk and turned the vase upside down.

The instruments and bottled of drugs and pills in the cabinet were slightly better organized than the rest of the office. There were six small 'bottles of morphine tablets; it seemed to be the doctor's mainstay. On the same shelf was a small blue notebook with a stub of a pencil tied to it with scrawled but legible hand, a notation of each drug dosage given was ma e with the date and patient's name. MacQuarrie scanned down the name column with his index finger, until he found the entry he had hoped he would find.

"July 14th; Kessel; 1/4 grams morphine."

That was the day after the fight. And there was several other listings with Ward's name on the days that followed.

"Mrs. Everett, did the doctor give morphine for things such as broken ribs?"

"I wouldn't think so. He tried not to give people dope unless they were in serious condition; ever since Eli Mason became an addict from too much treatment, after Doctor had to amputate his leg (caught in a harrow when he fell off a wagon). Doctor said, 'It's as if all the devils in hell were let loose in them; if they once get started and can't 'break themselves. He used to sneak a shot of morphine to Eli once in a while when he would come screaming at the door at night, until one morning they found Eli hanging by his neck in his own barn. Somehow he had climbed a ladder and hung himself from the hayloft. No, I doubt Doctor would give anything strong if it was nothing more than broken bones."

MacQuarrie looked through the papers on the desk, but it had obviously been searched before. He wondered how they had missed the drug cabinet. There was nothing more that ~~11tc1c~tGd h'~1rn~ he th0nn~~ Mrs. Everett, and went back down the street toward Cyrus's house. Suddenly he stopped; he wondered where the Harwood boy lived. It might be well to talk to him. He walked back to the Doctor's home. Mrs. Everett had seen him returning and was waiting at the door.

"Anne Harwood and her family?"

"I guess so; young boy named Matt."

"That's them. Matthew is the youngest boy. Nice folks; the Harwoods." She pointed, "Two blocks, then left at Poplar, about four houses down on the south side on the street. You can't miss it; name's on the mailbox."

"Thank you."

He watched the door close and then he turned and followed her directions. The sun was now out and MacQuarrie was glad there was spring to stir him back to life after every winter.

"Good morning, Mr. MacQuarrie."

He looked up into Margaret Cross's eager eyes.

"Oh, hello; how are you?"

"I'm fine," she said, putting her hand on his. "Are you to be in Crescent long?"

"Probably just today."

"I wish you would drop by for tea."

"Might just do that; haven't listened to a piano solo for ages."

She smiled coyly at his remark. "Tea, then?" she asked for reassurance.

"Probably."

MacQuarrie was aware that her walk had a slight, teaø He hadn't had time to think of such activities since the last time he was with her on their first meeting. That would indicate that either age was catching up with him or the past year had sobered his mind. Then, on the other hand, both of those reasons fizzled out like a couple of balloons losing their air; he had been just too busy. Then there was Gloria; one could always dream. But, before the day was over he probably would drop by. Just for tea.

Matthew was very happy to have MacQuarrie visit him.

They sat at the kitchen table with the bright sun almost blinding them as it invaded the room through the large panes of the kin3ory. "A happy house," MacQuarrie thought as he listened to the sounds of the Victrola coming from the front room where the Harwood sisters were singing along with the latest record.

"Mr. MacQuarrie; just in time for lunch with the children," Ann Harwood said as she busied herself at the kitchen sink.

"I'm really not here to put you to any bother," MacQuarrie said, but the smell of hot bread and beefy vegetable soup simmering on the coal stove forced him to put his protest in muted tones. "Sure he will, b-o- Mr.MacQuarrie will eat with us," Matt added.

"And you'd really be more bother if you didn't eat," brought them up to be.

"Matthew, Id say your mother was giving you a lecture at the same time she was giving me an invitation."

"Oh, it wouldn't do a bit of good," she said.

"Now, Mom."

"It wouldn't and we all know it. All grown up. Did you tell Mr. MacQuarrie how grown up you are?"

"Of course not; that only just come."

"Girls, girls; come now; soups on the table," Ann said at the peak of her voice. "Of course, it isn't, but it will start them thinking of getting in here by the time it is," she added with a smile.

"I thought you were grown up, Matt."

"Oh, she" talking about my trying to join the Navy; you know how mothers are."

"No; I'm sure, Matthew, that he'd never know how mothers are; only a mother would know that," his mother said and turned back to filling the bowls.

"Joined the Navy? The war is over. When?"

"A week ago; but they're not ready for me yet. Might not be until the end of the month, or not at all if they don't need me.'"

"Margo, will you come slice the bread, dear?" Ann shouted through the door. "And they wonder why mothers and fishwives have the same size lungs."

The lunch was ample and as taste as MacQuarrie had 'back steps in the sun and talked0

"Haven't taken up the nasty habit of tobacco, I see, Matt."

"Dad doesn't smoke either; he always said he had more important vices, but I don't know what they are."

"I went to see Ward on my way down."

"Did you? How is he? Good, I hope."

"He's fine I guess; but he's sure he is going to die and that we can't help him0"

"It's not fair, Mr. MacQuarrie. I'm damn sure Ward didn't kill Morgan for any other reason than the he had to."

"Did you see Morgan try to kill Ward?"

"No, damn it, no!"

"Did you hear him say he was going to stab Ward or anything like that?"

"No; nothing."

"The men who were with him; did they say anything?"

"I was too 'busy fighting to know. Besides they weren't really 'men'; just kids like me."

"Kids?"

"Joined the Navy? The war's over. When?"

"A week ago; but they're not ready for me yet. Might not be until the end of the month; or not at all."

"Margo, will you come slice the bread, dear?" Ann shouted through the door.

"And they wonder why mothers and fishwives have the same size lungs," she quietly said to MacQuarrie.

The lunch was ample and as tasty as MacQuarrie had 'back steps in the sun and talked0

"Haven't taken up the nasty habit of tobacco, I see, Matt."

"Dad doesn't smoke either; he always said he had more important vices, but I don't know what they are."

"I went to see Ward on my way down."

"Did you? How is he? Good, I hope."

"He's fine I guess; but he is sure he's going to die and that we can't help him."

"It's not fair, Mr. MacQuarrie. I'm damn sure didn't kill Morgan for any other reason than that he had to."

"Did you see Morgan try to kill Ward?" "No, damn it, no."

"Did you hear him say he was going to stab Ward or anything like that?"

"No; nothing."

"The men who were with him; did they say anything?" "I was too busy fighting to know. Besides they weren't really men; just kids like me."

"Kids?"

"Well, Morgan and one of the others weren't; they 'were grown up all right. But two of them were just plain kids."

He was a bastard, you know," Matt quietly added, looking back to be certain his mother wasn't near. "Talked about screening all the girls so he could pick the best ones for the night. And then he'd laugh. I wish it had been me that killed him; I really would have turned that courtroom upside down. Would have told them everything he said, foul like that."

"And you don't know any of their names?"

"Oh, I know one of them." "Don? The one Ward mentioned at the trial?"

"No. This one is Paul, Paul Crawford. He used to work at Case's store in Flintsville after Morgan got killed0"

"Doesn't he still work there?" MacQuarrie asked with excitement and stood up.

"No, He quit I guess. Someone else, an older fellow got the job then."

"Where does he live I" "I don't know."

"Matt, this is important. If you want to help save Ward's life you'd better find out."

"I don't know."

"Where did you say he worked?"

"Case's store; right in Flintsville."

"Then he probable lives in Flintsville," MacQuarrie said, doing his thinking out loud. "Matthew, can you get a 'buggy and drive me to Flintsville, now?"

"Sure; I guess I can borrow Ward's surrey from Gilbert. I can't use the horse from the feed store since I quit."

"You quit; why?"

"Sure did; Mr. Dodson kind of asked me to if I was going to take Ward's side in the trial."

MacQuarrie shook his head: "Matthew, you get the buggy and meet me at the godson house in a few minutes. I'll pay you for your trouble." He was so excited he could hardly breath. This might be the boy who could back up art's testimony.

When they arrived in Flintsville Mr. Case was busy but he took long enough to tell him that Paul Crawford had 'been drafted seven months before. His parents lived on the west side of town on a small farm.

"How convenient for the prosecution," MacQuarrie grumbled: "take all the witnesses and ship them in the army. The goddamned army."

Paul's father was doing his spring plowing, but didn't seem to mind pausing to talk. He left his horse and plow standing in the field and leaned over the fence.

"I could have put in a complaint and had Paul deferred, I 'speck; but then it would have been rough on family pride and all, so I didn't. Things haven't been the same at home since; with him gone and Evelina, that's my wife, not talkin' to me. 'What kinda man did I marry?' she keeps askin' every-one else. Kinda man who would send his son off to be killed when he coulda kept him at home'. But she just says nothin to me. Thought for years it would be nice havin' complete silence; but it aint. In fact, it's almost noisy, it's so quiet." "1~. Crawford..."

"No,,] vow inst call me Joe'."

"Didn't have too many." "Did you know a boy named Don?n

"That would be Tracy's boy; same age as Paul, but his Pa kept him from the Army to help with the chores,"

"Where do they live?"

"Well, sir, you are in luck, because the Tracy farm is right next door, right here. Miranda will talk your head clean off. Miranda; she's a talker, same as my wife. They're sisters."

"Did Paul have any other friends?"

"No, not that I can remember. Use to have one called 'Larry'; someone at the store in town, but he drowned in a flood or something. You could write Paul except he's in England waiting to come home,"

"Thank you very much, Joe."

"Nice to have talked with you. Better heed the signs at the Tracy's; the dogs are mean as hell. They'll chaw your leg clean off, if they get their teeth in ya."

Don Tracy was thin, tall and very muscular and his deep-bet eyes were dark and suspicious; exact copies of his father's and older brother's.' The three of them stood on the other side of the high picket fence and glowered at MacQuarrie and Matt, while the five Shepherd dogs snarled and displayed the sharpness of their teeth.

"That's him; he's one of them," Matt said quietly.

"You sure?"

"He's the one, all right."

"We just came to talk to your son.

"Don ain't talkin' to nobody; I fixed it with the government. The war's won and he ain't goin' in no Army and if they try it, there'll be another war right here, right now. So go."

"Mr. Tracy, we're not here to talk about the Army or anything like that; they're demobilizing anyway. I just wanted to see if Don could help us bring about justice in this state."

"Speak more plain. If you ain't from the draft, who are you?"

MacQuarrie lied, "I'm from Governor Dodson's office; may I come in and talk to you and your son?"

"And you ain't here from no Draft Board?"

"No!"

"Boys, chain them dogs up then, and let the man in."

"Sorry to bother you," MacQuarrie said, "'but a man's life depends on whether or not your son can help us."

"Miranda, come clean the crap off the couch and chaise; we got visitors," Mr. Tracy called as he opened the front door to the small cluttered room.

Miranda was round and jolly; it told in the creases around her eyes and mouth. But she was not as talkative as fl--hrn-ho-in1-w -Rn-, nrpd hi-, -?--r- thought it probably would change with family. ', fortunately they would not be here long enough to witness her back fence space technique.

Inside the fence, Mac and Matthew were treated with dignity and warmth. When they were seated in the Tracy living room. Miranda served strong coffee and bread and 'butter with currant jelly, and Mr. Tracy, after hearing what MacQuarrie wanted, calmly put his cup on the floor in front of him and said "Donald, is what Mr. MacQuarrie said true?"

"Yes, Pa."

"Then I guess his questions better be answered, wouldn't you say?"

"Yes."

"Tracys ain't lawbreakers: you ask your questions, Mr. MacQuarrie0 I voted for Cyrus Dodson, and if we can help him in any way, we're going to do it. And, Don, you tell the whole truth, understand."

Donald opened up, but stammered and locked at the floor. He seemed eager to get it off his mind. His version of the night at the Grange was similar to Ward's. Don and Paul had held Matt's arms while Morgan hit him. Morgan had told them before they started the fight that he was going to cut Matthew up good so he wouldn't come back to Flintsville. "You know, Larry Morgan was tough; he 'said 'after we 'beat the shit out of this Crescent dude, we'll dunk his ass in the river and let him float away if he ever showed up in Flintsville again. That's what he said and he'd done it."

"Donald; your mother is in the house. Watch them damn cuss words when she's around." His father snapped.

"Sorry, Pa."

"That blacksmith whacked out heads together, and I thought I was going to die. Paul went right out and the next thing I knew, Larry was slashing away with his knife. Then it was all over; Harwood here kicked him right in the nuts and he folded up and puked all over the floor."

"I said mind your tongue, Donald!"

Beads of perspiration formed on Don's forehead as he relived the fight.

"Don, what happened after the fight?"

"Morgan called us together back by the stove; it's back in the rear of the Grange, in the corner. He said he was going to kill both of them before he got through. We didn't think that was too good; that is, Paul and I didn't. Al, a friend of Larry's, thought it would be all right, but we talked them out of it. They decided to just beat them up some more."

"Weren't you a little afraid of Ward Kessel?"

"Hell, yes. Larry wasn't of course; he said he would cut his guts out just like he did with pigs when he butchered them. And we figured we'd surprise him. Larry had a plan: we would go out and if the blacksmith followed us, we would hit him with a club; then Larry would cut him up."

"Son, you don't sound like a Tracy. Were you drunk?"

"Yes, Pa; bein' honest, I was; and so was Paul and Al and Larry Morgan."

Donald.

"You'd gone somewhere," Don said to' Matt, "we thought you had probably gone home or something, Besides, by that time we were all out to get the red head. In fact, Larry said 'If you are afraid, you two, go ahead and take off. You hit him and I'll take care of him myself."

"Did you go then?"

"Sure; 'but first we hit him with a 'brake handle."

"Son, who do you mean when you say, 'we hit him'?" Tracy asked.

"We were there together, Paul and me," Don said looking at his father, hoping he had explained enough. But he hadn't. His father's eyes narrowed and Don continued, "I guess I was the one who really hit him."

"Did you run over him with the wagon?" MacQuarrie asked.

"I don't know for sure, 'but I think we did; Paul thought we did anyway. We were afraid we had killed him if we really did."

MacQuarrie leaned back in his chair. He wished that Miranda Tracy would offer him another cup of coffee, but she didn't; she just sat next to her husband staring at their son.

"Mr. Tracy; all Don has done is get in a fight. You don't have any worries at all and neither does Don. What he has told us will probably save Mr. Kessel's life. I think we can get a new trial."

"I can't believe my Donnie would do something like this," Miranda Tracy sighed.

J U -UluGUJ1c

"I don't know; guess because nobody asked me. They could have hanged an innocent man," Mr. Tracy said.

"The prosecution wouldn't be likely to ask you, Don; some of the men in the legal profession can only think of one thing; to get a conviction whether it's right or wrong. And it looks as if Ward Kessel's attorney didn't try to track you down. I don't understand what he was thinking of when this case was going on," MacQuarrie pondered.

"Son, no sense me threatening you; yer Ma and me, we love ya too much to lay a heavy stick to ya every time you do something wrong. But I hope you learned yer lesson. Maybe you'd have been better off in the Army; there they wouldn't have coddled ya."

"Let's don't talk that way," Miranda interrupted. "We're disappointed, son, but your dad, as he says, just loves ya too much. He was the one that wanted to be sure you didn't go to that war."

MacQuarrie was beginning to feel uneasy about the family talk and the unnecessary sadness. "I would like to buy dinner for you and Mrs. Tracy at the hotel in town this evening; the boys included."

"It would be nice," Miranda said, "but I don't know what I would wear."

"We'd better leave Don home to watch the dogs," Mr. Tracy said.

"I'd like him to come with us," MacQuarrie was quick to say, "We will need to have him sign a paper about the things he has said so we can put the brakes on and save Ward Kessel."

In town MacQuarrie took Don to a lawyer and had an affidavit written up and signed, then took the family to dinner at the Caufield Inn, and later returned them to their home. It was after eleven when he and Matthew arrived back in Crescent.

"Matthew, we were damn lucky today. Ward can be thankful he had you along, or he actually would be heading for the gallows."

"I don't know quite what we've done; but I guess it's good."

"It is, I can assure you. We'll make Cyrus sit up and take notice of this. He'll have to give a stay of execution."

MacQuarrie rolled over and over in bed that night until the sheets looked as if he had tied them in knots. Before going downstairs to breakfast he tried to straighten them out some so Myrtle and Cynthia wouldn't think he was insane, then packed his bag and finished dressing. He would leave immediately for the capital. He breathed deeply, with a feeling that he must be dreaming. Either the trial or this latest news had to be fiction; they just didn't fit in the same picture.

"Mac," Myrtle said in a rare moment of informality, "we like having you come visit us. Don't judge Cyrus too harshly; I believe you'll find that in the end he will do the right thing, because he seems to admire you and respects your judgment. And the rest of us..." she patted his hand, "At least a couple of us wish you were a permanent member of the family. Oh, damn; I wasn't going to cry."

MacQuarrie was touched by Myrtle's sudden tenderness. He had never felt close to her before. You never knew about people's feelings, he reasoned, especially those who were shy or had been beaten back by others.

He thought as he left town down Elm Avenue, that it was going to be the last time he ever saw Crescent. For such a small place it had gouged a big piece out of his life. He smiled: he hadn't dropped by for tea with Margaret.

Chapter 26

Cyrus had been busy with legislative business and Keith Hampden had sat for two days in the governor's anteroom waiting to see him because he wanted to apply for the stay of execution according to protocol. Finally, MacQuarrie called the governor's office.

"Hazel, you tell Governor Dodson I will be there at one-thirty, right after his lunch; and if he isn't there, I'm going to the 'Statesman' and make some newspaper headlines of my own without talking to him."

"I'll tell him, Mr. MacQuarrie, as soon as he comes in."

"No, Hazel, that isn't good enough. You find him and send a message to him where ever he is, because I mean business and he'll damn well find it out if he tries to stall me anymore."

He slammed the phone down. "Give him some of his own phone-slamming business, he thought as he took a taxi to the Governor's Mansion. He had to talk to Gloria.

"I knew he was bitter, but this doesn't sound like Cyrus," she said.

"It isn't Cyrus; it's the 'new Governor' on his way to the top, afraid he's going to slip. I told you, Glory Be, that he was in for a hell of a shock. Now you can see what that shock had started to do to him."

"He hasn't changed, except where his job is concerned."

"He doesn't know where his personal life starts and his official life ends, and you know it."

"Mac, I know it has to be that he just has too much on his mind."

"Gloria, there is just one day left; and then it will all be over. Unless Cyrus acts, Ward will die and his blood will be on all of our hands because we didn't force some sense into Cyrus. He's already killed one man."

"Who?"

"Clarence Calder; Cyrus killed him."

"Clarence Calder was crooked, it's all in the paper; and Father has documents. So don't say such things."

"I'm sorry, Glory," he said, not wanting to push her too far, "but where Ward is concerned, we have to move now!"

"Mac," she said.

"Gloria, I don't want to fight with you over this. I guess it's just that I want you to understand how I feel about this disappointment in your father."

"You don't have the right to be disappointed: Father is doing the best he knows how. If Ward is innocent, Cyrus will do everything in his power to help him. But you saw the reports of the trial; Ward admitted that he killed the man. How could a jury do anything but convict him?"

"I want you to read something; carefully."

"What is it?"

"An affidavit, just read it," MacQuarrie said and sat down on the ornate Victorian loveseat.

Gloria read the document very slowly, going back to read parts of it to be sure they were clear in her mind.

"Oh, how horrible," she said at one point and continued reading. When she was finished she handed the affidavit back to Mac and sat down next to him.

"Poor Ward. How ugly; they must have been like animals."

"They were. All men are capable of turning into that kind of being under the right stimulus; and drunken brawls are one of the prime drugs in making such conversions."

"But seriously, what kind of men could do such things?"

"Morgan was about the only man in the group. The rest were just boys; ordinary, homegrown, boys, with mothers and fathers. And, when you ask Donald there 'why?' He can only shrug his shoulders and shake his head. He doesn't know what got them started. But if you look at it carefully you'll see that it was Morgan who worked them up in the first place."

"None of this was said in the trial?"

"Yes, Ward tried to tell it, but it looked as if he was lying as there was no one to back his story up; no one. Not even Mitzie Kawalski. Here is one more statement. This is one that I had taken down from what Matt Harwood told me regarding Mr. Morgan's ideas on sex and women. See if you don't feel that he was the kind of man who would do the things Don Tracy describes. The two statements should convince anyone that the decision in this case creates a great doubt where justice is concerned."

She took the papers MacQuarrie gave her and read them quickly this time.

"He must have been vulgar and crude; those horrible things he said."

"Many men talk that way, Glory Be, and I suppose some think that way. Where the mix-up starts in their minds I don't know, but they are perverted whether they know it or not."

"And he really said these things to Matthew?"

"Yes, and many others that Matt didn't have us put down."

"When Father sees these, I'm certain he will take action."

"He has to, Gloria; but I have a feeling that I might not be the one to convince him. When I quit him we had some very harsh words and feelings. We are at opposite ends of a tug-of-war when it comes to ideas; so I have to have you back me up."

"I don't know how I can help," she said, looking away from him.

"Oh, yes, you do. You have more influence with your father than all of the politicians in the world. He is distrustful of the rest of us; but he knows that you are on his side."

"Father will do what is right without anyone trying to influence him," she said defensively.

"Gloria, there was a time when things were that simple in the life of Cyrus Dodson, but those times have passed. Giving this stay of execution will be the hardest move he will ever have to make."

"I don't know what you mean. If it's right, it's right."

"If Cyrus gives the stay, he will ruin his career in politics. Just like that, with one stroke of his pen, he will sign his own political death warrant. The wolves will be after him; the opposition will make him look like the most hideous obstructer of justice in the history of the world, and the voters will be out for his head on a stick. They will say he gave the stay to save his daughter's husband from the gallows. Ward Kessel, a man the court convicted and sentenced to die, given back his life just because he was related to a governor who deceived the public into thinking he was going to bring honest government to the state."

"You are exaggerating," she said. "You should be serious at a time such as this."

"I'm really not stretching the point one bit, and Cyrus knows it. I will never have to give him this line of reasoning because Cyrus has been an able and brilliant student in the arena of statesmanship, Gloria, and he knows what the odds are and just how the cards have been cut. There is nobody else who can make the decision but Cyrus, and that is why he won't see Keith Hampden, Ward's lawyer, and why he won't talk to me on the phone. Under fire, your father can be treacherous; that is why he turned on Clarence Calder. He thought the news of Ward's arrest would put him in a bad light, and Calder had threatened him, so he destroyed him."

"He didn't, he didn't, Mac."

"Gloria, I am sorry, but he did; and he told me in his office when we had our last violent argument that if I didn't leave him alone he would do the same to me. I don't know if he understands that Calder and I were of two different breeds and the weapons he used on Clarence won't faze me because I don't give a damn."

"What do you want me to do?" she said softly and took his hand gently in hers.

"Talk to him about Agatha and her baby, and the love she has for Ward. Show him that the most significant thing is not how important he is, but how right he is in his decisions; that his honor and love is more to all of you than his damn job as governor. You see, Gloria, Cyrus is really the kind person who thinks in these terms, just like the boys that turned on Ward are good, normal, young boys. It is only when they get their emotions fired-up that they do the wrong things. Right now, Cyrus, I am afraid, might have his emotions overflowing down a dangerous dead-end street. If he understands your love and his friends' respect are on the line along with Ward's life, he might be turned back into the rational man you call 'Father'."

"I'll talk to him."

"Think about it for a long time today, first, Gloria."

"I'm confused, but I'll try."

"That is a wonderful thought: 'I'm confused, but I'll try. It about wraps the lot of us up in one little package and puts a fluffy satin bow on it. As I said, think it over carefully and then just honestly tell him how much he means in your life."

"What made you say that?"

He stood up and walked toward the door, then turned and shook his head, "I'm worse than all the rest; here to ask you to help save Ward's life, with just a matter of hours to go before a tragedy cuts us down, and I let jealousy bother me."

"What are you talking about?" she said following him.

"I never thought I would ever be envious of anyone, Gloria, but suddenly I am, of Cyrus, because he has you."

"Mac, dear Mac, you may not know it, but you have me, too."

"One of these days, GloryBe; you never know. Right now, it is damned silly."

She motioned a kiss to him with her lips. "I'll talk to Father tonight and do my best."

"I'll be in his office after lunch; I hope he's there so we don't have to have a fight over it in public."

"One minute you are so understanding, the next you want to fight as if you were part of that brawl."

"There is a difference; we are fighting for Ward's life, they were out to take it away."

He kissed Gloria on the cheek, wishing it were more, and left her standing in the large hallway. She seemed saddened by his visit. He knew how she must feel, how there were many doubts as to the truth of what he had told her. She idolized Cyrus and refused to have him attacked, MacQuarrie hoped she would not lose that adoration. For Ward's sake, he hoped that Cyrus felt as much for Gloria, as his stepdaughter did for him.

When MacQuarrie arrived at the Statehouse, Cyrus was waiting for him in his office. His desk was stacked with neat piled of legislative documents, transcripts of meetings and appointment rosters. He smiled as MacQuarrie was led in by Percy Snow, Cyrus's new secretary: a rather chubby-faced little man with a small, dour mouth and a pair of steel-rimmed glasses.

"Hello, Mac; Mr. Hampden, here just submitted a request for a stay of execution on the Kessel case and I've agreed to consider it carefully."

"Uh, the governor has a copy of the two affidavits and the listings from Dr. Phillips' drug book and your description of the trial's omissions," Keith said nervously.

"All of it will be gone over very thoroughly," Cyrus said, clearing his throat. He turned and extended his hand to MacQuarrie. "I'm very sorry about not being able to see you before, Mac; I didn't realize the gravity of your visit. But, winding up this legislative session and all has just given me more to do than there is time for. You didn't tell me how much work there was going to be when you asked me to run for Governor, or I probably wouldn't have accepted."

"You've forgotten, Governor, it wasn't me who asked you; it was Clarence Calder."

"Yes. And, and now about the submission from Mr. Hampden on Kessel's behalf."

"He goes to the gallows at noon tomorrow, unless you grant this stay, so we can file for an appeal."

"That soon?"

"I covered it in my previous letters," Hampden interrupted.

"I was without an experienced secretary after Mr. MacQuarrie left me and things have just stacked up, I guess."

"And he is innocent of murder. The jury didn't have all of the facts presented to them. Take a look at those affidavits. They'll prove to you that Ward was trying to defend himself when that man was killed."

"I'll consider it fully."

"Mr. Governor, I urge you to make this decision now; there is no time to wait," Keith Hampden said so loudly that Cyrus turned and looked at him for the first time since MacQuarrie had arrived.

"Mr. Hampden; where matters of life and death are concerned, I make my judgments without duress; I want you to remember that."

"I'm sorry, Governor, I didn't mean to pressure you."

"Well you damn well better pressure him," MacQuarrie broke in, "Governor, this is not something that you can leave until tomorrow noon."

"I am aware of that, Mac, but I do have other duties as well as watching after the welfare of my wayward family."

MacQuarrie held himself back.

Cyrus continued: "There are some nominations for the courts that I have to make to the joint session at three."

"Yes, I read about your decision regarding Victor E. Burton and his appointment as a justice on the Court of Appeals," MacQuarrie said. "Poetic justice, retribution, compensation and a pound of flesh all in one recommendation."

"Justice Burton is only one of several appointments," Cyrus said with irritation in his voice.

"Were the others as pressing?"

"Mac, I believe this interview has gone on long enough."

"Governor Dodson, I'm positive that the truthfulness of Ward Kessel's testimony will be born out by the affidavit," Keith started to explain.

"Mr. Hampden, if you have done an adequate summary with your submission, I will be able, to draw my own conclusions."

"Keith, I would like to have just a couple of minutes with the governor alone. Could you wait for me in the other room?" MacQuarrie asked.

"Of course, Mr. MacQuarrie"

"I am very busy, Mac, and I really don't have the time."

"It won't take much time. Keith, please."

"Yeah, oh, sure.

After Hampden had closed the door the two men seemed to relax.

"I am sorry about not being able to see you before, Mac."

"I don't 'blame you for trying to put it off."

"I'm not putting anything off."

"Of course you are."

"Look, a man was murdered and Ward Kessel has been sentenced to pay for it."

"Oh, for Christ's sake don't be redundant with me. Come off the pedestal. Hampden's request is backed up with all the legal proof you need to be justified in giving that stay...even if Ward weren't Agatha's husband."

"What are you trying to say?"

"Just that! That is the reason you are trying to keep from giving the stay of execution."

"That has nothing to do with it. He's a murderer!"

"I thought you said that you had been too busy to even read our letters on the case. You don't mean to tell me that you are making a judgment in the case even before you have read our evidence?"

"Of course not. I've done a great deal of research on the case, and I've concluded that Ward Kessel is a killer. If you don't believe me, read it for yourself; the whole file on him from Whalen, a mining town in Pennsylvania. You read it and you'll know that he's killed before and will kill again if we let him free."

"I've read it. And it has nothing to do with the case that was tried at Colton. Ward Kessel is innocent."

"He killed a man."

"And so did you, Cyrus. You killed a man."

"That's ridiculous and let's not go through it again."

"No, Cyrus, you can't face the fact that you and Ward are both 'killers', as you put it. And there is another great similarity: you both committed your crimes in self-defense. Clarence Calder threatened your life and you killed him. Ward killed Morgan who was threatening his life."

"How stupid! If I killed Calder as you claim, he deserved it and besides, I didn't do it on purpose."

"Perfect parallel: Ward was in a fight and he killed a man: you were in a fight and you killed a man. Where in hell lies the difference?"

"I am sorry, Mac; you've got to leave."

"What a coward. All poised to kill again; that's you, Cyrus. This time you think it's Ward that is threatening you, and so you'll sacrifice his life just to be safe."

"Mac, you're going insane. If I believe Kessel is innocent, I'll certainly grant the stay; or if I think that your new evidence has any possible chance of proving anything new in the case, I'll grant it. That is all there is to it."

"And the fact that your career is on the line has never entered your head?"

"All right. Of course I know what will happen if I grant that stay: I will slit my throat from here to here."

"Now we're talking sense; just as long as you admit that to yourself, they you might have a decent chance of an impartial hearing of the facts you are about to read. There is a whopping lot of good in you, Cyrus; let it show itself. Don't deceive yourself and others into believing the myth that you are managing to build up around yourself, because that isn't going to last forever, even if it makes you believe for a moment or two that you a hero fighting for right and all that shit. If you kill to get where you are going, you'll lose every friend you ever had, including yourself."

"Are you through?" the governor coldly asked.

"Almost, Cyrus. If you think that Ward's execution will save you, you are wrong, because I'll make damn sure that every newspaper in the country gets all the facts that were presented to you today. So the public can have a chance to make up their own minds as to your honesty and integrity."

"You are not being very practical, Mac. Calder threatened me and he paid for it; so don't you threaten me or I'll make certain that you never get to write for another paper as long as you live. And if you want to give the papers your story, go ahead. I've already gone over it with my lawyers. From the information in Hampden's letters they're convinced that there's enough doubt with this file from Pennsylvania to cancel any reason for a stay or a retrial."

"Then you have made up your mind?"

"No, God no, I haven't. Mac, stop digging at me. Do you realize what you are asking me to do? There are a million things to consider."

"There really aren't, Cyrus; there is only one: whether Ward Kessel should have a chance to fight for his life."

"I do have to go, Mac; I'm sorry but I do."

"Cyrus, just consider what you lose in either case; on one hand you'll lose yourself and all the respect you have for Cyrus Dodson, plus the respect of the people of Crescent and Walker County, that is, the ones that really count: your family, Glory, Myrtle, Agatha, Matthew Harwood and your first grandchild. You won't be their special god any longer. And on the other hand, if Ward lives, you'll lose a job and a little power; and you never know, you might even win that back someday when people forget or when they learn the truth. It's like an election, you have to make your choice; you can't vote for both candidates. Being governor isn't everything. You might want to be grandfather or just plain Cyrus Dodson, champion of Crescent."

"I'll consider it thoroughly."

"You know, Cyrus, it is ironical that it was Ward's campaigning that put you in the position you are now in; having to make the choice between the two men inside you who are battling it out for your favor."

"It is complicated enough without all of your fancy platitudes. Now, Mac, thanks for your time; the legislature is waiting."

"Don't let them panic you with their praise, Cyrus; the glory will turn cold in retrospect when they're gone."

Cyrus left before MacQuarrie did.

"Nellie, tell Mr. Snow that I have left for the session."

"What did you accomplish?" Keith Hampden asked MacQuarrie as they watched the Governor's figure disappear down the long marble corridor.

"Nothing."

"Nothing?"

"Shall we say nothing except to rub a callous or two off of his skimpy conscience? At least he will think about it in serious tones, if nothing else. He's in a spot where he can't win regardless of which way he decides."

"What do you mean?"

"Oh, it's a long, mixed up damn mess. Why don't we have a drink or two, Keith? I feel as if I were about to attend my own funeral. We might as well start the wake early."

"I don't understand; you people act as if this weren't going to happen tomorrow. It's like a nightmare; it's horrible, but nobody seems real. Kessel is going to die in about twenty hours if that stuffy, pompous, holy prick doesn't do something about it," Hampden shouted, his voice echoing down the statehouse corridor.

"Why didn't you talk that way when you were facing him?"

"I don't know."

"Well don't clean your lungs out on me. After we have a few drinks we'll have dinner and then we'll go back to the vigil, just to keep Cyrus aware of the importance of his move. Not that he needs it; but just in case."

After they had left the building and walked about a block down the street, Hampden regained his courage and spoke.

"For someone who supposedly hates the governor's guts, you are certainly concerned with his welfare," Hampden said stammered.

"Keith, just a couple of friendly drinks. Don't try to put me on the defensive, because I'll turn on you and cut you into a bloody pulp."

"Fine, just a couple."

"First of all, I don't hate Cyrus. He turned into just exactly what I knew he would. They all do. It's just that you dislike seeing a decent person fall into the trap; and you see, Keith, I didn't do anything to help him out of it when there was still time."

"You've lost me."

"Come on, right in here, the hotel has a very quiet bar for guests; and the bourbon isn't that bad."

"All comedy aside, Mac; what are we going to do about Kessel?"

"We've done it."

"You mean to say that you are just going to walk away and let him be executed?"

"Come on, Keith, just wait until I get a drink in me; then we'll talk, We might as well sit at the bar; then we don't have to look into one another's eyes."

"What will you have, Gentlemen?"

"A couple of double bourbons with a chaser for the man on the left," MacQuarrie answered.

The bartender poured and MacQuarrie drank his in one gulp; then, motioned for a refill. "Now, Keith; ask me your questions."

"I only have one; isn't there something else we can do? You know very well that prissy bastard isn't going to do a thing but sit on that petition. How in Christ's name he ever got to be so big; I don't understand."

"It is an occupational disease, Keith, it sets in about two minutes after the winning results are tabulated and starts a general degeneration of the patient's mind until within six months he has been translated up to heaven, much as Enoch of the Bible, and finds himself in the presence of God. But it doesn't stop there. Such perfection in the mind of the victim often in some cases of extreme infection, results in the patient even taking the place of the Lord. The only possible cure of this terrifying ailment is defeat. Plain, hard, devastating defeat. Most often it kills the patient, so you might say the disease is incurable."

"Answer the question."

"We have done everything; you know yourself that the appeal court is in recess and that there isn't one of the judges of that austere body in the state to grant an appeal; so we have done all there is to do."

"Then it's all over."

"It's a wait and see proposition. We have presented our arguments and our campaign slogans to the voter, and so have the opponents. Now, we don't know all there is to know about the voter's prejudices, and weaknesses, and strengths, and warm, vulnerable spots, so we just have to sit and wait until the counting is done and hope what we've said has made sense."

"It's over then; he voted against us the minute we walked in the door to his office," Hampden said.

"Another couple of drinks, bartender."

"There is no similarity whatsoever."

"Nobody sees a similarity if they are part of it, Keith; but just stop trying to draw me out of my corner. Tonight I'm in a fighting mood. And a fight between us is not going to help Cyrus make up his mind."

"All right: I'm sorry."

"Then it's all over."

"It's a 'wait and see' proposition. We have presented our arguments and our campaign slogans to the voter, and so have the opponents. Now, we don't know all there is to know about the voter's prejudices, and weaknesses, and strengths, and warm, vulnerable spots, so we just have to sit and wait until the counting is done and hope what we've said has made sense."

"It's over then; he voted against us the minute we walked in the door to his office," Hampden said. "Another couple of drinks, bartender."

"Keith, I really have faith he will vote our way. You see; he isn't near the polls yet. What you saw was just the backlash of the campaign itself. Cyrus will start to make up his mind during the night, and it will be one hell of a night. You see, Keith, you and everyone else would try and make this out to be a simple decision. But is it? Cyrus Dodson has been asked to decide by which means he wants to commit suicide. He has put if off as long as he can, so in the next few hours he'll consider all the facts and relive his life and think about the future and the present, and then decide how he is going to kill himself."

"And that arbitrary decision to make Victor Burton a Supreme Court Justice is beyond belief. That's the post of an impartial advocate and Burton is nothing but a butcher, a legal butcher, whose only goal is to convict men, innocent or otherwise."

"Keith, you could be disbarred for a statement of that nature."

"Well, he is."

"Burton is a member of the sacred legal profession of which you are a part. Where is your loyalty? Don't you know that one doesn't attack the establishment if one wants the support of the establishment?"

"Dodson, even if he made perfect decisions in all other matters for the duration of his term, would be a farce with that one appointment."

"Keith, don't you know that Cyrus is sick over making that appointment? He's made himself vulnerable; he's exposed one of his tools of operation, one of his techniques. Cyrus Dodson has made more political enemies in his own party in his first few months in office than most men make in their entire lifetimes. If he makes a mistake they'll cut him to shreds, and if he lets Ward live they will have all the ammunition they need. There are still a lot of Clarence Calder's friends around who will remember Cyrus's Machiavellian touch. He knows that he's standing there naked because of that appointment, and he's a very modest man when it comes to such things."

"Then why in the hell did he do it?"

"Now wait a minute, Keith. You were an absolute flop as a defense attorney. If you had done any kind of job at all, we wouldn't be sitting here asking for a governor's plebiscite because Ward would have been free."

"That's a damn lie!"

"It is not! You did a very sloppy job and as a result, Ward was convicted. If you had presented an affidavit of Donald Tracy's during the trial, the jury would never have returned a guilty verdict, never."

"Well, what in hell do you want me to do; commit suicide because the judgment went against me?"

"No, of course I don't; but you want Cyrus Dodson to, don't you?"

"There is no similarity whatsoever."

"Nobody sees a similarity if they are part of it, Keith; but just stop trying to draw me out of my corner. Tonight I'm in a fighting mood. And a fight between us is not going to help Cyrus make up his mind,"

"All right: I'm sorry."

"Besides, Keith, let's not go down in defeat until we know the count; I sincerely feel that Cyrus will vote for us; so you keep beating the drum, and I'll play the flute."

Chapter 27

Gloria tied her long hair up on top of her head with a thin red scarf of chiffon and slowly slid down into the tub of warm, scented water. The soft, oily liquid caressed her legs, her thighs, her stomach, arms shoulders and neck. She writhed in its comfort and breathed in the steam rising from the surface as it enveloped her. Her bath had become her consoler, her confessor, even her lover, for other than Cyrus that once when most of the servants were off duty, and she served him more than his usual amount of wine, she had never felt a man's full power other than the night Willard Helms had awakened her after choir practice.

She thought about that night whenever she curled in her bath; just as she thought of how it would be with Ward, Matt, or MacQuarrie. Now that she had missed her monthly time twice, she wondered how she was going to handle the situation with Cyrus. Maybe tonight, she would bring it up after dinner; she might do that, it would be an ideal time to discuss it. She rubbed the bar of soap languorously over her body and then scrubbed her face with a sudsy washcloth. She sighed and regretted that she would soon have to get dressed. Since they had moved to the Governor's Mansion, she had taken more and more to longer and longer baths. When she dozed in her tub there were no tensions and the warmth and pressure of the water and her own touch seemed to give her vitality.

But tonight she would have to hurry. She had arranged with Hans, the cook, to prepare Veal Scaloppini, a newfound favorite of Cyrus's, which the chef at the Parisian Gardens had introduced him to. She had laid Cyrus's personal mail, which had been sent to the house by his secretary, on his desk in his study. Among the letters were one each from Myrtle and Agatha. The latter had been sent direct to Gloria, in a double envelope, so there would be no mistake about Cyrus getting it.

She and Cyrus would be dining alone, as Peggy had been invited to attend the theatre with a young army captain and his family and Alfreda was going out for the evening with Mr. Snow, Cyrus's new secretary. Wouldn't it be something if she, Gloria, turned out to be the old maid of the family? She had certainly complicated her life. There had been time when they were all certain she would be the first to get married, she more than all the rest. And, now, there were no prospects, none. Oh, MacQuarrie teased once in a while, but she was certain he was far too set in his ways to ever get married again. If he had ever asked, however, she might have considered. Cyrus, she would always have him as a dream, nothing but a dream, however, as there times together could be nothing more than what they were. What had happened was actually her own doing. And, Ward, Ward was... She sat up straight in her bath and the sense of pleasure disappeared.

Ward was going to die unless Cyrus decided otherwise tonight. The thought gave her a chill and she dried herself quickly with a heavy Turkish towel and put on her robe. She could remember when Ward had helped her into the wagon the time they went to the wedding. His hands were strong and big and gentle. It was hard to conceive of them without strength, without life.

"Miss Dodson, the Governor has arrived and is in his room," the maid called through the door to Gloria.

"Thank you, Nancy, for letting me know. I'll be down in a moment to be certain things are ready for dinner."

The changes in their lives in the past two years had made a great difference to all of the family, especially Gloria. It was nearly impossible to remember the town of Crescent, as it was when she lived there; and she sometimes longed for its simplicity. In Crescent there had been more going on; more people, the house full of people, things to do, that each person was responsible for doing. And a closeness that Cyrus, in spite of his strict attitudes, had created in holding them tightly together as one, Here in the Capitol there was none of this.

The servants ran the household, indulging the requests of the masters as they were made, but without worry or bother from the outside; as only they, the servants, knew the system and the routine. It was all very complex and one found oneself alone in the long hallways and sitting rooms and never saw a servant between meals or unless one rang for them, It was a paradox; a mob without a mob; twelve servants including the two gardeners. Who in their right minds would want twelve people always snooping around without your knowing they were there? They must talk in whispers, for you never heard them, She knew that they must talk about the governor and his daughters, but there was never a snicker or a glance of surprise. Servants were amazing, Gloria thought, but she would be better without them; she had become so useless.

In the dining room, Gloria inspected the table setting, lit the candles in the tall candelabra at each end of the large oval table, and adjusted one of the gladioli in the floral setting in the middle of the mantle piece. She wondered how the gardeners grew such large blooms, especially out of season.

Cyrus's study was next; there she turned on the lamp on his desk and the one by the large easy chair next to the fireplace. There was even a fireplace in Cyrus's bathroom and another in his bedroom. Imagine; nine fireplaces in one house. What an extravagance. The study had the pleasant fragrance of narcissus in the air, from the plants the gardeners had placed in the window solarium. The walls were lined with stiffly posed oil portraits of nine governors who had preceded Cyrus to the post. What a stern and serious lot, she thought as she shoved another easy chair close to the fireplace. She would have the coffee served in front of the fire tonight. She and Cyrus would be alone.

Again she checked Cyrus's mail on his desk, rearranging it so that Agatha's letter was on top of the pile.

"I would like a glass of wine or something before dinner," Cyrus said, standing in the doorway watching her.

She looked up with a guilty, surprised expression on her face.

"I didn't hear you, Father."

"Something bothering you, dear?"

"No, it's just that it's a big, big house to wander in all day long and sometimes I find myself going back over the tracks that I have made earlier."

"You should go out for a walk."

"Now, Cyrus, I do go for walks and I am not complaining. I'm glad you are home early, though, because you and I are going to dine alone tonight. The girls both have engagements for the evening."

"That will be nice; my favorite woman all to myself."

"Father, you do sound provocative. Shall we have brandy instead of wine? I need something to warm me up inside. I feel cold."

"Fine, if you'll pour while I browse through my mail," he said, picking up the silver letter opener with its ornate dragon's head handle. "Then we can relax and talk about your wanderings around the cottage; and my wanderings around the Capitol."

"Cyrus, you must have had your brandy already?" she teased.

They laughed and he picked up his letters.

She watched him as he put Agatha's letter to one side, then and went through the others. Then Gloria went over to the liquor cabinet and poured the brandy in the delicate wine glasses Governor Simpson had sent Cyrus as an inaugural present.

"Your mother is feeling better; Crescent seems to be good for her. It's strange that she disliked it so much here. With all the help you would have thought she would enjoy it. The way she talks, you might think she had gone home to die."

Gloria turned to look at him as he continued reading the letter. He sat down at the desk and leaned back in his chair. She put his glass close to the mail.

"Thank you; Dear. The medical director here at the hospital says she is in excellent health and will probably out-live us all; just a matter of the change of life. He says it makes them unsure of themselves and prone to finding ailments that are not really there."

"Father; to you," Gloria said, holding up her glass."

"What is the occasion?" he said, not paying much attention to her.

"I don't know; just felt like toasting you."

"To you," he said. "Matthew Harwood is going into the service next week; enlisted in the Navy; unless his uncle pulls strings and gets him sidetracked. That is ridiculous. I told him I wanted him back to run the feed store. All he had to do was answer my letter and I would have done as I had suggested."

"Cyrus," she said, standing behind him, rubbing the back of his neck. "You have to read that letter now? I get jealous, and want all of your attention when we are alone."

"You're saying that just so you can look over my shoulder and read my mail without my knowing what you are up to."

She kissed his neck and then sat down in the chair by the fireplace. "I'll sulk."

"That is an excellent, daughter-like thing to do."

"Dinner is served, Governor Dodson," Nancy said as she walked into the room and went to the mantle, struck a match and lighted the fire.

"Didn't really have a chance to do much relaxing," Cyrus said.

Nancy ignored his remark. "Miss Gloria, will you want to serve the wine with dinner tonight?"

Gloria nodded her head. "Just as always, Nancy; I arranged it with Quincey this afternoon."

When Nancy had left the room Gloria laughed, "I think she asks that every night as a means of aggravating me, but it doesn't work. I'm just waiting to see how long we can play the same game."

Cyrus had not paid any attention to remarks and continued reading in silence.

"Father, we better go in. Hans has prepared a surprise for you."

"You go on in, Gloria, and get them started; I'll be in a minute."

"Father, there is no one else to get started; you and I are dining alone; remember?"

"I'm sorry, Gloria, I've had so many things on my mind. Your mother is trying to, indirectly, run the government again."

"What is it, Father?"

"Nothing of importance."

"Ward?" she asked and then closed her eyes and wished she could have swallowed the word.

Cyrus didn't look at her, but finished drinking his brandy and then stood up, putting his arm around her waist as they walked slowly toward the dining room.

"Yes, Ward; and I noticed that I will have to hear Agatha out, too, before the night is over."

Hans was excited about the meal; Gloria could see his expectant face asking for approval through the butler's pantry window every time Nancy or Pamela went into the kitchen. The tender slices of veal in their white wine tasted delicious to Gloria, but Cyrus just picked at his food and drank a few more glasses of wine than usual. They skipped dessert and had coffee served, as Gloria had planned, in front of the fire, which was in full flame by the time they went back into the study.

It was going to be an awkward evening; Cyrus seemed depressed. He didn't talk but just looked into the fire and sipped his coffee. Several times he seemed to be asleep, but she knew he wasn't. In the other room she could hear Nancy and Pamela clearing the table. Then the front hallway light was extinguished and their footsteps faded into nothing, leaving just the crackling of the cedar logs.

"I should be practicing my budget speech for tomorrow morning; but then, I'll probably just read it and not add too many frills," Cyrus finally said without opening his eyes.

Gloria got up and refilled his cup from the ornate silver service and added the sugar and cream, the way he liked it after dinner.

"The Ways and Means Committee is threatening a holdup on expenditure bills unless I agree to keep the new child labor legislation from being put in the hopper this session.

"You didn't finish your brandy before dinner. Shall I get you some fresh?" Gloria asked.

"No, tonight is not the night to hide behind drink, I'm afraid; though it is certainly a temptation."

"Father, are you all right?"

"All right? I wonder. Yes, Dear, I'm fine, it's just that I'm much the same as the members of the Ways and Means Committee who don't want to stand up and be counted on something that is going to be so unpopular. They know very well that the businessmen, especially the manufacturers, are going to react violently if that child law goes into effect. It will cost them money; so right or wrong they want it killed. But, Gloria, they don't want to take the blame for killing it. If they can't find a scapegoat, their popularity on one side or the other will diminish; so, they believe they can place me in the middle."

"Would you like one of your cigars?" Gloria asked, trying to get his mind off date business, even though she hated his cigars.

"That is more to my mood tonight."

"I'll get it," she said as she went to the humidor on his desk for the cigar and brought it back; and lit it for him.

"Gloria, you shouldn't be smoking cigars, even as a kindness to tired old men. It puts you either in the class of a back-hills woman, or an intolerable suffragette."

"It isn't dark, but it would be if you turned off the lamp," she jested.

"Obliged," he said, reaching up to switch off the lamp.

There were still several coals changing themselves into a variety of shapes and effects of moving color in the grate. Cyrus threw his cigar into the fire and it suddenly burst into flames for a second and then became a dark spot on the coals. The clock in the hall chimed ten and then there was no sound but the ticking of Cyrus's pocket watch. He patted her head and stroked her soft hair.

"Cyrus."

"Yes."

"I love you."

He patted her again and she turned and kissed his hand.

"I've wanted to tell you for so long, but couldn't."

"I love you, too," he said; but his words sounded hollow. He could have tried again, but what was there to say after someone said, 'I love you', except 'I love you, too'? It would always be a second-place remark. But, he did love her, although he had never put it in his mind in those words before.

"I knew I loved you the time I came to your room and fell asleep in your arms," she said. "Do you remember?"

"Uh huh," he answered, thinking about his speech, and MacQuarrie, and the committee, and Ward, all at the same time.

"Of course I remember."

"And that love has grown stronger as I've watched you grow, Cyrus. And you have grown and changed, but you've kept all the qualities that I loved before."

She slid up into his lap and kissed him on the mouth. He held her closely and returned her kiss.

They didn't talk until the clock chimed ten thirty, then she stirred and shifted in his lap.

"Cyrus, if you could, would you marry me?"

"Well, I guess you have a right to ask impossible questions, the same as everyone else these days."

"Are you offended, Father?"

"Offended, Dear? No. Flattered, but obviously the question cannot be answered, because I can't marry you, and you can't marry me. I love you though and I didn't know it before tonight. So I am glad you awakened me; I might have slept through the dream."

"Father, you are learning politics, just as Mac says you are. You answer important questions by not answering them."

"How could I answer that question?"

"You could have been gallant and said 'Yes'. I wouldn't have quoted you."

"Perhaps."

She kissed him again and they watched the last ember fade.

"Cyrus."

"Yes."

"What are you going to do about Ward Kessel?"

His body stiffened and he felt the tensions of the day surge back into him.

"I don't know; I haven't completed my study of the case."

"Father, you know the case better than anyone."

"Then, I haven't made up my mind," he said in a cold, hard voice.

"Father, there is only one answer you can give."

She waited for him to answer; but he didn't.

"You can't let him die. There is only one thing you can do."

Again he didn't speak.

"Father, you can't let them execute him."

"Yes, I can, if I decide that is what should be done."

"You don't mean that; you don't. This is real, Father. You can't just stand by and watch it happen to one of our family."

"Gloria, you don't understand."

"Of course I understand; and you do, too. Ward is supposed to be executed tomorrow."

"Look, Gloria, stop going over and over it. I know what is supposed to happen. Besides discussing it with both attorneys, I've read all about it and I've heard all about it from everybody from Matt Harwood's mother to MacQuarrie, from you and your mother and it doesn't change the facts one bit."

"Father; facts you ask for, and the only fact that is important is that when people are dead they are dead and you can't bring them back. You just can't let them kill Ward," she said standing up and walking over to the lamp and turning it on. "That would be murder, too."

"Gloria, we are not living in the dark ages. This is a civilized nation that is governed by laws. And the law states that if you kill another man you must pay for that killing with your own life."

"Is that what your law says, Father? Remember, everyday they were sending boys into the Army to kill and be killed and what does the law say about that?"

"The war was different, it has nothing whatsoever to do with civil law. They are two different standards; the military law and the law of our courts."

"Different? There is nothing different about a man who is dead. He's dead, whether he's in a uniform or out on a farm."

"Gloria, I haven't made up my mind."

"You can't order a man to kill one day, telling him that it's legal because you have a war going on and that he must kill to defend his country; and the next day kill him because he has killed someone while he tied to defend himself."

"I haven't decided and this discussion is getting out of hand."

"I won't let you kill Ward Kessel."

"Is that why you told me that you loved me, Gloria; to influence my judgment?"

"Cyrus!"

"Well it won't work, Dear. Nobody is going to tell me how to run this state." He stood up and shook her by the shoulders. "Nobody is ever going to tell me how to be governor or what decisions I am supposed to make."

"I do love you, Father," she said, starting to cry, "I do; and I know you won't do this horrible thing."

"I don't want your love, Gloria, if it has strings tied to it. This is my business and my responsibility."

"You're wrong, Cyrus, so wrong."

The light in the hallway went on suddenly, followed by the sound of Alfreda giggling.

"Your father, the Governor, is destined to be the finest Governor the state has ever had," Percy Snow said.

"Oh, Mr. Snow, do you think so?"

"There is no question; the way the newspapers are talking about him and the way the senators and representatives ask his advice about all their problems. Why, he dictated thirty-six letters today. We had to bring in an extra girl and a court reporter because of that and the speech he is going to give tomorrow. He wrote that speech himself; not very many governors do things such as that."

Alfreda giggled nervously again, "Do you think so?"

"No question about that." Snow went on with great authority.

"You are so intelligent, Mr. Snow."

"Good night? Miss Dodson; things will be hopping at the Statehouse tomorrow so I must get my rest."

"Good night, Mr. Snow."

Cyrus stood looking into the black fireplace, while Gloria dried her eyes with the handkerchief she kept tucked in the satin band around the waist of her dress.

"I'm going to bed," she said to no one particularly.

Oh, Gloria; Mr. Snow is such a conversationalist; and so devoted to Father. You should have heard the stories he told about the things that are happening at Daddy's office."

"I'm glad, Alfreda. Good night." Gloria said, "I'm very tired and am going to bed."

"Oh, Daddy, I wish you could have been with us. You would have enjoyed every minute of it, Mr. Snow is really quite charming and so well informed about your government."

Cyrus wanted to ignore her, but he couldn't, "I'm very happy that you and Percy enjoy the same things," he said as he looked past Alfreda and watched Gloria leave the room. His hands were shaking and he felt a throbbing starting in his left eye. Another headache; he must get some sleep; then he would feel better and think better.

As he walked past the desk, he noticed his stack of half-opened mail and Agatha's letter put off to the side by itself, He picked it up; and took it with him. He would read it after he had taken his bath and gotten into bed. Going up the stairs, he straightened up to his full height, pulling in his stomach. He must be getting old. He felt tired, his shoulders were starting to get rounded and he found his head wasn't held as high as it used to be.

Chapter 28

The clock said six twenty-five. He was late, as the chairmen of the various committees had been invited for breakfast at the mansion at eight. He hurriedly went through his morning shaving routine and dressed. It bothered Cyrus to be rushed; he was afraid something might be missed. The fact that he had fallen asleep without finishing his work last night bothered him. He gathered the pages of his talk and arranged them in order. Agatha's letter on the bedside table annoyed him with its presence. He picked it up as if to open it, then placed it in his inside coat pocket; there wasn't time for that now.

"Sir, Senator Randolph has arrived early. Shall I seat him in the library?" It was Quincey, the head butler, at the door.

"Isn't Gloria there?"

"No, Sir."

"I'm nearly ready anyway, Quincey. Since it is to be an informal breakfast, put him in the dining room and serve him some coffee."

"Thank you, Sir."

He wondered what was the matter. It wasn't like Gloria not to be ready to greet all the guests and he was certain she knew of the breakfast.

He put his white carnation in his buttonhole, pulled himself high and with dignity went down to meet the legislators. He felt stronger now. He would let them read the confidential summary of the budget talk during the meal. Keep them informed and they can't fight on the grounds that they don't know what is happening.

He was starting to think as MacQuarrie did. All of the figures and proposals of the year's expenditures, including cuts in some of the fatty areas of Simpson's projections; were ready for them to read ahead of the session, He smiled to himself as he thought about some of the comments and demands he would make, which were not part of the actual budget report.

The breakfast had served its purpose, he had achieved his goals; and Cyrus could feel the closeness of the men about him; he sensed that he slowly was winning them over, even the Democrats.

Only two of the guests asked him about the stay of execution and both were satisfied with his answer: that he had been studying it in depth and would give it full consideration; and act in accordance with the dictates of his office. Senator Killsborough, Chairman of the joint Ways and Means Committee was the only guest Cyrus felt wasn't in the spirit of the meeting. The speech itself, however, would take care of that problem, he thought as he studied Killsborough's face from a distance. He wanted to remember his face now so he could check the reaction when Killsborough heard his expose' of the attempted child labor bill holdup.

At nine-fifteen they dismissed to go the Statehouse, with Cyrus apologizing for leaving first to make final arrangements for the day's activities. Percy Snow was there to help him at the office,

"Good morning, Governor Dodson, I have the retyped the final copy of your talk. I had them triple space it so it would be easier to read. And, Sir, there is a Mr., Jacobson, a reporter from the Statesman, who wants to talk to you about the Ward Kessel execution today."

In the House Chambers there was hardly enough standing room for all of the reporters; and the gallery offered no additional space: the public was out in full force to see Cyrus in action. Cyrus looked around, but could not see Gloria anywhere.

"Attention, attention, gentlemen," the Speaker of the House said, as he pounded the podium with his gavel.

"The hour is ten o'clock and this joint session is about to convene. Please take your seats and lower your voices; our Governor is waiting to address us."

His gavel thumped away until the wave of sound subsided; then he officially opened the meeting.

When Cyrus entered the chamber, there was a standing ovation for him. He was calm as he spread the pages before him on the lectern and reached into his inside pocket for or his glasses. Though, he momentarily winced as his fingers touched the haunting envelope once more, he smiled, as Mac usually insisted. Carefully he put his glasses on and read the speech. He felt in command. True, here and there, he could have used more of MacQuarrie's flair for words, but the applause, where he wanted it, was more than satisfying and these were his words, no one else's. He paused to wait for their quiet each time, so they would not miss any of his points, and he spoke slower than usual, as Mac had once told him to do. He was amused by the expressions on the faces of his own party members when he complimented Governor Simpson's basic preparation of the budget.

"Many times the cries of 'poor government' should not be directed at the administrative branch. You gentlemen in this room are the ones who can make this government honest, by enacting the right laws at the right times and giving the administration the tools it needs to work with and for us to accomplish all of our goals."

The talk was a complete success and there were a sizable number of 'well wishers' from both sides of the aisle and the gallery. They had gathered out in the corridors to congratulate him. The press wanted pictures and a statement. He posed for the pictures, but said he would give them an interview after lunch.

He had some other pressing business that needed attention. From the House chambers, he quickly took the back stairway and cut through the State Treasure's, conference room and the connecting door to his own office. Once there, he locked the two doors and sat down in his chair exhausted. He reached in his pocket and pulled out his watch; eleven-twenty. Twirling around in his chair, he opened the credenza and poured a glass of the sherry Governor Simpson had left behind. Sipping the wine, he closed his eyes and tried to get the faces of the senators and representatives to leave him to himself, but they wouldn't. He could see them as clearly as if they were in the room with him, cheering him, and he could feel the touch of their hands as they gathered around him and pressed close to him. There was even Governor Simpson as he congratulated him.

Suddenly there was someone pounding on the doors to his outer office; and Mr. Snow's screeching voice crying "You can not go in there; you must not do that. I will call the Sergeant at Arms."

"Damn it, Cyrus, open up; we've go to talk," MacQuarrie was yelling as he continued to pound on the doors. However, after a few minutes of disturbance, things quieted down.

Cyrus let a sigh escape his lips; then he opened his eyes and pulled the stack of files on Ward Kessel's case toward him, turned to the plea for a stay and then read the affidavits of Matthew Harwood and Donald Tracy. He had read everything else in the case over a dozen times.

When he was through, he took Agatha's letter and slit it with the letter opener. Agatha's fine, delicate handwriting spoke out:

"Dear Daddy Cyrus,

"You know why I am writing. I have no tears left to give you, but if there is a God he will be watching you, and He'll remember. If there isn't a God, I'll remember, and the child that was to be your grandchild will remember...."

He folded the letter without finishing it and laid it on the desk, then stood up and walked to the window and looked out at the spring day. His fingers clutched into fists, the nails cutting into the flesh of his palms. He stood there as if in a trance for a long time. Then he relaxed, as a complete calm came over him. He didn't even have to reach in his pocket for his watch; he knew by instinct that it was noon.

Keith Hampden, long after two-thirty, was still sitting in the outer office, dried tears drawing tight unseen lines down his pale, now gaunt face, waiting to see the Governor. It was almost as if, in the intoxicating void of his grief and failure, a frantic, yet numbing desperation had taken over: he wanted to ask for reconsideration of the brief.

The reporters from the various newspapers had stopped their prolonged grumbling and cussing and left for other venues. They would get the same story elsewhere, since the staff, even Mr. Snow, could give them nothing here, where the news actually took place.

MacQuarrie, however, after his violent protest and demonstration of anger, that had sent Hazel, the staff and even some members of the press cowering into the far corners of the room; realizing there was no further hope, pounded on the heavy doors one last time, then stormed out of the Statehouse, heading for a bar.

Cyrus did not hear Mac's final outburst or even the defeated Hampden; he had by twelve-fifteen gone out through the State Treasure's office and down the back stairs. He walked briskly along the back streets to the Mansion and what had once been the stables, now the garage, at the rear of the property. From there, through the latticed walkway, he went unnoticed to the hall by the kitchen. Perhaps he and Gloria would have a late lunch. He would discuss it with the cook.

"No visitors, none," he snapped at Nancy as he passed her in the hall on his way to the narrow back stairway.

She looked up at him as he bounded up the dark stairs to the second floor; a bewildered expression on her face. She had never seen him exert so much energy or move as quickly.

Cyrus barged into Gloria's bedroom without even knocking. He looked around, but she was not there, so he turned to leave. Annoyed, suddenly he felt the emptiness of the room: her brush set and perfume bottles were not on the dressing table. It took him several seconds before he started to comprehend. He crossed quickly to the far wall and opened the double French doors wide; her large walk-in closet was empty, not even a shoe, or a hat, was left, just a slight trace of her scent left to claim the space.

The staff, gathered in the hall, at Cyrus's request; however only the butler, had anything to report: she had packed and left by the carriage she had telephoned for.

It was reasonable to assume she would have gone to the station, probably to catch the train to Colton, on her way home to Crescent. Cyrus would call and have the railroad officials intercede. The train wasn't leaving until four. When she went to get her ticket, and they called him, he would go himself and pick her up and bring her back. She was just upset; she would get over it.

Cyrus was perplexed at her disappearance; but he brushed it aside and went back to his study, where Nancy brought him a cold lunch of sliced roast beef, potato salad and rye bread. He asked her for mustard, and frowned at the bitterness of the coffee. No one seemed to serve it right, other than Gloria.

The four o'clock train departed for Colton on time. Gloria was not on it; and there had been no report from the railroad ticket office; nor from the Station Master on her arriving at the depot.

He would make a telephone call to Myrtle later and ask her to have Gloria call when she arrived; he was certain that it was where she would be going. He needed to talk to her, yes, even to hold her, to touch her and let her know that he cared for her.

Cynthia answered the telephone in the front hall; "No, Father; we have not heard from her; and Mother is very ill. She is so disturbed by this horrible tragedy. The doctor has given her something to make her sleep."

"When she's better, have her call; and have Gloria call me, immediately."

"Yes, Father," and there was silence: Cynthia had calmly hung up the receiver.

As it started to get dark in the study, Cyrus called the hotel where MacQuarrie usually stayed. Mac would probably know where she was; he had become so close to Gloria over the last year or so. However, the desk clerk, seemingly unimpressed by who was calling, said in a flat, expressionless voice, "Yes, he's registered; but we haven't seen him or Mr. Hampden since yesterday morning, right after they checked in. I'll leave a message, that you called, in his box."

Chapter 29

Agatha had been sitting in the Warden's office since eight in the morning waiting for any possible last minute word from the Governor's office. Orville Banks, who had held sway over the workings for the State Prison for thirteen years, sat opposite her in his squeaky swivel office chair, quietly watching her as she rested her head on his cluttered desk.

He wasn't certain if she were asleep or awake; but he ached inside for her and for Ward Kessel. He had become so personally attached to both of them; never had he felt this way before about a prisoner. He was convinced that, if Governor Dodson did not give a last minute reprieve, it would be a gross breach of justice. Several times during Ward's incarceration he had gone out of his way to visit him; and their talks had been varied and honest beyond any he could remember ever having with anyone, even members of his own family. They had even laughed about themselves, their friends other prisoners and the guards. It was all extremely improper, but he didn't care: there had been a miscarriage of justice; that much he knew, full well.

He looked over at the old school clock above the doorway; listening to it's immutable, resonant ticking. Orville felt an emptiness welling up in him, almost to overflowing: eleven-thirty. As he got up and went around the desk toward the door, he gently patted Agatha's head; then closed the door as he went into the clerk's office. From there he called the Governor's office; but the secretary, Mr. Snow, advised him the Governor was not accepting any calls.

"Don't give me that, he has to talk to me, or this man's going to die. You tell him I need his word to call it off."

"I'll tell him you called," Snow said; with a new found sense of cold efficiency.

Twice more, before noon, he would call with the same plea; but even Snow refused his calls, leaving Hazel, the clerk, to repeat the same answer.

At five minutes to twelve, Orville Banks, the only one standing between Ward and death, sent word down to put the execution on hold; much to the disappointment of the members of the press gathered there to witness the event. At twelve-twenty another desperate call was placed. This time Snow was in his private office and accepted the call.

"Governor Dodson has left his office for the day. There is no way for us to contact him."

The prissy voice both sickened and infuriated the warden. He wanted to argue; but what was the use. What recourse was there? None, even if he quit right here on the spot, they would hang Ward within minutes. How long could he stall? He went to the water cooler, took a paper cup from its rack, filled it and drank slowly.

After that he went out into the hall and walked it's full length three or four times, stopping at the windows at each end to stare blankly down at the exercise grounds on one end and the prison incinerator and garbage dump at the other.

Finally, after what seemed hours, he went back into the clerk's office and picked up the phone. It was thirty-five minutes after one. "Tell them to proceed," he said sadly to his deputy. He would be damned if he would be a witness.

Breathing deeply, to regain his composure, he opened the door to his office. Agatha was sitting in his chair with her hands folded across her swollen belly, her back to him. She was looking out of the window at the blank, grey wall of the nearest cellblock.

"Mrs. Kessel," he said; and his voice told all there was to tell.

She stood up, not answering, and walked over to him, looking up into his eyes, that she knew were sympathetic. He put his arms around her, as a shield, and held her tight for an illusion of time that spanned eternity.

Agatha's eyes were dry, her breath shallow, her hands cold, but her arms strong, as she held the warden tight with all her strength. She should cry, but couldn't.

Suddenly her stomach writhed with the force of her baby's kicking and a severe contraction; and she slowly pulled away from the warden, the only man she had left in her life.

Orville looked at her, questioning.

"It's about time anyway, I guess," she said in a matter of fact manner.

He was not sure if she were talking about Ward or about her to be born child, or both.

"Maybe, I had better call the nurse," he said gently.

She looked at him for a moment as if to question, "Why?" Then she had another cramp and she clutched her abdomen tightly.

Orville reached over the desk to the phone and called the dispensary, "Emergency, Ralph, this is the warden, emergency, my office."

Within five minutes Ralph and his assistant were in the office and between them they carried the protesting Agatha, to the small prison hospital.

The examining doctor was the one who only a half hour previously had pronounced Ward Kessel "legally dead". He scrubbed his hands and prepared his patient for the delivery of her baby.

It was the first child ever born in Colton Prison: a nine and a half pound, screaming red headed boy. Borrowed scales from the kitchen were required to weigh him. It had been relatively fast for a delivery, but not an easy one. Because of the size of the child, stitches were needed to repair the damage to the mother; but she would recover well after a week or so in the Holy Cross Hospital where the doctor conducted his regular practice. The next morning, after "Mrs. Kessel" had rested and the sedation had worn off, he would have her transferred by ambulance.

Orville Banks had held Agatha's hand all during the hours of labor and birth; and had wiped her brow of perspiration with the sponge the doctor had given him. Now, near midnight, as she slept, he looked down at her and thought of his own daughter. The excitement had helped him forget the hideous happening of the afternoon; but now remorse trampled in, as a herd of wild beasts rushing in and over him, crushing all other emotions. He sat still holding her hand, his head resting on the bed. Ralph watched his boss for a moment; then turned out the light, leaving just a faint glow from down the hall.

Gilbert Henri pounded iron on the anvil all afternoon, in between lengthy swallows of homemade corn whiskey. Then he sat in the darkness of his room in the blacksmith shop all evening, until he could stand himself no longer; then with a bottle in his pocket, a bucket of black pain from the shop in his left hand, and a paint brush in the other, staggered the length of Elm Avenue, painting wide black bands around each of Crescent's cherished, electric street light poles. After each band was painted, he would sit on the wooden sidewalk and take another drink; until by the time he had reached Burnett Street and headed toward the Dodson house, the painted bands were more and more uneven, and Gilbert finally dropped the bucket, slid to the splintery sidewalk a last time and passed out, leaning against a light pole, just a hundred feet from his goal. Willie Clay found him there on his way to the police station at six the next morning and helped him back to Ward's shop; putting him to bed, fully clothed. Later, Willie would make Gilbert clean up the messy aftermath of the protest he had made to mark his inner outrage.

MacQuarrie looked in the small, hotel mirror: red eyed, head aching, groggy, tasting and smelling the sour, dank fuzz that had collect so solidly in his mouth and stomach. He tried to remember when and how he had gotten back to his room.

Even in this saddened state, his wisdom told him that he must at this very moment make a ninety-degree turn and start a new path if he were going to continue to travel a "meaningful road" in his life. His self-pity, so craftily disguised as rage, was going to kill him or at least destroy him as useful human being. He truly had become, as Calder commented so many times, "a sloppy, no good lush".

He poured some water from the pitcher into the washbowl and pushed his face down into the cool dampness, then slowly dried his pained features with the towel that hung over the back of the room's only chair. Next he brushed his teeth; but the rancid odor was still with him. He would have to buy some Listerine when he got down stairs. He must get back on track. He wondered where Hampden was. He had not seen him since noon, yesterday. When he thought about it seriously, though, he wasn't even confident that it was yesterday he had seen him, or if the vague images in the back of his consciousness were real or just the sporadic particles of some mixed up dream.

He pulled on his clothes, not bothering with a tie or suit coat, and took the elevator downstairs on his way to the barbershop for a shave, and later in the barber's back room for a long bath and a massage. After three cups of coffee and a piece of toast, he stopped at the desk and checked for messages. There were three: two from the Governor and one from Gloria that simply said "Call Northside five sixty three, room twenty six."

He used the lobby phone to call the Northside number.

A gruff male voice growled "Front desk; what do ya want?"

"I'd like to talk to room twenty six," Mac answered in the same tone.

"Well; you'll have to wait. There's no phone in the rooms ya know. I'll have to go up and get her; I guess it's that new dame ya want."

The wait was at least ten minutes; and Mac wondered "wonder where she is?'

Finally, Gloria's softy answered, "Hello, Mac."

"How in hell did you know it was going to be me?"

"No one else knows I'm here. Mac, can I come see you? I need to talk to someone."

"Are you all right, Gloria?"

"No; I'm in a mess. Can I see you?"

MacQuarrie paused in answering, visualizing the turmoil in his room. He was certain its stench would curdle anyone's stomach; besides he wanted to get some clean, maybe even new clothes to rid himself of the malaise he had awakened to earlier. Hell he might even give up cigars, and trim down on the hooch.

"I'll meet you, wherever you are. Is that all right?" he countered.

"I'm at the Orpheum," she said.

"God, sounds like a theater, not a hotel," he laughed.

"No theater is this bad," she laughed back.

"Where in hell is it?"

"On Third West, across from the depot. Room twenty-six. Can you hurry?"

"In about an hour," he said remembering that the bellboy had taken one of his two suits to be cleaned and pressed when he first checked in.

"See you," she said, obviously relieved, and hung up the receiver.

Mac tipped the bellboy a quarter for the cleaning and went back to his room; the odor was foul, as he opened the door. After shoving the window, quickly to the top, to let in the air, he dressed, putting on clean underwear, shirt and socks. He took great care in tying his red and grey, college-striped tie into a perfect fore in hand knot.

After polishing his shoes with the towel from the back of the chair, he grabbed his fedora hat from the hook on the closet door and headed for Third Street. He would get the mouthwash or Sen Sens on the way.

As he walked the six blocks to the station, his thoughts were split in two: first those of Ward, his death, and how Agatha would survive, and second, those of concern for Gloria. It did not surprise him that she had moved out of the Governor's residence after Cyrus's lack of action. He remembered the effect Ward Kessel seemed to have on her when she mention him during that first visit to Crescent, but he wondered why she had not gone home to Cynthia and Myrtle. Why was she holed up in a cheap railroad men's hotel.

In the shabby, dingy lobby of the Orpheum hotel, he made his way through the smoky haze to the desk. He didn't ask for her by name, just the room number.

"Upstairs, third door on the left," the clerk said with complete disinterest, not lifting his eyes from the betting sheet in front of him.

It sickened Mac to think of her even walking into this place, let alone staying here.

He knocked lightly. He could hear rustling inside and a door close; finally Gloria opened the door a crack and looked out before taking the chain off the lock.

"Oh, I'm glad you are here," she said, her voice trembling slightly.

"You had anything to eat?"

"No. I don't think I could eat."

"I think you had better. We'll go over to the beanery at the depot," he said as he reached for her arm, but she pulled away from him and stepped back into the shadows of the dimly lit room.

"Mac, just hold me for a minute or two first; just for a minute."

Squinting to see the expression on her face, he looked down into her eyes; they were dilated, excited; almost wild. He put his arms around her, cautiously, not quite sure what to expect, not wanting to upset her even more. She was shivering noticeably as she folded her body close to his and held him tightly for warmth.

In the near dark, they stood for a long time without speaking, almost without breathing. As her tremors eased, he looked into her eyes again and saw that they were less stormy; then he held her even closer for a second.

"The beanery it is, Glory Be. We will come back for you things," he said, reassuring her, even though he didn't have the slightest idea where he would take her, his publisher was expecting him back in Springville by the end of the week.

She did not answer, question or protest; just followed him down the stairs and across the street to the sterile, railroad restaurant. They sat at a table in a far corner; away from the trainmen, red caps, clerks and passengers-to-be. Gloria had agreed on scrambled eggs, fried potatoes, tea and toast; and she had cleaned her plate. Mac had more toast and coffee.

After they had eaten, he was tempted to light a cigar, but realized he had brought none with him. Maybe he would give them up. He knew she hated cigar smoke. Maybe that would be part of his new ninety-degree turn, his new path. He chuckled silently.

"Mac, I am so ill over this; honestly, I thought that, in the end, he'd sign it. God, I did; poor Agatha," she said softly, as she looked down at her empty plate, "But, he didn't."

MacQuarrie, for probably the first time his adult life, had nothing to say in return. He reached over and held her hand. She sat across the table from him and clenched her teeth to keep from showing any further emotion. He studied her again without speaking.

"I can't go back!" she said in a determined but soft voice.

"There's the four o'clock to Colton," he said after a pause for contemplation.

"That would be even worse: Crescent. No, I just can't."

"You still want to marry me?" he laughed, trying to lighten their mood. "I'll even try to give up smoke and drink, to make it more palatable"

"Whoever said I wanted to marry you, Mac?" she finally said, without seeming to respond to his attempt to brighten the conversation.

"Oh, I could just tell; you were always so eager," he laughed again and pulled his hand away.

"Not a very bright idea. Mac, I'm pregnant."

Suddenly, the background sounds of the restaurant filled the void between them and neither of them made any effort to break their own silence to compete with them. After wordless moments, Mac reached out for her hand again.

She covered her mouth with her other hand and looked at her empty plate.

"Do you want to get married," he asked seriously.

She just looked at him; and shook her head.

"I feel so cheap, so stupid. It was my fault, not his. My fault. I caused it on the couch in his study. He doesn't know," she finally said.

"Will you marry me, Gloria? I mean it."

"I use to think about it all the time, Mac; but it wouldn't work. Not now, it wouldn't work."

MacQuarrie, again, had nothing to say. He had speculated about what her answer would be if he had ever decided to change his ways and ask her. Now he knew, and it hurt him to feel that now he could even lose her.

"And how about you, Mac; what are you going to do from now on?"

Once more MacQuarrie felt as if he were mentally tongue tied, so he took the easy way out: "You mean now that your stepfather has won?"

After speaking, he knew it had been one of those "your cat crapped on the kitchen floor" remarks; that was not going to go over well. What was the matter with him; he should be kind instead of straining himself trying to be witty, when she was so obviously torn up inside."

"Cyrus hasn't won anything." she smiled, "unless you let him."

"Well, I am due back in Springville to start covering the Statehouse, over there, in a couple of days."

"Do you have to go?"

"It's a job, Glory; besides, what's here?"

"I don't know," she said looking straight into his eyes, "Me, I guess."

"And what does that mean?"

"Yes; I suppose."

Mac smiled and said almost in a whisper "On second thought, I'm not exactly a winning horse; been running pretty wild for the past sixteen years, since my wife died. I would try my best though, I'll guarantee you that."

"I need someone, Mac."

"Want another cup of tea?" he quipped as he stood up, and took the two cups to the counter.

When he came back with her tea and his coffee, she was looking down at the table.

"I am so tired, Mac, so unhappy. I need to be close to someone; I really do. Maybe you."

"Want to play it by ear; or are we going to be married? Or it could just be 'in name only' if you want." he finally asked with complete sincerity; but it struck them both funny and they started to laugh.

"I, honestly don't care which way; but let's," she said with a sigh of culmination.

"We will have to go to Springville, until I get things cleared up; and then we can split for wherever you want, New York, San Francisco... 'Podunk'."

They left their cups half full, then crossed the street to the crummy Orpheum Hotel, and climbed the stairs to room twenty-six. Gloria slipped the chain into its catch, locking the door behind them. In the dark room, they held one another as he comforted her; and then finally, after several hours, she finally fell into a restless sleep while he remained wide-awake, thinking of Ward's death and how miserably he had failed in trying to prevent it.

Edwards Brothers Malloy
Oxnard, CA USA
February 6, 2015